HER
CROWN
OF
FIRE

RENEE APRIL

DEDICATION

This book is dedicated to my Mum, who taught me to make a cup of tea, read in her chair whenever she got a chance, took me to the library, and bought me secondhand books. The depths of my appreciation can't be expressed in a small paragraph, so I hope a lifetime of unconditional love will suffice.

Thanks, Mum.

*A bird falls from the sky, its glossy feathers shuddering against
the icy wind. Its eyes are dull and dark, its beak clamped closed.
Wings catch the air; for a second, the bird soars.
Then gravity's cruel hand smashes it against the cold earth.*

CHAPTER ONE

THE BIRD IS fresh, not long dead; I've nudged it with my shoe to make sure. A lump swells in my throat as I stare at its tiny corpse. I glance around, searching for trees, power lines—anything it could've fallen from. The stretch of pavement I stand on remains bare overhead.

"What's wrong, Evermore? You getting teary over a dead sparrow?"

I roll my eyes as Tyson, my best friend and biggest pain in the arse, lumbers over.

"No." My voice is clear and strong, and I'm grateful. He would tease me all day if it cracked. "I'm trying to figure out why it's here."

"Because it's a dead bird? They're everywhere."

I point upwards and he, too, squints at the cloudless sky. "There's nothing above us."

Tyson shrugs, adjusting the strap of his backpack across

his expansive chest. "Maybe he had birdy cancer. Corked in mid-air." He flaps his arms wildly, then pulls a face. I'm struggling to remember why I'm friends with this idiot when he turns serious. "For real though, why are you so worried?"

I chew my lip. "I dreamt about a dead bird last night."

"A sparrow?"

"I don't know, just a bird. It was black, like this guy." Another nudge. The shining feathers dimple for a second.

"'Their song might be brief, but how greedy would we be to ask for more?'" Tyson quips, and I raise my eyebrows. He rolls his eyes. "It's from the book *you* lent me, dipshit. Read it again. So you dreamed about a dead bird, and now you're getting the sads over one you found on the pavement."

No. In the dream I watched the bird falling unnaturally from the sky, limp and lifeless. I woke with tears on my cheeks, chest heaving. Finding the sparrow on my walk to school stopped me in my tracks and made my stomach drop.

Arms gather around me, picking me up. Tyson throws me over his shoulder and, showing off why he's chosen for every Narralong High sports team, begins the short jog to our school.

"Put me down," I say. His shoulder jabs into my stomach, but worse, he's starting to cheer me up. He ignores me, like I expected. "Tyson!"

"She's a witch!" he warns Molly Barnes' posse as he trots past. I bounce on his back and return Molly's bemused wave. "A soothsayer! Seer of dead birds and prophet of destruction."

2

Though my cheeks burn, I have to admit that one's pretty badass.

By the time Tyson deposits me before my first class, I'm struggling to hide a smile.

"There. Feel better? By tonight the birdy will be gone."

I twist my face as I imagine him scooping it off the pavement. He guesses why.

"A cat will eat it or something, Evermore. Don't be gross." He turns to leave as students file into the classroom but pauses and tugs something from his backpack. "Almost forgot. Thought you'd need breakfast."

It's a lukewarm can of energy drink. I snatch it. "You legend—I totally forgot. I'll buy next week?"

"You know it." He salutes and walks backwards, bumping into other students. "Oops, sorry. Bye, Rose!"

"Idiot," I mutter, but I'm grinning as I crack the tab. We've been friends for too long. I slurp the sour soda as I cross the creaky threshold into my classroom.

"Welcome, everybody, welcome. Sit down; we've a lot to get through today." Mr Burgess hastily swigs from his stained mug of coffee. His collar sticks up on one side, and there's a smear of shaving cream on his jaw. He shuffles a bundle of papers. "Today we start our mid-semester career counselling."

I settle into my favourite desk towards the back, the one coated in a buttery layer of sunshine every morning, but even that can't cheer me up from my teacher's words.

Career counselling... how could I have forgotten it's today? I was all prepped to pull a sickie and everything.

Stupid dream.

A sheet of paper like a white slip of doom is laid on my desk. A happy face is printed in the upper corner as though it'll make planning your entire life at seventeen any more bearable. I trace it with my pen.

It makes it slightly more bearable.

"You've got twenty minutes to fill out your papers. Then come up and make a one-on-one appointment time with myself or Ms Wesley."

The chatter reluctantly ceases. I glance at the first line.

"When I graduate, I want to be..."

Inexplicably, I flash back to me and Tyson having this conversation when we were nine.

"A cat!" he'd proclaimed loudly, outlining an overhead cloud with a stubby finger. "They get the best stuff. Food whenever they want, sleeping all day... Man, that's the life."

I imagine writing 'cat' in my career counselling sheet and can already hear Mr Burgess' sigh.

"Rose, you have to write something." I realise too late I've written nothing, and my teacher really is standing behind me.

"I know, I just..."

Just what? This time, the demanding voice in my head is my mother's. I curl my fists.

"I haven't thought about it," I say finally.

A disc of light flickers on the wall as Mr Burgess checks his watch, then he jerks his head toward the door. "Why don't we go have a chat? You can have the first appointment."

The classroom next door is empty. Mr Burgess takes prime spot at the desk, then pulls up a chair and gestures to it. I sit, placing my blank paper beside me.

"You haven't thought about what you want to do when you finish high school?" he begins. "You know that's the end of this year, right?"

Stress grips me. "I know. I'm well aware."

"Do you want to go to university? Take a gap year?"

I frown. "Gap year?"

He nods enthusiastically. "It's a year off from studying. You can do anything, but most people travel. I enjoyed my time in the United States last year; I'd highly recommend it."

America. The image of a bald eagle soaring over a canyon plants itself in my mind. Something lifts in my heart. "That could be cool."

"Career-wise, though, is there any path you'd like more information on? I know your mother works in the hospital; have you thought about following in her footsteps?"

I shake my head. "I don't like blood." I've seen her return from emergency call-outs pale and wan, her eyes filled with what she saw. Last year, there was a pile-up on the National Highway just outside Narralong; she came home a different person.

"You like reading. Video games," Mr Burgess presses. "Anything related to those spark your interest?"

So far, the only thing that has is the idea of leaving Narralong and traveling. I imagine returning, attending

5

our tiny university and getting a meaningless degree, then settling into the nine-to-five and marrying a local boy.

That will probably be my next fifty years. I huddle into my oversized coat. "No. I think our appointment is up, Mr B."

He glances at the clock, then out the window where the nine-thirty appointment hovers anxiously, concern on his freckled face. "Oops. You're right, Miss Evermore. Off you go. Think on what we talked about."

The unsupervised class yells and laughs, sheets forgotten. I sit at my cold, shady desk, realising too late that I left my career counselling page in the other classroom.

CHAPTER TWO

CRISPY BURGERS IS packed with students fresh out of school. Almost every table is crammed, and the booths overflow. Behind the counter, a loaded grill sizzles while the distracted cook yells over his shoulder to the pretty serving girl. She grins, then turns to serve the next student digging through his wallet. I tear my gaze away as Tyson slurps his soda and slams it on the table.

"And the ball definitely went out, I saw it, but the ref didn't call it." He shakes his head and rips a monstrous bite from his burger. "*So* rigged."

"Every game you lose is 'rigged,'" I point out. "Remember when you thought you'd found the underground betting ring during Milo cricket? We were five."

"Could you for once not play devil's advocate? And I *did* find money changing hands."

"It was our registration fee!"

I shake my head and steal one of his chips. I'm here disappointing my mother further by having burgers instead of preparing her dinner. Remembering this, I pull my phone from my pocket and shove it deep into my school bag.

"I want to go," I say when we've finished our meals. "Do you wanna come to mine?"

He stands and swings his school bag onto his back. "Nah. I've actually got some assignments to do."

I smack him with my bag. "Loser."

"Let me guess, you've already done the essay for Ms Wesley."

"I may have."

"Can I copy?"

"No!"

He keeps wheedling as we step into the cold evening. The faux fur on my coat collar shivers in the breeze, reminding me of my dream.

Glossy feathers shuddering against the wind...

I shake my head, returning to the present. I stop walking when I realise Tyson has, his head cocked slightly as though listening to something. I hear it at the same time.

"So how you liking the country, city boy?" someone sneers behind the row of parked cars.

A dull thud sounds. Anger heats my cheeks, and I step towards the source. Tyson's hand shoots out to grip my arm.

"Don't," he says, thick brows furrowed.

I wrest my way free. Weaving between the parked cars, I don't take long to reach the scene: our small-time high school bullies and one city kid, Russell, who's curled up on the ground. His schoolbag has been emptied onto the pavement, and his career counselling sheet careens past me in a gust of wind.

"Oi!" I yell above their taunts. "Quit it, will you?"

Their leader, Jacob, has been in my classes since we were in daycare together. He started going off the rails in our senior year of primary school, with a few detentions linking into a suspension by the time we graduated. I heard rumours he even spent a night in lockup a few weeks ago but didn't believe them.

"Shove off, Evermore," he sneers. His hair has grown long and lanky, and there are bags under his eyes. "Gonna go dob on us?"

"Just leave him," I protest, though I realise my first flush of bravado was anger in disguise. Now it ebbs, leaving me unsure. "What'd he ever do to you?"

Jacob wipes his mouth with his hand, and I catch a whiff of sour spirits.

They're drunk.

"Piece of city shit, thinking he's better than us." He whirls and kicks Russell in the ribs.

"Hey!" The anger is back, and I launch forward to grab Jacob's arm. He wrenches free.

"You're not disproving the theory!" I shove him as hard as I can, but he hardly falters. Unfamiliar arms grab me clumsily from behind. I fight their hold.

"Enough." Tyson emerges from the parked cars. He's shed his backpack, ready for a fight. "Let her go, Smith."

The jerk releases me, and I quickly trot to Tyson's side. My heart thunders in my chest.

"The rest of you can disappear, too. Go home," my friend orders. I can't help but slink behind him when Jacob levels a drunken glare at me.

Together, they lumber into the darkness, heading for the woods that ring the development this side of town. Tyson helps Russell up as I watch them go. Until now, I'd really thought Jacob harmless—now he seems set to transition straight to small-town crook.

"You okay?" I ask Russell as he stands, wincing.

"I'm fine." He gathers his things with shaking fingers. "I hate this shithouse town!" he bursts out before limping towards the restaurant.

"Come on, Rose. He'll be fine in there." I let Tyson scoop me under his arm, and together we head to my car.

It's late when I pull into my driveway after dropping Tyson home. I let myself in and sling my bag onto the shoe stand. Out of habit, I scuff my shoes on the frayed rug that covers the floorboards—an act my mother has promised she'll gut me for, but one she's unconsciously picked up.

I meander through the living room and switch on the TV; I tell myself it's for background noise, but I know I just want to pretend more people are here.

In the fridge is a four-pack of my favourite energy drink, usually saved for gaming marathons, but my eyes itch with fatigue and adrenaline still runs through my body. I tear a bottle from its cardboard prison, twisting the cap and listening for the satisfying crack.

I sip and savour the sour taste as I head for the kitchen to start Mum's dinner. I open the freezer and peer into its depths.

"Bingo." I slide out a big, frozen steak.

I pull a fry pan from the cupboard and light the gas stove, giving the lace curtains above it a half-hearted tug. Mum swears at them every time she cooks, but I like them. I drizzle some oil into the pan and leave it to heat, returning to the living room to curl up on the couch.

I've had a few scuffles in the past, mainly when I was young enough to tolerate pigtails and lose the occasional baby tooth. But not since—tonight was my first real brush with violence. For it to come from someone I know...

Distracted, I pull at the label of my energy drink and shred it as TV commercials flicker with bright colours and happy jingles. I zone out as the game show wears on. The orange glow on the screen doesn't register.

Then the flames crackle.

"Shit!"

I drop the bottle, darting into the kitchen. Seizing the mop bucket, I fill it with water, then dump it on the flames. The fire roars and explodes upwards in a ball of black smoke.

I can't tear my eyes from the boiling, orange flames that have begun to spill onto the counter, the bucket empty in my loose grip. Shades of crimson and gold swirl in the pillars of fire. Golden sparks settle on my sleeve as I move forwards. My hands tingle, almost buzzing, and a yearning tugs at my heart.

The ghost of a faded scar whispers along my wrist, stretched almost to invisibility by time. As a child, it took me a few years to grasp the concept of 'hot'; I always grabbed at flames, lit matches, birthday candles. I lick my bottom lip and stretch a palm towards the nearest column of fire. My heart freezes when it dances eagerly towards me.

"Rose!"

I yank my hand back, the heat of the blaze suddenly washing over me. I cough. My lungs burn. Through the haze I recognise our elderly neighbour, Mrs Rogers, who grabs my arms. With surprising strength, she hauls me from the house as sirens wail down the street. Smoke billows through the living room, roiling against the windows, and I see the bottle I dropped leaking its contents onto the rough carpet as fire licks at the threshold. My throat tightens.

Mum will be pissed.

She throttles the packet of cigarettes. Through gritted teeth, she says, "I said cook dinner, not burn the house down."

I cringe. "I know."

"You know? At seventeen I'd hope you could be left alone for a few hours. Do I need to enrol you in after-school care again?" She shakes her head and turns away.

A man in uniform, mask open so he can talk freely,

approaches my irate mother on our damp lawn. Behind him, the fire crew marches in and out of our house. I welcome the reprieve as she starts talking to him instead of shouting at me.

"Can we go inside?" I ask tentatively when the man leaves us.

"We have to wait for the building inspector to sign off." She rubs her face with one hand. Still in her scrubs after clocking out of a ten-hour shift, I know she'd hoped to get into the shower and pyjamas. Instead, she'd come home to the entire metropolitan fire unit on her front lawn. "You got any of those shitty energy drinks?"

I offer her a crushed stick of gum instead. She waves it away and pulls the pack of cigarettes from her pocket, squeezing them as she builds up to whatever she's trying to say.

"Mrs Rogers said you were staring at the fire. Reaching out to it."

Her voice has changed—softer, intimate. Nerves slink into my stomach. "I went into shock. Didn't know what to do."

She's thumbed open the packet and now fiddles with a cigarette butt. "Rose, if there's anything you ever want to tell me..." Mum looks up, creases between her tired eyes more noticeable. "I promise I'll listen."

Her newfound concern takes me aback before I refocus. "There's nothing."

She meets my gaze. I remain blank-faced and wait for her

to look away first. How can I tell her I was freaked about a dream with a dead bird? How can I explain the call of the fire, how much I wanted to touch it and feel it burn? I knew I could make it dance if I wanted.

I press my lips together and stuff my hands deep into my pockets.

"There's a traineeship opening up in reception at the hospital." Mum changes the subject like she always does when we almost breach a serious topic. "I was thinking of putting you up for it. Now that you've finished your exams for this semester, you can do part-time if you want. The pay will be rubbish—"

"Can we talk about this later?" I interrupt. Even now, she's thinking of my life after school.

She rolls her eyes. "Fine."

That night, after all the paperwork is signed and the strangers gone, I can't sleep. Acrid smoke and the smell of burnt plastic and mothballs have soaked into the familiar house. I creep out of bed, my socks silent on the stairs. I rummage through Mum's 'secret' drawer. When my fingers close around the little plastic cylinder, I know I've found it.

A single click; a bright flame springs up eagerly, illuminating the hallway. I dart a finger through the white-gold teardrop. It flickers. Shadows close in around my single form, but the flame stabilizes, staving them off. This time, I drag my finger over it slowly.

No burn.

I change tactics. With my palm open, I lower it over the lighter until the flame flattens against my skin.

My breath catches.

There's still no pain.

I'm fireproof.

The floorboards overhead creak with muffled footsteps, and I drop the lighter. It extinguishes before it hits the carpet; still, I'm annoyed with myself. I retrieve it, return it to the drawer and sneak it closed. The bathroom door squeals open. A minute later, the pipes screech as Mum turns the shower on. I stand in the dark until I hear the shower curtain's rasp, then pad upstairs and back to bed, my heart pounding wildly as the fire continues calling me. When I lie down to sleep, all I see are flames.

CHAPTER THREE

ENSURING MY BEDROOM door is locked tight against snooping parents, I focus on the task before me. I had another dream about a bird, and when I trundled outside to check the mailbox, I found a dead sparrow on the drive. I stepped over it with the bundle of letters Mum instructed me to collect the day before.

There have been other dreams. In one, Russell, the redhead kid from the bullying incident a few weeks ago, caught the eye of Molly Barnes, widely deemed the hottest girl in school. I recounted it to Tyson, who chuckled along with me. Our jaws dropped when, at recess, we saw the two canoodling on the hill.

"So now it's not just dead birds, but also high school flirtations," Tyson remarked over burgers that night. "Worst. Superpower. Ever."

I agreed, but he didn't know about the fire.

Holding Mum's new Zippo lighter in one hand, I make a pinching motion with my fingers. The tiny flame strains toward me, pulling against its gas anchor. Little beads of sweat grow on my brow as I press my fingers together harder. Suddenly the flame pops free and lands on my skin briefly before flaring and disappearing.

I'm stunned for a moment, then I shoot to my feet and jump on my bed in victory.

"Not just fireproof!" I proclaim, holding the lighter above me like the Olympic torch. "I command it too!"

I need a bigger fire.

The silent house eggs me on as I thunder down the stairs and snag my worn jacket from its peg. The lighter is crammed in my pocket as I shoulder the laundry door open with its signature screech. I hop the back fence, leaves crunching beneath my sneakers as I walk under the branches. Cold wind plays across my face.

My fingers snatch the first dry branch I find, then the second and third. I stuff my pockets with brittle leaves for tinder, cradling my armful of branches. I make several trips to the yard, dumping the wood beside my old swing set. The pile grows to waist-height before I dust my hands on my jeans and open the lighter, holding it near the leaves. They blacken, grey smoke curling from the edges. A thin line of fire gleams at the corners but dies almost immediately.

At a loss, I shut and squeeze the lighter. Then I remember the bright red jerry can in the garage and scramble to my feet. Concern tugs at me briefly, but I brush it off.

I need this fire.

I need to see what I can do.

Petrol sloshes inside the cold plastic. I splash it liberally over every branch. The smell hits me in the face, and I gulp some fresh air as I carry the jerry can away.

I stand still as the streetlights flicker on and the wind sweeps my thin, brown hair from my eyes. Then I open the lighter and drop it.

Fire explodes, eating the branches like they're a gift. Heat seeps through my clothing as the newborn flames stretch tall and pale like ribbons. They rise to my full height, and I know I should step back. Instead, my foot drags through the dirt towards the burning pile. Yearning pulls at my soul.

"Give it," I whisper to my fire. "Please."

I watch a small flame creep and ebb towards my palm. It tickles, crawling down my fingers.

I let out a surprised breath somewhere between a laugh and a sob, drawing my hand back. A little pool of flame remains in my palm, dancing. When I spread my fingers, the flames sink deep under my skin, threading across my veins in molten sparks. Jewels of fire lace up my arms and across my chest until I'm awash with embers.

"More," I urge, and shove my hand back into the blaze.

Fire sweeps along my arm. The fabric of my jacket sizzles. Again, I feel no pain—only the heat of the flames warming me from the inside out.

I'm holding the fire—not a tiny flame, but a real, live fire. I laugh.

"Rose!"

The fire melts through my jacket and I shout in surprise. Suddenly the pain I've expected from the start is there, sharp and insistent, and with a shriek I fight to free myself from my burning clothes. Slender hands slip across my shoulders. The jacket hits the ground, smouldering.

I glance up into my grandmother's shocked eyes. "Uh oh."

"Of all the irresponsible things." Grandma paces across the kitchen as I sit at the table, feeling five years old again. "Christina, talk to your daughter!"

Mum cringes, leaning against the doorway. "I don't really—"

Grandma latches onto her. "It is *your* lack of discipline that caused this. I come to visit and catch your daughter lighting herself on fire. And the kitchen? That was her, too, I assume?"

I've never seen her this angry. She smacked me plenty of times when I was little and gave me stern words and scowls, but she never shouted this way. It hits me: she's scared. She saw me on fire—not screaming in pain, but laughing.

But the kitchen fire... that was an accident. Right?

I grip the edge of the table as Grandma and Mum argue. When silence falls, I look up.

"That's not fair," Mum says. Every hair on my neck

stands. I've heard that tone twice—both times, I'd been in big trouble. "Do not bring Rose's father into this."

I can't help pricking my ears. She's mentioned him about three times in my life and I know nothing about him. He's a topic best avoided.

"Well, surely you must realise as she gets older—"

"Enough!" Mum stands to her full height and advances on her mother. "Rose, out."

I slink into the living room just as the shitstorm of the century explodes in the kitchen. I curl into a ball on the window seat, watching the quiet street outside. Try as I might to block my ears, I hear several phrases hissed from the kitchen.

"You don't think I know that?" My mother's voice holds cold fury. "You don't think I know she's my *biggest* mistake?"

A knife jabs through my numb shield. Their voices blur like I'm underwater, and not until I hear the front door slam do I realise Grandma has stormed out. I brush away my tears and step cautiously into the kitchen.

"I'm sorry," I croak. Mum sits at the table, a lit cigarette between her fingers, her gaze on the floor.

It has darkened outside, and only the embers of my fire remain in a guilt-inducing heap. The kitchen light glows above us, the soot-streaks of my previous fire coarse against the black-and-white chequered lino. Mum lifts the cigarette to her lips; the tip flares sickly orange. Finally, she speaks, blue smoke punctuating her words.

"Is there anything you'd like to tell me, Rose?"

I glance at the cat clock above the sink. I watch the swinging tail count off the seconds, then place my phone on the table and switch on my flashlight app.

A minute later, the power goes off, plunging us into darkness. The bright beam of light from my phone illuminates us.

The cigarette flares with a hiss. "Same question."

"I knew the power would go out because I dreamt it," I say. "This and a few other things have happened in the last month."

The clock, battery-powered, keeps ticking. The silence stretches forever.

"Your grandmother wants you to see a psychiatrist," she says around her smoke. My heart plummets. "And I agree with her."

There's a pause, then I throw my phone at the wall. It hits the wood panelling with a thud and slides to the floor, the torch still stubbornly lighting the kitchen. "Even after I proved it to you? I gave you a demonstration—"

"You set yourself on *fire*!" Mum shouts, finally losing her temper. She stands, towering over me, and throws the cigarette to the ruined floor. "What next, Rose, you check whether I'm flammable too?"

Anger swells. I rise. "How could you even say—"

"What if she hadn't come over when she did?" Her voice grows louder. "Would I have come home to the news that my daughter burned herself at the stake? Or worse, would you have turned up in the burns unit with *this*?"

She seizes my arm and yanks me toward her. She turns my wrist this way and that, examining closely. Her eyes widen.

"That's not possible," she whispers. "She saw you on fire. Your jacket is melted in the yard. How are you unburned?"

I curl my fingers into a fist and snatch my arm back. Tucking it against my side and rubbing it with my free hand, I look at the ground. "I held the fire."

There is no answer and I cringe, waiting for the retribution. But when I risk a glance upwards, Mum has gone sheet-white in my phone's pale light. A second later, she squares her shoulders and turns to leave.

"You and Grandma," I begin slowly. She halts at the archway that separates the entrance hall and the kitchen, her face turned away.

"What about us?"

I cross my arms and huddle in on myself. "You discussed my dad."

Her fingers tighten on the frame. "Not now, Rose."

"Why not?" Something has soured between us today, breaking an already fractured relationship. It's the first time she's let me hear her call me a mistake. The word rose, once, when I drew on the walls as a child. Confused, I'd offered her an eraser. "I want to know."

"When you're older." She heads for the stairs.

I pick up my phone for light and follow, pressing the attack. "I'm older *now*. I'm seventeen."

Halfway up, she turns, glaring at me, and I realise I've pushed her too far. I take a step back down.

"You are a *child*. I can't trust you in the house, can't trust you'll make the most of the opportunities I fight to give you. You stay out past curfew and you don't lift a finger to do any housework. You've squandered any ounce of responsibility I've given you. You are a child in every sense of the word, and I don't trust you with the information. Is that clear?"

I clench my teeth, willing the blooming tears away. "You're right. I am a mistake."

The word doesn't have an effect on her. She rolls her eyes. "Go away, Rose."

I remain there long after she disappears. Even when the power returns, the house stays dark.

CHAPTER FOUR

I HARDLY SEE my mother the next few days. We operate on different schedules, living separate lives.

It suits us both.

I get a call from the traineeship rejecting me. My essay that I'd thought myself so clever in doing early is returned with a 'see me' note. The brochures Mr Burgess gave me about gap years wilt on my bedside table.

As my life unravels, the dreams strengthen.

"That kid is going to trip." I point at a stubby youngster, who face-plants on a loose brick three seconds later. "Molly's lunch is about to be stolen."

Tyson muffles a laugh as her shriek echoes across the yard. A triumphant seagull scarfs the sandwich as she and her group watch in horrified fascination.

"More," Tyson demands. I entertain him on the way to the canteen with split-second predictions.

They aren't really. Somehow, I've dreamt this entire day. The dream showed me everything. Every time Tyson laughs or gapes in wonder, the past few days peel away. I'm regaining control.

"Can of soda and a Dagwood dog, please." I hand over the coins and wait for my order as Tyson hovers beside me, hoping for a pity handout. "And some chips," I add, and his expression turns gleeful.

"Thanks. It's broke week." He digs into the chips with a shovel-like hand. "Why'd you get a Dagwood dog? You hate those."

"I know." I scoop the battered hot dog in a dollop of tomato sauce. "But I dreamt I ate one last night."

We sit under our favourite tree, a gnarled old thing that has survived generations of children climbing all over it. The teachers hate it and try to make us stay away—too many kids have fallen, too many young couples can hide in the tall roots.

"You know it's not seeing the future if you act it out, right?" Tyson queries as I grimace at the first bite. "Dreaming you had a Dagwood dog then buying one is self-fulfilling."

He's right; I *do* hate Dagwood dogs. I relinquish it after a few more forced bites and he chomps it down as I crack the tab on my drink.

"You've never failed me, sugary can of delicious." I lift the brim to my lips, but the soda barely touches my lips before I'm pulling it away. "Gross!"

"What's wrong?"

"That's disgusting. Way too sweet." I peer at the sugar content like that'll tell me if I got a dud. "Here, try it."

Tyson sips, then shrugs. "It's fine. Are you sure you don't want it? This is the one you like."

I give it another go but shudder and push it into his hand. "Have it. I'll just get some water or something."

As Tyson scarfs his bonus lunch, I rinse my mouth with tepid water from my untouched bottle. It's been at the bottom of my school bag since who knows when, a forgotten effort to make myself drink more water during the day. I watch the yard, seeing more of my dream come true before me. A teacher handing out detention to a kid throwing rocks. A flock of seagulls screaming and swooping Molly's group again, forcing them to pick up their bags and run. One kid getting tagged so hard in a game of chase that he trips and slides on his face for a good half-metre.

"What're you going to do without the traineeship?" Tyson asks as the kid howls. He picks his teeth with the Dagwood dog's empty stick. "Get another job?"

"Might study. Do business or something versatile like that."

He prods me with the damp stick, making me recoil in horror. "Versatile *or* useless?"

"Versatile!" I repeat, swatting it away. "I did some research and—"

"No you didn't."

"Yes I—fine, I didn't. But I have to do *something*."

"Why? You gonna move out?"

I could move out. The idea of my own place, like a little flat, seizes me. A different kind of fire surges through my veins.

"That's brilliant! I'm going to do it."

Tyson, like a puppy, is immediately hooked by my enthusiasm. "Yeah? This'll be great. Party at your house every night!"

The bell rings as I hit him, and we're caught up in a mock fight on our way to the next class. By the time I head home, I'm humming with excitement. Even the house, with its darkened windows and peeling paint, can't deter me.

I have to start saving. I research a few real estate and job websites as night falls. Thirst for independence has drowned out any need to play with fire. I scrawl notes in a workbook I've owned since primary school, tearing out a few pages of crayon stories. I'm not a child anymore.

I'll show her that.

I'm in a glass case, my fists pounding on the edges. Beyond my prison, a stone building burns. It's replaced by a silver pin on a pillowcase in a dark room, then a city viewed through mottled glass, and fire...

So much fire. It twists and curls, then plunges down towards me. I scream and throw my arms up to protect myself from the pain, but it doesn't come.

There's a temple in the ocean. The waves beat against worn rocks. Chimes sound in island air. A towering sea monster rises above a city, illuminated by a flashing storm. A thousand horses gallop past, ridden by armour-clad soldiers with faces hidden by steel.

"Help!" *I scream at the sky. The dream swirls around me, pulling me in a million directions. I can't breathe, can't find the way out.*

Wake up! *I beg myself.* Wake up, wake up, wake—

Now there's pain. Needles thrust into my skin as I crawl along the pavement I walk every morning. I pull myself towards the bird's crumpled body, my hand stretched to hold it. I need to feel the feathers against my skin, to know I'm not alone in this horrid world. A raw growl escapes from me as something tries to tear me back, but I jam my knees into the concrete even as I'm dragged away, leaving threads of bright red blood. With my every molecule, I strain towards the bird.

Suddenly, the scene changes. I'm standing by the river, just down from the bridge where cars roar across like metal monsters. I shy away from their flashing silhouettes, seeking out the river instead. The water is still and glassy, comforting compared to the rush of the road above.

I want to jump and escape the loud world. I shed my jacket, hanging it neatly over a nearby branch.

Won't be a moment...

My shoes sink into the soft bank, and water wells up in the depressions. My socks are wet already, but it doesn't matter— soon I will be enveloped in the cold, quiet river.

Leaning forwards, I spread my arms wide, ready and eager for the river's icy embrace. I tilt past the point of no return, my hair brushing from my face as the water kisses my cheeks and—

I catapult upwards in bed, releasing the breath I held to go underwater. Blue light shines from my phone: a text from Tyson.

Found a cool place for you to check out! I sent the link.

I remain that way for a long time, my fingers gripping my phone so tightly it leaves indents. It's 6 am. My thumb brushes the lock button. The phone lights up again, searing my eyes. It's way too bright; I shield my eyes and shove it under my pillow. In the distance, a police car howls.

I join my phone under the pillow as a headache grips my temples. I need fire like I need air. My fingers fumble in the drawer beside my bed, beads of sweat growing on my forehead. When the flame lights my room, I pinch it from the metal base, draw it onto my skin and cup it in my hands. It calms me immediately, shutting out the world. I roll the flame back and forth as the room slowly lights up, then curl my fingers into a fist, extinguishing it.

Time to face the day. Something in the world has changed, and I'm pretty sure it's me.

Whatever new enthusiasm I had yesterday is gone. Tyson bounds up to me on the path, wearing a goofy grin that fades as he draws closer, concern clouding his eyes.

"Rose... You look like shit."

I turn my face away. "Leave me alone."

"What happened?" He bounces alongside me, and my ire rises at his tone. "Was it something with your mum again?"

"Leave. Me. Alone!" I yell and watch his face fall.

"Fine. Call me if you want."

He slings his bag over his massive shoulder and strides off, sulking. A needle of guilt slips into my stomach and I hover, torn between calling after him and taking refuge in this mood. But I can't get the words out, and eventually he rounds a corner out of earshot.

It takes me an hour to give up on school. My feet lead me away from the stale buildings and dead grass. Shadows fall across my skin as the paperbark trees lean in to tell me a secret. Somehow, I'm in the floodlands beneath the bridge—a soggy area filled with twisting trees and marshy inlets. I walk along the boardwalk, skipping lithely over the broken sections. Finally, I reach the river.

I shrug my jacket off as I approach. The bridge roars overhead like in my dream, and I hunch inwards, away from the noise. My heart slams in my chest, wrestling for control. It won't win. I sling my jacket over the branch, feeling some thrill from fulfilling a premonition again.

"Rose?"

I whirl on the spot, furious. Tyson pushes through the trees, confusion lining his face.

"What are you doing out here?" he asks. "It's gross under the bridge, you know that."

"I was just..." I set my lips together and fold my arms. "I needed a walk."

His face hardens. "I thought something was off. Come on, get away from the river."

All the willpower in the world wouldn't be enough to pull my foot from where it's rooted in the mud.

"No," I whisper.

He lowers his bag slowly. "I will pick you up and carry you. You know I can do it."

I can feel the emptiness at my back, and the urge to fall in is almost overwhelming. Tears prick my eyes.

"I don't want to."

"Don't want to what?" Tyson echoes. Panic creeps into his voice. "Let's talk, Rose. We can go to the burger place. We can go to the rail yard. Just... come on. Talk to me. Is this about the fires? Your mum? I know this year hasn't been easy on you, but this... we've talked about this before. It's not the way for you."

In my mind's eye, the bird falls. "You'll be fine," I tell him, letting myself tilt backwards.

"*Rose!*"

His hands catch the hem of my shirt and in the split second I have, I try to fight him off. But it's too late.

The water submerges us both.

CHAPTER FIVE

THE CURRENT TAKES us immediately. I smash against the riverbed's soft mud like the bird in my dream. In that instant, I know regret.

The river is dangerous—all Narralong children are taught this from a young age. Narrow and deceptively calm, its glassy surface hides a tumultuous current. People have fallen in and drowned; once, a car plunged off the bridge and disappeared beneath the murky surface, never to be seen again. They couldn't even find a wreck.

Now I've jumped in, pulling my best friend with me.

We're strong swimmers—we both attended the same after-school training with our parents. I kick my shoes off and let them sink, knowing he's doing the same. My arms pull towards the surface.

Instead, I bump into the silty mud, raising clouds of mouldy dirt. I panic. What I thought was up is down, but when I try to swim in the opposite direction, I find only more sludge.

My air is running out. The pressure in my chest tightens, and I know I'll soon have no choice but to open my mouth and let the river into my lungs. I've heard stories of people drowning, the survivors describing the excruciating pain.

I need to breathe *now*. I kick off from the river bottom one last time, my chest burning, and part my lips to heave in the water. I can't stop it.

Instead of water, I suck air. I thrash in the river, hair plastered like cobwebs to my forehead. I crack my eyes open to see Tyson.

"Rose!" he splutters. "You good?"

He's a little way away from me, a dark head in the steely water. I nod, looking around. I can just make out a muddy bank enveloped in a haze of rain, and we surge towards it. Around me, the river boils and heaves, threatening to pull us under. I strike out towards the bank and seize handfuls of sharp, spiky grass as Tyson holds onto some exposed roots.

Suddenly, strong hands grip mine and someone hauls me from the river like I'm a soggy fish. My legs nearly fold when my rescuer stands me up on my feet, and I resist the urge to collapse.

"Stay there, girl." A rough blanket that smells like hay and mould is thrown around my shoulders, then the man heaves Tyson from the river. I don't recognise him from our town.

We're being kidnapped is my first thought as the strange

man leads us through the twisting trees. I glance back at Tyson, who's staring at the man's back like he's sizing him up. I shake my head, lips tight. This man, with a thick chest and wide shoulders, towers over us. I have a feeling he could throw Tyson back into the river with one hand and throttle the life out of me with the other. We have no choice but to obey him.

We emerge from the trees, and the fear in my stomach deepens. Gone is Narralong's eighty-four-year-old bridge with its patchwork of repairs in the stone walls. Gone is the sound of peak-hour traffic. The car park with its uniform gravel and neat log fences is nowhere in sight. Instead, we slosh through black mud. Rain pecks at our faces, and my shivers increase as our feet find a hard-packed road. Up ahead, I make out buildings, blurry in the drizzle.

"W-w-where—"

"Not to worry, not to worry." He reaches back and takes my wrist, pulling me faster. Tyson waddles to keep up, squelching. "I'm taking you to my daughter. She'll get you both sorted out."

'Sorted out'? Like in a serial-killer kind of way?

We reach the first house. I trip on the threshold, kicking up a small chunk of earth. The man glances around as he shoves us in with iron strength, then the door closes behind us. I almost miss the metallic sound of several locks fastening against the gloom.

The house looks like nothing from my century, or the last. A fire with a cooking rack struggles against a buildup of damp wood in the middle of the room, the few wisps of smoke siphoned outside by a small flue above. Dirty flagstones line the floor. A strong, grassy smell emanates from the drying herbs along the back wall. I jump when I realise a young woman stands behind the fire, watching. Her wide eyes meet the man's, then she moves forward into the light.

"Sit, please." She ushers us into sturdy chairs beside the fire. I sit when Tyson does. She bends over the cooking rack to stir something inside a pot, and I take the opportunity to study her.

She's about my age, maybe a touch older. Her cheeks are thin, her shining brown hair tucked into a bun at the nape of her neck. She wears a faded, green dress bunched at the waist, the hem dirty. I can just make out a long, leather strap around her neck, but her dress hides whatever hangs on it.

"My name is Laela," she offers, turning back with an earthenware mug. She gives it to me with a small smile. Warmth lends me strength as Tyson receives one too.

"Where are we?" I ask.

Laela glances at our rescuer hovering near the door. He shifts his weight too quickly.

"We'll explain soon," he says, but his voice is unsure.

I sip, distracted when the taste of cinnamon and cloves dances on my tongue. "Wow. What is this?"

"Mead," Laela says, and she smiles again. Hidden golden highlights glitter in her dark eyes. "I find it the best remedy for a dip in the river."

"Thank you," Tyson adds, but he puts his cup beside his chair.

My mood lifts at Laela's teasing tone. I take another sip. When I'm done, I hand back the mug and to my delight, Laela fills it with more mead as another woman enters the room. Her dress, covered by a stained apron, is much rougher than Laela's, and a chequered cloth restrains her hair. She stops dead in the act of wringing her hands on the apron when she spots me and Tyson. Her face reddens, and the hulking man by the door cringes.

I bury my face in the mug, sensing a shitstorm. The woman suddenly slaps my rescuer on the arm. They have a hushed argument I do my best to hear.

"I don't believe you! We discussed this and I said *no*, it's too dangerous, Markon. Your only hope now is walking them to the Academy and begging forgiveness."

"*Two* of them, Carrie! We got two."

"Excuse me," Tyson interrupts. "Can we have *some* explanation for all this?"

"It's not our place," Carrie, who I now realise shares Laela's button nose, says tartly. "We'll be taking you to the Academy—"

"You're going to learn magic," Markon says, his face open and hopeful. "Up at the school. And when you do, please remember our help."

My lips part in shock as Tyson snorts. "*Magic*? You're insane. We're leaving, Rose."

Laela places a hand on his arm. He can fight her off, but he lets her push him back into the chair. "Magic is real."

Tyson looks at me with pleading eyes for help I cannot give. Instead, I lift my hand to the struggling fire and call with the itch in my blood. Sparks soar from the pit and land on my bare skin. They flare bright on my palm, bursting into flame—cheap heat, unsustainable by themselves.

Laela's eyes brighten at the sight, and she gives an encouraging nod. Her mother crosses her arms and looks away. The flames flicker and die, and I tuck my hand into a wet pocket before risking a look at my friend.

He stares at me with wide eyes. I meet his gaze, silently begging him to understand. Eventually, his lips tighten and he nods. Something in me relaxes.

Laela, however, looks at her father with polite confusion. "He should know about his magic by now."

Markon says nothing, and Carrie breaks the silence with a taut sentence.

"You brought a *humanborn* non-magi here?" she asks me, and I quail under her stare.

"I didn't bring him anywhere! He grabbed me when I went in the river, and—"

She holds up her hand. "No more. We cannot know what goes on when the Headmasters call you from The Other." She turns to her husband. "They'll kill him if they find him."

The man nods. "Laela, get the bag."

"Whoa, hang on." Tyson stands now, towering above

the girl, who has scurried deeper into the house. "What's happening?"

Voices sound from outside. Carrie and Markon exchange a look before the woman goes to the window, twitching aside the worn curtains.

"They're here," she breathes. Ice fills my veins.

"We have to go," Laela tells Tyson, returning with a satchel over her shoulder. She appeals to her father, who's gone white and doesn't respond. She tugs harder at Tyson. "*Now.*"

"Tyson." With all the sincerity I couldn't muster when I told him to leave before I jumped into the river, I say, "Go."

"No, I won't—" He shrugs Laela off. "I'm not going anywhere without you."

Laela's tiny gasp draws our attention to the door. The iron locks glow orange. Smoke curls from the blackening wood beside them.

Carrie said they'd kill him. "*Go*, Tyson, damn it. I'll be fine."

Laela yanks at his arms. The cooking fire between us sputters and flares wildly as tears choke me.

"I'll be fine," I repeat.

Tyson clenches his jaw, then lets the girl pull him from the room just as the locks give way. I wrap my rough blankets tighter around me.

A man appears in the doorway, silhouetted against the grey sky. His unfriendly gaze sweeps across the man and woman. "Where is the other?"

No one says anything. The man moves indoors, almost sauntering. He wears a cream tunic trimmed with gold, and a crest on his left shoulder depicts a bird wrought in silver thread. Around his waist is a belt, looped and tied off, from which hangs a sword, a small dagger and a leather purse.

"My report said two students were pulled from the river."

"Your report was wrong," Markon croaks. He clears his throat and stands to one side. He gestures at me, his head down. "There was only her."

Tears remain on my cheeks; I wipe them on the blanket. When I'm done, the stranger is looking not at me, but at the fire burning behind us.

After a second, he nods. "Come with me, miss."

"Where am I going?" I demand. The fire warms my back, the mead tingles on my tongue, and the kindness these people have shown me makes me want to stay. "I'm not going anywhere until I know who you are."

"He's from the Academy," Markon says. His shoulders slump. "You must go with him."

The man gestures out the front door. I glance back up at Markon, who inclines his head gently. I step outside. The wind slices through my wet clothes, and I hunch as I emerge from the house. Two men stand on either side of the door—large, thick with muscle. Did they think they'd have to fight to get me out?

"It would be wise not to mention your little excursion to anyone at the Academy, Miss Evermore," the man says.

I follow him onto the street, trying not to look behind for Tyson.

"Why not?" I challenge. He doesn't answer.

A small, glossy white wagon pulled by a tall horse waits out front. My guide helps me into the back as I eye the horse nervously, then hands me another blanket. It's soft and made of pale wool, unlike the one Laela gave me. I pull it tightly around myself as he leans toward the other men; when they remain at Laela's house, my stomach sinks. Our horse lurches into motion, springing into a trot that soon takes us through the township.

"Who are you? Where are you taking me?" I force through shivering lips. My eyes fall on the knife at his waist.

He looks at me. "Everything will have an answer soon."

Though the cobblestones are rough and uneven, the wagon merely bounces along. Sturdy brick buildings surround us, their window glass polished to shine. We ride through a square, parting people pulling carts, big mules braying angrily, and pedestrians in dresses and coats. I sink lower when their eyes linger on our wagon.

I see no cars, hear no planes, smell no exhaust fumes. The people don't wear jeans or jackets—one woman has a shawl tied around her shoulders, while another wears trousers and a long coat. The man opposite me sits tall and proud, almost preening under the people's attention. He looks younger than me, with a strong jaw and reddish-brown hair. His eyes are muddy brown and heavily-lidded, but he wears an air of importance and responsibility. The crest on his shoulder is hand-stitched; closer up, I see the little deviations in the thread, the wonky wings of the bird in full flight.

"Welcome to the Stanthor Academy," he announces, and I peel my eyes from his form as he turns to gauge my reaction.

Another square, this one much larger. A castle made of strong, grey stone rises before us, dwarfing the other buildings. Leadlight windows pepper the front, and two narrow towers stand tall on either side of the main door, stretching above the battlements crowning the building.

A large, wooden gate opens, and the driver steers the wagon expertly through. We emerge into a loud, bustling courtyard of horses and people, our horses' hooves clacking against the damp cobbles. A flag flutters overhead, and clear rainwater sputters from the pipes running down the side of a stable. A young boy in overalls wrestles with a horse, trying to pull it out of our vehicle's way.

My guide sighs. "Commoners." Then he stands, apparently at ease with the swaying motion of our cart. "Out of the way, Thompson!"

The boy tries to bow and keeps up the fight with his horse who, sensing freedom, jerks on the reins and breaks free, prancing on the spot. As the wagon halts, the horse trots beside us, reins trailing.

"Hello there." I scratch its velvety nose and it whuffs at me, the warm air brushing my hair back. I bunch the reins in one hand and pull them off the ground, then hand them to Thompson, who comes running. His face is the colour of the blood-red flag curling in the breeze.

"Thank you, miss, I'm very sorry, miss. Please forgive me—Echo is bigger than she seems."

"That's all right." I'm unwilling to show more interest, though the child seems close to tears.

My guide jumps down and cuffs the boy. The boy turns away, then leads Echo back to the stable.

"Hey! What was that for?" I ask angrily.

He cocks his head, eyes wide and questioning. "Don't concern yourself with him. This way, Miss Evermore."

I ignore his helping hand and dump the blanket he gave me in the wagon. I disembark, teeth chattering, and follow him through the yard. We pass under the second-story balcony and climb a small flight of stairs, then push through double doors and emerge in a hall unlike anything I've ever seen.

The ceiling soars far above my head, the stone ancient and carved with thousands of tiny shapes in gold. It's so high I can't make them out, but my fingers tingle like they do with fire. I itch to examine the shapes in the torches' light and find myself on my tiptoes. A nearby flame flickers green, then reverts to pale gold.

"Miss?" My guide has finally realised I stopped following.

"What are they?" I point up. "The little pictures."

He shrugs. "Decorations. Come along."

By now I can't feel my toes. Leaving damp, little footprints, I clutch my elbows.

I wonder where Laela took Tyson. Did they return directly to the river? Is he already home? Something colder than the air tightens around my heart at the idea of being left alone in this strange world.

The man leads me down a set of stone stairs twisting into the floor. Flames in brackets light our way, and for one crazy second, I consider pulling them from the iron and hurling them at my guide.

The nearest lamp flickers, and he looks over his shoulder at me. "Not far to go, Miss Evermore. Please remain calm."

I leave the fire.

The floor levels after a tower's worth of uneven steps. My legs wobble when we reach the tiled floor. Here, the lamps are tinged with green and too stable to be naked flames; somewhere down the staircase, they changed to gas lamps. We're in a small chamber with a large double door on the side farthest from me. There's a stone basin in the corner. Long cords hang from pegs on the nearby wall.

"Where are we?"

My guide leans over the pedestal, splashing himself with water within. He dabs a bit on his forehead, muttering something, and I move forward, unsure if I'm expected to do the same. He holds up a hand to stop me, then chooses a long pendant from the wall beside him. A small, round, iron token on the end is carved with another intriguing shape. He pulls it on over his head.

He gestures to the door. "Please, Miss Evermore."

It might be my imagination, but he looks far paler than he did aboveground. His stark brown eyes stand out, lined with worry, and the hand he holds to the wooden door shakes. Warily, I take a step forward.

He grips the bronze handle and heaves. The door creaks open, the darkness beyond yawning farther back than the lamps can see. A cold gust of wind blasts from the abyss the door had hidden.

"This way, miss." He jerks his head, and I follow his instructions, unsure what else to do.

I step beyond the doors into the inky darkness.

"My name is Eustace Greatree, Miss Evermore. I am first page of the Academy, and I wish you luck."

His voice echoes past as I twist to look back over my shoulder. I catch one glimpse of his worried face before it seals.

"Hey!" I hold my arms out, searching for the door. "Let me out!"

My hands meet cold stone where the door should be. My fingers search for cracks, handles, anything, but they slide over the unnaturally smooth surface.

Ghostly, grey light dawns behind me, revealing my reflection against the mirror-smooth stone. My frightened face looks back.

There's sure as hell no door there.

I take a step back, removing my hands like they're burned. I tuck them deep into my wet jean pockets, shivering from things other than the cold now.

When I look back at what was a dark pit, a long cave now stretches before me, pockmarked with jagged rock and broken stalagmites. Some are so large I could lie flat on them. The cavern reaches far above my head, where moss hangs in dripping strings from the ceiling, and I crane my head back, trying to see farther. I get an eyeful of cave water instead.

As I'm digging my knuckle into my eye, a faint noise reaches me on the thin breeze. I squint towards it. The mouth of the cave is just visible, looking onto snowy moors. My belly drops; there was no snow during my escort to the big palace thing.

But when I recognise the noise, my blood turns to ice.

Someone is crying.

I can see them hunched on a rock just inside the front of the cavern. My foot shifts towards them, but I hold back.

Clearly I'm meant to go investigate, and *clearly* that's playing right into the hands of... whatever this is. I turn, scouting the biggest rock I can find, then scale it. My fingers dig into the dusty crevices, my bare feet slipping as I haul myself up. When I reach the top, I have a better view of the entire cave, including the crying intruder. I squint at them but have no clue who they are.

We remain in this tableau for a long time. My knees ache from the hard surface and my muscles scream from being in the same position. But my gaze never moves from their huddled form.

The snow keeps flying; the distant wind keeps howling. The crying never ceases, but it does rise and fall in pitch. The longer I remain on my rock, the more I'm reminded of a bugged-out video game cutscene. The thought plants a little nugget of self-satisfaction in my chest: I've managed to throw a spanner in the works of whatever this cave is supposed to be.

I perch on the rock like a goblin and praise myself for a solid twenty seconds before it all turns to shit.

The light at the cavern front dims, as though the sun is sinking behind the blanket of grey clouds. The wind dies away, but the crying increases. My insides writhe and I crouch lower on my rock, trying to be invisible.

The light vanishes completely as something shifts in the gloom to my right.

I listen to the crying far away in the darkness and try not to join in. I've never been so frightened in my life. For one petrified second I imagine what I would do if the crying started up right below my rock and nearly lose my mind in the dark. Maybe I should play along with whatever this is. I lower a tentative foot.

A yip echoes through the cavern, bouncing from wall to wall. I go still in my precarious position, hardly daring to breathe. Something skitters below and I fight the urge to yank my foot up, just as a spine-tingling howl soars across the rocks.

I fall from my perch.

The impact slams the air from my lungs. Adrenaline fires through my system as the yipping is punctuated by snapping barks and growls. I get my feet under me and run back the way I came, toward where the stupid door disappeared.

My reflection rushes at me as I close in on the wall, lit by a light I cannot see. The terror in my eyes comes too close, and I squeeze them closed as a breeze gusts over me. When I peel them open again, the girl in the rock is holding a handful of fire.

Copying her, I lift my shaking hand and call the fire. Small edges of flames race along the sides of my fingers. It nearly dies when a scream follows the barking.

The creatures are attacking the crying person.

My foot shifts towards the sound, my heart hammering. Every breath I take is too shallow and I hold still, wasting time, until a second scream flies through the cave towards me.

My step forward isn't so hesitant this time, nor is the one after that. My fire illuminates the way through the cave. I stumble over loose debris and nearly stack it on a large branch. Struck by an idea, I grab the branch, sending ripples of fire down it. With the burning torch held high above me, I charge into the fray.

Dark, nimble shapes dart, and I swing the branch with both hands at the nearest one. It hisses at me like a cat, but it's too slow. Patchy black fur begins to smoke, and the creature howls as it bursts into flame.

With the burning... *thing* giving us more light, I get between the stranger and the others.

"Stand behind me!" I command.

The stranger nods, sniffling, a hooded cloak disguising her face. More creatures rush at us, and I smack another with the torch. It, too, ignites and runs away screaming. On my next swing, the branch dashes against the floor, sending embers scattering. To my surprise, the rock also goes up in flames.

It's forgotten as teeth sink into my arm, tearing my jacket. I yell in pain. Fire rushes down my arm, lighting the creature's face. Beady eyes glare into mine even as it burns, wet blood gleaming around its yellow teeth.

I drop the torch and smash the creature against a large rock. Pain seethes up my arm and I hit the creature again and again until its grip loosens and it flops, lifeless, onto the cave floor.

Pain wracks my body. I cry, holding my arm as I sink to the floor. More howls join the first.

I want to go home I want to go home I want. To. Go. Home!

Fire explodes through the cave, bright even to my closed eyes. Heat washes over me, soothing and calm. Slowly, I look up.

Flames crawl up with glorious abandon, illuminating the entire cave. Rock that shouldn't burn feeds the fire as it reaches the ceiling and begins to consume the moss there.

Everything is ablaze. I stand amidst an inferno I created.

CHAPTER SIX

THE PERSON I rescued stares blankly at me, her face hidden in the shadow of her hood.

"Who are you?" she whispers.

I lick my dry lips. "I'm—"

A screech cuts through the crackling flames. A dark shape swoops towards us. I flinch as a large bird with glossy, black feathers lands neatly on my shoulder, his talons gripping my jacket without breaking skin. Intelligence glitters in beady eyes as he cocks his head at me.

The woman gasps. Then she flees into the night, her boots kicking up the edge of her cloak.

"Wait!" I call. "The snowstorm—"

Darkness swallows her like she never existed, leaving me with a bird and a cave on fire. But the corpses on the floor melt into the stone, leaving inky puddles where the toothed creatures lay. Flames on the walls sink back down, washing along the length of the cave in molten waves of gold. When the bird seems unbothered by the overwhelming heat that neither sears nor burns me, I follow the fire away from the entrance. The stone floor smooths into glass as shiny and reflective as the back wall that was a door. I nearly fall over when shapes form beneath the surface.

A little flame flares on the largest shape: a landmass. When I turn, it brightens like a beacon.

It's the magical equivalent of *You are here* on a huge world map.

Other landmasses have appeared, and I take a tentative step onto a cluster of islands west of my position. The air around me warms, carrying the scents of jasmine and summer. I breathe in, and the bird on my shoulder ruffles his feathers happily. There's a faint clunking, like wind chimes in a sea breeze.

Intrigued, I tread on the island to the east. Heavy perfume washes over me, something metallic wrapped within. The clashing of steel reaches my ears as I backpedal. The land to the north is almost as big as the one I'm on, and when I cautiously slide a toe onto it, the noise nearly knocks me out. Music, laughter, and stringed instruments blend together as a desert breeze engulfs me. Flecks of sand sting my exposed skin. When I remove my toe, the sound dies.

Two other countries to the northwest have icy winds that chill me to the bone. A haunting song rises from one, raising goosebumps on my skin and making the bird squawk. I quickly return to my original position.

"So this is our country," I tell him. I glance around the cave. "What the hell am I meant to do now?"

Time slithers past. The fire died when it reached the end of the cave, but that grey light has swept in. Eventually I sit, resting my chin in my hand. With the other, I lazily call up some fire, smiling a little when it comes so easily.

Then I'm falling.

In all honesty, it takes me a second to notice. When the bird takes off from my shoulder, I assume my hair is going everywhere in the breeze from his wings until I look down.

A white floor rushes up to meet me, and I yelp once before I'm engulfed. I hold my cringing position for a few seconds before I realise I'm still falling, except now I'm soaking wet.

Clouds. I'm falling through clouds!

These are not soft and fluffy, not at all. The one time I'd been on a plane as a child, I got the window seat and stared out at the snowy landscape with wonder, imagining the softness—a big sky of pillows for a little girl to relax on and shape to her amusement.

"Bleh!" I manage to yell as water streams back from my face into my hair. I flail experimentally in case I've learned to fly in the last few minutes; if anything, I drop faster.

But the land below looks very familiar. I was standing on it just seconds ago, except I'm definitely falling more to the south than where my little flame was. Remembering the magical smells and sounds of the other countries, I decide this is just a more close-up look.

I laugh in delight.

The wind chills my face and I'm soaked from the clouds, but I'm having the time of my life. I tuck my arms and legs in, shooting through the sky like a Rose-shaped bullet. Then I spread my limbs wide, slowing just a little.

Below me, roads spider-web across the landscape. Fields of green, yellow, and brown patches are punctuated by deep, dark forests. A river twists across. Dirty grey smoke rises from flat squares—rooves!—and I'm close enough now to see little wooden fences and the roof tiles of the big castle I'm heading for.

Boy, they're getting close.

I push my hands before me as though trying to hold the world away.

"Hey!" I yell to nothing, and my voice is whipped away. "Hold on!"

I struggle harder against the wind as the courtyard comes into view. A small, familiar stableboy looks up and drops his shovel as I scream.

Then I smash into the ground.

The pain wakes me first. Four deep pockets of it on my left arm that sting when I groan and sit up in an unfamiliar bed. I peel back the loose sleeve of a fresh shirt someone's put me in, and it takes a moment to register the white bandages wrapped around my arm and stained with brown patches.

The strange creature's bite was real. I groan, clutching my head with my good hand. Images of the ground

52

rushing up to meet me flicker in my mind, and I hastily pat myself down; I'm all accounted for, just a little sore. My body drags itself back down, my head meeting the feather pillow gratefully. The room I'm in is small with stone walls and a pretty, stained glass window beside the only door at the foot of my bed. A carved wooden wardrobe stands solemnly beside a writing desk, topped by a genuine, bona fide quill.

I throw back the soft quilt and shuffle my butt to the bedside. Loose trousers flop over my feet, slightly too long, like all the other pants I've ever owned. The stone beneath my feet is cold and uninviting, but I pad over to the desk and pluck the quill from its stand. The nib is heavy and intricate, the feather long and glossy black. I pretend to write until I accidentally stab myself with its sharp point.

Holding my injured arm close, I open drawers in the wardrobe, finding trousers, clean shirts, and socks with no elastic. I don a pair, ignoring how they sag. Tall, leather boots are tucked beside the wardrobe; I tug them on, stuffing in the overly long pants. I fish out a soft leather jacket, doing up the ties across the plain white shirt I apparently slept in.

My arm twinges as I press my face to the window. A stone balcony stretches in both directions as far as I can see, and I twist the knob in the middle of the door, stepping over the high threshold.

A cold wind sinks deep into my clothing and brushes my hair from my face. I peer over the balcony into an empty yard with a manicured lawn in the centre and shielded lamps on the pillars. Light rain drifts as I collect my thoughts, ticking off the things I know of this world.

I fell from the sky, and I'm fine. A creature sunk teeth into my arm, and it *hurts*. Someone dressed me in clothes that aren't mine.

I need to find Tyson.

Other doors line the open-air corridor facing the courtyard below. My breathing shallows as I edge towards the corridor's end, to the staircase spiraling down the right and deeper into the building. Blank windows glare accusingly.

I watch the ornate knob on the door to my right as I pass, waiting for it to turn. A noise from my left snaps my head to the side, but the room stays quiet and still. I release a deep breath.

Then voices echo up the staircase as someone climbs.

"She shouldn't be awake yet, but I'll check." It's a woman's voice, harshened by the spiral tower. "But if she is, I'll take her straight to the Headmasters."

That sounds like a punishment. I back up, nearly tripping over my own feet. Forgetting my injury, I catch myself against the rough stone.

"Ow!" I lean against the offending wall. A tiny shower of dust coats my boot as I suddenly sink back farther.

Did the wall just move?

I back up as the footsteps draw closer; surely they must be near my floor. I glance down the corridor with the waiting doors and mysteries lurking behind, then re-examine the wall. The stonework is a slightly different colour than the wall beside it, and a shadow outlines a small, rough doorway.

The gamer in me recognises it immediately. *A goddamned secret passage.*

I push against it; nothing happens. My fingers search the gaps, but the mortar is hard and unyielding. I look around for an ornament, a lever, anything, but the only decoration is a gas lamp.

My hand searches the brass stem of the lamp. When I find the lever, I pull it.

Stone scrapes against stone as hidden hinges unlock. I scramble to the wall and push, falling into the darkness behind. I shove it closed and hear the click of the hinges re-latching just as someone rounds the nearest stairwell corner. They walk right past my hiding spot.

Only then do I wonder if I've locked myself into the wall of the Academy. I feel around with my foot, finding another stair behind me like the one I just escaped. Carefully, with my good hand on the wall, I wobble down the hidden stairs. Several creatures skitter away. The air tastes stale with a hint of mould. I wrinkle my nose and try not to screech when I walk into a cobweb strung across the stairs. To avoid it, I lift my right hand and try to call the fire, but besides a spark or two that lights the dark stone in a flash, there's nothing. My injury sears with pain, and I abandon the effort. No fire for me.

When light finally seeps into my secret tunnel, I breathe a sigh of relief. The hidden passage emerges as a slender crack in the wall behind a statue, and I squeeze past the marble figure, thinking skinny thoughts. Though I take special care, I bang my arm on the statue's thigh and blanche with pain.

I emerge in the hallway Eustace led me down just a few hours—or was it days?—ago. It's empty, and I scuttle down until I reach the courtyard.

The stablehands are flat out, and I walk unnoticed across the yard. When a cart laden with firewood nears the gate, I follow it out, looking bored and plucking at a thread in my cuff.

The hairs rise on the back of my neck as the Academy looms behind. The townsfolk pay me no attention; they're busy with sacks of grain over their shoulders, children around their feet, horses at their heels. When the shopfronts turn into houses, I break into a little jog. My boots skip unevenly over the cobblestones.

Where did the cart bring me from? I hasten through the square and shoulder someone aside to see down the next alley. The overhanging rooves and deep drains don't look familiar, so I waddle on, trying not to look too panicked.

If Tyson has gone back, can I do the same? Just jump back into the river, have it turn into a washing machine and spit me out onto the banks of Narralong? Or—my stomach sickens—were they caught? The guards remained at Markon's house. Did Laela return thinking the coast was clear?

I'm so lost in thought that when a hand grabs me by the arm, I jump almost a foot. It's a man—tall, well-built, with black hair salted white at the temples. His eyes were made for frowning, two deep, dark wells that bore into mine.

"You shouldn't be out here."

I look at him, wide-eyed, like I don't know what he's talking about. Then I yank my arm free and start running.

I get about two seconds' head start before the man gives chase. Pure adrenaline pours into my system and I fly through the little alleys, taking each turn as fast as possible.

"Stop!" he calls as I hurtle down a narrow street.

But some architectural genius built a house directly across the street, and the arch beneath it is piled high with pallets and crap. Without stopping, I take a running leap at the junk and try to climb. A strong arm snags me around the waist.

"You are determined, I'll give you that." He lifts me as I wriggle and kick. "But you don't belong out here, little mage."

"Let go!"

He puts my feet barely on the ground. I struggle to gain better footing, but he holds me tight.

"You're going back to the Academy, hopefully before they realise you're gone. How did you get out anyway?"

I lift my chin and stay quiet as he scoots me back through the alleys. We're both filthy. Mud has splattered halfway up our trousers, and his leather apron leaves soot marks on me. My arm aches; fresh blood stains the bandage. He notices.

"What've you done?"

I shrug. "Got bitten by something."

He puts me down but keeps ahold of my shoulder. His face furrows in indecision that clears as another stain blossoms. "Come on. Back to my shop."

I dig my heels in as he tries to lead me away. He sighs. "I'll fetch a guard; how does that sound?"

I pause in my struggling as I mull it over. I didn't like the look of those guys that came to Laela's house. "No guards."

As he hauls me through the streets, I feel again for the itch in my blood that has been ever-present since I washed up on the banks. It's louder than it was in the secret passage, and it'll hurt to conjure, but it's there now. I'm not defenceless against this man.

The mud deepens as we leave the district. Stone houses become wooden ones, their rooves thatched with golden straw. Wood smoke thickens the air as hammers ring out.

"In here." He nudges me towards an open shop. A forge sits in the centre, fire glowing, but the coals brighten as I approach. He looks over me. "Another fire mage. Been a while since they've had one."

"What do you mean?" I perch on the wooden stool, enjoying the fire's warmth on my damp skin.

He waves my question away. "I don't wanna tell you anything they haven't."

I scowl. "They haven't told me anything. They dumped me in a cave and made me fight off strange creatures. Then they dropped me from the sky onto my face."

The man snorts as he peels the bandages from my arm. "Gods-touched. You're twice cursed, girl."

"Gods-touched?"

"To fall from the sky and walk away? Yes. The gods are watching you. You have my pity."

I wince as he pulls the last layer away. It is heavy with new blood, and the punctures throb anew. The blacksmith whistles.

"Did a good job, whatever it was. You don't know what bit you?"

"Some kind of wolf, but it was smaller. Patchy fur."

He brings over a torch, and in the golden light it's clear the wounds aren't healing. A greenish tinge rings each tooth mark.

"Did they yip?"

I remember the ringing barks in the cavern. "Yeah. Hunted in a pack."

He begins mopping my arm up, but some of my blood has dripped, staining the hay.

"No more than seven?"

"I didn't exactly count them."

"Mm." He leans back, rubbing his jaw stubble. "Let me think for a bit."

More blood runs down my arm, and I pale. "Take your time."

He sits beside me, deep in thought. Finally, he moves to a bench on the back wall. As he bends to dig through a bag, the clink of glass bottles catches my attention.

"Are you gonna introduce yourself?" I ask finally.

"I think the less we know about each other, the better."

He returns with a small, dusty bottle. "You've got a lot to learn about Lotheria, little mage."

Lotheria. I finally have a name for this place. The thought somewhat relaxes me.

Sudden pain tenses my every muscle as the blacksmith pours, and I wince.

"Sorry," he says, not sounding sorry at all.

Green liquid trembles atop the open wounds before sinking in. A new kind of panic hits me.

"What was that? What did you put on them?"

He plugs the cork back on the bottle. "The antidote to the fangs' venom. Whoever patched you up at the Academy didn't know what they were looking at. Probably a southerner."

I don't ask him to elaborate. Too much information has filled my head, none of it Tyson-related. He wraps clean linen around my forearm in silence.

"I'm going to take you back to the Academy now. For reasons you'll understand soon enough, I won't come in with you. Can I trust you'll remain there?"

"I'm not promising anything to a man who won't give me his name."

He sighs. "You're welcome for patching you up. Come on, girl."

I hop off the stool. I hate to admit it, but my arm already feels better. The steady throbbing has warmed into a seemingly manageable ache. Following him from the shop, I emerge, blinking, into a waning grey day.

When we reach the main square, he stops and points to the main doors. "Go through those. Don't tell them where you came from, and if I'm very lucky, we won't see each other again."

I nod, but I don't really understand. "Okay... Thank you."

He waves it away, already returning to his shop. I watch until the traffic hides him. Then I trot away from the stone castle and back amongst the people.

I have to find Tyson.

CHAPTER SEVEN

THE RAIN HOLDS off as I head to the other side of town, away from the blacksmith and his shop. No one pays me any mind as I trundle down the streets. I keep my head down when I spot two men wearing black armour, but they're smoking and laughing. They don't notice as I pull my hood up and continue.

Houses and taverns thin, replaced by open workshops. I watch a carpenter turning a length of wood, shavings falling to the tiles. Next door, a young man stacks pallets of clean glass, his face screwed up in concentration. I wander the craft district, passing painters and potters. No Tyson.

My feet carry me to the river, where a large building towers on its banks. Two little boats bob in the water. Men load them with barrels as one yells orders. The air smells sweet and heavy, thick with the scent of sugar and alcohol. Large letters painted on the building spell out its name.

V.B. Brothers Distillery.

I watch a little longer, fascinated by the boats—long, wide crafts that sit low in the water with a single mast and furled sails. The barrels occupy almost all the room across the deck.

"Oi!"

Two men climb the slight hill that leads to the river's shore, their eyes fixed on me. Both have patchy stubble clinging to weak chins, and their loose trousers and shirts are badly stained.

I take a step back as they approach, and one groans. "Thought you said she was pretty?"

The other drags the back of his hand across his mouth. "Didn't get a good look til now. You watching the boats, girl?"

"I was just leaving," I mumble, then walk back towards the busier streets.

They follow. "Oi, nah, they're good boats. You should stay and watch the launch."

"No, thank you."

One jeers, something about thinking myself too good for the likes of them. The other agrees in a loud, sneering voice. I begin to wonder if this is why the blacksmith told me to stay in the castle.

Flustered, I take a wrong turn, then stare furiously at the dead-end I've just walked down. The back of a shop blocks what would've been a thoroughfare, and when I twist on the spot, both men are blocking the entrance of the alley.

"You know, I don't mind that she's not so pretty," the first says, advancing with a grin, exposing the yellow stumps of his teeth. "Grab her, Jeren."

I hold up my hand as the other goes to lunge at me. The fire comes easily, adrenaline blocking out any pain from the injuries. Both pause at the sight of flames on my fist.

"A baby mage." Jeren raises his eyebrows. "Well, I never."

The first man hitches his trousers. "Praise to you, girl, you just became more valuable to us."

"Leave me," I command, but it comes out weak. "I mean it."

They ignore me. "You still got that cousin up north? The trader?" Jeren asks the other man.

The other nods. "Aye. He's looking for new stock, and he'd pay pretty for an untrained mage."

They grin at each other, future riches gleaming in dull eyes. I cuddle my left arm close, knowing I'll have to rely on my right to do all the fighting.

I pretend they're the jackals in the cavern.

Jeren comes in to get me first, and I swipe at him with a closed fist. He leans back as sparks wash over his greasy shirt.

"Come on, girl, nice and easy now."

I'm too frightened to reply. As he makes a grab at me, I dodge his first attempt, then plant a burning hand on his shoulder. The material catches easily, and Jeren yelps when he realises he's ablaze. As he frantically tries to put it out, I take a running step forward and kick him between the legs.

64

On fire and in pain, he staggers away while his mate swears at me. "None of that, little bitch. Come on, now."

I turn to face him, emboldened by the fire in my blood and my first victory. This man is smarter, going for the arm I'm trying to protect, but on a whim I crouch low and punch him in the stomach. His shirt doesn't catch immediately like Jeren's, but the wind is knocked from him and he reels back with an 'Oof.'

I try to shove past him. He seizes my right arm. Without stopping to think, I headbutt his face. Blinding pain spears through my skull, but I blink it away and run as he swears, clutching his head. Jeren is still on fire.

With a glance at them, I dart from the alley back into the town.

The stableboy, Thompson, lets me back into the courtyard with a puzzled look. As the wooden door fastens behind me, I relax slightly with some regret; there's no way the men can get to me here, but I'm no closer to finding Tyson now than before I left. Panic tightens my chest. I have to find him soon; he doesn't have magic fire to shoot at bad guys, though I imagine a kick from him will hurt a lot more than mine.

I rub my face with my right hand as I cross the yard to the open arch that leads to the hallway. I'm thinking of crawling into bed to get a few hours of sleep before my next search when I hear men at the end of the corridor and a voice, rapid-fire, bargaining for freedom.

I dart across to my niche and cram myself behind the statue that occupies it. The crack in the wall that leads to my hidden staircase is inviting, and I'm halfway through it when I recognise their quarry and smother a gasp.

Markon, the man who hauled us from the river.

I stay frozen behind the marble. When I hear Laela's father plead again, I grip the statue's arm so tightly that my fingers go white.

After a second's consideration I slide out from my niche, silent as a shadow. The men turn the corner at the end of the hall. The rational part of my brain tries to steer me up the stairs to safety, but instead I trace the men's steps through the labyrinth castle. None of the party glances behind and I grow bold, closing in, unwilling to lose them.

They drag their quarry around a corner, but I pause and hunker down on the floor. The corridor they walk is bare of decoration. No niches, no vases, no statues—not even a tapestry to hide behind. I'll be completely exposed.

I crawl forwards, recognising my biggest advantage: they don't expect to be followed. Markon's voice covers the whisper of my boots against the thick carpet, and we're nearly to the end of the corridor.

A bite of pain lances through my injured arm, and I stumble, almost face-planting into the floor. The party halts. I stay in my huddled position. This far inside the castle, the light is dim; a single, dusty chandelier swings far overhead from the tall ceiling, with fat little candles that sputter. I tucked myself against the wall when I started crawling. I lie on my face now, my breath disturbing the bits of fluff that have attached themselves to the carpet.

An age passes before someone speaks. "Told you this place is haunted."

Another voice laughs. "It has every reason to be. Come on."

They hoist the man between them and disappear around the corner. I rest there for a moment, heaving shaky breaths before I get my feet under myself and waddle after them.

I round the corner cautiously. A door slams, bouncing off the frame and letting the weak torchlight spill across the carpet. I crouch beside the door and listen.

"Ah, Markon. I was hoping it wouldn't come to this."

"Then don't let it." Markon's voice is stronger, but I hear the quavering note. I hug my knees to my chest.

"You know the rules."

I peer around the door at the familiar voice, glimpsing the room inside. Three men in black armour stand between Markon and the door. Markon stands before a table, across from two strangers—a man and a woman. Another man in blue robes is off to the side. His face is almost unreadable, but a muscle ticks in his cheek.

The woman steps forward with a cold look. Her white hair, laced with strands of black, is tied into a loose rope that rests over her shoulder. One eyebrow lifts slightly higher than the other as she takes in the man before her. "We wrote to the governor, and he agrees with us. Never in our time has someone had the audacity to take a humanborn student into their home before the Academy finds them."

"Headmaster Netalia, she was cold!" Markon protests. He lifts his hands and shakes his head. "I only—"

"You were waiting for her," the man beside her rumbles. I look him over. Every head in the room turns towards him when he speaks, but he doesn't appear to notice. His eyes bore into Markon's as he steps closer to the table. "You wanted leverage over her."

Silence thickens. He continues.

"Your daughter, I'm presuming. Recently out of work, unmarried, non-magi. A nothing person, really. No special talents or looks. You needed an in. You needed a student."

I think of Laela serving me hot mead with a sly grin, and my temper rises in my gullet.

Prick.

"As for the second you pulled from the river—"

"There was no second. It was just the girl."

I press my knuckles to my lips at his lie. He did it well, with just the right amount of humility and shame.

"Sergeant Hall is slipping with his reports," the man murmurs to the woman, Netalia, beside him. Then, louder, "The penalty is set, though we had to sift through archives to do it. Your audacity, Markon Pike, will get you killed. But not today."

My relief is temporary when I hear movement in the room. I crane my head around the door again—they've got Markon with his hand outstretched on the table, and one of the men holds something that glints silver in the lamplight.

My heart leaps into my throat. I can't look away.

"Do it," Netalia orders. The hatchet falls.

I pull myself back, chest heaving. My empty stomach roils, then I'm fighting to get my legs under me.

I race down dark, unfamiliar corridors, panic flooding my mind. I could so easily get lost in this castle. What would I do if I did? Wait for sunrise? Sleep in a wall niche?

Markon's cry of pain, muted in my ears, replays in my head. I skid to a stop and cover my mouth with my hands, fighting tears. I take a deep breath, steadying myself, then turn another corner.

"Good evening, Miss Evermore."

The velvet voice slinks through the dark. Fire lights on the man's palm, rust-coloured like old blood. His dark, elegant features are lit by the flames, and I take a step back.

He was just in the room with Markon, insulting his daughter, threatening him. How can he be here before me?

"It's very kind of you to join us, finally." He takes a step forward. The heat from his fire warms my tear-stained cheeks. "You were missing from the address today."

Anything I say, he'll know to be a lie. I grit my teeth and wait for him to continue.

He comes closer, towering over me. "Tonight, I will let you return to your rooms. But learn from his mistake. Remember what you saw."

I won't be able to forget. My day in the town, my defiance of this new world, is thrown into the sharp relief of this man's fire and command. I nod, but a new kind of heat warms my stomach.

Anger.

He brushes past me, leaving me in the cold, dark hallway. "Goodnight, Miss Evermore."

CHAPTER EIGHT

THE CLANGING BELLS wake me from a restless sleep. I sit up against the headboard, still dressed from the previous day, my boots in a discarded pile on the rug. Old sweat stains my brow—I was dreaming of home.

I squeeze the blanket in my hand, my heart hammering. Tyson spent his first night alone in this alien world. Did he sleep in the gutter, or did he haul ass back into the river?

There's a knock at the door. I jump, then clamber off the bed, my fingers combing through my hair. "Come in."

A young woman enters, her face sour and drawn. She bears a silver tray. "Breakfast, my lady."

I wrinkle my nose. "Call me Rose. Please."

"Where would you like it, my lady?"

I can hear from her tone where she'd like to put it. I don't answer, and she sighs, then sets the tray on my dresser with a bang. The door slams behind her.

The tray contains a plate with two pieces of toast and a small teapot. I lift the lid and sniff the fragrant steam cautiously, then slip the toast into my pocket. After pouring a cup of tea, I carry it from my room to the open hall outside.

The courtyard is empty except a few tiny birds flitting from the low hedges. I sip the tea.

Scenes from last night flash through my head. The silver hatchet, the sickening thump, Markon's anguished cry.

Bile rises in my throat and I lean against the railing with my eyes closed, setting the tea aside.

They only took his finger, I think, and hate myself for it.

What I saw last night only raises more questions I dread answers to.

I rub my face with my hands. If that's what they did to one of their own, what will they do to Tyson if they find him? Laela's mother said they'd kill him. Until last night, I didn't believe her. No world could truly be that harsh. Now I understand a little better.

Someone climbs the stairs, soft leather shoes tapping against the stone. The maid who brought my breakfast skitters to the top, holding her skirts in one hand. She sees me and her face sours again.

"You're not meant to leave your room without an escort, miss."

I look at my open bedroom door, then back at her. "You never said."

She scowls. "As long as you're not going to run off again.

Politics' Master Alena has gathered the other humanborn downstairs."

The word sticks. "Humanborn?"

She approaches and steers me back into my room. "If you'd been at the Headmasters' Ceremony yesterday, you'd know." She digs through my dresser. "Others like you, who came through the river."

I stand in the doorway, my teacup now cold in my hands. Something lifts in my chest. "There are others like me?"

"Four." The maid dumps a pile of fabric into my arms, bumping the wounds and making me wince. "Do you need assistance?"

I guess she'd be about as gentle as the creature that injured me. I shut her out and don the soft grey clothes, then lace the boots from yesterday. When I reopen the door she's standing guard like a tiny sentinel in a linen cap.

"Come on, you're already late." She leads me across the balcony and down the winding stairs. A strong, female voice sounds from the hallway beyond, and she shoves me towards it.

The woman paces the hallway like a drill instructor, hands clasped behind her back. Four people stand before her. "Finally, Miss Evermore. Where's her cloak, Greatree?"

The page who fetched me from the Pikes' house comes closer with a wooden box. I take it roughly, making my sore arm complain once again. I fiddle with the golden latch.

He watches, concerned. "Miss Evermore, if you need help—"

"It's fine," I say, tugging at the ornate clasp.

Eustace watches me a second longer before taking the box and opening it easily. He extends it with a flourish, and I pull the length of slate-grey material free. He finally gets the message and drifts away with the empty box. I swing the cloak around my shoulder as the others do the same.

Politics' Mistress Alena clicks her tongue. "Girls fasten on the left shoulder, boys on the right. Come on, Miss Evermore, it's not that difficult."

I force myself to ignore her, my fingers fumbling with the silver clasp. Just as I'm about to tear the heavy clothing from my shoulders, lithe fingers replace my clumsy ones.

"Stand still." A girl with dark, curly hair fixes the clasp, then adjusts the folds of the cloak so they fall evenly.

"Thanks," I mutter as our mistress observes the boy trying to do his. "What's your name?"

She smiles. "Dena."

"I'm Rose." She finally gets the silver bird to sit flat. I clear my throat. "Thanks. Probably a whipping offence to not present this right."

"I hope not," a girl says on my other side. She's a curvy blonde with a soft face. "I strongly suspect whipping will be bad for my complexion."

I snort with laughter despite myself, and Dena stands beside me as our mistress inspects our group. I shoot the friendly girl a sideways look, curious about my classmate. She's a little taller than me, her skin dark. Her eyes are warm brown behind her glasses, and she smiles at me as the woman polishes a nonexistent speck from my clasp and steps back to address us.

"Though you will not bear your Silver Wings until graduation, you will represent the Academy with pride," Alena says. She's only a few years older than us, with dark brown hair coiled at the base of her neck and deep blue eyes. Her mouth is tucked into one corner, and I wonder if it's because she's been put in charge of the humanborn. She holds a hand to the archway. "This way, everyone. Welcome to Fairhaven."

Those in the entry courtyard nod as we pass, and unlike the previous day, the heavy gates are open to the village. A brisk wind sails over the cobblestones as we cross the square in the shadow of the Academy. I pull my new cloak tighter, suddenly grateful for its warmth.

There were gloves in the box, and I pull them on eagerly—it's cold. Colder than anything I've known in Narralong, even winter. Alena leads us around the sizable village, ignoring the villagers' stares and bows. We're shown a mural depicting a fishing scene on the river I was pulled from, the oldest tavern in Fairhaven, and a plaque declaring the opening of a new townhouse. I look at everything as we thread through the streets and pass a dilapidated stone church. Dena walks beside me, bright and alert, taking great interest in everything from the construction of the buildings to the fashions of passersby.

"Isn't it wonderful?" she asks, watching a horse-drawn cart loaded with noisy sheep.

I don't reply. A person getting their fingers cut off for simple hospitality doesn't fit my definition of wonderful.

We encounter a small square lined with shops and garden beds. Flowers bloom in the dark soil, bobbing in the breeze. In the centre is a large stone statue of a woman with one arm raised above her head and a look of wonder. A fountain burbles with clear water around her feet.

"This is our second queen. Known as the Lily, Queen Fleur led an age of peace roughly fifty years ago. Since then, her legacy has ensured that all of Lotheria lives harmoniously."

She could be reading off a script. Even Dena looks a little bored as Alena continues, extolling the virtues of a dead monarch. I look around while the lecture wears on, noting that the shops here look much more expensive than anything we've seen yet. It's quieter too, with fewer people going in and out. I notice a few men watching us from the alleys, their hands clasped lazily behind their backs, feet shoulder-width apart.

"We'll head into a tavern for lunch now," Alena says loudly, and we all snap back to attention. "If you'll follow me?"

Lagging, I'm the last to pass the Queen Fleur statue. I glance at the brass plaque hammered into the front of the fountain and halt.

She will rise again!

The bold proclamation has been scrawled in white paint, dripping crudely across engraved words and splattering onto the tidy cobblestones below. Intrigued, I drag a thumb through the first word. Chalky residue clings to my skin, and I dust it on my pants before Alena notices.

The paint is fresh—someone just did this. Is it for our benefit? I cast a casual glance around the square again. No one has noticed my lingering, nor has Alena mentioned the graffiti.

"Miss Evermore!"

I jump like a guilty child. One of the lurking men—a mage, I now realise—has emerged from the shadows. His face is half-familiar and twisted in annoyance.

"What have you done?" he asks angrily, peering at the graffiti. "Was this you?"

"It just appeared," I say, still wondering how it could've in such a short time. Then I realise how it sounds and spread my arms wide. "You can search me if you want. No paint."

He pats my form and I loathe the feeling of his hands on me. I recognise him now; he held Markon down for his punishment last night. Is this the man who reported two students being taken into the Pike's home? When he finally straightens, I'm surprised he can't feel the heat of my glare.

"Fine. But this—"

"Excuse me!" Alena has finally noticed I'm missing and strides toward us. "Why are you manhandling my student?"

"Making sure she couldn't have done this, ma'am." He watches her closely as she examines the paint.

"I have no clue where that has come from," she concludes

finally, stepping between me and the guard. He still peers at me like I'm a criminal, and a bite of fear lodges in my throat. Will I have all ten fingers tomorrow?

Alena addresses me over her shoulder. "Miss Evermore, the others are waiting."

The guard stops her as she tries to leave. "I'll have to report this, ma'am."

"I'd expect no less," she snaps. She grabs me by the upper arm and hisses in my ear, "Are you done wandering off?"

As I protest, she pulls me along the street like a chastised child. Something silver flits overhead as we meet up with the others, but I can't get a good look before it disappears in an icy sliver of sunlight.

The others are huddled in a group outside a tall building with a balcony cresting its second floor. We are led up the interior stairs to a room with windows standing open. I brace as the curtains billow inwards, ready for the midday chill, but none comes. On either side of the room are tall fireplaces, flames dancing. Their heat seeps across the patterned carpet and presses against my back when I take my offered seat at the long table. I remove my gloves as the others do, glad to find myself next to Dena.

She leans close. "You got lost?"

I shake my head and keep my voice low. "Not quite. Had a run-in with a guard."

She stares at me with wide eyes and I distract myself with wine. It's dark and fruity but musty, like it's been left in a cellar for far too long.

"I hope you don't expect this to be a regular occurrence," Alena tells us as she hands her gloves and scarf to the servant. "But we'd like you to get settled in, show you what the country of Lotheria has to offer you. I know some of you aren't thrilled to be here," she says, her gaze lingering on me, "but believe me when I say others have felt the same, and in a month or two, you won't want to remember where you've come from."

She turns away to consult a menu, and conversation returns hesitantly to our table.

"That got rather dark," Dena says.

"That's Lotheria." I want to say more but decide not to isolate one of the only people who've shown me kindness here.

Lunch is pot pie served with flaking butter pastry and chunks of meat in rich gravy. I stare at it miserably. If Tyson is in Lotheria, I doubt he's eating like this. I remember how sharp Laela's collarbone was. I tear into the pastry, wondering if it's our final meal.

We eat in silence, stealing glances at each other across the table. The only boy in the group hasn't touched his pie, and the red-haired girl beside him eyes it eagerly. The blonde notices and carves a chunk from her own, sliding it onto the other girl's plate.

"Thanks," she mumbles, then devours it in a few mouthfuls.

"So you're new?" Dena asks.

I raise my eyebrow. "I think we all are. And if I'm not

mistaken, they'll call us humanborn." I remember the way Laela's mother said it: like a bad taste in her mouth. "You came by the river?"

"Yeah, it was real pleasant." Her gentle face falls. "Do you think we'll ever go back?"

A guard in black armour stands like a sentinel in one corner, but he's close enough to hear. I keep my eyes on him as I answer.

"No. I don't think we will."

The corner of his mouth twitches as Dena slumps. "In that case, shall we compare notes?"

I push my glass of wine away. "Sure. I know almost nothing, though, so it's going to be a one-way exchange."

She laughs, and the sound melts some of the tension from my shoulders. "That's fine. I thought I didn't see you at the speech last night."

If I hear about this stupid speech I missed one more time... "Yeah, I got held up with something."

I saw nothing of Jeren and his friend as we walked the town. I glance up the table to where Alena sits. She defended me fiercely when the guard grabbed me—what would she do to the men who accosted me?

Dena flicks her hair over one shoulder. "Well, we're here to learn alongside the nativeborn mages, and most of them seem real snobby. There are two Headmasters, Iain and Netalia, who run the place."

My stomach squeezes, threatening to return the pie. "What do they look like?"

"She's pretty small, white-haired but not old. Blue eyes, smells like flowers."

"And Iain?" I already know how they look. I want her opinion.

"Tall, terrifying. I don't know." She flaps a hand, flustered. "When he started speaking, everyone went quiet. *Everyone*. They all hung onto every word with almost... reverence? His voice is amazing. I could listen to him for hours."

I think of the low sentence that slithered through the dark.

Good evening, Miss Evermore.

I shiver. "Anything else?"

She ticks things off her fingers. "Headmasters, mages... oh, magic."

"That little old thing."

Dena brightens, grinning at me. Her brown eyes sparkle behind her glasses. "Have you used your power?"

I think of the burning cavern and the man on fire. "Um. A little."

She shows me her progress, flicking her fingers until cold light flashes from her fingertip. At the head of the table, Alena smiles approvingly and Dena beams like a good little student before continuing.

"We'll learn everything—theory and practice, history of Lotheria, geography of the entire world, and I think they mentioned something about majors?"

I nod. Typical school, got it.

She smacks a hand on the table, and the redhead looks at us sharply. "Oh yeah! We get soulmates."

"What the heck is a soulmate?"

She props her chin on her hand. "Someone who shares your life, your soul, your thoughts—apparently all mages have one. A companion for life, but I got the feeling that anything romantic is uh... heavily frowned on."

"Gross." The idea of letting someone into my life, having someone that close to me, makes me shudder. "Can we opt out?"

Dena laughs like I've made a joke. "Apparently we'll find them naturally, as we study. Isn't that exciting?"

I shrug. "If you're into that sort of thing."

Her smile dies a little, and I know I overdid it. A small bite of shame nips at me, but I don't apologise. We finish our meal wordlessly.

Our mistress finally breaks the awkward silence. "If everyone could gather their coats? We're needed back at the Academy this afternoon." Alena accepts her short grey coat from the serving girl, and we all stand.

The sun has leapt over the village in a disappointing sunset, and guards hidden in the long shadows accompany us. Even my heavy cloak can't keep out the fierce chill. I'm not the only one with chattering teeth when we reach the Great Hall, where Eustace and some other Academy pages await us. They take our cloaks and gloves and turn away as the Headmasters, Netalia and Iain, enter from the other side.

"We hope you all enjoyed your outing." Netalia smiles thinly, somehow not showing a single iota of emotion. I remember her voice, ordering the man to 'do it'; I take a deep breath as revulsion unsettles me. "Before dinner, we'd like to get you processed so we can proceed to the important parts of your schoolings. The other mages have waited for this their entire lives."

Well, they can wait a bit longer. I'm still fighting my stomach.

"Who are we seeing first, Page Greatree?"

Eustace consults a list like more than five names are on it. "Miss Dena Brungarra."

Dena shoots me a frightened look, and I flash what I hope is an encouraging smile and not a 'Thank God it's not me' smile. Eustace bows as she disappears into a small room off the side of the hall. Feeling a bit lost without my new friend, I pace and hug my arms, pretending my fingers aren't getting frostbite. The doors to the courtyard are still open, and I watch Thompson wheel a barrow of hay taller than him to the stables, leaving a small trail on the muddy ground. An older man cuts him off halfway, pointing at the towering stack of hay and obviously berating him for overloading it. Distracted, the boy lets a side of the barrow lean and loses the entire lot into the sopping mud. The older man cuffs him hard around the side of the head.

I'm heading towards Thompson when my name is called. "Miss Evermore?"

Dena emerges, looking shell-shocked. Nerves erupt in

my belly. I redirect my path, feeling the other humanborn's eyes on the back of my head as I step through the arched doorway.

"Come in, Miss Evermore, and close the door behind you."

I obey. The room is even smaller than I thought, and rather dank. A desk occupies most of the space, and lit torches compensate for the lack of natural light. I wouldn't be able to discern night or day if I didn't know already.

"Miss Evermore, please take a seat." Netalia gestures to the chair at the desk. Iain is posted in the far corner. I look away from him and sit. "Now, I'm sure you have many questions."

I do, but they die suddenly on my tongue. I stay quiet.

"Please know you can go to any of your teachers with your concerns, especially Politics' Master Alena." She flicks through a book. Today her long white and black hair is twisted into a severe bun, pinned in place by a jeweled comb. Her glasses have gold rims, and the rings on her slender fingers are encrusted with gems. Her pale robes are finely made with silk trimmings, the silver bird of the Academy embroidered neatly upon her breast. A brooch gleaming of pearl fastens her lace tunic shut, and the smell of lilac perfume is almost overpowering.

Apparently this job pays well.

"Now, my dear." She rests her clasped hands on the book. "All we're going to do today is some very boring paperwork and a quick jab with a needle. Does that sound all right?"

The pie rolls in my stomach. I hate needles. "What's the jab for?"

"A little booster of certain vitamins and immunisations." She flaps her hand as though having strange concoctions injected in me is nothing noteworthy. "We've noticed throughout the years that our humanborn mages tend to get sick over the first few months of their new life. Our medical team came up with boosters to help them recover and return to their studies."

That sounds well enough. I look around for this medical team, but it's Iain who sits beside me.

"Your arm, please, Miss Evermore." I hesitate, and he looks at me with dark, unreadable eyes. "I promise I am capable of delivering this booster."

"Oh, you promise. Well, all right then." I try to fight back the snip, but having a needle sprung on me puts me on edge.

I make myself still as the Headmaster takes my arm and rolls up my sleeve. When the needle pierces my skin, I look but grudgingly admit he was telling the truth.

"All done." He presses a piece of clean linen to the site, calming the burn a bit. "How does it feel?"

It hurts. "It's fine."

"Excellent," Netalia says, her pen poised. "Your full name, please."

I'm pretty sure she already knows it. "Rose Lucinda Evermore."

"Date of birth?"

"Um… third of June."

Iain, having discarded the syringe, consults a wooden chart with numbers and symbols carved into it. "Twelfth of Candle Moon."

"Right in the middle of autumn," Netalia says with a little smile, apparently trying to make it sound like a treat. "A fine day for a birthday. And your mother?"

"She exists."

Netalia glances up with a 'Come now' expression: pinched lips and raised eyebrows. I simply hold the cloth to my arm.

"Father?"

"Doesn't."

"Miss Evermore—"

"That's the truth," I say, my eyes on the floor. "I can't tell you because I don't know."

If I hadn't looked up, I would've missed the look she gives Iain. My face heats.

"Has anyone in your immediate family disappeared within recent years?"

I frown. "What?"

Netalia flicks through a tome. I peer at it—hundreds of names, listed in alphabetical order. "Sometimes we can reunite humanborn mages. There's always a line of magic in each humanborn we take. To date, there are seventy-five lines producing mages. There are no Evermores in here."

I shrug. "Probably on my dad's side then. Dunno what his last name is."

I refrain from adding that I don't care whether I have relatives in this world. I'm getting Tyson, then we're busting out of here.

Her expression sours as she reviews the neatly written lines, maybe because they'll have to find a way to add me in between the Eugenes and Falkes.

"So, a non-magical mother, no father to note, and no immediate magical relative. What an odd little creature you are, Miss Evermore." She tries but doesn't quite manage a teasing tone. "Here is your new birth certificate."

The parchment is embossed with golden foil, my name and new birthday in flowing handwriting. With my thumb, I deliberately smudge the 'e' on the end of 'Evermore.'

"Can I go?"

"In a minute." Iain returns to the seat beside me. My heart begins a slow descent to my boots when I see the empty syringe he holds. "We need to evaluate the quality of your magic, Miss Evermore, and for that we need your blood."

I look from him to Netalia, birth certificate in my lap. "But... No, you said just the one needle."

"A tiny fib," Netalia says.

My heart hammers in my chest. I had a blood test once. I still recall the aching pain as it was drawn. "No, thank you."

"Miss Evermore," Iain says. I chill at the warning in his tone. "You must."

"Why?"

"Every student must comply. It is the rule of the Academy."

I clench my teeth, working my jaw backward and forward. Then I stand from my uncomfortable seat, not really minding that the birth certificate flutters to the flagstones.

"You treat me like I'm your possession," I say harshly.

"A crude way of putting it, but yes," Iain says, standing with me. "We will teach you to use your power and create something with it, and in return you will serve us. Once your years are up, depending on how well you toe the line here, you're free to pursue a life anywhere in Gardhillan."

"Oh, goodie," I retort. "Thanks ever so much. Do I get a choice in this?"

"Does the poor man get a choice in being born poor?" Netalia asks sharply. "No. Status from birth frames a stable community. Be grateful your station is higher than most."

I think of Markon losing a finger, Thompson getting hit in the head, and I snap, calling my fire. Iain moves quicker than I thought possible, his strong hands fastening around my wrists as flames coil up around my legs and torso. I seethe inside my fireball, the temper I've always fought finally free to wreak havoc. I want to lash out at Netalia for her callousness, for Markon...

Netalia's quill falls limp in her hand, her lips parting.

"Calm yourself," Iain says. The bass of his voice reverberates through his touch. "Breathe."

He doesn't know I'm fully in control. As part of me tries to attack, the other suggests a better alternative, and I lunge for the door while wreathed in flames. Iain's hold of my wrist loosens, but he doesn't release me, even when my fire sets his sleeve smoking.

His other arm snakes around my waist like the blacksmith's did to peel me from the pallets. My fire flickers and dies as I instead try to escape the man's grasp.

He opens the door I nearly got through.

"Page Greatree? Miss Evermore needs to be taken to her room. And order the smelling salts from Carrier Bayde, please."

"Smelling salts?" I echo, pausing. "Why would you need—"

There's a sharp pain in the back of my head. Then there's only black.

CHAPTER NINE

MY HEARING RETURNS before anything else. A tiny sigh, the brush of a foot against the carpet. Then other sounds filter in: birds in the courtyard, a horse's neigh outside the window. I lift my eyelids slowly, wincing as they scrape against the white gauze wrapped around my eyes.

"What's going on?" I stretch my hands out, trying to make contact with something. "Hello?"

"It's all right." A hand catches my wrist, guiding it back to the mattress. "Just take a breath."

Her voice, though soft, sounds like she's talking directly into my ear. I flinch away.

"Why can't I see?" Blurry white light filters through the fabric, but I'm blind to anything else.

A wave of perfume washes over me, making me dizzy. Alena's next words are hesitant.

"You lost control of yourself. The Headmasters took precautions to keep you and the other students safe."

I turn my head from the overpowering smell of lilies and hear Alena move away.

"Sorry. I tried to wash it all off before coming to see you."

"They took precautions by poisoning me?" I ask through gritted teeth.

"It's a serum to keep you still, but it seems to heighten people's senses. They haven't worked out why."

A bolt of pain shoots through my skull when I try to move, but I force it anyway. "Where are the others?"

"Getting their magic ignited with the nativeborn mages. It's a shame you had to miss the ceremony."

"Yeah, a real shame," I say dryly. Frankly I'm becoming uncomfortable. The fibres of my mattress grate against my skin, though it felt soft enough last night. The crook of my elbow aches fiercely. Apparently they took my blood anyway.

Before Alena can speak, there's an earth-shattering clang from above. The noise reverberates, pressing against my skull, and I cry out unintentionally. A pair of fluffy earmuffs slams against my ears, but I can still hear the bells tolling the hour. Warmth trickles from my nose, but a cloth wipes it before the blood can drip.

Finally, the bells stop. The cloth and earmuffs are removed, but my temples thud with a newborn headache.

I hate Iain for this.

"I'm going to leave these." The earmuffs are placed at my side. "The bells only ring every four hours, but you will hear them."

She stands to leave, but I hear the scrape of her shoes on the flagstones as she turns back.

"Are you settling in, Miss Evermore?"

I look to her voice. Already, my muscles are relaxing. I relish the simple movement. "It's only been a few days."

"Yes, but..." I feel her hesitation. "You know you can talk to me."

I roll onto my side, away from her. I don't feel like talking, not when I can hear every breath, every click of her tongue against teeth. "I want to sleep."

I don't need heightened abilities to sense her disappointment. "That'd be best. I'll come to you tomorrow. You can probably navigate to the privy by yourself."

"I'll be fine," I say gruffly.

When she closes the door, it's gentle.

I'm wide awake when dawn breaks, listening to the sounds of the waking Academy.

For a moment I lie still, encased in a warm cocoon of blankets. Grey light fills my room, making everything monochrome and soft on my eyes. Then I push the covers aside, suddenly eager to be up. My muscles ache as the last vestiges of the Headmasters' poison fight for control of my body, but I ignore the pain and it fades. It's cold enough to warrant my cloak, which I pin on my left shoulder. The folds swish around my legs.

Having laced my boots, I step outside my room into the fresh morning air. I pause, reveling in feeling better—a migraine doesn't spear my temples, and I don't hear everything within a hundred-metre radius.

I'm one of the only people moving around the castle besides the Academy servants. They bow to me as they go about their business, opening shutters and putting out gas lamps. The Academy hasn't opened its doors to the public and stands silent.

I learned from Alena as she and Eustace tended to me that the Academy isn't just a school. Iain and Netalia, in conjunction with the Governor in the capital city, rule the entire country and conduct their business from the castle. It makes sense—a building this size is far too grand to be just a few dozen teenagers' schoolhouse. Merchants, nobles, petitioners, and businessmen all visit the Stanthor Academy during daytime.

The small hall for student dining is full when I arrive. Lit by a large hearth fire at one end, two rows of wooden tables and benches line the flagstones, laden with hungry students. I can't spy Dena and quickly take a seat. A serving page brings me a bowl of thin onion soup and a hard crust of bread. My stomach warbles in anguish as I realise this is the entirety of breakfast.

"You'll get used to it." A mage boy with dark brown hair plonks opposite me and receives his own bowl. He doesn't thank the page. "My mother warned me about the Academy, so I adjusted my diet before coming."

A fleeting memory of a battered hot dog on a stick and a sickly sweet can of soda flickers.

"Do we always eat like this?" I ask, dunking part of my crust into the lukewarm soup.

He shrugs and gnaws the end of his bread. "There are a lot of people in Lotheria who eat worse. I suggest you eat all of it, by the way."

I watch him use the bread as a spoon for a few moments, then the obvious comes to mind.

"Are you my soulmate?" I blurt.

He looks up, half the crust hanging from his mouth. "I don't think so? This was the only seat left in the hall."

When he resumes eating, I pivot cautiously. He's telling the truth. This was the only place he could've sat.

Relief sighs through my system and suddenly the dregs of soup taste delicious. Alena told me that the pairing of soulmates, the one Dena warned me of, is gradual, the only bit of good news she's brought as far as I'm concerned. Apparently we'll make unconscious decisions that lead us to our second half.

"I'm Rose." I stick my hand out.

He takes my hand firmly over our bowls. "Petre Lyon. I'm the son of the Lord of Riverdoor."

I hesitate in our handshake, wondering if a curtsey or something is required. He senses it and laughs.

"As a mage, you rank equal with me. You'll discover that soon."

After breakfast, we're told that we've been given the day to make friends and wander—a thin ploy to match up a few soulmate pairs, in my opinion. Petre invites me on a walk with two students he knows; a redhead mage with pale, freckled skin, and a girl with deep brown eyes and flawless tawny complexion.

"Orin, Amisha, this is Rose," Petre says. The girl, Amisha, takes my hand.

"A humanborn," she remarks in interest. "You could tell us so much!"

"I could, but I don't think I should," I reply uneasily. "I... don't think the Headmasters would like that very much."

She relinquishes my hand but smiles mysteriously. Perhaps she's gotten the measure of the Headmasters better than I have.

The day has bloomed into a slightly warmer one than yesterday. We quickly discover Orin has far too much enthusiasm for little things. He leads us out of town to where the waterwheel splashes in the river. I keep my head down as we pass the cluster of houses where I'm pretty sure Laela lives, but I don't see any sign of the friend she took. My heart beats wildly. I'm wasting time when I *should* be looking for Tyson.

"This mill has been here since the Academy was founded," Orin tells us proudly. Amisha nods, politely interested, but Petre catches my eye and hides a grin. "That means it was here before most of Fairhaven was built."

As Orin turns his soulmate's attention to the paddles'

craftsmanship, I undo my cloak and sling it over my arm, sweat beading on my brow. My stomach clenches so tightly that I think of the Headmasters' poison, but I know it's guilt hurting my belly this time.

I'll find him, I promise. *Later.*

But what if he's hurt? What if they've found him? I clench and unclench my fists, making Petre glance down.

"Are you all right, humanborn?"

My mouth goes dry as I think quickly. "Explain something to me," I say. "There's a statue of the queen in the square, but no queen?"

He raises an eyebrow. "Did all your monarchies survive?"

Good point. "So Iain and Netalia rule Lotheria, then?"

"Not officially. That title falls to Governor Ryman in Castor. He has a puppet council he doesn't consult and has managed to re-elect himself term after term by rigging the votes." An edge creeps into his voice and his cheeks tinge pink.

I take a wild guess. "You don't approve."

He shifts uneasily and avoids my gaze, just like I hoped. "I didn't say that."

"There's a wayhouse just a bit farther along." Orin, setting a steady pace, has produced a map of landmarks for us to visit. Petre suddenly looks as though he regrets bringing his friend. "I'm ready for a spot of lunch. Anyone else?"

The onion soup in my stomach gurgles for company. Surely a wayhouse would have better fare to offer? "Yes, please."

But the little building just off the road is almost empty. A sour-faced woman behind the counter serves us a slab of sagging bread for an exorbitant price. When Petre produces an extra silver piece, she adds a dish of thin sauce.

We decide to sit outside in the sun, something no one can charge us for. A spindly table and chairs keep us out of the dirt, and Petre sheds his cloak as Orin tears a strip from the bread. Both boys are sweating already, but Amisha looks comfortable.

"Used to the heat?" I ask.

She tilts her face to the sun, her rich brown skin glowing. "I love it. Reminds me of home."

I suddenly remember the islands from the big map in the cave and think of sun-soaked wind chimes and sea breezes. Is that where Amisha comes from?

"Too hot," Petre says, folding his cloak. "Never this hot in the mountains."

My thoughts wander back to my excursion to the township. "Alena took us to Queen Fleur's statue yesterday. Someone graffed it."

"Graffed?" Amisha queries.

"Drew on it in paint," I explain. "They wrote, 'She will rise again.' But hasn't she been dead for, like, fifty years? Would've thought she'd be pretty crusty by now."

Amisha laughs gently as Orin rolls his eyes. "Monarchists," Orin says. "They're a political group who wants the return of a standard monarchy. They idolised Queen Fleur and are convinced she's coming back to Lotheria."

"They've not done much in the last century," Orin continues, twisting a coil of bright red hair, "besides organise the odd strike and write bizarre slogans on walls. I can't imagine Fleur would be too proud of them."

"So when Fleur died, the crown didn't pass to anyone else?" I bite into the pasty. "Most of our monarchs were brought down by public indignation and revolution."

"Fleur died peacefully at an old age after the War of the Lily. Her husband was killed in it, though, and she never bore any children. After that, there was no need for another queen. A council, and now the Academy Headmasters, stepped in to fill the gap."

I frown. "So no distant cousins stepped up to claim the throne?"

Amisha and Orin share a look. It strikes me how easy they are together when they've apparently just met; maybe there's something to this soulmate thing after all.

"I don't think you're quite grasping how the Lotherian crown works," Amisha says finally. "Whereas your monarchs, and my Empire, go by bloodline, Lotheria has a... different way."

Orin sighs. "It's not crazy. I can hear the disapproval, Amisha." His soulmate lifts an eyebrow and smiles innocently as she nibbles some bread. He continues, "In Lotheria, the land chooses the monarchs."

I mull it over as I work some bread from its stubborn perch in my teeth. "Cool. Does it write horoscopes, too?"

"He's serious," Petre says.

I stick a finger in the untouched sauce. "But how? It's not a sentient being." I glance around at the dusty road. "Is it?"

"Apparently." Orin picks up the last piece of bread and uses it like a pointer. "Or at least, that's what the older history books will have you believe. That stuff is starting to become myth instead of fact."

It's hard to keep the derision from my voice. "And it chooses your monarchs?"

"Again, more speculation," Orin says, though his mouth tucks in at one corner, apparently displeased.

"Well, I'm totally up to date now." I smile at him. "Thanks. You guys are really nice to hang with." Their horrified expressions prompt me to add, "Not hang, literally. It means to spend time with."

"Your lingo doesn't translate well here," Petre mutters, a hint of amusement in his tone.

I sigh. "I know. I'm trying."

It's evening by the time we wander back into Fairhaven. The daytime warmth has lapsed, leaving us pink-nosed and shivering. Orin tells me we are moving into winter, a prospect which first depresses then delights me when he promises snow. Narralong isn't suited for snow, and I've never seen it firsthand. We thread through the traffic and lamplighters, and my stomach lurches when I recognise a girl moving through the night traffic. My heart quickens.

"I'll see you guys later." I peel away from my new friends.

I don't hear their hurried goodbyes as I chase Laela

through the alleys. She's quicker than me, having grown up in this labyrinth of cobbles and close houses.

"Laela!" My shout echoes down the alleyway. Several people look at us, but she stops and addresses me over her shoulder.

"I don't want to talk to you."

I falter, then resume my pace. "What happened wasn't my fault."

She levels a glare that pierces me. "Doesn't mean I have to like seeing you."

Ouch. That hurts more than it should.

I move around to look her in the eye. She meets me steadily. "All I want to know is what happened to Tyson."

Her lips thin, and she readjusts her grip on her basket. "Your non-magi friend."

The one who caused all the trouble goes unsaid but we both hear it. I chew my lip. "Yes. My best friend."

She pauses for a second and I wonder if it's some small revenge for what happened to her father. Then she sighs. "He's here in Fairhaven. He found some work with a smith."

I'm so relieved I can't help the small laugh that follows her sentence. She smiles ruefully, like she's trying to fight it.

"I guess you'll want his address?"

"Please," I say eagerly.

She tucks the basket into the crook of her elbow, tugging my hand from my sleeve. The cold evening air bites as she removes my glove. She grips my wrist with slender fingers, pulling a reed from the messy bun of rich brown hair at the nape of her neck, and draws a tiny map on my palm with thin ink. The pen nib tickles my skin, and when she leans in to add a street name, I smell the flowery scent in her hair.

"Laela," I say when she straightens. "I really am sorry for what happened to your father."

Her bitter smile is full of regret as she returns my glove. "It was never going to work. I guess desperation does funny things to people."

She turns with that dry smile and walks off as a chilled wind ruffles my hair. I watch the hem of her skirts swish until she turns a corner.

Bells from the Academy towers toll across the square. Guards in black armour light the lanterns on their belts, moving through the throngs of evening traffic. Indecision claws at me; do I try to find Tyson now, amidst curfew? I take a hesitant step away from the Academy, but a hand clamps on my shoulder. I look up into a familiar, unwelcome face: the guard from the statue.

"Well," the guard sneers. "My little artist."

The way he says it makes me sick. I wrench free, tucking my bare hand into my cloak so he can't see the map Laela drew.

"I was just heading inside," I say.

He sneers again, or maybe his face is permanently stuck that way. Sunken eyes examine me closely. "I know you dirtied that statue. You had paint on your fingers."

"Because I *touched* the paint, yes." I start sidling towards the enormous castle, though I don't turn from him. His eyes watch my every step. "Goodnight, sir."

"It's Sergeant Hall," he calls when I finally look away. I stop dead. My heart has sunk down to my boots. Hall is the one who reported *two* people coming from the river.

He knows about Tyson.

I lick my dry lips. "Goodnight, Sergeant," I say over my shoulder.

Then I scramble behind the rest of my classmates into the castle.

CHAPTER TEN

I REFRAIN FROM rubbing my eyes, my bones aching to return to bed. The urge to sneak out again *almost* beat my fear of Sergeant Hall; instead I spent the night awake and worrying. Petre nudges me as we walk, tearing my tired gaze from the slip of paper in my gloved hands and nearly knocking it from my grasp.

"Ignore the schedule, they'll change it anyway," he says, trying to tug it away.

I cling to it. "They might change *yours*. I'll be happy going to these for as long as they'll let me."

He cranes his neck to read my parchment. "Beginner Theory? Starter Casting? Rose, you won't be in these classes longer than a week." A slender flame slips along the leather of my glove, leaving it untouched. Petre taps where it disappeared into my palm. "See? Five silver says you get bumped up to my level next week."

I bat his finger away. "I don't *have* five silver, so you're on."

He grins triumphantly as we approach the closed wooden door where our classmates gather, and everyone surges forward when the door unlocks. The nativeborn mages rush in first; as Petre said on our way down, they'll get their schedules reassigned when it becomes clear what they can already do. I recognise Dena.

"Go with your kind, then," I tell Petre, shoving him a bit. His attitude has started to piss me off. "Get your real classes."

He pouts, but there's an eagerness in his step as he disappears through the doorway.

"Oh, leave him," Dena says as I sulk over to her. "The other mages are excited to finally be here."

My response is a dark look. She sighs, leading me into the room with the other humanborn behind us.

Rows of wooden tables cluster the room. Three arched windows show the grounds far below, letting in shafts of cold, grey light. Exposed wooden beams cross the ceiling, and two hanging brass candleholders illuminate the farthest corners. The whole place smells of some dried herb. I relax slightly.

The bang of books on a desk puts me right back on edge. With sharp, commanding clacks, a man scrawls his name in chalk on the slate that fronts the classroom.

"Sit down, hurry up. My name is History Master Jettais." He drops the chalk into its holder and goes to his desk to consult something. I use the distraction to scramble into an empty seat, Dena right behind me.

"Now, before we get started with actual work, you must choose a subject to major in. Though you'll receive basic tutelage in all of them, your later years will be focused on your major. Once you leave the Academy, certain careers have higher institutions for you to attend," Jettais continues. "Page Myla is handing out your options."

A slip of parchment flutters before me, settling on the desk. A list stretches through three columns.

"You have five minutes. Don't dawdle."

"But, Mr Jettais... The humanborn just got here, shouldn't they—"

"What?" the teacher asks, interrupting Orin. "Get special treatment? Some consideration? No. They will be treated like the rest of you. Hurry up."

He strides back to the front of the room and pulls a large hourglass from beneath his desk. Sand trickles into the lower orb as I clutch at my parchment.

Alchemy
Archery
Cartography
Cooking
Enforcement

Healing
History

Horticulture

Metallurgy

Politics

Runes

Smithing

Sword

War magic

Weather magic

Dena has already scrawled an 'X' next to healing. The redhead next to me scrutinizes the page like she wants to choose everything, and I hover dangerously close to cooking. The image of an inked smiley face seems to flicker in the corner and my stomach tightens, but Mr. Burgess isn't here to give me encouraging words. I glance up as History Master Jettais rakes his coal-dark gaze over the scribbling class.

He catches my eye. "Time's almost up. If you don't choose, one will be assigned to you."

I wish I'd sat next to Petre. What the flip is metallurgy? I'm not strong enough for smithing. If enforcement means joining the ranks of guard muscle, they can forget about it; no way am I carting people in to have fingers chopped.

As Jettais comes closer and closer, I jab my pen at an option, then hand it to him without looking. He does, though, and his brows lift.

"Runes?" To my surprise he tries to hand the page back. "You can choose again if you want."

"It's fine. I'd like to try runes."

He tucks my form into the stack with a smirk. "You'd be the first in years. Have fun with your new... mentor."

A few of the other students snicker. I can't help but feel like I'm the butt of some joke.

He moves along and I lean into Dena. "What the hell are runes?"

"What the shit is horticulture?" she counters. "Orin was right; we should've had time to be coached on these. It's unfair."

I remember Markon. "We've got it just fine. Trust me."

We peel off from the other mages once we're released from History Master Jettais. Petre waves a jaunty goodbye. Our small group of humanborn visibly relaxes when the others disappear from sight, but we toddle in silence. As the bells toll in the towers above, we're let into a smaller classroom with Politics' Master Alena. While she begins teaching the basics of our new power, I find myself losing interest in the bucketloads of theory she dumps on us, my thoughts returning to Laela's map I scribbled in the back of my notebook.

When the lesson shifts to practical magic, I'm the first humanborn to summon fire at will, but it's Dena who first conjures a weak ball of light. The redhead—Theresa, as she reluctantly introduced herself at the beginning of the lesson—absorbs information like a sponge, with the blonde humanborn, Yasmin, a close second. I keep up, but my notebook holds only a few scrawled lines. I sketch lazily for the rest of the lesson, thinking about when I can next sneak from the castle, but I think of Sergeant Hall's hand on my shoulder, the men by the river, and my enthusiasm fades quickly. I *will* return to the township, just... not yet.

Getting let out of the room is a relief, and we move on to our next class according to our new schedules. It's a cold, clear day, our breath frosting the air. I walk with my new mage friends, pulling my cloak tight like a sausage, and wish I'd remembered my gloves.

"There's going to be a frost tonight," Orin says eagerly, testing the air with a finger.

"First snow, more like," Petre replies, and a mini-argument breaks out over the likelihood of one so early in the season.

I stop listening halfway through, more excited about snow than the others are. We leave the building, entering a large, open space lined with trees. The sun falls across my face.

"What about you, Phoenix?" I turn as Petre addresses someone unknown. "Snow, ice... will feel just like home, eh?"

There's something unkind in his voice I haven't heard before. Another mage boy with a solemn face and taller than everyone nods in our direction, then walks on.

"Stop it." Amisha swats him on the shoulder. Petre, apparently annoyed at her reprimand, watches her closely when she turns away.

"Who's that?" I ask.

"He's from the north," Petre says shortly. That's all I get as we cross the field to a man awaiting us.

The man gestures. "Students!" We meander over, a small group of giggles and shouted conversation. As we reach our new teacher, the voices wilt into nothing.

The man before us is from the Tsalski Islands, like Amisha. Tall and lithe, he waits patiently for us to finish talking. It doesn't take long under his hawkish gaze.

"I am Swordmaster Yu." He examines each of us. I clutch my cloak. "I will be your teacher, this field your training room. I'm to instruct you in the ways of our fighting styles and weaponry. You will be given the opportunity to select your choice of weapon"—we must look too hopeful, because he suddenly scowls like thunder—"once you've convinced me you've earned it. First, evaluation. Please accept your new clothes from Page Greatree."

Eustace hands us each a small, beige bundle. I receive mine last and hold up a sleeve.

"Be careful," the page whispers to me with a nervous smile. "Blood is awful to get out of this fabric."

We redress back inside the castle and emerge, shivering, into the bright sunshine. We keep our boots on over the long pants, but the wind goes straight through the sleeveless tunic. I huddle against Dena.

Yu faces us, hands laced behind his back. "We start with laps. You run until you can't. Last one standing is granted a prize."

"Laps of what?" Yasmin asks, arms folded across her generous chest.

Yu gestures across the field. We squint; pages are standing

at different distances—our markers. "Page Greatree is your first stop. And... go!"

I stumble, then fall into a slight jog. Several mages sprint off straightaway, but as he didn't say anything about most laps completed, I maintain my steady pace.

I reach Eustace, manage a small smile, then trot to the next one. I've quickly become one of the stragglers, Yasmin panting beside me. I was worried about my boots pinching, but the inside is supple and soft, moulded to my foot like a sock. Crisp air sears my lungs and I feel the stitch in my side as I slow. I squint ahead for the others. The humanborn boy, Dylan, plods along just in front of us. Dena admirably keeps a decent pace, but Theresa outstrips us; she's amongst the other mages. I've lost sight of the northerner, Phoenix, while Amisha heads the pack.

"Faster!" the teacher snaps when we pass, and I spare the energy to scowl when we're safely away. We've been lapped already, but we don't care.

"Oh my God," Yasmin gasps. She staggers to a halt and braces herself on her knees. "I'm going to puke."

I slump to my knees, then lie facedown. My chest burns and my heart races. My stomach debates whether to upchuck everything from breakfast; I fiercely regret the cottage cheese. Feet rumble past, but I don't look up. Long strands of grass tickle my nose as I turn my head toward Yasmin.

She paces, hands on hips, face to the sky. "I hate this. Oh, I hate this," she pants.

Once we recover, we stagger back to the starting point, keeping a safe distance from Yu. Slowly, others join us, watching those continuing. The sprinters have retired, out of breath and flushed.

Eventually they are whittled down to two. Phoenix and Petre keep neck-and-neck, looping lap after lap. The sun moves across the sky, shadows lengthening as the two run past again. After an age, Petre returns to us, puffing and panting. Phoenix's chest heaves as he comes in, his tunic stained with sweat, but he doesn't seem to be in any discomfort.

"Well done, northerner. For your prize, you get to choose your weapon first." Yu gestures to a wheeled cart that the pages open. Phoenix approaches slowly, almost warily, as though he's waiting for a cruel joke to be played. When no one stops him, he surveys the selection.

Weapons of all shapes and sizes hang from their brackets. While we watch, envy burning off the other mages, Phoenix stoops and picks up a longsword in a dark leather scabbard. He examines the silver trimmings, then draws the sword confidently, like he's done it a hundred times. His muscles flex as the blade gleams in the sunlight, and he holds it before him, apparently measuring the dimensions.

"You've chosen well," I hear the teacher say, his voice low.

There's no response as the younger man takes the sword in both hands. Petre glowers and I brim with more questions, but they die in my throat as the northerner turns back to us. He is looking at the sword—not proudly, but like someone who's used one before.

CHAPTER ELEVEN

BARELY FIVE HOURS after being forced to choose our majors, I have my first Runes class. The Academy page I asked for directions refused to take me, pointing to a stairwell that curled down and under before trotting off as fast as she could.

I have descended so far down the stairs that I'm sure I'm underground. The gas lamps down here are tinted green for some reason, lending the air an eerie quality. Why have they placed Runes so far under the Academy? Is this part of the joke everyone but me seems to be in on? I step over damp, mossy flagstones, but my cloak trails, leaving a muddy streak as I continue down the never-ending hallway. Finally, I turn a corner and spy a door, almost slipping on another lichen patch in my haste to reach it and the people behind it. These dungeons are freaking me out.

I knock on the solid wood, and I think I hear the clink

of a bottle and a muttered curse before a low voice growls, "Enter."

I hesitate, then turn the knob and peer inside, taking in the towering shelves lined with thick books whose pages face outwards. A branch of candles lights one corner and a heavy, parchment-covered desk. Behind it sits a man with a mane of ash-blond hair.

"Uh... hello," I begin. "I'm looking for the Runes' Master."

Shrewd eyes examine me through the mass of hair. After a second, the man continues scribbling, and I hover before entering and closing the door.

"So you're my student."

I shuffle closer. "Student? Just one?"

"I usually only get one. And unless your name isn't Rose Evermore, we're waiting on someone else."

"That's me."

"Good. What do you know about runes?"

Absolutely sweet stuff-all. "Not much."

He huffs like I should know more. "Right. Starting from basics, then."

I sit heavily in the only chair and pull a blank notebook from my satchel. He immediately removes it.

"Hey—"

Another notebook is placed before me. "Use that."

I leaf through the new book. On every page is a linking design of shapes. "What are these?"

I finally get some reaction; unfortunately, it's barely disguised disbelief. "Those are runes."

"Oh, cool," I stare at the designs, hoping to feign interest. "What for?"

"This is where you'll draw *your* runes. At the end of the semester, the book will be destroyed, but until then, those designs will stop anything you draw from activating."

"Mint," I remark, taking the cap from my pen and gently tracing one of the runes.

"You're humanborn, aren't you?"

I look up at my teacher. "Yep. Why?"

"I have no clue why you just called that an herb."

"Oh."

This has happened a few times with Amisha, Petre, and Orin. Besides the 'hang with' comment, I've also received polite inquiries on why I called one of our teachers a certain part of the male anatomy, and Petre was mortified when I agreed with something enthusiastically while invoking an oath; apparently those are taken more seriously here.

"You don't normally get humanborn?"

A slight head-jerk that I guess means 'no.' "Last year I didn't get a student at all."

I continue tracing the rune. "Maybe no one can find the class."

When he doesn't answer, I glance up in time to see his mouth quirked in what might pass as a smile. When I look closer, it's gone.

"What are you doing?"

A completed rune bleeds into the page, the ink running

along the fibres of the rough paper. "Oh, I just copied one of the ones from the top."

He spins my book toward him. "Hmph. Good enough, for a first go."

I thin my lips and spin my pen. I wasn't even trying.

"Draw it again."

I copy the rune three more times before breaking the silence. "Um, sir. You haven't told me how to address you."

"Arno."

"Just... Arno?"

"Runes' Master Arno to be proper."

"Do you only teach runes, Runes' Master Arno?"

"It's my area of expertise. I'm one of two living Rune Masters in Lotheria."

I realise the neat lines on the pages aren't words but rows and rows of tiny, perfect shapes. "What are you working on?"

"Designing. A dam near Mornington is weakening, and I've been commissioned to fix it."

"With runes?" Disbelief is heavy in my tone.

He pauses, then lays his pen down and opens a drawer on the other side of the desk. He reappears with a solid slab of granite that clunks against the wood. "Runes are the most powerful form of magic in a Master's hands."

I watch quietly. He daubs shapes onto the stone from a small jar of white paint. A rumbling reaches the lowest ranges of my hearing, but my teacher ignores it, even when the candles burning on every surface begin to jitter.

The runes upon the stone flare golden, and the granite rots away from the edges until the entire slab looks like a mouldy cake. Runes' Master Arno cleans the paintbrush with a small cloth, then nudges what used to be stone. It crumbles into black sand, which he swipes to the floor.

"What did you do?" I ask breathlessly.

"Resealed some fissures under the south wing. I've been meaning to do it for a while, but you reminded me. Gotta do it every half-year."

Ink drips from the nib of my pen, marring one of the imperfect runes I was half-assing. "But how?"

He lifts a bushy eyebrow. "How what?"

I point at a few granules of sand—all that's left of the granite slab. "You painted pictures onto a rock. That can't be all there is to it."

He sets his elbows on the desk and looks me over. Finally, he opens another drawer and, with a grunt, heaves an identical granite slab onto the desk, flattening my new practice book.

"Look at that, humanborn, and tell me what you see."

I lay down my pen and look. The stone is polished to a deep shine; my reflection stares curiously back. Flecks of white are embedded in the black rock, glinting when the candlelight hits them at an angle, and the whole thing is cut neatly into a rectangle with tapered edges. I run my fingers along the sides, searching for imperfections, then try to scratch the polished surface, but my nail slides off without leaving a mark.

I don't know what he expects from me, so I lean back and say, "It's pretty."

He scoffs. "Pretty? Is that all?"

Okay, not what he wanted. I look at the rock again. I've always loved granite. Cool to the touch, with sparkles hidden in the depths. I run my fingers over the smooth surface, reminded of the countertop in my grandmother's kitchen. She was so excited the day it was installed, but not about the price. I was there when the guy fixed it in place, bored out of my skull as he described how hard it was to cut and polish, thank goodness they had diamond-tipped powertools these days, blah blah blah.

My eyes fly open, and the hand caressing the slab stills.

Arno looks at me. "Yes, little humanborn?"

In Lotheria, they *don't* have powertools. "How on earth did they polish this? Cut it?" I look at the tapered edges. They're perfectly straight. "This must've taken *ages*."

He nods. "Yes, this particular piece took several weeks in a workshop. Hundreds of non-magi hours were sunk into this rock."

I thought it was pretty before; now it's beautiful. I sweep the backs of my fingers across the surface, reveling in its smoothness.

Arno lifts the slab and re-deposits it in the drawer. "My works relies on non-magi craftsmanship. The more hours and effort involved in creating a material, the more energy that the runes drawn, carved, or painted on it can pull from."

I nearly reach for my notebook, overcome with the notion to take notes. Another thought sneaks into its place. "So you have to work with... the non-magi."

Those shrewd eyes seek me out again. "Don't tell me that lot upstairs have already gotten to you?"

I shake my head quickly. "No, but I got some funny looks when I chose Runes as my major."

"A lot of them up there don't like me," he says. "And that's all I'll say on that topic, Evermore. Now that you've seen what runes are capable of, do you want to learn?"

Something in the way he asks it makes me wonder how many students have declined his offer.

I sit forward. "I do."

Arno makes me draw a rune over and over in my practice book. My hand cramps around the pen, and the lines blur as hours wear on. My mentor returns to his own designs, but he fades into the background as I begin dissecting and correcting my own drawings.

When one of the runes at the top of the page flickers with a faint golden glow, he speaks. "Pen down, Evermore. Well done."

I stretch my fingers, wincing as my knuckles pop. "Does that mean I did it right?"

"My runes are suppressing yours, so yes. You've done your first runework."

I look at the one that finally did it, noting the clean pen strokes that resulted in a tidy overall shape. "What does the rune mean?"

"*Burn.*" He opens a drawer, and several objects roll to the front with a clatter. He lifts a white candle and stands it on the desk, then hands me a small knife. "Carve that rune into the wax, exactly like you did on your page."

I take the blade with shaking hands. It took me so many tries to get it right on paper; what will happen if I get it wrong on an actual object?

I nestle the candle in hand and take a deep breath. There's a low hum in my ears, and I let my vision relax onto the rounded surface of the wax. It's clean and pure, begging to be marked.

My hands steady.

With the rune design in mind, my right hand carves deep cuts into the surface of the candle. My fingers guide the blade confidently, and when the wick bursts into flame, I release a breath that nearly blows it out.

"Good work, Evermore. We'll leave it there today."

The burning candle illuminates my bag for me as I pack. I close my rune book with a tangled sense of excitement and sadness; I want to learn more, draw more.

Only when I leave do I realise I haven't thought about Tyson in hours.

CHAPTER TWELVE

WHEN THE TOWN square lamps are lit, I descend my secret stairwell, fingers tracing the familiar patterns in the brick. I'm wearing a plain brown cloak of simple fare instead of my Academy one.

Sure enough, when I reach the courtyard, the gate guard pays me no mind, thinking I'm a servant. I hurry through the opening, my eyes to the cobbles, heart pounding. The little flask nestled in the crook of my arm is a reassuring weight. Dena brought it when I complained of a false headache, promising it would dull the pain. I examined it closely, but as it's from the Academy Carrier, I can only assume it will do what the label says.

The pale blue liquid sloshes inside the glass as I hasten down the alleys. The main square's comforting light fades behind me, and my eyes adjust to the gloom of the commoner's district. The beggars are nowhere in sight—

my breath mists, and I can only hope they've found shelter tonight.

Having searched the warren of houses unsuccessfully before, my heart eases when I recognise Laela's house. A light glows in one window even at this hour. I step under the eaves and go to open the door, but when my eye catches the burnt wood around the molten lump of metal that once served as a lock, I reconsider and knock sharply.

Voices flurry within. A thin curtain is pulled back from the window, and Laela peers out, eyes wide. I lower my hood and jerk my head towards the door.

After what feels like ages, it cracks open a sliver. I press my advantage and hurry inside, then close it, wondering if locking runes exist.

A single candle lights the main room. Markon lies on a bench in the centre, next to the unlit cooking fire. My stomach falls.

"Are you happy?" Laela asks, stepping between me and her father. Her arms are folded and her brow is furrowed, but worry has made her thin-cheeked and vulnerable.

I stay where I am. "I never asked for this."

She shakes her head as she returns to her ailing parent. I follow tentatively, wishing I'd chosen healing as my major or at least thought to bring Dena with me. But I can't trust her yet—not with this.

"How's he doing?" I kneel beside the stricken man.

"I don't know." Raw honesty breaks her voice. "When we saw what they'd done to him at the Academy, we were relieved."

I look up, eyes wide.

"They usually take much more," she explains softly. "My mother thinks they like him because he works hard and talks little."

Now Markon isn't talking or working at all. I reach across him and feel his arm, the heat of his fever burning my skin. Calling the tiniest bit of fire to my thumbnail, I examine the limb further.

Bright red streaks claw up the arm. I swallow hard and rock back on my heels, the magic extinguishing in a holy unimpressive way. How can I tell Laela her father's blood is infected? That the whole thing will have to come off if he's to have any chance of survival?

"It's poisoned, isn't it?" Laela's mother enters, carrying a brace of rabbits. She doesn't meet my eye as she tucks them out of sight. "Once I saw those marks, I knew."

"You have to take him somewhere," I urge, then dig the flask from its hiding place. "This should help, but only temporarily. Where do you go to treat ailments?"

Laela takes the tiny flask. "We don't have a clinic anymore. No one could afford it, and the carrier moved on. Now there's only Bayde at the Academy, and he doesn't bother with the likes of us."

That isn't true. I remember Carrier Bayde at Markon's punishment. His face was hard but not impossible to read—he didn't condone what they'd done to a hardworking citizen.

"He'll help," I say. "I'll speak for you."

Laela's mother turns. "Do not."

Her tone cuts me to the core. I clear my throat and look down.

"If the Academy discovers you were here, a finger is the least of our worries," Laela says.

She's still holding the flask; it's something. I'll find a way to get more to them. I quickly slip into the night, leaving behind a broken man and his grieving family.

I pull out Laela's crumpled map. My heart is heavy for the first few steps, but excitement quickens my pace. The idea of seeing someone I love, from my old world, reignites my vigour in the frozen night. I hurry through the streets as icy wind streaks under my cloak, but my fingers and cheeks are warm with the promise of reunion.

I wind through the streets, slinking from shadow to shadow as the silhouettes of mage guards cross the roads before me. I tuck myself into a nook when a pair passes, crudely discussing a dancer. One laughs loudly—Sergeant Hall. I press myself deeper into the shadows as they go by, my heart slamming in my chest. I remember Jeren and his friend from the river.

This is crazy, I think, but fire heats my blood.

Finally, I find it. The smith shop Tyson's taken work at is tucked into the corner of a courtyard, a wide wooden door fastened shut against the night. Above it is a small loft. Flickering golden light glows through the slats of the window shutters. With my boots, I feel around for a stray rock.

The first stone bounces off the siding, making a small clatter. I try to wait with baited breath, but impatience surges and I toss another. This one connects with the middle of the shutters, a hollow tap sounding back down. The clack of the shutters unfastening sets my heart pounding.

"I've told you kids, if you don't—"

Tyson's dark head sticks out from the opening, and I let all the excitement in my belly glow through a jaw-aching grin. He stares down at me, lips parted.

"Holy shit" is all he says before withdrawing.

I see his shadow flicker over the other side of the room and wait for the door to open. A smaller side door is yanked almost off its hinges, and I let him sweep me up in a massive hug. I wrap my arms tightly around his neck and bury my face in his shoulder as he lifts me. Relief makes me dig in my fingers as my lip trembles. He only clutches at me tighter when he feels me shake.

"It's okay, Rose," Tyson murmurs.

"I thought you would leave me here," I manage before tears choke me completely.

"Never." His fingertips bruise my back, as though trying to make up for all the hugs we've missed. "Never ever."

Tyson closes and bolts the door, then sneaks me upstairs. I follow, hidden in his massive shadow. He shoulders open the door to his room with a creak, then hurries inside and picks up shirts and socks, ditching them in a pile in the corner. He straightens the bed covers, then gestures. I sit as he fastens the window shutters. Then he settles on a rickety wooden chair beside the fire and kicks a small canvas bag out of sight.

We just study each other for a couple minutes. My heart beats so fast I think I'll be sick.

"Well, I'll start, shall I?" He laughs nervously, like a kid on a first date, and I smile at the awkwardness. "Ah, jeez.

"Well, that girl bailed me out the back door and into the streets. She had a hell of a time doing it, too." He nicks at the corner of his eye with his thumb. "I kept trying to go back, but she was stubborn as hell. Worse than Molly."

I remember the girl from our high school soccer team. "Oh, shit."

He grins. "Yeah. But it's a good thing she didn't let me. I have nightmares sometimes about what would've happened."

I don't know what to say. He takes a shuddering breath.

"She set me up with some other clothes. Lost my favourite shirt—she burned it in a barrel. Then she gave me some money, said I looked like I could lift heavy things, and steered me to this area. Then she had to go back, and I think she got me deliberately lost because I couldn't find my way out.

"So I wandered the district and spoke to every journeyman I found. Eventually one of them knew that Craige was looking for a workshop assistant. He took one look at me and had me start hauling coal for the forge,"

Tyson finishes. "And I settled in to wait for you to show up. Saw the girl, Laela, a few more times."

Another feeling peeks through the layers of guilt and fear. Something tiny but red-hot. "Oh?" I say a bit too quickly.

A little colour comes to his cheeks. "Yeah. I didn't know anyone except Craige, so it was nice of her to come check on me. She, uh... brought me something."

I hold my hand up with a grimace. "Pineapple."

He waves our long-standing 'too much information' safeword away. "Nothing like that, you jerk. She taught me to knit."

Sheepishly, he pulls the bag from under his chair and opens it. Balls of rough yarn in bright red, sunshine yellow, and blue-green jumble around in the bottom.

"Oh my God." I pluck one free. "What are you making?"

His expression clears, and he pulls out a small, misshapen circle of yarn with two wooden needles speared through it. "I'm trying to make a hat. She said not to make something too hard first go."

I'm allowed to hold and inspect the hat, which he tucks away before showing off the blue socks Laela brought him when she last visited.

"She seemed a bit distracted, though," he says, lowering his pants leg. "Asked a couple times if you'd come to visit."

I tuck my legs underneath, a bit miffed. "You realise I have to sneak out, right? You think they've got guards wandering only the streets?"

Since term started, there's been a considerable step up in security. Guards in rotating shifts now patrol the front of the Academy, forcing me to climb the fence behind the stables and creep along some poor soul's balcony. Luckily, I've struck a bargain with a stableboy, so I won't have to do it on the way back tonight.

"So what's it like in there?" Tyson asks, adding a split log to the tiny fireplace. He sat me near it after noticing how it flared and flickered in my presence, saying he usually only gets green wood that smokes the place out. Tonight, it burns clean and hot. "Is it all fancy and shit?"

I think of the awful food and scant halls, but then look around at his lodgings. He's done a good job cleaning it up, but there are exposed bricks behind the cracked plaster, and the rug on the floor is frayed and thin. His bed has three blankets, and the windows no glass. A winter breeze rattles the frame.

"It's big. And lonely." I explain how they've scattered the students across the estate so none of us are roomed next to each other. Petre has taken to jogging to my room every morning so he can take me to our first class. "But I don't have to pay for lodging or food," I say, trying to look at the positives.

"Plus," he adds, poking the newest log with a length of scrap iron, "you're actually *meant* to be here."

Something that sounds awfully like resentment weighs heavily in his tone.

"Tyson. Are you okay?"

"No?" He looks up through his flop of hair, sounding unsure of even his own discomfort. "I don't know. It's just... I watch the guards patrol the streets every night and feel prisoner in the rooms I pay lodging for. I'm always hungry because there just isn't enough food. I burn myself every day. I get cold every night. I have nothing to do except knit when the day turns dark early. Mainly, I'm terrified what will happen when they find out I'm 'humanborn.'"

We sit in silence. New flames curl around the fresh wood, bright and playful.

"What can I do?" I ask.

He meets my eyes, as serious as I've ever seen him. "You can find a way to get us home."

I start to protest out of habit before I realise he's right. Of course he's right. Tyson can't stay here. Neither can I. I think of the Other: my comfortable bedroom, our favourite burger place, my classroom. Where neither of us has the threat of discovery hanging over our heads, where our families are desperately searching for us.

But I see Yasmin jogging and laughing beside me, feel the burning candle seated in my hand with a fresh rune carved into it. Laela's skirts swishing around a corner as a brisk evening closes around the township. Petre's wistful look talking about his homeland and the mountains surrounding his estate. I want to see it one day. I want to see it all.

But I reach forward and take Tyson's hand as his gaze searches mine. "I'll get us home," I promise.

CHAPTER THIRTEEN

TYSON LETS OUT a shaky breath, then pats my hand and leans back in his chair. "Well, we're not going by the river."

"We're not?"

He looks at me out of the corner of his eye. "I, uh... tried it my first night alone. Stood in it waist-deep. Even dunked my head under. Didn't feel anything like the washing machine ride that brought us here."

Heat rushes to my cheeks. "You tried to leave without me?"

He holds up his hands. "What else was I meant to do, Rose? For all I knew, this is where you're *meant* to be. Maybe this is where you *want* to be! I saw fire come to you, sit on your hand. That shit doesn't happen back home. It happens here."

The fireplaces flares. "You don't get to decide where I belong."

He meets my gaze, then visibly relents. "I know. I'm sorry. I was scared, a coward. To be honest, doing that—trying to go home without you—has haunted me since day one."

I exhale and blink with damp eyes. The fire dies back down. "I'm sorry, too. The idea of being here without you... That's kind of stuck with me. Whatever we do, we do as a team."

He nods. "Agreed."

We talk into the night, and when my eyelids begin to close, I know we have to say goodbye. We cling to each other and promise further visits before I scuttle back into the streets, wariness of the ever-patrolling guards banishing any thought of sleep.

Getting back into the building is easier than leaving. A silver coin a few days ago bought Thompson the stableboy. He stands on tiptoe to reach the latch and I slip inside, flicking him another coin.

"Get some sleep, kid." I plant a gloved hand on his dirty blond hair as he goes to comply, yawning.

I'm waning too, thinking of my soft bed and tidy room upstairs. I'm alone in the corridors, my footsteps muffled by the thick runners of crimson carpet that line the inner halls.

Then Iain rises from where he's been sitting on the stairs. My blood turns to ice.

"Good evening, Miss Evermore."

The greeting is pleasant and laced with danger. I take a step back. My heart pounds, and I'm convinced he can hear it. I take a deep breath and shove my hands into my pockets.

"Good evening, Headmaster Iain."

He stretches to his full height, towering over me. "Nice night for a walk."

Lie! My brain scrambles to come up with something in the two seconds between responses.

Something embarrassing. Something I wouldn't want to discuss with the Headmaster that isn't totally illegal.

Got it.

"It is," I respond, a little breathy, and I hitch my cloak higher as though trying to hide my neck, drawing his attention to that spot. "I just wanted to clear my head."

"Of course," he says. My finger works busily under the cover of my cloak. "These past few weeks have been intense for the humanborn, I know."

I agree with a noise in my throat, my eyes on a faraway spot.

"But some have been fitting in better than others," Iain continues. I'm reminded of a panther's sinewy strength as he nears. "Drop your cloak, Miss Evermore."

I buy a few more seconds by looking politely confused, but then he lifts his hand as though he'll do it himself, and I relinquish my grasp on the cheap cloak.

The patch of skin burns hot, and I know it's bright red—I bruise and mark like a peach. I let myself redden conveniently, and Iain sighs as he leans away again.

"Miss Evermore, I must ask that you stay in the Academy from now on. I won't ask you for his name."

I feel the heat from my face as I look down. Carefully edging around the man, I head for the stairs to my room.

"Miss Evermore, you should know..."

I turn back when he lets the sentence trail. He's staring at me across the floor.

"Any non-magi caught in a tryst with a mage, or any kind of friendship... The punishment is severe. There's a reason we discourage relationships between different kinds of blood."

I remain frozen as he heads farther away, then shake my head and race up the stairs.

The next day, I stand at the window and watch the rain. A thousand worries roll through my mind. Is Tyson's flat waterproof? Will there be leaks? If he gets damp, he could get sick or the flu—there's no popping down to the chemist for some Ease-A-Cold in Lotheria. I already know no carrier tends to the non-magi.

"Rose?" Amisha's tentative voice shakes me from my reverie. "We're going to the library to study. It's too wet to go outside."

I nod, turning from the window reluctantly.

"Are you all right?" Amisha asks as we walk together. She readjusts the strap across her chest, apparently still adjusting to the long canvas map tube slung across her shoulders. "You seem pensive today."

I shrug. "I'm fine. Just a bit homesick."

She nods. "I know how you feel. I miss the islands."

The long corridor holds no other students. Either they've

found cosy places to tuck up in for the day or they're out braving the deluge to find some food not from the Academy kitchens. I don't blame them.

"How's the map coming?" I ask. Amisha has chosen cartography as her major.

Her eyes light up. "Very well. I'm starting small by just mapping the interior of the Academy. My teacher, Cartography's Master Suvran, is... interesting. I don't think my mother would like her." She sounds pleased by the idea.

We pass a descending staircase, and familiarity smacks me in the face. Goosebumps rise as I peer into the darkness, remembering my trek into the bowels of the castle. I had no idea what I was in for.

Amisha, too, shudders. "That place worries me."

"You were taken down to the cavern?"

She looks at me. "I think we all were. But it wasn't a cavern for me."

Together, we halt at the first step that disappears into the yawning dark. A breeze, stale and musty, sweeps up from underground. Though we're alone, voices mutter past my ears.

Fire gleams on my palm, sending light dancing across the stone arch. But it doesn't penetrate the inky black, and another gust of old wind flaps our cloaks as it soars up the inside of the inverted tower past us into the castle.

"That's a long way down," I comment, pulling back. "So, if not a cave for you, what was it?"

Amisha clenches her jaw. "An island in the sea."

I wait, but she goes quiet. I can tell by her gaze she's a thousand miles away.

Did we all see different things? What did they mean?

I wonder if I should tell her I fell from the sky and lived but shrug it off. How do I even begin that conversation?

"I don't like it here," she announces. With a lingering gaze at the stairs, she continues towards the library. I skitter behind her.

Around the corner and along the hall, the Academy library doors are swung wide. I breathe a sigh of relief. A polished wooden desk with library pages scribbling behind it greets us, but we move past and disappear into the stacks. I run my hands over the spines. I've already raided the Runes section of the library, a small collection of dark novels tucked away at the bottom of a shelf.

Rain spatters against the tall, wide windows that look down into the courtyard gardens on the first floor, where a few Horticulture majors dig despite the weather. Orin is tucked into a red, cushioned chair with an open book on his lap, though his eyes watch the water running in rivulets down the glass. Petre sits on the ground before a similar chair, engrossed in a manual. Amisha steps over him and takes a seat, slinging her map tube behind it.

"Finally," Petre comments, not looking up. "Thought you two weren't coming."

"How was Runes?" Orin asks as I settle in.

I search his question for any hint of sarcasm, but all I get is polite curiosity. "I like it. I think I'll stick with it."

Petre snorts, earning a soft boot to the shoulder. "What do you think of your mentor?"

"Arno seems like he'll be a fine teacher." I'm trying not to let him get to me. "And your major?"

He snaps the book closed, looking gleeful. "Watch."

Petre slides a small dagger from the sheath on his belt: a small, leather-wrapped hilt with a long, unsharpened blade. It looks well-made. I itch to scratch a rune into the steel.

Brows furrowed, Petre draws a finger along one edge. My breath catches; I expect a bright line of red to appear on his skin. Instead, a spark of grey light brightens the steel. Metal shavings fall to the carpet as the blade sharpens itself, and Petre finishes with sweat beaded on his brow.

He holds it out. "Look."

I take it. One edge is dull, the other deadly sharp. I scrape it across my palm.

"So this is war magic? You can sharpen blades?"

He gives me a withering look and straightens. "That's not *all* I can do, it's just what I've done so far. I can strengthen swords, protect their wielder... War magic is a varied element of different strategies and tactics, *which* a lot of people don't realise are diff—"

Orin groans. "Not again. I can't hear it all again, Petre."

Amisha shares a look with me and we hide a smile. Petre frowns.

"Fine. Tell them about your major, weather boy."

Orin runs his palm along the glass. The rain on the other

side of the window follows the path, bending horizontally to do so. He smiles slightly.

"There. That's weather magic."

Petre looks so miffed at the short explanation that I can't help laughing. As they turn to grill Amisha about her cartography magic, I wander the closest stacks. I pull a few books here and there, finally returning with some to skim through. Amisha is the only one to notice.

"*Rivers and Inlets of Southern Lotheria?*" she reads. "I thought I was the cartography student."

I shrug. "I need a break from Runes."

We return to studying in silence. Orin gives up any pretence of reading and plays with the rain on the window, Amisha sketches the interior of the library, and Petre dances silver light on various weapons, apparently sharpening and dulling them for practice.

I pore over the book, seeking any information on the Fairhaven portion of the Lotherian river—the portal. I find a mention of the magical capabilities before the author proceeds to the river's importance for shipping and ferrying of ale and other Fairhaven exports.

I'm not surprised. I didn't exactly expect to find a book called *Don't Like Lotheria? Here's How to Escape!*. I can't imagine the Headmasters letting it lounge in the library. I gnaw my lip as I close the book.

How can I possibly keep my promise to Tyson?

Breakfast the next morning is a strained affair, and not just because it's the wateriest soup we've had yet. The hall is thick with the hearth fire's smoke; the wood was too green when they brought it in.

"Better than what they have in the township," Petre says, covering his mouth with one arm. "They won't have wood at all, if this is what our pages brought for us. The Headmasters will bar people from the forests so we can have a store of firewood for winter."

"So what's everyone else meant to do?" I ask angrily, keeping my voice low. I remember Tyson's glee at a clean-burning fire. Imagining his tiny room without a fire, I feel the chill right to my bones.

Petre shrugs. "They'll steal it or rug up. Sometimes they get a communal hall going where they pool their resources, but it's not much."

I rest my forehead in one hand as I stir the dregs of my soup. It's lukewarm and so thin it resembles plain water, but the non-magi will always eat worse.

Suddenly, Laela's mother with the brace of plump rabbits comes to mind. She'd been hunting. No wonder she couldn't look me in the eye when she brought them in.

I hope they're tasty.

"What are you planning to do with your day off?" Petre's asking when I return to the present. He's opening his daily mail, handed to him by the flirty page with dark red hair.

"Not sure. Might read for a bit, go for a walk." Really I'm

going to visit Tyson, but I'm trying to make it sound boring so he won't ask to come with me.

True to form, he pulls a face. "Books again? Rose. You need a rest."

I trail my spoon through my breakfast soup in a perfect *burn* rune shape. Since my first lesson, I've found myself half-doodling runes in my other books, stopping just before they activate. All the books in my room have been replaced with every tome I could acquire in the Academy library that mentioned 'runes' anywhere in the description.

"No I don't, I just... really like it."

Something mischievous glints in his grey eyes. "You have a book in your bag right now, don't you?"

Five Times Runes Saved the World is tucked deep into my school bag. I was going to read it in Tyson's shop while he worked. I push the bag farther under our table.

"No."

He hooks a foot around the shoulder strap and tries to yank it toward him. I stuff my boot into the actual bag, accidentally kicking *Basic Runes to Change Your Life*, and am half-pulled under the table when Petre lifts the bag onto his lap.

"*Two* books! You need a hobby."

"I have one!" I reach over the table and snatch the satchel back. "It's runes."

He makes a face again as Amisha and Orin sit at our table. Jasmine perfume washes over me when the Tsalskinese girl flips her long black hair over one shoulder.

"We're walking to Saint's Crossing today," she says. "Would you like to join us?"

"It's too cold for the Crossing," Petre complains.

"For swimming, yes," Orin says. "But the apple trees will be in fruit soon, and I've heard the small tart ones are actually the sweetest."

Petre grins. "That's no way to talk about Rose, she's right there."

Amisha laughs as I flick my spoon at Petre. Pale droplets of gross soup hit him in the face, and he yelps.

"Thank you, but no," I reply as my friend wipes his face. "I'm going to get some studying done."

"She has books in her bag," Petre says disdainfully. "She's going to *read*."

"I'm glad you've found an area that interests you so much," Amisha says with a smile. Her dark eyes flick to Petre. "You should be glad she's taking up a subject with such enthusiasm."

The two bicker as I watch the iron hands of the massive clock on the wall. When the bells toll, I wave to Orin and Amisha as they drag Petre with them for a day of eating apples by the river. Only a tiny sliver of regret slinks into my belly as I head into town to meet my old friend.

Finding his shop is easier when the district is trading and working. I dodge mules and carts, workmen and flustered apprentices, until I recognise the loft above the street. The main door is open to the road, and I watch two large men argue over a wooden cart of coal. Inside, watching the exchange, Tyson waits with a hammer in hand, a large leather apron covering most of his body. Fresh, shiny scars cover his arms—the burns he referred to the other night. He's pushed his hair out of his eyes and left a large smudge of soot above his brow. More than one delivery girl lingers near the opening of the smith, clutching baskets and trying to peer in without being obvious.

"Rose!" Tyson's call scatters them as he places the hammer on a workbench and approaches. In my plain cloak, I look like any other trader in the Workman District, and more than one lingerer shoots me a glare as my friend wraps an arm around my shoulders. "Come meet Craige."

"This is good charcoal!" the trader is arguing when we reach the pair. He picks up a piece and crumbles it; we all hear the hollow crack as it falls apart. "Good lumber burned down in hot clay. You are arguing for the sake of nothing again, Craige."

"Three good pieces in a barrow full of shit." The smith crushes some in his fist. Splinters of unburnt wood bounce off the ground. "The same trick you tried last time, Garren. Don't come by my shop again."

The trader heaves the handles of his barrow and scurries away, disgruntled, as the smith shows Tyson the coal.

"Oldest trick in a charcoal trader's handbook," he warns. "A few pieces from a good burn scattered in a barrow full of crap. Be wary; we need good charcoal to burn hot, and this won't even fire pottery." He throws his handful to the ground. "I'll make sure to tell the guild Garren is trading again."

Tyson nods solemnly, apparently forgetting I'm tucked in his armpit. I nudge him with my elbow and he looks down. "Oh! Craige, this is Rose."

Craige looks down at me, and the second we meet each other's eyes, I recognize him. A mix of emotions swirl in my stomach—happiness at a familiar face, nerves about what his reaction might be to seeing me again.

He looks back at Tyson. "Into the shop, boy."

I let Tyson sweep me into the forge as Craige closes the door. Without the icy grey light of day, the main fire lights us in dancing orange.

"You're a mage," the blacksmith says, his eyes boring into mine. "He knows?"

"Yes, sir," I manage.

He rubs a wide hand over his jaw, the rasp of bristles reaching all the way down to me. Then he grunts and clips Tyson in the ear.

"Idiot. You know what the penalty is for dating mage girls. I told you on your first day."

Tyson rubs the offended ear. "I'm not dating her, sir. She's my friend."

"That's how they all start," the blacksmith calls as he makes his way to the other side of the shop. "You two just stay out of the guards' sight, or it'll be hell to pay." He sticks one arm through the sleeve of a long leather coat as he considers. "Probably my hell to pay, as you're under my care, Tyson Welles. So don't get caught."

Tyson nods, "Yes, sir."

Craige hovers by the smaller sidedoor. "And you, girl; you're lucky I believe in the fates. Treat my shop and my boy well."

Something uncoils in my chest and I slump as he disappears.

"Of all the shops," I say miserably. "Of all the shops you could've taken work at, it's his."

"You've met before?"

I remember the smith plucking me from the streets of Fairhaven and delivering me back to the Academy's doorstep. "Once, when I was out looking for you."

Tyson nods. "I like him. He has this way of seeing through people." He shifts uneasily and refuses to meet my gaze. "Marika, the baker's wife up street, says it's because he's from the north—"

The forge fire flares as I clench my fists. "You told him. Damn it, Tyson. You *know* how dangerous that is!"

He sighs and hangs his hammer in the tool rack. "Calm down, Evermore. He knew already. Took one glance at me and said I looked like a rounding hammer when he wanted a fuller." He seems to revel in my blank stare for a moment before clarifying, "Different hammers for different jobs."

I shake my head to clear it. "Your boss knows you're humanborn non-magi."

"Yes."

"And he was okay with this?"

He shrugs one shoulder. "He just seemed miffed that he

had to teach me more than he normally would. He says I'm big enough to make up for it, though."

I rub the bridge of my nose and squeeze my eyes shut. I see Iain sitting on the stairs again, waiting for me to slip up. Now another person in Lotheria knows Tyson is not meant to be here.

"Hey," he says. His arms close around me and I press my face into his chest. He smells like iron and leather. "It's going to be all right."

I return the hug, and we rest in the easy embrace before another voice scares ten years off both of us.

"I *knew* it! I told you she was banging someone."

The forge fire flares again as I snap, "Petre Lyon, what have I told you about using that word?"

All three of the supposed apple-hunters are standing in the doorway. Petre lowers an accusing finger. "Did I not use it right?"

Actually, for the first time since I taught it to him, he has.

"I'm guessing these are your friends?" Tyson says, stepping away from me like I suddenly have germs.

"That's a strong word for him." I eye off Petre, who cracks a shit-eating grin.

"You adore me, Evermore. How dull your life would be without me." He punches me in the shoulder when he gets close enough. "Petre Lyon, son of the Lord of Riverdoor."

To my surprise, Tyson bows neatly. "My lord."

Petre accepts the bow with an inclination of his head. I roll my eyes. "I would know your name."

"Tyson Welles, apprentice to Craige LeFeyellen, fourth

Master of the Blacksmith Guild of the Southern Lotherian Region."

A hint of something I've never heard has crept into his voice; it takes me a moment to realise it's pride. Something squeezes my heart, and I have to clear my throat before introducing Amisha.

"Lady Amisha Ni Luh, from the Tsalski Empire, here to study under the esteemed tutelage of our Headmasters." I say the last bit through gritted teeth, thinking of Iain's threat, but Amisha curtseys, even though technically Tyson is below her station.

"My lady," my friend says with another bow. I start to wonder if the whole morning will be introductions.

Orin bounces forward, a hand outstretched. "Orinius Thoreau, first son of the House of Thoreau. Call me Orin." He seizes Tyson's hand and shakes it. "So you're Rose's non-magi friend?" He waits for my nod before turning back to Petre. "You owe me five gold."

Petre argues that there's no evidence of us not being romantically involved, though in far less delicate terms.

"You're a smith?" Amisha asks politely, drawing our attention from our friends now haggling over the price of my non-affair.

"An apprentice, miss."

"Have you been at it long?"

It'll be too obvious if he cites the start of term. I open my mouth to supply an answer, but Tyson says, "Only since the fourth of Dawn Harbour, my lady."

What the hell is the fourth of Dawn Harbour?

Amisha smiles, clasping her hands before her. She's the picture of the perfect noble. "Are you enjoying it?"

"Very much, my lady," Tyson says with a smile. "May I show you some of my work?"

He gestures to his work bench but doesn't dare touch her as they approach it. I watch her walk away, noticing the way her crisp blue cloak is cut so it doesn't drag on the ground and how her soft leather boots clip neatly across the flagstones. I peer down at my own boots; I trod in mud a few days ago and never cleaned it off. The ugly brown splash covers almost the entire toe of my right shoe. I scuff it on my too-long cloak, feeling frumpy.

"You created all these?" I hear Amisha ask, and look despite myself.

She's holding a small twist of metal in one palm, and I drift over for a closer look. At first it seems like nothing but scrap, but then the shadows flicker the right way and I realise it's the outline of a small bird, made entirely from one piece of iron. I take it from her as she collects another one to examine.

"I did, yes. Craige likes that I've taken an interest in artisan blacksmithing as well," Tyson explains. His cheeks tinge red as Amisha turns over another metal animal shaped like a fish with long, flowing fins. "I use them for practice after we close the shop at night."

"This is *lapuni*," Amisha remarks, her tone laden with surprise. "How have you seen a *lapuni* in Lotheria?"

"That's 'moonfish' in Basic. We're in Lotheria, dear." Petre, as though sensing an opportunity to be a condescending prick, has joined us. "We don't speak Tsalskinese as well as you do."

I punch him in the shoulder when no one else does.

Tyson looks directly at me as he says, "Craige took me with him on a supply trip to Norrisville. There were some in the river. Just past the bridge."

I return his look with pure confusion while Amisha exclaims in surprise about the presence of Tsalskinese fish in a Lotherian river. As Tyson wiggles his eyebrows in his infamous 'C'mon, you idiot, it's so obvious' gesture, I realise we surfaced from the Other—just upriver of a bridge.

Why would foreign fish be there?

"We'd better get going to the Crossing," Amisha says. "I told Dena we'd bring her some apples."

"Oh… you're leaving?" I'm suddenly terrified of them spreading the word about Tyson. "Maybe I should go with you?"

Amisha flashes a smile. "I think you're in capable hands here. And Rose? We won't say a word to the Headmasters about him."

Orin nods enthusiastically, and Petre agrees because he apparently got to keep his money even though he was wrong. I shunt them both to the door as Amisha bids my friend goodbye. When she hugs me, I feel the hard shape of the iron fish inside her cloak pocket.

"You have lots of friends already," Tyson remarks behind me.

I bar the shop door and turn back to him, arms folded. "You don't have to sound so surprised."

He spreads his arms wide. "Yet here we are. I'm serious, Rose, you've never been one for making friends so easily. How long did it take you to talk to me?"

I remember the crayon-eating idiot all too well. "About four weeks of primary school."

"You've been here for, what, not even that? And you've got three. *Three*."

"I can count. I know how many there are," I snap, mildly annoyed.

He claps an arm around my shoulders. "I'm proud of you. I mean, I know we're leaving, but I'm proud of you."

He whistles as he tidies his ironwork animals, and I ignore the tiny pit in my stomach. Something else niggles at me.

"What is the fourth of Dawn Harbour?"

"Just a date Craige and I agreed on as my start. He thought it'd be too obvious to tell people the truth."

I sit on an anvil next the forge. "So he's been mentoring you?"

Tyson pauses his tidying. "I think 'mentoring' is too nice a word for what I've been through."

I frown. "But you make him sound so great."

Tyson turns and leans against the workbench, fiddling with a small iron cat. "I understand Craige. I know where he's from, which is why I don't mind when he snaps at me or expects me to understand something after barely a sentence. The north... Rose. It's a different place from here."

I remember the tall, dark-haired mage. Phoenix. "What do you know about it?"

He shakes his head and I doubt he even realises he's doing it. "Not much. The people from there... They're bred differently, they think differently. They're made of something else. I've never met anyone as strong as Craige; I've seen him lift anvils and bend iron bars with his bare hands. He can burn himself and not notice or react. He never shows an ounce of emotion. Sometimes I think he'd kill someone and never say a word." He looks up, something unreadable in his eyes. "So when he told me he'd hire me but that I had to learn everything first to make my story believable, I trusted him. When he packed me onto a wagon leaving for Norrisville, early morning in the freezing rain, I rode that damn thing four hours north so I could learn everything about the place. Now, when people ask me where I'm from, I can answer confidently. Craige made me create an entire family tree.

"He's built for something other than the comfortable life the working classes lead here." Tyson holds my gaze fiercely. "And as long as we're here, I need to be too."

CHAPTER FOURTEEN

AT BREAKFAST THE next morning, I get my first proper taste of why northerners are so hated. A small contingent of armoured soldiers from the southern capital arrives in the hall flanked by Netalia, who points out a student to them. Netalia remains at the door as the captain crosses the hall, and I wonder if it's because she doesn't want to dirty her shoes on the canteen flagstones.

The student is a girl I've never spoken to, but the fear on her face as the soldier approaches immediately makes me sympathise with her.

"No," she moans as he gets closer, and we hear it even across the hall. "No, please."

The captain takes a knee beside her, murmuring. Tears thicken in her eyes before streaming down freckled cheeks, and a brunette boy beside her wraps his arms around her as she sobs.

"Another raid," Petre mutters. I turn to see him throttling his fork, knuckles white against the steel. "Where?"

"I know her. Anieke of Longrock." Orin has paled beneath his copper curls. "Her brother, Alyn, was fighting when I left."

"Longrock?" Petre asks, a cold note in his tone. "Are you sure?"

"Our parents are old friends. They stay with us every summer."

Amisha clutches Orin's hand as Petre thins his lips. I stay quiet, feeling very out of touch with my friends.

When it becomes apparent Petre won't tell me, Amisha explains, "Longrock is the only stronghold between Riverdoor and the Orthandrellian border."

I know Riverdoor is one of the biggest cities in Lotheria, sistered with Numin, which lies across the longest stone bridge in the country. I thank Amisha internally for making me review maps with her while she studied cartography.

Petre's family lives in Riverdoor.

Anieke cries. We watch the captain in black armour rest a hand on her shoulder out of the watching Headmaster's sight. As students surround their grieving peer, the bells toll the beginning of classes.

"To class, everyone," Netalia says, her voice piercing the hall. "Anieke, with me please."

As everyone packs up, I watch the Headmaster and the girl. Netalia leads her from the hall, but her hand doesn't rest on her shoulder, and no emotion crosses her brow.

"They don't like us talking about it," Petre says in a quiet voice as we leave. "Don't let any of the teachers hear you mention it."

"So why did they tell her in front of everyone?"

"It's custom for immediate family members to know within forty-eight hours of a death. A messenger would've ridden hard all night to bring Netalia this news, and she was bound to deliver it to Anieke within the time limit." My friend looks down at me. "Not even the Headmasters dare defy the old laws."

Anieke doesn't appear in classes for the rest of the day. It was her brother, we find out in hushed whispers, fighting in an illegal guerrilla group for lost farms around the turbulent border. Alyn's body was recovered and is being sent to the Longrock stronghold.

Anieke is denied permission to return home for the burial. Their reasoning: being so near the dangerous region is too risky for her. It seems unnecessarily cruel to me.

No one says a word about the incident, but during our study session, small voices hold a banned conversation.

"Did you know him well?" Amisha asks, her fingers winding Orin's curls into a small coil.

He shrugs, but his bronze eyes are pained and heavy with loss. "I guess. He was older than me. Came with Anieke and her parents to our estate every summer and helped with harvest. We used to swim in the lake." He pauses and nicks a thumb at the wayward tear in the crease of his eye. "Yes, I guess I knew him well."

"What will happen to Anieke?" My voice is quiet. I feel out of place amongst the grieving mages, but Petre's hand slips over mine. "Will she be allowed home?"

Orin and Petre exchange glances and Amisha looks around, but we're alone. We're tucked in a small nook of the library near one of the large windows overlooking a garden, but it's dark and we see only our own reflections in the void.

"Longrock will be lost in the next fortnight or so," Petre says, his voice low. "When it is, the Headmasters may decide that its strategic value is worth the half-thousand or so lives it'll cost to bring it back under southern rule. If not, the estate will be inhabited by rogues and bandits, and the populace of the village around it at their mercy."

"That's a lot to assume after the death of a single man," Amisha whispers.

"I knew Alyn of Longrock almost as well as him," Petre responds with a nod at Orin. "I knew which group of fighters he led, and I knew that they—not the Headmasters, not the War Council in Gowar—were our best hope against northern invaders. If Alyn's dead, the entire legion is. Longrock will fall."

My fingers tingle. I turn my hand so Petre can lace his fingers through mine. Our strength mingles, and my breathing steadies.

"What will happen to Riverdoor?" I hear myself ask, and when Petre turns steel-grey eyes on me, I wish I hadn't.

"Enough canoodling!" Library Master Yan, a short Tsalskinese man with a temper, rounds the corner. "The library closed an hour ago!"

"We're allowed a study session," Amisha argues.

"You are *allowed* to do so," Yan replies and gestures with a pointed finger. "But I see no *books*."

"We're studying arseholes," Petre says as he stands to his full height, and though his tone is even, his fingers clamp around mine. "Thank you for providing us with a prime example."

A squeak of outrage is all Yan dares emit. We gather our bags and leave, my cheeks flaming.

"I hate it when you do that," I mumble to Petre.

"Me too," Amisha says from Orin's other side.

"I don't," Orin says.

We all look at the usually mild-tempered redhead. His knuckles are white against Amisha's brown skin.

"Alyn was my friend, and Anieke still is. If the Headmasters won't allow us to grieve, then we must find somewhere we can."

I hold Petre's hand the whole way back to the main hall, where we all know we must split ways. We're stopped by unspoken words until Amisha turns.

"We don't know what's coming," she begins hesitantly. "But with the raid on Longrock, all I know is your civil war is getting worse. We may not be students for much longer, and we must be our strongest selves if that time comes."

Petre releases my hand. "Amisha—"

She lifts her chin. "You both need to find your soulmates. It would've been a tidy thing if you'd paired, but you haven't. There are two mages out there who belong in our group."

I look from face to face, puzzled. "How do we find our soulmates? I thought it was supposed to happen over time."

No one answers me immediately, but when Amisha parts her lips to speak, Petre lifts a hand and cuts her off.

"No."

"Yes." She lances him with a hard glare. "We're going to the soulwitch."

On our next free day, four days after Anieke's news, we're allowed into the township with our meagre allowance. I lead my friends through the alleys to one of my favourite bakeries, eager for food not from the Academy kitchens.

"Put that away." Petre slaps my bronze coin from the shop counter. "We'll have two, thank you."

He pays with exact change and delivers a hot pastry to my gloved hands. The baker bows but the young lord doesn't see it, so I wave goodbye as I bite into the pie.

"You have to stop buying me food," I tell him, flakes of pastry dusting my lips. "I have money."

"You should return as much as you can to the Headmasters' pockets at the end of your studies," he explains, biting neatly into his own lunch. "Or they'll count it against your docket and it's a financial debt for you as well as a timed one."

I've heard mentions of this docket thing that apparently all mages graduate with, but before I can inquire further, Amisha and Orin round the corner of the stone building before us.

"Where's mine?" Orin asks indignantly upon seeing the pies.

"He only had two." I'm not going to tell him the meat is tough and stringy and the gravy flavourless. I know the baker can only work with what he's got.

"Tyson is meeting us there," Amisha tells us, lacing her fingers together. Her gaze lingers on me just a little too long, but I don't know what face I'm making.

"You asked him to come?"

She grins. "Where we're going, the Headmasters won't see us. The guards won't see us. I thought you'd appreciate the opportunity to spend more time with your friend."

"That's very kind of you," I say, but my brain is working overtime. They've been in contact outside me, if they set this up. When, how, where?

How careful is Tyson being? I know him. A pretty girl flashes a smile at him and all reasoning goes out the window.

It's probably how he keeps such a steady head around me.

Amisha leads us into the commoner's district. It's an icy cold day, with plump grey clouds overhead promising snow. Frigid wind streams between the buildings and cuts through our gloves and cloaks. I huddle behind Petre, finding some shelter behind his six-foot mass. He doesn't notice until we're almost to the communal hall.

"Are you using me as a windbreak?" He grips me by the upper arms to shunt me before him. "Too bad I can't do the same."

I swat at him as he tries to waddle behind me, but I can't wipe my smile. A few flakes of snow catch in his dark hair, and the sky lightens his eyes beyond their usual grey. My heart beats a little quicker, and by the time we're on the rickety wooden steps of the hall, my cheeks are pink from something other than the cold.

"Hi!" Tyson hurtles towards us, hands bare. He tucks them into his armpits and stomps ice and mud from his boots. "Sorry, had to finish a commission."

"Thank you for coming," Amisha says with a small smile.

"Yeah, thanks for the heads-up," I mutter to him, but he doesn't hear. Petre nudges my shoulder as we ascend the stairs.

The non-magi communal hall seethes with people. My smile fades as we push open the door, revealing the cots and ragged curtains. Entire families have taken shelter here for the winter months that loom overhead. Some have attempted to put up partitions with old sheets and blankets, whereas others lean against the wall with nothing but an old pack and worn-out boots. Murmurs of people and crying babies are everywhere. A spoon clangs against metal, and smoke fills the air with an unhealthy, greasy odour.

"Oh my gods," I breathe.

Amisha's good mood dissipates. "She said she'd be here. She has to stay hidden."

We press through the crowd, trying not to tread on children or belongings. A puppy pushes past me, ribs sharp against his fur.

"Why does she have to stay hidden? Who from?"

"The Headmasters don't like soulwitches," Petre says. His voice is a comforting presence at my back. "They're a reminder of failure."

Amisha told me about soulwitches a few days ago. A mage who loses their soulmate before pairing can sometimes hone their soul sense onto other mages. Sometimes, mage students like ourselves seek out those who practice it, eager to be united with their other half.

Petre is dubious. "I've never heard of this woman."

"You wouldn't have," Orin answers. "After her soulmate died, the Headmasters ousted her from the Academy and struck her name from the records."

"Ouch," Tyson says from the back, and I know he's frowning.

"Something to keep in mind," Petre murmurs in my ear. "The Headmasters don't take kindly to failure."

In the corner of the ramshackle hall, a faded red curtain hides the small nook. Amisha pushes it aside and speaks with the person in a low tone before nodding back at us. Tyson lets the curtain fall behind him, and the haze from a nearby scented candle envelops us.

"I am Serra," the woman before us says. "Thank you for coming."

We sit on flattened cushions around a small brazier.

Tyson tries to sit near Amisha, who's seated herself next to the witch, but I step in front of him and plonk down before he can argue. Instead, he picks one across the fire, as far from Serra as possible. Just as I wanted.

Petre's apparent disapproval of the woman rolls off him like fog from the lowhills around Fairhaven. Serra's blonde hair is long and dirty, her eyes wide with the stunned expression of one addicted to what the non-magi call 'Neverdead.' I spy a bottle poking from the cushions behind the witch, the brown glass neck tilted toward her left hand as though she's just tucked it there. Her dress is old and worn, the pale red fabric coming loose at the seams, and long strings of beads hang from her taut neck to pool in her lap.

"Who are the unpaired?" she asks Amisha. I can't help but think it's a bad sign if she can't already tell.

I lift my hand as Petre reluctantly half-straightens his index finger from where it rests on his knee. She reaches for him, her arm dangerously close to the brazier and the hot coals within. As she grips Petre's hand, I beckon the fire to me and pull its heat from the witch's direction.

"Oh my," Serra says, a smile stretching across yellowed teeth. She looks past Petre, as though seeing someone behind him. "So much pride, young man. You think a lot of yourself?"

"Not particularly," Petre says, trying to pretend he's not leaning away. "I think a lot of my potential."

Serra is nodding. "Good, yes, and your family... Very strong. Very proud."

A heaviness falls over the air around us, and silence drowns the sounds of the hall. The hairs on my arm rise as the witch turns to the fire, her fingers still entwined with Petre's. She glances into the ruby embers before looking up at me with those wide, still eyes.

"Might I have my fire back, young mage?"

I uncurl my fingers with only a small amount of embarrassment. Heat surges back to the coals as Serra throws several dried sticks of something smelling like millipedes on them.

"Humanborn," Serra says, her eyes darting through the smoke as though she's reading a book. Her hand is tight against Petre's. "Strong-willed, stubborn."

Tyson looks sideways at me, and I hold up my hands in protest. "We know it's not me."

But I know who it is. Yasmin is the only unpaired humanborn left. Dylan paired with the foreign mage, Brin, and spends most of his non-class time with their friends. Dena and Theresa accidentally paired in class one morning.

"Yasmin," Serra breathes. She looks around for confirmation. "Is there a Yasmin in your year?"

"Yes," Petre answers, looking a tiny bit stunned. He hasn't tried to pull away from Serra. "Yes, there is."

"She's an unpaired humanborn," I explain when he continues staring into the distance. "It's probably her."

The soulwitch lances me with a steady gaze. "There is no 'probably' about it, young one."

My cheeks heat as she pats and releases Petre's hand. She

and Amisha talk quietly, then the chink of coins reaches my ears as a purse passes between them.

Smart girl. Whatever she might have heard, whatever she might believe, Amisha waited for proof before paying her.

"And you, handsome?" Serra asks Tyson, reaching for him.

"*He's* fine," I answer quickly, holding my hand out to stop her from touching him. "Happily matched."

The woman purses her lips and tears her eyes from my friend. What was Amisha thinking, bringing him here? If this woman sees unforged connections between mages, what will she see if she touches a humanborn non-magi?

"So you're next." Serra winds her fingers through mine. It's like having my hand held by an old willow tree; I don't think I could pull free of her if I tried. "Oh. Another humanborn." She turns to Amisha. "A good crop this year?"

"We're very lucky," Amisha says with a smile, eyes on me. I return it, some tension melting away.

As Serra reaches for her embroidered bag of herbs, I realise she's about to reveal who my soulmate is. With thoughts of Tyson's discovery and the Longrock attack, my brain hasn't spared a thought for what life would be like after my pairing.

She tosses dried sticks of cinnamon then a pinch of what looks like rosemary. The smell of the spices rises with the warm air, but Serra frowns as she reads the blossoming smoke.

"An interesting match," she murmurs to the fire, and

I see the half-look she throws Petre before saying, "Your soulmate is from the north, young humanborn."

His name hangs in the air like a curse until Petre shatters it. "No. It can't be. Not Phoenix."

"Why not?" I challenge as the soulwitch slips her fingers free from mine. "Why can't it be him? It has to be someone."

But he's shaking his head furiously. "I won't have him in our group. I can't… The things he's done."

My blood chills to ice. "Things such as…?"

"Petre," Orin warns.

"She should know. If she's going to pair with him, she should know what he's capable of—"

"Not here," Orin snaps. I've never heard the mild redhead so incensed. "Think, man. How would you want to find out?"

"Will someone please tell me what's going on?" I whisper. I'm holding my hand out before me as though it's dirty, and tears dampen my eyes.

"He's from the north," Petre spits.

I clench my fist. "That's not enough explanation anymore, Petre! I need *details*."

"Not yet," Orin says, his eyes softening when he turns to me. "In due time."

Amisha's eyes are wide, and I see an apology growing on her lips. I open mine to tell her not to worry when Tyson yelps.

As one, we turn. Serra's hand is clamped around his wrist. She tosses a small bunch of peppercorns onto the coals.

Her eyes widen, and my stomach sinks. "Non-magi... Humanborn?" she whispers.

Amisha's lips part in shock. Petre's expression darkens as Orin turns raised eyebrows to me.

Lies cluster on my tongue. "I—"

The fire explodes, sending sparks and embers flying around the nook. Flames dig into the cushions and curtains and take hold. Screams erupt from the hall around us. I stand, throwing my hand wide, stretching with the inert power that roils in my veins alongside my blood. I feel the air sing as the heat slips between my fingers and into my skin. Smoke rises to the patched ceiling even as the flames stutter and dim, their energy sapped. When everything dies down, the cushions don't even smoulder.

I brush my fingers against my shoulder, sending a few wayward sparks to the floorboards as the scene clears. Petre and Orin are on their feet, and Amisha has thrown herself across to Tyson. Serra is nowhere in sight.

"Where is she?" I ask the others, who shake their heads blankly. My stomach sickens as I remember her words.

"Hoods up," Petre commands. Amisha and Tyson get to their feet as noise builds in the hall. "The guard will be here soon. We need to be gone."

I pull my hood up while Tyson does Amisha's. A flurry of emotions scatters across my chest as the two exchange quick, unheard words.

"Come on." Petre grabs my hand and pulls me between cots and mattresses, women and children. A few of the men grab for us while the rest yell at us to get out with furious voices. All five of us burst into the frozen daylight as snow swirls in flurries down the street. "We need somewhere to hide."

"My forge," Tyson says. He tugs Amisha down an alley.

We follow, our boots slipping on occasional hidden ice, slush staining the hems of our cloaks. Snow melts on my face, feeling far too much like tears. Tyson's shop is a welcome sight, but only when we duck under the large door do we lower our hoods.

Tyson fastens it with an iron lock. "Craige knows how to get in, but I don't want anyone else following us."

He turns to the group as the other three mages stare at him. There's a beat of silence before I step between him and them.

"It's my fault," I begin. "I pulled him through the portal with me."

"You're really humanborn?" Petre asks.

I feel him nod reluctantly. "Yeah."

I close my eyes, remembering all his hard work fabricating a false life for himself here. All done away in an instant.

"If the Headmasters find you—" Orin begins.

"—they'll kill him," Petre finishes. "They barely tolerate non-magi, let alone a humanborn non-magi. He holds no value for them."

Anger heats my belly. "Hey."

He steps back. "I'm just telling the truth, Rose."

A hand rests easily on my shoulder. "We already knew this." Tyson lifts his voice. "We've been trying to find a way to get me home. So if anyone has any ideas, that'd be great."

Everyone goes quiet. The slumbering forge fire pops as it recognises me, then doesn't stir again.

"You're trying to leave?" Amisha asks in a tiny voice. Something in her tone has Petre, Orin, and me trying to be invisible all of a sudden.

Tyson clears his throat. "I have to, my lady. That fellow just said it. They'll kill me if they find out the truth."

Orin kicks a piece of black coal along the dirt floor. "Then they won't find out."

I peer over my shoulder at Orin, who shrugs. "Not from me, anyway."

"Nor I," Amisha follows.

"Or me," Petre finishes. "I don't owe the Headmasters anything."

Relief almost knocks me flat. "Thank you. We owe you."

"Serra knows," Amisha says. "You heard what she said."

I nod. "We have to find her."

"And then what?" Tyson asks. "Pay her off? You could do that, right?"

"It's amongst the possibilities," Petre says with cold eyes, and I try not to imagine the other options. "But as far as I'm concerned, no one outside this room knows the truth. We'll keep it that way."

Tyson nods. "Thank you, my lord."

The noble shrugs. "Amisha said it. We have to be our best selves in the face of what's to come."

CHAPTER FIFTEEN

"SHOP ONE-ONE-FOUR, DUSTMAN's Way, got it?"

Thompson repeats the address with silent lips, then nods over the bundle he carries. Silver coins jangle in his pockets as he trots out of the courtyard, unseen amongst the bustling traffic. Amisha and I watch him from the shadows.

"Thank you for the Tsalskinese candies," I say as snow drifts to the mud around us. "He'll love them."

Amisha takes a hand out of the fur muff she carries and waves my thanks away. "Mama always sends too many. She makes them herself, you know."

I wish my mother made sweets.

The weather has turned nose-bitingly cold, and the drafty halls and corridors of the Academy aren't much better. My talent with fire has never been more helpful.

I light a small one on my palm for comfort. "Will you go back to the Islands when you graduate?"

"I'm not sure. I can travel home as soon as I graduate, which is rare, but I don't know if I'll stay."

We turn a corner as I start to ask what she means by 'rare,' but the question dies in my throat. Phoenix descends the stairs before us and continues toward the training field without looking back. I watch my soulmate disappear out of the double doors.

"Are you all right?" Amisha asks. I shake my head.

"The boys won't tell me why Petre reacted that way." I snuff the fire out, preparing for the cold. "Makes me think horrible things. I'd rather just know before pairing with him."

Amisha nods sympathetically. "I'd tell you if I could, but I feel the conflict in the north is closer to their bones than mine. They'll tell you."

"When they feel the time is right, and not a minute sooner, I'm sure." Bitterness fills my tone. We hover just inside the double doors, propped open despite the shearing wind. Slush makes the flagstones slippery, but I jog on the spot anyway. "Can you believe Yu is making us train outside in the middle of winter?"

Amisha smiles wryly. "He did warn us."

We bow our heads and press out into the snowy field. Ice crunches beneath our boots, and snow dusts our hair coiled and bound at the nape of our necks. Beneath our heavy cloaks, we wear the thin linen of our training outfits; I hoped we'd get some protective gear considering we've progressed to sparring, but as though determined to mash my spirits further, History's Master Jettais has been present at every lesson for a very specific purpose.

"You again," I call to him as we get closer.

"Watch your tone, Evermore," he replies, but even he sounds bored with the admonishment. Over the months, we've established a dry line of communication. "Trust me, I'm not here for the company."

No, what he *is* here for is much more important than dabbling in conversation. As fire calls to me, metal calls to him. Over the years, he's honed the talent of softening the blows of swords against skin. Whilst the skill wouldn't save him from a midnight stabbing, it can save us from concussions and the most serious of bruises.

"Take your swords from Page Greatree and warm up. The carrier has told me we're not to be outside longer than an hour today," Yu snaps, as though temperatures below freezing are excellent working conditions.

Reluctantly, Amisha and I strip off our coats and gloves. The icy air bites almost immediately, stripping away any reserve heat from my clothing. I accept a longsword and thin gloves from Eustace with shaking fingers.

"I thought you islanders hated the cold," I remark, taking position with the sword against my shoulder and my legs bent. I chop downwards in a powerful cut, slicing through the air, my muscles seized and cramped. "Yu seems fine."

"I don't think the rest of us have the fortitude," Amisha replies through chattering teeth. She takes the same position and tries the same cut, but it doesn't have the effect. "Oh, I'm always so terrible with swords."

"Make the power come from your hips," I suggest as the rest of the class mills around, flattening the snow beneath sodden boots. I do the cut again. "Your feet are allowed to move. Use your whole body."

"Excellent advice, Miss Evermore." Yu has come up behind us, and I wonder if he heard the rest of our conversation. "You may choose a sparring partner first."

Ah, crap. Every time I've sparred, I've chosen Amisha or Yasmin, but the class has turned to watch who I pick. I can't pick either of them again—my skin crawls to admit it, but I've progressed in the discipline much faster, and my skill with a blade far outranks theirs. I spy Theresa, Dena's humanborn soulmate, resting easily on the pommel of her sword. Her pale eyes seek mine, and she nods.

I've watched her spar. She's an excellent fighter.

I jerk my head at her. "Come on."

Excited murmurs break out in the group as we both head deeper into the snow. From the corner of my eye, I see Jettais follow closely, lifting his boots over the larger snow drifts. The class circles us, stamping their feet or hopping in place to keep from cramping up.

I take position in my favourite guard, the point of the sword aimed at the steel-grey clouds, the rest of the blade nested against my shoulder. Theresa settles into a planted stance with her sword above her head, the point aimed at me, her hands crossed on the hilt. Her eyes betray nothing.

"Students ready?" Yu asks.

We nod. Our resident metal mage moves in farther. Yu drops his hand between us then steps back.

We stay frozen in place, then Theresa whirls into movement. Her sword swings overhead, aiming for the place left open by my guard: my head. I step back, place the strong of my blade in her path, and knock her off line.

She falls back, but I press my advantage and lunge forward, capturing her blade in my crossguard. Lifting the sword high, I aim the point at her shoulder, but she disengages with a sidestep and escapes my reach.

We scramble back, cheeks pink. Our breaths frost in the air. Steam rises from our bare arms as we retake our guards.

She's good—and fast. I would've had any of my previous partners with the crossguard lock—if they'd even tried to attack me at that point. But she expected it.

Theresa isn't just fighting. She's playing with me.

I grin at her across the snow, the sword comfortable in my grip.

She strikes at my hip, forcing me to block. The clash of steel rings out, eliciting hoots and whoops from our audience. Theresa doesn't falter, pressing closer. I stumble back, trying to lengthen the distance between us, but she's caught me in a loop blocking her attacks. I growl in frustration. The sword in my hand jolts from a particularly heavy hit.

Again, she whips her sword around to attack my exposed shoulder. But she's tired, and her laboured movement gives me time to duck as I mirror her movement.

My sword flashes, slicing through the air. Jettais only just catches the sword with his affinity before it makes contact with her ribs, slowing but not entirely softening the impact. She grunts from the hit but swings through. I cross my hands on the hilt, using the length of my blade to cover my entire body as her attack finally lands—not on bare skin but on solid metal.

I take another step back in case Yu hasn't seen the hit, but he holds his hand up. "Point!"

Theresa puts a hand to her side, but no discomfort crosses her brow. She rests her sword point-first on the top of her boot. "Well done. I wasn't expecting that."

"You're fast." My chest is heaving, but I'm smiling. "You almost had me."

A wry grin. "Almost."

"Well done, well done. Next pairing," Yu calls, clapping his hands sharply.

Theresa and I leave the ring as Phoenix and another mage step forward. Petre pushes toward us, leaving students mumbling.

"Excellent swordsmanship," Petre says, clapping a hand on my damp shoulder. "You've picked that up very fast, Rose. You should be studying war magic, with talent like that."

"It wasn't a long fight. I doubt I'd do very well in a real confrontation," I argue, but his compliment is nice.

"The fight was longer than anyone expected." He turns to Theresa. "Have you studied this before?"

She lifts an eyebrow and hefts her sword onto her shoulder. "Where?" she asks plainly, then turns to disappear into the crowd before he can answer.

Petre looks at me. "I forget she's humanborn sometimes."

"We all do." It's true. Theresa has found her place here.

The clangs and clashes of the next match commence, but Petre doesn't turn to watch.

"I mean it, Rose, your guards, your footwork, your form—"

"Are you commenting on my form?" I ask with a grin.

He returns it with a new, mysterious look. "I'm *complimenting* you on your form."

I start to respond, but an anguished cry rings out over the crowd. As close as I am to Jettais, I hear him grunt and watch as he's pulled forward through the snow by something unseen. My heart in my throat, I turn.

"I'm sorry," Phoenix says in his deep voice. His eyes are wide, his cheeks pale as he leans over the form of the prone student. "I'm so sorry."

Blood speckles the trampled snow, and the broken half of a sword blade, sheared off near the hilt, has a smear. Phoenix's sword is whole.

My eyes widen. "He broke it at the strong."

The other student bears a large, bloody mark the length of his cheek. Yu and Dena crouch near him as blue magic flickers over the gaping wound. Dena, the only student majoring in Healing, has become our form of first aid. She shakes her head.

"We need Carrier Bayde. His cheekbone is shattered beyond my repair."

Phoenix's knuckles whiten on the hilt of the sword he still carries.

"Barbarians," Petre snarls under his breath. He looms behind me. "He doesn't belong here."

I remember Tyson's words: the northerners are built for something other than this life.

The story circulates quickly. Both young men were fighting hard. The other mage, Larren of Knotts Hill, used illegal strikes against Phoenix. Rumours fly that it was in retort for the raid at Longrock.

"And then he just struck back," Orin tells us at dinner, demonstrating the hit with his fork. A piece of boiled cabbage flies off, forcing Amisha to duck the greasy missile. "I've never seen such power. Larren tried to block, of course, but Phoenix's sword went through it like butter and got him in the face. Guess he's lucky we don't fight with sharps."

"I doubt Dena could save a cleaved head," Amisha agrees. "Why didn't Jettais stop the blow from landing?"

"He tried. Looked like he'd been pulled forward on an invisible rope, didn't you see? Phoenix's strike was so powerful he couldn't hold it back."

I twist in my chair and peer over my shoulder. Phoenix is hunched in the corner, his plate untouched. A book rests open before him, but he doesn't turn pages, seemingly studying the brickwork instead.

The Academy pages start coming through with the evening mail, and I pick at the broiled vegetables. Mail time always saddens me a little, though I've started looking forward to the candies promised with Amisha's care packages. Someone brushes by me—the flirty page with eyes for Petre. She's been around for a few evenings now, and as she hands him a letter, I wonder what would happen to her if something was between them. Do Academy pages hold more status than regular non-magi?

"Thanks," Petre says brightly, and though she lingers, he turns back to us.

She leaves with a sigh, and I raise my eyebrows at him. He begins peeling the ruffled envelope.

"She's only trying to marry up," he explains, digging his finger under the seal. "I don't think she's actually interested."

Amisha gets a package wrapped in oiled canvas and I peer inside, eager to examine the treasure trove of treats. Candied flowers and bitter bamboo biscuits decorate the top of a new dress wrapped delicately in fine paper.

"Your family must be loaded," I remark, reaching in and grabbing a biscuit. I pull it apart with difficulty; my arms always ache after sword class. "To keep sending you this much stuff."

"Loaded with what?" she asks, puzzled.

The screech of a chair makes us look to Petre, who's

holding the letter he received. His eyes dig into it, as though searching for information written between the words.

"I have to see the Headmasters," he says.

"What's wrong, man?" Orin asks, but Petre winds around the table and strides through the hall.

The three of us look at each other in confusion, and I stand. "I'll get him."

I chase him past the other tables, leaving curious conversations in our wake.

"Petre!" I lunge for him and miss. "Slow down. The Headmasters, really? Are you sure?"

He drops the letter over his shoulder and I catch it, trotting to keep up with him. Only a few phrases are decipherable due to the hasty writing and fast pace he's setting.

... not in his bed...

... ransom... three thousand gold and an oath...

... no response...

We're in a wing of the Academy I've never seen. It's bright, clean, and open. Gilded vases, rich tapestries, and golden gas lamps line the halls, and the pages here are older and more distinguished.

This is where the Headmasters live.

A deep voice halts us. "Master Lyon." Referring to this man as a page seems wrong. He's older than me and Petre combined, with dark hair combed neatly back from a high forehead. He steps forwards with a raised hand. "Might I ask what brings you to the Headmasters' wing at short notice?"

"*Lord* Lyon. I have to see them," Petre demands. He barges past the page.

Petre dodges the man's attempt to grab his shoulder and knocks on the enormous wooden doors, pushing one open. I follow and poke my head inside.

A fire burns at one end of the room, the dry wood burning without stifling smoke. Shining ceramic plates are laden with heavy food against an ivory table cloth. Tall windows let in the moonlight. Our two Headmasters, Iain at the head of table and Netalia at his right, start at the intrusion. Their furrowed eyebrows and furious expressions would normally scare the shit out of me.

Instead, my belly, upon seeing creamy porridge in a bowl topped with a golden swirl of syrup, growls anxiously.

"What is the meaning of this?" Netalia asks. Despite the hour, she's wearing a heavy dress with a high neck, a glittering brooch pinned to her shoulder—her Silver Wings. "Lord Lyon?"

Petre squares his shoulders. "I've come to formally request that a contingent of mages be sent to Riverdoor to assist my family."

"There's nothing formal about the way you've come in here," Netalia says. She raises her hand, preparing to send us off.

I glance towards Iain, solemn in dark leather with a clean plate before him. His eyes flick to me then my panicked friend.

"What is the nature of your request?" he asks.

Petre fumbles for the letter. I hand it over.

"My younger brother has been kidnapped. He's the second heir to my parents' estate, a young lord of Riverdoor. You're obligated to help us retrieve him."

I groan internally as Iain's gaze hardens.

"Let me remind you that we're not 'obligated' to do anything, Lord Lyon. Your brother's disappearance is tragic, but who's to say he didn't leave under his own steam?"

Petre's eyes narrows. "He's four."

"Did he test for magic?" Netalia asks, scraping rich butter across soft bread.

"No," Petre says through clenched teeth. "He did not."

Netalia bites delicately into the buttered bread and says to Iain, "I told you."

Iain doesn't spare his soulmate a glance. He heaves a sigh and goes to speak, but I interrupt.

"What would happen if Riverdoor turned?"

All heads swivel my way. Even Netalia stops eating.

Iain's gaze is lethal. "What did you say, Miss Evermore?"

"Like Petre said, his brother is the second heir to the Riverdoor estate. A nice little bargaining chip. What would happen if the Lord of Riverdoor started supporting the rebels instead of your rule?"

My heart slams in my chest when I finish. It may be a last-ditch attempt to get them to help, but it's the most dangerous thing I've done since arriving.

Netalia's cheeks colour, but she says nothing. Iain considers me closely. I drop my gaze.

"We will send soldiers," he begins. Petre looks up. "To

Thurin. We can consult with the established War Council there."

"Thurin is nowhere near Riverdoor," Petre says dryly.

"That is our decision."

We're forced back out the room as another page closes the heavy door in our faces. Petre breathes heavily, his grey eyes watering.

"Come on," I urge, pulling him away.

He refuses, but I dig my heels in and finally manage to lever him from the spot. He at least waits until we're a few halls away before exploding.

"The nerve of them! After all my family has given, after all they've been through—"

"Petre—"

"The support they've given! Now they have to go through this alone, it's—"

"*Petre.*"

He finally stops talking and I pull him in for a hug. He resists before wrapping his arms around my torso. His lips rest on my hair, trembling.

"He's my little brother."

"I know."

"How can they—"

"They can't," I whisper. "It's wrong of them to place no value on his life because he's non-magi."

Petre squeezes me harder. "I have to go to Riverdoor."

I let his words melt over me as I go stone-still. "Think seriously for a second—"

"I am. The northerners have taken him to coerce my father into joining their cause. Riverdoor is too big for takeover by force. They're staging a coup."

"They'll keep your family safe." I dare not tighten my grip on him in case he realises I'm trying to keep him from running away.

I feel him shake his head. "My father will not bow to their demands, no matter how small. The Lyons have governed the eastern states for centuries. He will not be the one to let it fall."

I feel the weight of his risk. One small boy over thousands of lives.

"Come home with me," he murmurs.

My heart pounds in my chest, and I break our embrace but keep a firm grasp on his hand. "You don't know what you're asking."

His fingers tighten around mine, and his grey eyes are made of steel. "I'm asking my friend to help me."

"You're asking me to break the law," I say. "You know we can't leave."

There is no sympathy in his gaze. "I've broken the law every day for you."

It cuts me to my core, and I rest my forehead on his chest. "Petre—"

"Rose."

I press my lips together, weighing each word in the silence of his damning sentence. "What will we do when we get there?"

He sighs. "I'll collaborate with my father and the guerrilla groups up there. We'll find the raider's camp and… negotiate for Samlin's return."

I turn cold. "You mean, kill for his return."

"If it comes to it."

I'm shaking my head. "I'm not ready for that, Petre. Please don't ask me to do that."

He grips my hands so hard it hurts. "I need your word that you're strong enough for this."

"I can't give it. Not even for you."

"Evermore. Lyon." We jump apart as Jettais calls us. The lantern he holds illuminates his face, graveled and concerned. "Why aren't you in bed?"

"Petre had to see the Headmasters," I tell him, stepping away from my friend.

"Then I don't envy you." Our teacher gets closer. "Off to bed with you, Lord Lyon. I trust you can find your way. I'll escort Miss Evermore."

Petre leaves reluctantly, unsaid stanzas of our argument in his wake. I know I haven't heard the last of this trip.

"You all right, Evermore?" my teacher asks as we head towards my staircase. "You look rattled."

"I'm fine. We just argued for the first time." My voice is small.

I climb the first few stairs of my spiral staircase as Jettais lights the way with his lantern. "Don't let him bully you, Evermore. The noble-born mages have a funny notion of always getting their way. Talk to me if you must."

The gesture takes me by surprise and I halt, one hand on the curving stone wall. "That's nice of you, Mr Jettais."

He rolls his eyes and leeches any kindness from the offer immediately. "Just doing my duty. But by the gods, call me Jett when we're not around others."

I climb a few more stairs into the darkness, mulling over his offer as I reach my room. But as I dress for bed and put out the small candle that leans into my hand like an affectionate kitten, I think of telling him that Petre plans to return home. That he wants to take action where the Headmasters refuse to.

By the time my eyelids drift closed, I know I'm headed there too.

Planning the getaway falls to me.

"You're far more cunning than I am," Petre explains. "You know who'll help and who will keep their mouth shut. It's a talent, really."

A useless one, I want to say, but I shut up and get on with it.

Thompson has already risked too much taking care packages to Tyson every Sonsday. The older stable hand is no good to me, plus I won't work with him after seeing how he treats my young friend.

Maurice, the farrier, is old and grizzled, fond of drink. Once, I saw him dunk himself in the horse trough, obviously trying to wash away a hangover. His back was crisscrossed with whip welts; he's denied the Headmasters before.

In the cold afternoon, I weave through the stable, dodging barrows and boys. Horses shift uneasily in their stalls as I pass, and one black gelding sticks his nose over the half-gate for a sniff. My hand lingers on his velvet nose as I watch Maurice work on a familiar mare—the one Thompson lost control of when I was brought in.

Academy horses are for use by messenger pages and students as required. Some mages, like Petre, brought their own. I spy his dappled grey gelding in a stall and resist the urge to inspect him before talking to the farrier.

Steeling my resolve, I straighten my cloak and approach the older man. He takes note of me but continues picking clean the hoof between his knees.

"Miss," he says begrudgingly. "How can I be of service?"

"This mare. Can she be ridden today?"

He wipes the pick on his leather apron and squints at me under bushy eyebrows. "Aye. I'm not shoeing her, just a rough cleaning."

"Good," I say. "I'll need her tonight. And the grey down the back."

"The one that belongs to the Lyon boy?" Another fierce squint. "What're you up to, missy?"

I've worked my purse free and toss it to him.

He hefts it, testing the weight. "Shenanigans, I'm guessing. So two horses saddled and an open gate, is that it?"

"An open gate and *four* horses saddled," I correct. At this moment, Orin and Amisha are being informed of the situation. In the span of two short months, our little group has become bound by secrets. "For the extra effort I'll throw in a bottle of whisky. When the job's done."

He snorts, and Echo the mare turns her head to examine me with a large brown eye. Nerves bite my stomach; I've never ridden before.

"Good stuff. None of the shit they brew at the Wench."

Proper whisky will be hard to obtain. I wonder if the baker Tyson visits knows anyone who distils illegally.

"Fine, but you'll have to give me time to find one. You know what it's like."

He nods. "Aye. After the evening bell, you'll find your horses waiting in the stables and the gate guard missing. Don't miss that window, or it'll be my hide, not yours, getting the lash."

I leave the stable, my belt lighter without my day purse. I think of how much I have left for this monthly allowance and thank the gods that I'm frugal on a daily basis.

The sun heaves itself across the sky as Petre and I skip classes to prepare. Deep down, I know the Headmasters suspect we're up to something, but hopefully they think we're not foolish enough to actually leave.

Finally, night falls. Locking myself in my room, I pack my rucksack with extra clothes and what little food I could wheedle from the Academy cook. She's given me two stale buns and a strip of dried meat. Having skipped dinner, it takes everything to not eat it here and now.

My hand itches for a weapon as I sling the bag onto my

back, remembering the comfort of a hilt in my hand. I dare not visit the armoury. I can only hope we'll find food and arms at the Lyon estate.

I slip down the secret stairs to meet the others, hurrying along the corridors to the stableyard. A noise in the dark makes me jump.

"Where are you going, Miss Evermore?"

"Jett?" I ask, trying to place the voice.

He emerges from the dark in court clothes—a red velvet jacket and black breeches. He's not trimmed his stubble, which peppers his gruff face. His short hair is swept to one side like he's been running his hand through it. He holds a wrapped package at his side.

"The Headmasters know you're leaving."

I square my shoulders. "Then why haven't they tried to stop us?"

"They're giving you a chance to do the right thing."

"This is the right thing."

He examines me closely. I hover on a knife's edge, deciding whether to make a run for it.

Then he nods. "You're right, but I didn't say that. Take this."

I take the canvas-wrapped sword wordlessly.

"You get this glint in your eye when you're about to do something foolish, you know that? Once Iain and Netalia figure out you've managed to leave overnight, they'll send guards after you. If you make it to Riverdoor, get the Lord to offer you bread and ale. Once that's offered and accepted, you can't leave for at least twenty-four hours. Not even the Headmasters will defy the old laws."

"Why are you helping me?" I ask.

He lifts one shoulder in a half-shrug. "Sometimes I wish I still had reasons to run away in the night."

Before I can question him further, he turns away and begins whistling like he doesn't have a care in the world. I waste an extra moment trying to figure out what the hell just happened, then scoot along to the stables with my new sword.

My friends wait in the courtyard. Both Amisha and Orin agreed to come along. The gates are open and our horses saddled; I remind myself to source a bottle of good whisky for Maurice.

The horses' breaths mist in the lamplight as they toss their heads. I sling the sword onto my back and step to Echo's side, accepting Petre's boost into the saddle. I wriggle about and get comfortable while my friend mounts his horse.

"Petre?" I ask softly.

Astride his dappled gelding and dressed in his fine Academy cloak, Petre looks like a lordling ready to escape an arranged marriage. When his eyes meet mine, there is something manic in their grey depths. "Fuck the Headmasters."

CHAPTER SIXTEEN

ECHO TROTS AFTER the other horses as they clear the open gate, requiring zero effort from me. Petre is the first to ride into the village square.

A yelp splits the night. Petre's horse shies from something, but I see his concern is for the man lying on the ground. I dismount clumsily, Orin taking Echo's reins as I stagger towards the front of the line, readying lies on my tongue. One is half-formed as Petre dismounts. The man climbs to his feet.

Fear sparks in my chest when Tyson pushes back his hood. I see him recognise Petre then seek me. When he meets my eyes, I feel the accusation even across the distance.

"What's going on?" Tyson asks, glancing from one face to another. "You're all out late."

"We're going away," Petre says shortly as Amisha dismounts.

Tyson looks at me. "You too?"

I nod, the threads of a thousand plans knotting and unravelling in my head as I try to formulate a response. "You'd understand if—"

"If I knew. Well, tell me."

Petre and I look at each other as Amisha approaches slowly, wrapped in a heavy blue cloak. "Why were you coming to the Academy?" she asks.

Tyson produces a tiny box. "This was in your last care package. It's not something I should own."

"Oh." Amisha is reluctant to take back what is clearly a gift. "You should keep it."

"No, he's right," Orin says from his horse. I look back at him, feeling so exposed to the Academy that I may as well be naked. "They'll accuse him of stealing it if they find it in his possession."

Amisha takes back the tiny box with no further argument. I try not to jig on the spot.

"This is a really bad place for us to talk," I say. "Tyson, we have to go."

His lips thin. "You're not leaving me behind."

I flounder for a few moments before Amisha speaks. "He should come with us. It'll be safer."

"No, it won't," I tell her with a hard glare, trying to remind her what we're riding into. "Besides, he needs permission from his boss before he can take leave."

"Actually, Craige is up north for a meet of all Guild Masters of the Southern Region. He's given me leave while he's off."

I can't miss the enthusiasm in his voice. Poor thing thinks we're off for a holiday or something.

"He doesn't mean for you to leave town, surely," Petre says, coming to my rescue. "What if he returns early?"

"I can get a message to him," Tyson says sharply.

"But if—"

"Maybe I'm not making myself clear," Tyson interrupts. Petre looks like someone slapped him. "I'm not letting you take Rose without me."

Silence falls over our group. Something warm slithers into my chest and coils around my ribs like a hug. I meet Tyson's gaze, and he nods. It isn't Amisha he wants to come along for. It's me.

"It'll be safer for us to stick together." I relent, echoing Amisha's words. "Can you ride?"

Following Amisha to her horse, he eyes me. "Can you?"

Fair call. I mount Echo with Orin's help and guide her to the front of our group, mindful of the clopping of her hooves on the cobbles.

"We need to keep moving," I hiss to the others. "They'll be on us at dawn, and we need to break bread with Petre's family as soon as possible."

Tyson, mounted in front of Amisha, quirks an eyebrow, but Petre doesn't question the odd statement. Jerking his hood back into place, the noble leads a quickening pace into the icy night.

The exhilaration of a midnight getaway fades as frost coats my eyelashes. I pull a scarf over my nose and mouth as we ride farther north, grateful for my gloves and the warm horse beneath me. We press them hard along the great-road, the one thick vein that connects all of Lotheria, even Orthandrell. Though it has fallen into disrepair and deep ruts are scored into it from people trying to pull wagons through the muck, it is well-built and has lasted the test of time. In the pale moonlight, trees and shrubbery press in close. An ancient fear of the dark awakens in me as I watch the shadowed trees pass, wondering what could be watching us from the gloom.

"Petre." Orin pulls his scarf down to talk freely. His red curls are iced. "The horses are exhausted. We have to stop for the night."

I glance at Petre, who works his jaw before nodding. Having traveled this road to the Academy a few months ago, he leads us to a rest spot: a wide clearing in the trees with trampled grass and weeds. We hobble the horses and rub them down as Tyson lights a fire, and I watch him from the corner of my eye. I've never been as out of place as he is now. While the magic in my blood sings to the land around us, comes easily to my fingertips, and obeys my simple commands, he has none. His only connection to Lotheria is a misstep into a turbulent river.

Now, he risks his life to keep me company.

I sit beside him in the dirt as the new fire struggles against the damp wood. It flares at my proximity, lighting us both.

"You didn't have to do this," I say in a low voice.

My friend studies me. "I sure as hell wasn't staying behind."

"What if Craige returns in your absence?"

He fiddles uneasily with a stick. "I'll send a note as soon as we settle in. Where are we going, by the way?"

"My brother has been kidnapped by northern raiders," Petre fills in, sitting opposite us. "The Orthandrellians are pushing south and have already taken Longrock; now they want Riverdoor, my home city."

Tyson nods. "One boy in exchange for a city stronghold. It's a risky game."

Petre's eyes are dark. "Yes, it is. For them."

"Did you appeal to the Headmasters?"

"We tried," I say gently before Petre can wind up. "They're sending agents to the War Council."

Lines appear on Tyson's brow. "That's on the other side of the country."

"You're very well informed about a land that isn't your own," Amisha remarks. Her dark eyes reflect the firelight. She pulls the collar of her long fur coat up against the cold. "Not many Lotherians can tell you where their War Council is located."

"You forget I work for a northerner," Tyson tells her. Across the fire, Petre works his jaw back and forth, no doubt swallowing words best left unsaid. "And I could say the same for you."

She smiles. It seems out of place in this bleak setting. "It's my hobby to map different lands."

I think about the people sent to hunt us, who even now could be preparing to dash out into the early morning to retrieve us before we can reach our destination and be protected.

"We should sleep for a few hours." I stand, dusting my behind. "Tyson, you can share my bedroll."

Amisha's smile flickers slightly, and I wish I could tell her of all the times Tyson and I have shared a very platonic bed in our decade-long friendship. I wait for the boys to be busy around camp before taking her aside.

"You're a noblewoman," I remind her with a gentle whisper. "To share your bed with a non-magi would ruin you."

She bows her head. "But not you?"

I take a step back and smile wryly. "I'm not a noble anything, remember?"

As we ride through the hinterlands of central Lotheria, I realise why people flock to the Academy's shadow.

The thick forests of the south give way to stony moors and threadbare fields. A thin drizzle falls as our horses slosh through icy mud, and I find myself worrying more about Echo losing her footing. What if one of them throws a shoe? I squint into the haze, spying lumps in the distance that could be a village.

"Petre," I call. He turns back to look at me. "Can we stop?"

He studies me, then glances at Orin, who says, "Not here, Rose."

He's from here, I realise. He's been riding beside Petre for half the day, except now he's leading, not following. I urge Echo into a careful trot.

"Why not?"

Amisha slows her mount to hear her soulmate's response. Orin's hood is up, his scarf around his neck. His eyes flick not to me but to Petre, and the two struggle in a silent conversation.

"They shouldn't be this close to the great-road," Petre says finally. One hand rests firmly on the hilt of his sword. "They're getting brazen."

I squint at the shapes through the rain. "Who?"

Orin clears his throat. "Halvers."

Amisha presses her lips together, throwing the village ahead a sour look.

"What are Halvers?" I ask.

Orin looks at the road. I follow his gaze. A figure stumbles through the rain towards us, a hand outstretched from beneath a thin robe.

My friend pulls his scarf over his nose, leaving only bright eyes showing beneath his hood. "They're mages without soulmates."

We ride past the stricken man. His face is thin, making his eyes huge. I copy Orin, pulling up my hood and scarf.

"It's best if we're not recognised," Petre says as we leave the Halver behind.

"The Headmasters will move them soon," Orin says. "Probably out farther on the barrens."

"Why?" I can't help asking. Nausea sits deep in my stomach. "What's wrong with them?"

"You'll see."

The village isn't a village. It's a shanty town of ramshackle tents, some only half-built, with poles sticking out of the mud. One has burnt to a crisp, the skeleton of the tent still smoking despite the drizzle. People shuffle about, but their faces are blank and uncomprehending.

"Most of their soulmates died up north during the Headmasters' campaign to bring Orthandrell back under sovereign rule. Those who returned were left as... this," Petre explains. Amisha clutches at Tyson's cloak so hard it bunches. "The Headmasters move them about from time to time, but this is the closest I've seen them to the south."

Some Halvers stand on the side of the road, their wide, unblinking eyes following us. I lower my head.

"Why are they like this?" I ask quietly. The only sound around us is the patter of rain in mud and I don't want them to overhear.

"There are many theories," Orin begins. "Some mages took an interest in what happens after a soul is torn apart. Halvers don't feel cold, or heat, or pain, which leads to them falling ill or victim to frostbite when winter settles in. Sometimes they just let themselves die. The study ended pretty quickly; I don't think it was entirely ethical how they were testing."

I consider the debt all students owe to Iain and Netalia when they graduate. I thought that's how the two keep themselves wealthy—living on the repayments of the mages they trained. Why are these ones left to rot in the mud?

It hits me. "And they can't use magic."

Orin shakes his head. "Most of them can't, but some can. No one knows why. Before uniting with their soulmate, a mage can operate at relative capacity, but after the split, it's gone."

One Halver watches me closely. One of her eyes is scarred closed, but the other watches me with deep intensity. Echo veers from the road towards the woman, whose hold I find myself unable to break.

"Rose, what are you doing?"

I shake myself and guide Echo back to the others. A few watchers amble away at Orin's voice, back to whatever they were doing before we arrived.

But not the one-eyed woman. She stands like stone, watching us pass into the veil of rain.

The Halvers aren't the only people we meet on the road. Families flee the north, and traffic thickens as we near Riverdoor. It hampers our progress, and by the time the small city dimples the horizon, Petre's gaze is dark with frustration.

We crest a slight rise, and Petre's home city sprawls before us. Riverdoor, according to Orin's almost encyclopaedic knowledge of Lotheria, is famous for its quarries. Here they mine silverstone, a mix of granite and platinum unlike anything found in Gardhillan. The city is built from it except the Lyon estate, which crowns the city as a sandstone jewel. The hills are carved deep, and silver dust covers everything. Luckily, the tacky rain has traveled with us and plasters the loose dust to the cobblestones.

I wonder if the base metals for the Academy Silver Wings come from Riverdoor.

Petre leads a fast pace through the streets, and people get out of the way. Five cloaked strangers on horseback means trouble. I see the fear in a woman's eyes as she takes us in, scooping her children from the road.

The Lyon estate gates remain closed for about five seconds before a small team of manservants opens them. The drive up to the sandstone manor is layered in silverstone gravel, the trees that line it nothing more than sticks. The lawns grow wild, and Echo strains for them. I almost let her; it's been a hard ride.

Inside, the manor shows more signs of disrepair. The ground floor windows are boarded up, and the rich burgundy carpet reveals our footprints in a layer of silver dust. I cough into my sleeve as we follow the housekeeper into the main hall.

We let Petre greet his family first. Orin examines the artwork on the walls, though their canvases are stained and worn. Amisha sketches in the corner, mapping the road we used. Tyson, however, looks as lost as I do.

"You all right?" he asks. We close the door between us and the parlour, but the main hall is just as eerie and sets my teeth on edge.

"Just jittery. We need to have bread and mead with them before the Headmasters catch up with us."

He looks around, then plops into an armchair and sprawls when no one stops him, stretching his legs one at a time. "A few days ago, I went out to return Amisha's gift. I was going to spend the rest of the night knitting."

"Yet here you are," I say, sitting in the other chair.

My mind wanders back to the Halvers, and I rub my chest absentmindedly. "Wonder what's it like having a soulmate."

"Probably annoying as all shit."

I grin. "Yeah, I have no idea what it'd be like having some dork sharing almost every aspect of my life."

"Oh, come off it," he retorts, but he's smiling too. "Why, you thinking what it's going to be like with your own?"

That isn't what's on my mind, but I push the one-eyed Halver from my thoughts. "I guess. Just wondering what magic I have to look forward to."

He misses the wry tone. "You reckon you'll get more powerful?"

I haven't seen any mage increase in obvious power after matching, but I remember the pale northerner I left behind. The only other northerner I know scares the life from me: Tyson's employer, Craige, the most intimidating man I've met in Lotheria, even as a non-magi. Besides maybe Iain.

"I think I will," I say. "But not in the way you're imagining. I think I'll feel more... complete."

Petre returns to the parlour before Tyson can answer. A man, broad-shouldered and tall with a solemn face, accompanies him. "My father, Lord Hugh of Riverdoor."

I stand neatly as Tyson scrambles to his feet. I bob a brief curtsey, using my traveling cloak as skirts. Tyson bows deeply.

"Master Tyson Welles," I say with a nod to my friend. I offer my hand to the lord, who takes it. "And Miss Rose Evermore of the Lotherian Academy."

Lord Hugh nods to us, making no sign that he realises what I've done by introducing us both in the same breath. Petre, going to follow his father back into the hall, raises his eyebrows at me. I shrug. It's far too dangerous to let the Lord of Riverdoor know he's sheltered a non-magi.

We're taken into another room. Fine mahogany panels line the walls, reeking of old wealth. The carpet sinks underfoot, and the long table in the middle of the room is surely accustomed to holding grand banquets on its polished surface rather than the host of books sprawled along its length. Maps and charts are crudely tacked over the expensive walls.

Beside me, Tyson clenches his fist. A blacksmith will not see luxury like this unless he's crafting it in a noble's home.

"We've been tracking them," Hugh begins, pulling back the long curtains. The dirty glass they covered doesn't let much evening light through, but the lord has already moved to a map. He plants it with a crunch on the table before us. "We've narrowed down the area to Hallow Woods."

Across the table, Petre frowns. "The Hallow can't support an army."

Hugh looks up at his son. "Why in the gods' name would they bring an army?"

But I understand. "What are their demands?"

Parchment and books are pushed aside as the lord looks for a piece of paper. With trembling fingers, he shoves it into my hands.

Your loyalty or your son.

I fold the paper and draw my fingers down the spine. "They'll kill Samlin if you don't bow."

Anger sparks in the man's dark eyes, like he can't believe that I'd dare say the phrase aloud. I suddenly remember Arno's favourite saying: *A worse scenario spoken is a worse scenario tempted.*

I hand the paper back. "They need an army in case you don't give in. They'll be expecting you to avenge your son's death."

Hugh runs his hands through his dark hair at my words. I've never seen a Lotherian noble so flustered, but when I meet Petre's eyes, I finally see the Lord of Riverdoor he'll one day become.

"Rose is right," Orin says. He removes his gloves and approaches the map. Amisha, noting the dimming room, moves forward and lights the candles in an iron branch on the table. Their golden light bounces from Orin's curls as he examines the map. "Amisha, what topography would be ideal for a small unit of elite soldiers?"

The Tsalskinese noble rests a slender hand on the back of a tall chair. "To bring a unit this far south of a supply stop, they'd need a place to hunt small game. Fresh water would be tempting for them, and they'd want a thicket to hide them from view. A structure of any kind to keep out the night's chill and perhaps provide a vantage point."

Petre nods. "Deadman's Keep."

Hugh's head snaps up. "No. We'll not take the search there."

"What's Deadman's Keep?" Tyson asks.

"An old stronghold," Petre supplies. "But some think—"

"The place is wreathed in bad luck," Hugh interrupts. "Any who set foot in the Keep meets their demise soon after. A darkness has seeped into the rock around the castle, and none dare approach it."

A rumble sounds from the clouds above us. Outside, the thin tree branches whip as wind coils around their trunks and batters the boarded windows. The candles flicker, and I hold my hand out to steady the flames.

"Can we count on your support?" Lord Hugh asks his son. "You've not brought your friends all this way just to sup with us."

Petre nods. "We came with the intention to assist, but you should know the Academy denied us permission to go."

Hugh smiles. "You are your mother's son."

Our promised bread and ale are part of a larger dinner in another hall, the attending staff busy around us whisking empty plates and cups away before our cutlery can be laid upon them. I can almost feel their thankfulness at having something to do.

"Will the Lady of Riverdoor be joining us?" Orin asks as we finish.

"She is unwell. With Samlin taken, she prefers to dine in her rooms," Hugh says in a tone that reeks of finality. No more is asked of Petre's mother.

"You said Samlin was taken," I say, trying not to stare at how Tyson gulps his dinner. He ate very little on the trip here—a result of us not anticipating a fifth member. "From this estate?"

The serving staff melt from the room. Outside, the storm rages, but the lit candles and gas lamps on the walls don't waver. Above us, wreathed in dusty cobwebs, is a once-fine chandelier standing watch over our dining experience. Blood-red wine remains untouched in my crystal goblet, but Hugh's is freshly drained, leaving ribbons of maroon spangled across the surface.

"The bastards took him from his bed in the night," he begins, staring at the carpet. "I awoke to my manservant telling me my son was missing. In his place were their demands."

He looks across the table at me, sadness deep in his eyes. "They came into my home, and they took my little boy. My child, Miss Evermore. They stole him from his bed while he slept, smothered his screams, and carried him out into the wilderness. Every night for seven nights, he has been apart from his family, alone and afraid, starving and beaten." The stricken lord reaches forward, the creaks of his chair the only sound in the grand room. He plucks my untouched glass of wine. "So if the *Headmasters* think they can let him die without consequence, they're wrong. And if they think I'll forget this disgrace, their disrespect ..." He sips from my glass, his fingers steady on the stem. "They're dead wrong."

CHAPTER SEVENTEEN

THE RAIN CONTINUES through the night and makes for an uninspiring dawn. I rise early to practise with the sword Jett gave me when we left, wincing as my aching muscles protest. Days on a horse have left me bow-legged and sore-arsed. I find a relatively comfortable position half-squatting and run a few practice moves. It's a good sword, fitting nicely in my grip with a respectable reach, but I feel inadequate as I practice the few moves I'm okay at.

At breakfast, I'm impatient, my feet tapping a quick tempo on the plush carpet. Petre watches me across the table, his solemn eyes reflecting my mood.

At the head of the table, Hugh's chair is empty, a silent sentinel. His absence is obvious to everyone in the room, and though our gazes keep flicking toward the doorway, the lord does not appear until after we've eaten. When he stands in the doorway in full armour, my gut sinks to my boots.

"The men are ready," he says.

He leads us into the grounds. Tension mounts when we reach the stables. Villagers wait within the warm building, their faces grim. A few nod tersely as we enter, but niceties are put aside. They're here to find the lord's child, and there's a good chance they'll die doing so.

"Weapons." Riverdoor's finest blacksmith has been commissioned by Hugh to supply the search party. The others choose from the crate as I lay my sword on a hay bale to unwrap it from the canvas.

I let the apprentice run a measuring tape over my shoulders. A second later, a small bundle of leather and chainmail is deposited before me. I pull off my leather jacket, wearing only my thin cotton singlet until I shrug on the mail shirt. Black and fine, it falls across me like cold liquid, the weight reassuring. A leather corset reinforced with steel boning goes over it, pulling tightly around my waist and bosom. The apprentice does the hooks at my back as I buckle my gloves and boots. They're made like the corset, with metal woven through the thick leather.

Hugh told us last night what he ordered, but I'm still surprised at the speed and quality of the work. With my sword strapped over my shoulder, the hilt within easy reach, and fresh magic brimming in my veins, I begin to feel more comfortable.

"How are you doing?" Tyson asks as everyone gears up.

I try to finish buckling my glove. "I'm nervous. I'm scared we'll find what we're looking for."

Tyson nods as he does my buckle. He towers over me in his mail and leather armour, a gorget nestled around his throat. His chosen weapon is a two-handed longsword; apparently Craige has been training him during their slow times in the shop.

"No one's noticed I'm not a mage yet," he murmurs. "That's a win, surely?"

"Trust you to be the optimist." I can't help my tiny smile.

The others finish gearing up. Amisha wears her archer clothes, a light leather corset protecting her torso while long linen skirts her legs. Even in armour, she's graceful and light. Her longbow is far too large for her slender frame, but I've seen her draw it without so much as a tremble.

"Those of you who have volunteered to be here, I thank you," Hugh says. Everyone turns their attention to the commanding lord. "To the others, I also thank you. Today, we find my son."

The village men light torches, the pitch sputtering and smoking in the icy rain. I clench my jaw and keep my eyes on the ground as we march in a group down the road. This feels wrong. I'm not ready for combat. I don't want Tyson to experience combat.

We're a large party, torches bright and voices loud. I can smell the burning torches even at the back of the group as I follow along the cobble road. Villagers have clustered on the sides, taking in this rare sight of mages-in-training and the state lord dressed for battle.

A trail winds from the road, steepening as we climb.

Gravel crunches underfoot, loose silverstone left over from the quarries sunken into the landscape. In the distance, the Shayde Mountains of Orthandrell loom like thunderclouds. Before them, the moors of inland Lotheria stretch into graveled plains, and the wind howls as it soars over them. Scraggly forests tangle at the edges of the moor.

The party spreads out but I stay put, watching a large man in a fitted suit squint along the ground, searching for tracks. A thin man holds the torch for him, glancing over the plains. I squeeze my hands into fists as Tyson is drawn to Amisha, who turns to speak to him. Her skirts press against her legs in the fierce wind, and her long, dark hair strains to be free of the knot at her neck.

In some way I don't quite understand yet, I don't blame Tyson for being so drawn to her. I can only hope she forgives him for leaving when we do.

Forgotten on the edges of the group, I move towards the main quarry of Riverdoor that yawns in the distance. Stubby trees have managed to grow along the rim, and some protrude from perilous perches farther down.

Cautiously approaching the edge, I peer over. My stomach tightens at the drop. Far below, large boulders have rolled down the slope and crashed into the soft dirt floor, creating a depression in which water has collected. The surface of the resulting lake creases as cold wind skates across it, seeming as deep and deadly as hell itself.

I draw back from the edge with a shudder, then take a few more large steps just in case.

"It's something, isn't it?"

I jump but relax when Petre plants strong hands on my arms. "It's just me. We all separated on the moor, but I'm glad I caught you alone."

I frown, even as something warms in my chest. "Oh?"

He nods. "Rose… I know they're at Deadman's Keep."

The warm feeling shrivels into something frozen. "The haunted ruins."

Frustration bleeds onto his face. "It's not haunted. The generation before ours is a superstitious one, fed long-tales before bed to keep them obeying their nannies. I'm not letting a folkscare keep me from rescuing my baby brother."

I try anyway. "If you know that's where they are, maybe we should bring the others."

He shakes his head and takes a step back, peering deeper into the brush. "Father will forbid us from going. We have to at least scout the area and confirm my suspicions."

I relax slightly. "We'll just scout? You promise?"

Petre smiles and returns. "I promise. You won't see combat today, Rose Evermore."

I breathe a sigh that tangles in my throat as he presses his lips to my forehead. Our eyes meet too briefly, then he steps away.

"Later. We'll talk," he says.

Excitement flushes my cheeks, quickly replaced by dread. I follow him into the trees, ducking under branches and leaping over fallen trees.

I vault over a mossy log and land nimbly on toes that

whisk me to the next obstacle: a sheer rock face. I don't wait for Petre's helping hand as I plant one foot on a tiny ledge and catch the rim, pulling myself up. I dust my hands as he scouts forward, moving silently through the brush. My breathing settles. Hot blood surges through my veins. I'm ready for a fight even though I've been promised not to see one.

Adrenaline scours my body clean as I spy a crumbling stone tower in the direction Petre beckons.

Together, we close in on Deadman's Keep.

CHAPTER EIGHTEEN

THE RAINSTORM LASHES down as we look upon the enemy camp. A stone tower stands defiant against the ages, slowly being overtaken by ground creeper. The wide leaves and twisting roots seem to hold much of the mottled stone together. Smoke curls from the rotted roof.

Men in ragged cloaks stand beside a small tent of oiled leather. I crouch lower under my branch while frigid water drips from the leaves and slides under my mail. Mud squelches underfoot as Petre does the same next to me.

"How many?" he whispers.

My eyes dart around the clearing. The large fire they've tried to build in the middle is dying, sending out a blanket of fog-like smoke. Inside the tower through the open doorway, I spot more men around another healthier fire.

My heart beats rapidly in my throat. "Fifteen, at least. Petre, we can't take this many."

He lowers a hand toward the ground, signaling 'quiet.' I gulp back my fear and try not to shrink farther into the branches.

"We're scouting for information," he murmurs, and I barely hear him no more than a foot away. "We need eyes on Samlin."

The fire in the tower pulses to me. "I could give the fire inside a bit more juice. Light up the interior for a moment."

He nods. "Do it. Make it seem natural."

It's harder to speak to the fire through my gloves. I reach as far as I dare. When I clench my fist in a snap, the fire responds with a pop, like the sap in a log overheating. The resulting flare sends sparks up the inside of the tower and lights the small camp. The northerners barely glance at it. A few bedrolls, a thin cloth strung as a makeshift roof, and a drying rack for meat come into view. The light has almost faded when I spy the post hammered deep into the stony ground. A small form sits at its base.

They've tied Samlin to a post like one might a mule. I glance up at his brother, who watches the camp for signs of the little boy. I breathe a small sigh of relief but tense with indecision.

If I tell Petre he's tied up like an animal, I won't be able to stop him from storming into the camp. If we leave without a report, we won't return with more troops.

I drum my fingers on a branch, considering my words. "I think Samlin's with them."

His hand rests gently on my shoulder, but I feel the

desperation in his grasp even through my armor. "Are you certain?"

I nod, hoping it'll be enough, but the fingers tighten.

"Is he safe? Does he look well?"

"He seemed well," I say. "I only saw him for a second, Petre."

"Where do they have him? We have to tell Father as much as we can to plan his rescue."

"They have him at the rear of the tower."

"Near the rear?" Petre squints into the rain, and every nerve in my body locks in fear. "But there's only a post—"

He cuts himself off and I dare not move. The men shuffling around the muddy camp continue talking amongst themselves, but now I see their weapons sharp and close at hand. They're expecting us.

I grab for my friend. "Petre, please… Let us gather the others."

"They have him tied up like an animal."

I've never heard someone speak so coldly. His fingers are limp in my grasp, but I pull at them anyway. "Petre—"

He jerks his hand free. "They've tied my baby brother to a stake, Evermore. I'll not let this stand."

Tears spring into my eyes as his hand rests on the pommel of the sword at his hip. "We can't win this, Lyon. Listen to me."

"I've seen you with a sword," he snaps, his voice hidden under the cover of rainfall. "You're a natural. You far outmatch these petty bandits."

I grab his shoulders and make him look at me, terrified of moving so much but knowing we'll surely die if I don't. "You're overestimating what I can do, Petre. I'm not the ally you need right now."

He looks deep into my eyes, and I know then that he's lost. Fear and pain yearn in my soul as he takes a step back, drawing his sword. The naked steel is flecked with raindrops, but I know it'll soon be red.

"You're the only ally I have."

He steps out of the trees with his sword in hand, and I shrink back, hating my cowardice. I watch the northerners notice him, turn towards him. Their own hands wander to the weapons on their belts.

"I demand the release of the Lyon boy," Petre says, his voice ringing clear over the camp.

In the beat of silence, I dare to hope. Then one barks in laughter.

"Well, lads, that's us done, isn't it? Better hand over our hard-won prize," he jeers. He's taller than Petre, broader in the shoulder, and his cloak is trimmed in fur— the commander? "Who are you to heft such a confident request?"

"Someone with a personal interest in his safety," Petre replies. Part of me relaxes. If they knew the current heir to the Lyon estate and all of Riverdoor stands before them, the men would surely capture him instead. "And someone with the authority to enforce that request."

The man peers at him as he nears. "Well, the Lord of

Riverdoor is a lot shorter than I remember. He's the only one we're answering to, little lad, so best be off with a message for him." He leans down and says something to my friend that I cannot hear.

The fire in the pit flares timidly as Petre grips his sword. Silver light drifts in tendrils towards the blade—his war magic, ready to sharpen and strengthen the weapon.

"I think you'll find, sir, that I'm not a messenger boy." He lifts his sword.

My friend attacks faster than I can see. With a slash, blood arcs across the mud and splashes into the watery puddles. The big man grunts and falls to one knee, but as Petre brings his sword down from overhead, he stops it with a gloved hand that clinks with hidden metal.

His gaze darkens. "That was a mistake, boy."

He smashes his fist into Petre's chest. The noble goes flying, landing in the mud as the others yell and whoop. The commander advances on him, drawing a spiked war mace from his belt. Petre scrambles backwards, but the man is faster. I throw everything I have into the slumbering fire, pulling the heat towards me as I burst from the trees. The tiny fire explodes outwards, stunning the onlookers and burning the attacking man with tiny coals.

He rounds on me, his cloak singed and smoking. "You brought a little lass with you as well? One who speaks with fire, no less." A knowing look enters his eyes. "Two little mages, just like the ones we cut down in Longrock. We've dealt with your kind before."

I draw my own sword in two tugs, the longsword clearing the sheath easily. It's a motion Yu made me practice under duress, and if I survive this, I'll buy him all the bamboo candies this side of Gardhillan.

"Magekillers," Petre snarls, climbing to his feet. I shift before him, sword angled towards the most obvious threat: the commander. "You murdered my kin."

"Then the gods are expecting you too." The man charges.

I block his downward swing and attack in the same motion. The razor-sharp point of my sword snags on his cloak as he dodges, but the fabric slices and I'm free again as he turns to me.

"Get the boy," Petre tells me, and I nod even though fear races through every ounce of me.

They meet with sparking weapons as I run for the tower. The onlookers rush me. I barely raise my sword in time to stop the first slash from taking my head clean off my shoulders, but the strike was weak and I merely wind my sword until I control the bind. My muscles bunch as I push forward, and I've cleanly run the assailant through before I realise Jett isn't here to stop the blow.

The man I've skewered looks at me in horror, and I meet his gaze with wide eyes. "I'm so sor—"

He groans as blood trickles from the corner of his mouth and he slumps backward, sliding from my blade. Crimson smears drip from the steel, mixing with rainwater. Revulsion racks my body.

Silver light rushes down my sword. Strengthened with

Petre's war magic, I smash through my next opponent's shield, cutting him down with an overhead slash. His body lands with a splash. Bile rises in my throat. I settle back into my guard as the magekillers round me, wearied respect in their caution. I flex my fingers on the hilt, blade sparking with borrowed strength, and prepare to kill again.

Instead, white-hot pain blazes up my calf. I'm already half-falling when I see what used to be my right leg. A chunk, ripped by steel talons, has been clawed from it. I collapse into the mud, pain silencing my screams. The commander looms over me, his mass blurring into the iron-grey clouds.

"Little fire-whisper, know this brings me no joy," he murmurs, leaning on the pommel of his mace. My blood drips from the spikes and lands on my chest. "You fought strong and took lives. Now, I'll repay them with yours."

I want to close my eyes but can't look away. He lifts his mace. The strongest urge to live fills me, and my limp fingers search the mud for my fallen sword still glittering with imbibed magic. I barely graze the hilt when the mace begins its downwards swing.

"*No!*"

Petre's furious yell comes from somewhere deeper than his throat. The commander is thrown sideways, his mace falling beside my head. Instead of blood, mud speckles my face.

He's caught the northerner off-guard. I watch with rapidly fading vision as Petre gets one good stab in, his short knife disappearing into the man's bulk. The other men, who stood back to witness my execution, surge forward and grab Petre under the armpits, dragging him backwards. He kicks and fights, but they're too strong. His hair is dirty and matted. A large river of blood runs from his temple to his jaw.

Something shrieks in my head. *Tell them his name!*

My arms slip as I try to prop myself up, darkness still clouding my vision. "Wait."

The commander stands tall and tears his cloak from his shoulders. When it falls in a ragged heap, he reaches for the knife still lodged deep in his side. I can't tear my eyes from him, this large man unstoppable by mortal wounds.

The knife is jerked free, and he looks at it curiously.

"The last mages we fought did not try nearly as hard to save themselves," he mutters. He glances back at me as I try to form words through the descending fog. "Love is a powerful motivator."

"His name," I say with the last of my strength. "His name is Petre Lyon."

But as the breath leaves my lips, I realise I only whispered it to myself.

The knife is plunged up and under Petre's ribs. He jerks but doesn't cry out, even when the man twists it cruelly. His sword and mine flash and crack with power, then fall silent.

They drop Petre to the ground. His eyes, filled with pain, lock onto mine before something fades behind them.

Strength leaves my limbs. I slump backwards into the

mud. My leg has gone cold, pumping out hot blood. Even if they don't do the same to me, I'll be dead within minutes, but mine will be a comfortable death.

The man who killed my friend kneels to me. "I have no respect for mages. You are soft, weak behind your powers. But I have never seen them fight as you do."

He wipes the blade clean of Petre's blood on my leather armour, and another emotion wells behind the pain and guilt and grief.

The larger fire in the tower flares suddenly.

"You don't know what you've done," I whisper.

The commander chuckles, showing white teeth. "I'm sure you're about to show me, little mage."

He cups the back of my neck with unexpected tenderness, lifting my head free of the mud. I know I'm in raging amounts of pain, but I cannot feel anything below my waist.

Tears well in my eyes as I summon every ounce of magical strength I possess. The fire in the tower, hidden from the rain, has remained strong and fierce. I feed it a little of my intention, feeling it grow. I close my eyes and feel dampness roll down my cheeks.

"Your tears honour your fallen friend," the commander says gently.

When I reopen my eyes, I know there are flames in my gaze. "I'd rather honour him with your corpse."

The tower explodes. I seize the commander by the throat as his camp burns. My magic bubbles around the captive boy. Heat sears the stones beside him.

The man claws at the tight hand around his throat, my face, my arms, but something more than willpower possesses me even as ragged fingernails gash my cheek. The men's screams surround us as fire bursts from my hands and envelops the man in my grasp.

He burns, his screams falling on deaf ears as I will the fire to swarm. It digs into the folds of his clothing, hot air searing his lungs as he scrabbles at me desperately. When I thrust his body away a few minutes later, he collapses into greasy ashes.

I reach for my sword, pull it towards me, and sink the point deep into the mud. I stand slowly, using it as a crutch as I survey the area, ignoring the agony in my leg.

The other northerners fell early to my first fire. Their smouldering corpses flicker against the mud as the closest trees blaze, their canopies wreathed in golden flames that defy the watery deluge. I can feel my magic in every single spark, every ember.

I am tempted to burn it all.

But as the flames die, pain buries deep under my skin, taking precedence. I drag myself to Petre.

I rest a muddy hand on his cheek, then gently close his eyes. "I saved him, Petre."

Darkness takes me, and I let myself slide into its caress.

CHAPTER NINETEEN

THE MANSERVANT'S VOICE rings across the room, too loud and too brash. "The Lord would like to see you."

The answer is already on my lips. "No."

The manservant bows, but his face twists with dislike. How much longer will they turn their lord away from a room in his own house?

A carrier was summoned to fix me up after they found me on the moor with my leg mangled beyond repair. A rough cane leans against the table beside my bed, delivered by the woodworker from our hunting party. I'll never be without it for the rest of my life.

I lift my leg onto the covers and stare at it. Until an hour ago, I'd refused to look, but now I find sour solace in its ugliness. A badge of permanent failure that I'll never unlearn, never outrun. Most of the muscle in my calf had to be reconstructed, which the Riverdoor carrier, Rokun, had never done before. I felt its wrongness when I regained consciousness, knew on some primal level I'll never walk properly again.

It was with some wash of relief that I knew Petre's life cost me dearly.

"You have to let him come and see you soon," Tyson says, returning to sit beside my bed. He rests a small mug on the stand. It's for him; I've refused everything but water. "It's his house. Petre was his son."

"I don't care," I say. "I can't face him. Not yet."

Tyson's gaze rests on my leg. "They can't fix it properly?"

I shake my head. He sighs.

I don't tell him I scratched runes on my leg with a fingernail when I first awoke. The red marks faded quickly without magic flowing through. "He can't restore what's not there."

"He might if you tell him what happened."

I meet his eyes and hope he can't see the flames that overtook mine on the cliffs. "How would that change anything? We went to Deadman's Keep. They had Samlin. We lost the fight."

He shakes his head again and sips. "Being a smart-arse has never helped you, Rose. Not with your mother, not with me, not with this."

I look up with a clenched jaw as my oldest friend leans forward, gripping my hand.

"I know you're hurting. I know Petre was your friend. But we want to *help* you, if you'd just let us."

I finally look at him, but I'm not seeing Tyson the crayon-hogger, Tyson the footballer, or Tyson the blacksmith—I'm seeing him vulnerable, with a chest anyone could and would plunge a knife into if they knew who he really is. I blink and Petre's eyes stare accusingly into mine.

I turn my hand in his so I can hold it properly. He squeezes.

"You know, I like these." Tyson taps his cheekbone, and my hand lifts to mirror his action on mine. Three deep wounds are scored into my skin, torn by the nails of a desperate man. "I just hope you did them worse."

I drop my hand, eyes downcast. "I did."

There's another knock on the door. I tuck my leg beneath the covers again, my eyes fixed on where the person will enter. It's pushed open without a word from me or Tyson. A familiar man in black leather armour steps inside and closes the door behind him.

I reach for my cane.

"Relax, Miss Evermore. I mean you no harm." He nods to Tyson as he approaches and takes a chair from the desk in the window nook. I watch as he sits. Fair hair sweeps back from his forehead, and a small scar runs from his left eye to his cheekbone. His nose is fine and straight, begging to be broken; it seems out of place on a man so obviously dressed for combat.

He's the captain who told Anieke about the fall of Longrock.

"Miss Evermore, do you know who I am?"

I try to calm myself. I hold the cane at an angle, providing myself as much cover as possible. His armour is well-made and expensive. A small insignia is stamped into his left shoulder-plate, a bird between two crossed swords.

"You're from Castor," I guess.

"That's correct. Do you know why I'm here?"

I refuse to say what he wants to hear. "Holiday?"

Tyson groans as the man's eyes harden, and for a moment they're too like those of the men I killed. I lower my gaze.

"My name is Captain Griffin Marks. I was sent to return you and your friends to the Academy."

"I didn't think their jurisdiction stretches this far."

Amber eyes bore into mine. "Lotheria is the Headmasters' jurisdiction. As soon as the carrier gives permission for you to travel, we'll be escorting you back for punishment."

His words barely penetrate my stony facade. "It might be slow going."

"Are you sure? You set quite the pace on the way here."

I lift my leg back onto the bed. "Not all of me is returning."

His eyes flick down, then back to my face. A tiny flare of satisfaction loosens my chest; I caught him off-guard. "Exactly why the Headmasters don't let students leave before they're ready." He stands and towers above my bed. "I'll be back tomorrow and the day after that, until you're fit to return."

He goes to leave but turns back. He doesn't meet my gaze. "They're holding a funeral for the son this afternoon. You should go."

I look away as he leaves. Tyson shakes his head, then resumes reading a book from the Lord's library.

I attend Petre's funeral. Amisha helps me up, gets me used to the cane. She dresses me and brushes my hair. Her soft touch threatens to undo me, so I buckle my emotions down and meet any gentle enquiries with silence. Together, we walk to the family crypt with the rest of the townsfolk here to pay their respects. I limp uneasily with the cane, trying to adjust to its feel in my hand.

Riverdoor women wear black veils to mourn. Mine covers my face completely, lending a freedom I didn't expect. My eyes have been dry since waking, tearless and empty.

Dark trees lean over the graveyard. The gathered crowd bears the thin rain as a priest of Belatha delivers a gentle sermon, reminding us that life goes on and to heal with those we love. I ignore him, only cautiously interested in the fact that there isa priest at all; the worship of Belatha is dying in Lotheria, apparently. The church in Fairhaven was decrepit and unloved, serving only as a slim shelter against the icy night for beggars refused into the communal hall.

The lord and several men from the city carry the coffin into the family vault so Petre can rest beside his ancestors. A small procession of distant cousins moves forward so they can line his coffin with old possessions and treasured memories. Wooden toys and stuffed animals are placed inside to be sealed in with the bones of Lyons past.

After the service, the mourners gather to share memories of my friend. I leave the group to explore the cemetery, cane in hand. I flex my fingers around the carved grip as I lean on it heavily.

"Still getting used to it?"

The lilting voice belongs to a woman clad in black silk. Her grey eyes are expressionless, her dark red hair bound and twisted. My heart sinks. She is—was—Petre's mother.

"It'll be a long time until I do," I say. My leg aches, and there's a low stone wall nearby, but I hover between the graves. "I'm sorry for your loss."

Her mouth quirks. How can I explain the magnitude of failure I dealt her family?

"You spoke to him before—" Her breath catches. "Before he was killed, didn't you?"

I nod, my eyes on the ground.

"I knew Petre better than anyone. He was hot-headed, stubborn... He took you to the Keep with him. Everyone knows that."

I stay silent. Anything at this point would sound like an excuse.

"I can imagine what finding his brother chained up would've done to him." Her grey eyes fill with tears. "He was always protective of Sammy. I hoped he would be of..."

She trails off, but her hand lingers by her stomach. Something pierces the fog surrounding me.

"You're pregnant," I say.

She nods. "He didn't know. Not many do."

I should congratulate her, but it feels wrong. I stand and wait for her to direct the conversation, the honoured noblewoman, the matriarch of this family I've ruined. But she says nothing, and we look at each other through the rain.

"How is Samlin?" I ask. "Has he recovered?"

She hesitates. "He saw a lot of what happened. He doesn't speak much to anyone."

She finally breaks and lifts a silk handkerchief to her eyes. I let her cry but remain rigid where I am. My injured leg is numbing from overuse, but I ignore it.

"I'll leave you soon, I promise." She lifts her head and wipes her eyes. "But first I want to thank you."

My lips part in surprise. "For what?"

Her dress whispers over the damp leaves as she nears and rests a gentle hand on my shoulder.

"You gave up so much of yourself to save him."

I look away. "It wasn't enough."

She doesn't say anything, her hand cool on my shoulder.

"I was going to bring both your sons home. I promise you that was my intention, but I wasn't good enough." Tears finally burn at the back of my throat but I force the words again. "I wasn't enough."

She pulls me in close. "You almost were."

Back at the mansion, I stare at the ceiling and see burning men. Moonlight falls through the open drapes. A small, stunted candle flickers in the wrought-iron lantern on my bedside table, tired and wanting to be put out.

I feed a little magic into it, and the flame steadies like a loyal soldier.

My bedroom door creaking open makes me look up, aware but unalarmed. The candle flame grows a little when Samlin pokes his head around the door.

"What are you doing awake?" I ask the small lord. It's not his first appearance in my room. The night of Petre's funeral was his first visit, except he didn't dare wake me. I found him sleeping on the floor beside my bed, and he scarpered when dawn woke him. The second time, he tugged my hand and we talked until morning. Ever since these visits began, we've established a rapport no one else in the estate would understand.

"Couldn't sleep," comes the tiny reply.

He pads across the carpet to my bed. Without hesitation, he lifts the covers and crawls in beside me, bringing a blast of cold air.

I shiver. "Shut that, will you?" I tuck the blankets around him as he curls his little body near mine.

"Are you feeling better?" he asks.

"My leg hurts. My face hurts. And I'm pretty hungry."

"But you're alive?"

I consider my reply as he worms about on the pillow, making it dimple under my head. "Yes. And so are you, young master."

"It feels weird sleeping in a bed again," he says in a small voice.

They kept him at the post, even to sleep. From what we can make out of his side, he made a fairly decent escape attempt, legging it halfway home after pretending to be peeing in a bush. After that, he was kept under strict supervision. Matilda told me that since he came home, they've had to move his bed onto the floor, and he vomited the rich venison stew they'd tried to feed him almost immediately, settling instead for stale bread and water.

"You going to try and eat better this morning?" I ask, my eyelids feeling heavy again.

"Maybe."

"Bit of bacon?"

"Yuck."

"With maple sauce?"

"No!" His squeaky voice makes me laugh for the first time in weeks, and I poke him in the ribs. He squeals and tries to escape. "Let go! I'm a lord!"

"Yeah, but I'm stronger than you."

"Are not."

"Well, excuse me."

"One day I will fight like you." The childlike demeanour vanishes almost as quickly as it appeared. His little face is solemn, drawn. The ordeal on the moors has aged him far beyond his four years. "I'm going to attend the Academy and learn to fight like you."

As he settles and turns to sleep, I think about the future. Samlin will inherit his father's title. This includes the estate and all of Riverdoor, if it's still standing. Having seen the north's ferocity firsthand, I wonder how much longer this region will exist under southern rule.

I suddenly feel heavy. The warm bed envelops me and the boy is a comforting weight on my arm. At ease for the first time since the tower, I finally give in and sleep.

CHAPTER TWENTY

WHEN THE CAPTAIN asks permission to take us back to Fairhaven, I'm the one who gives it. Carrier Rokun protests that it's too early, but Captain Marks ignores him and orders us to move out. I pack my things slowly and take extra care with the sword I used during the battle. With my ruined armour discarded, the sword is the only remnant of the fight. It feels important to keep it nearby.

I clean it of blood so it doesn't rust, then wrap it in canvas for the journey.

I turn to examine the neat room, to make sure I've left it in an acceptable state, when the bird hits the window. I see it coming so I don't flinch, but the solid thud makes me frown in sympathy. It falls onto the wide windowsill and lies on its back, wings outstretched, claws curled. I crawl onto the bare mattress to get a better look and watch its tiny body twitch in the wind. It's definitely dead and stirs a half-eroded memory of a bird falling from the sky and another lying on a stone path.

Outside, my remaining friends prepare to be escorted back. Amisha speaks quietly to the stricken Lord Hugh, who does not look up when I walk through the double doors. Echo is saddled and waiting, Captain Marks at her side. His eyes bore into mine.

Matilda approaches me as Tyson dismounts his new horse to help me into the saddle. She is dressed in full mourning, the black silk fluttering in the breeze.

"Give the lord some time," she says. "He loved Petre. His family loved Petre. The perfect mage heir for his throne."

I glance up on a whim, spying a small face peering from a second story window. "Samlin didn't pass, then?"

In the sliver of sunlight, I see her mouth thin before shadows obscure her. "No, even with a second test after his ordeal. He will not be trained as a mage."

"Then he is a lucky boy," I say. Captain Marks seems distracted, but I know he's listening.

She's the only one to speak to me. When she clasps me to her chest, I smell dry, papery flowers and a hint of old perfume. Part of me wants to throw my arms around her and sob my soul out, but the other half—the half I strongly suspect held a man by his throat as he burned and screamed—turns me away. Tyson heaves me into the saddle then remounts his own pale mare, a gift from Lord Hugh.

The captain rides close to me. "I was sent to collect four."

I stare straight ahead. "Yes?"

He turns to look at Tyson, who chats with Amisha. "It appears you had another in your midst."

"Oh." I knew this was coming, prepared myself for it. "Our smith. Amisha is quite fond of his work, and... Petre thought it'd be a good idea to have him along in case the horses needed tending." It feels wrong, so wrong, to use his name.

A blacksmith is not a farrier, but Marks nods and apparently accepts it. We leave the estate as the sun fails to break through heavy clouds. His guards watch me closely until they realise I can't go anywhere fast even if I want to. A light sheen of sweat covers my brow as we ride out of Riverdoor, a city I hope to never see again. I don't turn when the others do atop the crest, preferring to keep the city with its lonely moors at my back. A guard rides either side of me, an imposing presence in black leather armour.

As we ride, the houses merge into fields, which become wild plains. The great-road slides beneath us as we begin our return to Fairhaven.

I close my eyes and let Echo's steady gait lull me half to sleep. Strength drains from every limb at the thought of returning to the Academy, and I wonder what solace I'll find back there. I try to remember the last time I was happy and come up blank. That hollow darkness grips my heart, and I want to fall into its despair.

I sleep for a bit and wake with Captain Marks hovering close on his cobalt gelding. He's close enough to reach out and touch me—was he making sure I didn't slide off Echo?

I sit up straight and wipe my mouth in case I was drooling. "Where are we?"

"A few hours north of Mornington. We'll stay there for the night and continue at dawn."

Mornington… We didn't pass a town with that name on the way here. I twist in the saddle and spy the purple shadows of the mountain range to the northeast instead of west.

"Why are we taking a different route?" I ask.

The captain's amber eyes watch me. "Trouble on the great-road. Not our unit's concern."

This road is thinner but somehow in better shape than the official highway of Lotheria. No deep ruts have been cut into it by stubborn wagon wheels, and the edges are trimmed and neat. The wind dances in rippling waves across fields of green grass.

Then, like a ray of warming sunshine, there's a change in the breeze. A warm gust brushes hair back from my face. Echo lifts her head.

Like a choreographed dance, the green fields around us open wide petals and a scarlet heath of flowers stretches as far as we can see, bobbing and weaving in the wind. A few of the horses in front have stopped.

"The wind is called the *uyvenberg*," Marks says. He seems as taken aback as the rest of us at the flowers' appearance. "Northern gabble for 'winter-breaker.' These are blood-poppies."

"Cheery."

"But aptly named. This field was the site of the Siege of Ten. Heard of it?"

I fix him with a look. "Petre studied war magic, not me."

He dismounts easily and hands the reins to a guard. I untangle my unresponsive right foot and he helps me down. He hands me my cane, and I hobble into the field.

"The Siege of Ten, longest battle in Lotherian history. Death toll was in the hundreds of thousands."

"Participants?" I ask as he surveys the landscape.

"Lotheria and Lotheria. Back then it was fairly united, none of this northern war business. The King and Queen had a disagreement; this is where it culminated."

"Why were they fighting?"

He shrugs. "If anyone knew, it wasn't written in the history books."

I struggle to remember the name of the queen in the town square. "Was it Fleur?"

He shakes his head. "Long before the Lily's time. This was Elijah and Ariana, around 724 or something. Married for three years before the war broke out."

We look out at the lonely landscape, and I can almost hear the screaming of horses and clashing of steel.

"The poppies grow in the most fertile soil in Lotheria, and this is the only place they can be found." Marks sits on his haunches and lifts a handful of dirt. "Seasoned with the blood of the loyal. Guess this is what happens when monarchs fight."

He dusts centuries-old bone off his hands. My cloak

ripples around my legs and the poppies bow as though acknowledging me.

I let the captain boost me back onto Echo, and we continue through the fields. When we reach the stunted woods around Mornington and the Stanthor border, the flowers have closed their petals again, recognising the *uyvenberg* for false spring, and we leave behind plain grass as we reenter our home state.

CHAPTER TWENTY-ONE

MORNINGTON WOULD BE nice without the civil unrest.

We've barely ridden into town when a woman strides over to our horses in long skirts and a bad mood. The silver brooch on her shoulder pins her as the town mayor—a mage who reports to the Headmasters and is responsible for paying taxes and sending harvests to Fairhaven.

I look around as she draws closer, taking in the ramshackle houses and thin townsfolk. A small gaggle of children clusters around a corner, their bellies swollen with hunger and eyes wide. Everyone in the square holds their breath as the mayor storms up to Captain Marks.

"I need to speak with you." She plants her hands on her hips directly before his horse. "Now."

Marks hesitates, then dismounts with a nod to one of his men. I expect them to go somewhere, but the mayor leans in and holds a hushed, hurried conversation. She looks furious, but Marks remains stonelike.

"We will send another regiment to move them as soon as we return to the capital," he says smoothly, but she shakes her head before he even finishes.

"No. I want them gone *tonight*. You know what they do for morale, which isn't exactly abundant here. It's hard enough with the tax increase and now—"

Marks lifts his hand to silence her, and her eyes bulge. She stops speaking, but I can't work out if she's obeying the order or just so angry she can't continue.

"I will send two men tonight to ask them to move along. If they don't go by the time we leave in the morning, I will send more to reinforce you. Do not engage by yourself. They're still mages."

It must be the Halvers. They've moved from the great-road. Why so close to a township? Are they nicking food? Supplies?

I remember what Orin said about them: mages with no soulmates, how they feel no pain. I clutch my chest, wondering about the ache that seems to have taken permanent residence there.

I listen as the mayor gives Marks rough directions to their camp, letting my eyes wander the village. When the captain turns from the irate woman, I'm picking something out of my teeth and looking completely unconcerned.

"There an inn around here, or what?" I ask.

Tyson looks at me and makes a 'You all right?' face.

He hasn't seen the children or the ones watching us from doorways.

"I wouldn't mind a hot meal," Amisha says.

We hitch our horses at Mornington's only inn, a tiny wooden building with few rooms. I pay for mine before the other guards come in, sending a few to the stables to stay the night with no small amount of grumbling.

"Bread and ale," I tell the innkeeper, and add an extra coin to his hand. I close the door between us before he can tell me there's no ale.

I sit heavily on the straw mattress and let my cane clatter. My leg aches fiercely, though I strived to keep signs of discomfort from the others. It jitters; I hold my hand down on my knee until it stops.

Instead of ale, a small loaf of rough bread and a wedge of fresh cheese are delivered. I eat the whole lot on my bed, keeping my leg elevated. I need it fully rested for tonight's expedition.

When night falls, I don my brown cloak and gloves, pulling the hood over my head. At least with my cane, it won't be hard to imitate the lagging shuffle of an elderly woman. I leave the inn and set off into the mist. Oil lanterns glow in the gloom. I pass the stables where our horses and some of the men are resting for the night and slow my pace as two guards emerge to fill buckets in the trough.

I'll have to avoid the two riders Marks promised to send. I limp along the trail by the light of a lazy moon, a thin crescent in the mottled sky, and soak my boots more than once in a hidden puddle. The Halvers' camp is difficult to find; no firelight flickers between their tents hunkered close to the ground. Instead, I find the dim glow of lanterns behind canvas.

A tent flap moves aside, and a pair of blank eyes watches me limp past. I hold the person's gaze, but they say nothing. A large man well over six foot tall shuffles into my path. His tattered clothing bares most of his chest, even though it's freezing. His dull eyes are the worst of them yet: stone-grey, cold. A slow, awful grin pulls his mouth to one side just as a female voice rings strong behind him.

"I hoped you'd come."

I start and wobble dangerously, planting my cane to avoid falling. The woman's hood rests on her shoulders, revealing her ruined eye.

"I wanted to talk to you," I say.

She assesses me for a moment, then jerks her head. "Come."

I follow her to a tent larger than the others. She lifts the patchwork flap and I enter. A small brazier burns in the middle with a kettle above the flames, and the rough ground is covered by thick canvas. Her bedroll, topped with animal fur, is against the tent's farthest edge.

"I don't feel the cold anymore, but I thought you'd appreciate the fire if you showed up," she says, passing me.

"Thank you." I sit near it and hold my hands near the flames. A few other Halvers enter.

The one-eyed woman settles on the hard ground opposite

me. Her pale skin is flecked with raindrops, her short black hair slicked with ice. "My name is Kaya. When I saw you on the road and your interest in our camp, I knew you'd seek us out."

I shift uncomfortably. "How?"

She smiles and doesn't answer, then lifts the kettle from the fire and pours into two battered tin cups. She offers one to me, which I take. The metal is hot, and though I don't feel the pain, I pretend to grimace; I don't know this woman, and I don't trust her or the creeps outside.

"Would you like to say a toast?" she inquires.

I think for a second, then lift the burning cup. "Fuck the Headmasters."

She lifts an eyebrow as I drain the cup. Hot mead scalds my throat and my eyes water as I resist the urge to cough.

"An interesting sentiment."

"One I thought you'd share," I say.

A few of the Halvers by the flap stir. I start to wonder if I should've brought my sword.

"Do you know what we are?" Kaya asks, pouring me a second cup from the kettle.

"Mages who lost their soulmates." I accept the cup. "Halvers."

She lets out an easy breath that turns into a laugh, and I relax slightly. "I haven't heard that one. Yes, we are half-souls. All that remains after a failed campaign to win back the pride of an old man and woman. Halvers." She toasts me with her own cup. "Fuck the Headmasters."

I grin for the first time in a long while. We drink a few more cups in silence.

"Why have you come here? Are you, perhaps, beginning to doubt the ways of our trusted leaders?"

I consider my reply; how much to tell a stranger? "I want to know what kind of people they are. I'm returning to the Academy after leaving without permission, and I want to know what to expect."

Kaya's eye widens. "No mage student has ever left the Academy before graduating."

"Well, now four have." The pit in my stomach, already deep and wide after Riverdoor, threatens to grow. "What will they do to us?"

"That I cannot tell you. What you have done is unprecedented. But they are fond of taking fingers, punishments that leave a mark. You will not be the same person after you return."

Ignoring the chills that run up and down my arms, I stretch my leg out before me. "That's already been taken care of."

Kaya examines it, holding her cup of cooling mead. "I swear you had two good ones when I saw you last."

That startles a laugh out of me, a rusty sound I haven't heard since Riverdoor. She smiles like she hasn't in equally as long.

"What happened?"

"I fought with northmen." I squint into my empty cup and force the next words. "My leg wasn't the only thing I lost."

Kaya remains still, looking at me with that one dark eye. "And you came to us for the same reason all Halvers group together: to find companionship in the hope it'll fill that vast, empty void in yourself."

I nod once and can't meet her gaze.

"Do you have your soulmate?"

I shake my head. "No. I haven't contacted him."

A murmur from the watching Halvers rumbles around the tent. Kaya leans closer.

"How long have you been at the Academy?"

"Months. Since autumn began."

"It is unusual that you haven't made contact with your soulmate, then. Is there anyone unpaired?"

"I know *who* it is. But we haven't paired yet."

"You are avoiding him."

She's right. "I didn't mean to at first. But now I—" I break off and detach myself from the words. "I work better alone."

Kaya says nothing. I take a deep breath.

"Tell me about the Halvers."

"Their story is not mine to tell," she says finally. "But I will offer my own.

"My soulmate was Jax, a mage from Castor. We met at the Academy, like all do. As the only Sudafraen, I thought I'd get special treatment from Iain, knowing we share a homeland, but that hope died quickly. After I graduated, I was given four years on my ticket."

I frown. "Four years?"

"Of service to the Headmasters. I was lucky; some got ten. Four was easy, a sprint compared to a marathon. When I discovered they were offering a year off anyone's ticket simply to enlist in the war efforts, I pressured Jax, who got six years, to come with me." Her jaw clenches. "He agreed. We went through basic training before being packed off to Gowar. We joined a caravan headed towards Thyssen, which they told us was a nothing town without strategic resources or positioning. We were told it would be an easy claim, to whet our swords and appetite for war.

"But it wasn't. Thyssen was a mining town for mirriam ore. Do you know what that is?"

I shake my head.

"It's the sister metal for southern silver, used in the official Silver Wings of the Academy. The northerners knew this and set up defences around its only known deposit: the town we'd all been sent to attack."

A few of the other Halvers are nodding with blank looks. Were they also sent to Thyssen?

"Only the best made it out of that town, none of us intact." Kaya taps her ruined eye. I reach up to touch my own scars. "I lost this but barely felt it. Jax took a sword to the gut; I felt that.

"When he lost his fight, I felt that too." Her eye settles on the fire. The pit in my stomach yawns, my heart pounding. "I'm not going to bother trying to describe the physical pain of my soul tearing, but I knew what waited for me on the other side and thought about throwing myself back into the war zone. But I didn't. I gathered myself, took my pension, and disappeared before I could be discharged."

"Discharged?" It comes out as a whisper.

"No one wants half-souls on the front lines," Kaya explains with a wry smile. "We're a liability, useful only as suicide units that forget their orders most of the time. No, I tracked down this camp somewhere around Thurin, got my resources sorted before I started degrading, and settled into my new life. It's not so bad. The chill is starting to set in, so I don't feel cold anymore. Gotta watch your fingers when that starts happening."

She drinks deeply and drags her hand across her mouth. "So you want to know what kind of people the Headmasters are?" She tosses the empty cup aside. "They're the kind of people who give you years on your ticket depending on your quality of servitude, who send green soldiers into unfamiliar territory for some pretty metals. They're the kind who sends armed units to clear out a camp of war heroes, who are grieving and hurt and lost, because they're a blight on the landscape."

She leans close, but I'm already hanging on her every word. "We gave them everything. Our hearts, our swords, our souls. *This* is the gratitude we receive in return."

Silence falls over the tent. The coals in the brazier dance with flames as I fight to keep everything inside—Petre, my fear of pairing with Phoenix, Tyson...

I take a heaving breath, and a slender finger taps my forehead.

"Gods-touched," Kaya says quietly.

"What?" I blurt, almost losing composure. *How can she possibly know?* "What's gods-touched?"

She smiles. "You. I heard of a girl who fell from the sky, a girl with green eyes and dark hair like yours."

I comb my hair back, twisting it into a long tail. "How did you hear that?"

She raises an eyebrow. "Do you think many fall from the sky and walk away? The news spread far, and quickly."

Great. I wonder why Amisha didn't bring it up when we found the stairs that day. "What does it mean?" I ask. "I fell through the clouds, smacked into the ground, woke up in a bed, poisoned by something that bit me in a dream." The absurdity of it all hits me and I laugh an unhealthy, loathing laugh. A small cup nudges my hand. "And no one's taken the time of day to tell me what it *means*."

Her hand curls around my free one as I heave a dry sob. Frustration boils to the surface, and I take a drink of the warm ale.

"I know." Kaya motions with her other hand. The Halvers file from the tent, and when we're alone, she takes my cup and sets it on the canvas floor. "I felt a connection with you the moment I saw you on the great-road. I do not have the sight, but I knew we'd meet. And here you are." She grips my hands tighter. *"Here you are.*

"I know you're feeling lost. You're scared. You're hurt. I will tell you *everything* you want to know, and I promise to tell the truth. Would you like that?"

I nod, knowing tears glisten in my eyes.

She jerks her head at the kettle on the fire and gives me a quirked smile. "Then I think we'll need more of that."

***

I drink and learn from Kaya until whispered word reaches us of the two men Marks sent to move them along.

The half-souls who haven't succumbed to the chill—as they call it when they can no longer feel pain or cold—escort me as far back to Mornington as they dare. Kaya promises to get word to me if they move closer to Fairhaven, but she doesn't want to move them any nearer the Academy than she must; some still carry memories of those who did them wrong.

As I slip into my room and light the stunted candle on the bedside table, I think of what Kaya told me. Of her time in the Headmaster's army. Of the northmen they fought.

I didn't ask her what 'gods-touched' meant; in the end, I didn't want to know. My leg shook whenever I thought about it.

The straw mattress is softened by the kettle of ale I've consumed. Kaya said she acquired it after seeing me on the roads. I asked if being a half-soul means she could see the future. She snorted and told me it just means she can read people better.

The ale dulls the memories that have taken to washing over me before I sleep. Tonight, when my eyelids drift closed, I don't see Petre's face in the mud or feel his cold cheek under my hand. The comforting embrace of alcohol numbs my heartache.

Instead, I see Phoenix, tall and quiet and sure. What will happen when we pair? Will I become complete? Will this hole in my stomach sew back together?

I think again of the pale northerner waiting for me back at the Academy, unaware that I've just murdered his kinsmen. I've told no one of the massacre.

When we prepare to leave the next morning, the mayor returns with a small jar.

"For you." She plants it in Captain Marks' hand. "Some of my family's preserve for the journey home."

He tucks the jar of what looks like blueberry jam into his pack. "Dare I ask?"

"We sent some farmers out to have a look this morning. The Halver camp is gone. Nice work, Marks."

I lift an eyebrow as I struggle into the saddle without Orin's help; I'm getting used to boosting myself up, but it still sucks. It sounds like she's ranking herself above Marks, but he's a captain. Surely that outranks town mayor?

I wait until Mornington is in the dust behind us before coming up beside him. Riding with no hands, he's smothering a chunk of bread with the jam. I hold my hand out until he sighs and hands it to me.

"Thanks." I bite into the bread. "This is…" I force it down with a grimace. "Good."

"Tastes like shit, Evermore, don't pretend." He's already loading up more jam. "Mornington doesn't have the greatest climate for growing fruit."

We ride in silence for about an hour, sharing bread as the rest of the group follows silently. When we come up over a little rise and spy Fairhaven in the distance, a small hamlet of thatched rooves and wispy smoke, he finally breaks it.

"Enjoying your last taste of freedom?"

I rub my eyebrow with my thumb. "What will they do to us?"

I think about what Kaya said, about how the Headmasters like 'permanent' punishments. "I honestly wish I could tell you." He looks down at me, suddenly seeming a lot older than he did in Riverdoor. "I don't really know them."

I frown. "You don't—"

He gazes at me steadily as my brain works it out.

"You're non-magi."

"One of the only in the Governor's employ. Oh, he's in Fairhaven as well. He wanted to see the wayward students."

And the Council of Three is complete for our shameful return. Something begins to gnaw through the shield of numbness I've taken refuge in since Riverdoor.

Fear.

Not for myself. I've come up against something hard and unyielding since Petre's eyes locked with mine and I saw his life slip from them like yolk from an egg. I'm afraid for Orin and Amisha.

But I'm terrified for Tyson. I wish I could get word to him, but Marks won't leave my side for a second. Instead, I catch Amisha's eye to my right. The noble has been left mostly alone by the contingent of guards, remaining quiet and pensive. I've caught her wiping silent tears for Petre, which seems to scare most of them away.

I jerk my head towards Tyson, and she nods before letting her mare drop back to him. I can only hope they'll find a way to separate him from the group before we reach the Academy.

The rest of the journey slips away, and before I know it, our horses step from the packed road onto uneven cobblestones. The Academy looms above the townhouses and inns, and the clouds darken. The two towers that flank the enormous main door stand stark against a roiling sky, and a gust blows dried leaves around the horses' legs as we enter the courtyard.

My heart thuds anxiously. Tyson is still with us. Soon, they'll close the gates, shutting him into the last place I want him trapped: the Academy.

I throw my right leg over the saddle as though I've forgotten my injury. It hits the ground hard, and I clench my teeth against the bolt of pain. My yelp is very real as I go tumbling to the ground—the same ground I smashed into face-first from the sky.

"Evermore, you all right?" The captain hurries over, having dismounted his own horse. Orin follows, looking concerned.

"I'm fine." I take my time accepting the hand Marks offers. I lean on him heavily as he pulls me up. "Damn leg."

I look around as the stablehands tend to our mounts. Tyson has vanished, and Amisha hurries forward, brown skin ashy against her royal blue traveling cloak and spattered with road filth. We share a knowing look. She nods. When I turn away, Netalia is standing under the eaves of the castle like a ghostly figure in pale silk. I accept my cane from one of the pages taking our gear and limp over to her, hoping she didn't witness Tyson's departure.

"Tell your friends to come with us," she instructs, making no mention of my leg.

I let out a shaky breath.

The tapping of my cane echoes in the empty halls. As we enter the main hall, dirty and grimy after so many days on the road, our classmates stand against the sides, clad neatly in their grey Academy cloaks. On the dais at one end, a large wooden table has been set up with matching chairs. Iain sits at the farthest end, unreadable. The man in the middle must be Governor Malic. Small and round, he verges on unimpressive, but his gaze is fierce and unbroken.

Netalia sweeps past us to her own seat on the dais, and we wait on the floor below. I take a few more steps to front the group and hear a rumble sweep through our classmates as I rest on my cane.

"Where is the fourth?" Captain Marks asks me from across the floor. "I reported four of you."

He means Tyson. On the dais, Iain seems engrossed in the report laid on the desk before him, but I don't believe it for a second.

"We hired a blacksmith to journey with us," I say as though it's a secondary thought. "I didn't want him caught up in the consequences when he couldn't refuse my order to begin with."

"Very gallant of you." Iain lays down his pen. "We'll now hear your reasons for leaving the Academy."

"Northern raiders kidnapped the youngest son of your sworn lord," I begin, trying not to breathe too heavily; even the short walk from the courtyard has tired me. "After an appeal to you for assistance went unheard, the former heir requested our help retrieving him."

This short statement sends ripples of conversation through the gathered students. There are a few tiny gasps of disbelief as the word 'former' sinks in.

Iain remains stony-faced. "And were you successful in this venture?"

I press my lips together, then pull up the hem of my cloak to show my leg. "You tell me."

The teachers have gathered at the back of the dais, and I see Arno frown as he takes in the injury.

"Lord Thoreau," Iain begins slowly. "Can you please confirm Captain Marks' report of Petre Lyon's murder during your time in Riverdoor?"

Numbness slices down my body as I tighten my grip on the cane.

Orin's words seem carved in stone. "Yes. Petre was killed while we were in Riverdoor."

"Would you say his passing was directly caused by the actions of your group?"

I wait, coiled and tense, for my friend's response.

"No, it was—"

"Did Miss Evermore go off by herself in an attempt to draw out the group you were hunting?"

"We lost them both at some point, but we were all—"

"So Miss Evermore had direct contact with the deceased before your group found her alone beside the body of Lord Lyon?"

"Yes, but—"

"Lord Thoreau—"

"How about you let him finish a sentence?" I say, unable to look away from the men and woman above us. "Or, if you're going to ask about what happened on the moors, why don't you ask the person who was actually there?"

More heated whispers rocket around the room. Guards in black armour, not the ones who traveled with us, step from the crowd of students and make their presence very well known.

"Miss Evermore," Governor Malico says. "If I may offer advice, it would be to remain silent at your murder trial."

I blink, finally thrown off guard. "At my... my what?"

Whispering goes out the window as voices erupt through the hall. One is louder than the rest.

"Murder?" Phoenix emerges from the crowd and slowly

walks forward until he comes to stand beside me. "What proof do you have?"

I don't look at him, though I can feel his presence at my side. It's strong and comforting. I wonder what he'll do when he hears what I did to his kinsmen.

"This is a manslaughter trial," Netalia says, lancing Malico with a stare. "Miss Evermore's actions on the moors resulted in the death of a valuable student and the heir of our sworn lord; justice must be delivered. And as far as we're aware, Miss Evermore has been refusing to share her version of the story to authorities."

"However, if Miss Evermore is to accept full responsibility for the trip and its outcomes, our sentence will be lenient," Iain states.

I want to burn the building with them still in it. I want to kick and scream and rage about how this is unfair, about how I received forgiveness from the mother of the man whose death I couldn't prevent.

Instead I lift my head, lean on my cane, and say, "I accept it."

"Rose, no." Phoenix steps close, and I inch away from him. "You don't have to accept anything without telling your side of the story."

I lift my shoulders and let them fall helplessly as I look up into his furrowed eyes. "My story will only give them more reason to carry through with their sentence."

Because this *should* be a murder trial. I killed at least seven men on the Riverdoor trip. Two fell to my sword, the others to my fire.

The smack of a wooden gavel makes us look up. "Sentencing will now commence," Governor Malico barks.

Amisha and Orin get three years added to their tickets. I get ten. It's unheard of for students to rack up years before graduating, but it's not over.

"In addition to her years, Miss Evermore will also receive fives lashes at the post," Malico finishes.

The room is dead silent.

It's not a finger, I tell myself as the guards come to escort me away. *I still have all my fingers.*

"Where will you receive your punishment?" one of the guards asks, and I recognise Sergeant Hall.

I lick dry lips as I think. "The courtyard."

Hall turns to the governor, who nods. They take me out there as a post is carried out before me. The students of the Academy file after us as we step back into the murky afternoon. It's cold; bumps rise on my skin.

The stablehands and yard boys watch with just enough curiosity to not get in trouble. Behind me, I hear Phoenix arguing with someone who I only hope is not Malico. Iain would never whip a nativeborn mage, but I suspect the governor would.

And a humanborn is free game.

I shed my cloak and jacket until I'm standing in the middle of the yard in just my travel-stained white blouse. I hand my cane to Amisha, who looks close to tears, and kneel before the post.

Don't look at Amisha, I tell myself, *or you'll cry too.*

As I'm told to place my hands on the wooden post, I see Maurice the farrier emerge from the stable, wringing his hands on his apron with a furrowed brow.

I will still have all my toes.

I'm given no warning as the first lash bites deep from shoulder to waist. My fingers dig into the wooden post. I grit my teeth and wonder how I'll take four more.

I will still have both arms.

I fight the urge to cry out at the second lash and the third. Through tears, I look up past the post I'm clinging to as though my life depends on it. Maurice and the other stable hands watch.

I will still have both—most—of my legs.

The fourth tears a sob from me as it flicks against another line already cut into my back. I barely feel the fifth through a haze of pain and anger.

Then someone helps me to my feet. They hand me my cane. I recognise the sandalwood scent and crisp blue robe of Carrier Bayde, the Academy healer.

"She is under my care and I invoke my right to do so," I hear him say, but it's as though he's speaking underwater. "You may punish her further after I've examined her existing injuries."

A corridor. A stairwell. A hall of light and colour. All pass in a blur as I struggle to keep my grip on the cane. I stumble into a dark mass that smells like wood smoke and jasmine. I'm lifted off my feet onto someone's shoulder as my cane falls to the carpet.

"I got her." The vibrations roll through my stomach, and I want to droop and let myself pass out, but I cling on instead.

Who is carrying me? Why does Bayde want to fix me?

I'm lowered face-first onto a soft, white bed. I can't help but sigh into the clean sheets, relaxing despite the raging pain. I suddenly remember Bayde, standing with a hard face in the corner as they cut off Laela's father's finger. Dena's excited recollections of her healing lessons with him sound in my ears as the man begins to mix things on the table beside me.

Bayde applies ice to my back. I suppress a groan as he coats all the cuts in his healing balm.

"Ridiculous. Whipping a student."

There's a soft *clunk* as a door is closed, and the next voice takes me by surprise.

"You could at least pretend to support them," Jett says. "Those people pay your wages."

"Like I care about any of that," Bayde snaps. The minty smell of the herbs reaches me, and I inhale, drawing comfort from the familiar aromas; Dena often comes to class smelling like them. "They keep me close on a leash because they know how I feel about them."

"So let me get this straight." The mattress under my legs dips as Jett sits on it. "You graduated with just one year on your ticket, topped your class at the Apothecary, then took a job working for the people you hate."

Pale flames flicker. I watch my shadow wobble.

"Keep your enemies by your side so you never wonder where they are," Bayde quips. "How are you feeling, my girl?"

I opt for a groan. It seems to satisfy the healer, for he turns me over with surprising strength. I brace for the pain from my back, but none comes when the soft mattress caresses my bare skin. With a carrier's trademark grace, he checks the scars on my cheek then my withered right calf, squinting through a warped glass.

"This is Carrier Rokun's work, isn't it?" he asks, but it's more a statement so I don't bother answering. He shakes his head as he walks back to his desk. "Sloppy stitch work—I wouldn't believe it if it wasn't lying on my examination table."

I look around now that I'm face-up. Bayde's office is more of a healer's studio: whitewashed walls almost entirely covered by small, square boxes holding crushed petals, dried roots. Some even hold live plants. Dena gushed about this office after her first lesson. I wonder where she is.

Tiny glass instruments cluster together like a small city landscape on his desk, some holding liquid, others with glass heated by fire. A mortar and pestle sit on his wooden desk, and the papers beside it are stacked neatly. Everything about Bayde is about as far as you can get from the subpar treatment I received in Riverdoor.

"You have done marvellous work on that leg, Miss Evermore," the carrier says, pointing at me with a willow switch. He resumes skinning it as he talks. "That was beyond even my capabilities, but Rokun has set it in stone. You'll be needing that cane for the rest of your days."

Though I've been expecting it, I slump. Then I remember how I lost it and shore myself against the disappointment.

"What about my face?" I croak.

The carrier looks at me over round glasses, then glances at Jett. "Fingernail marks. Deep. Those scars may heal in time, but not for many years."

I nod and stay quiet. It's a small price to pay for my life.

"Alsain, this student will need special care," Bayde continues. "Can I trust you'll see to her wellbeing?"

"You said she'll be fine," Jett says.

"Physically, yes. She'll get used to the leg, but mentally she will experience some trauma. In this environment, it is important she feels she is supported in every capacity."

Jett looks at me. I shrug. "I promise I'm doing okay."

I've never heard his last name before. I don't comment on it.

"Can I go?" I ask. Hunger pinches the sides of my stomach after the healing.

Eustace is sent to escort me back to my room. By the time we reach it, I can feel each whip weal again and my leg burns. I wonder if Dena can bring up more of the healing gel Bayde used.

"Wait," I tell the page as I rummage through the gear that's been brought up. Someone has searched it and made no effort to hide what they were doing, but when I find my purse it's untouched. I dig out my last gold coin. "Go into town and buy the best whisky you can with this. Take the bottle to the stables and leave it in Echo's stall before sundown. And send Thompson up, please."

Eustace takes the coin but looks at me warily. When he opens his mouth, I shake my head.

"No questions."

When Thompson comes up, he's on edge, looking around the balcony like child slavers are hiding up here with a written order for scrawny gits. I give him the jar of shitty blueberry jam I swiped from Marks when he wasn't looking and tell him to let Maurice know that Echo needs seeing to tonight at sundown before she's fed. The kid leaves, holding the half-eaten jar of preserve like a friggin' trophy.

Then I sit on my bed and finally let the tears come.

CHAPTER TWENTY-TWO

I DRESS IN my uniform the next morning and am gathering my books when Eustace ambushes me outside my door.

"Good morning, Miss Evermore. I have this for you."

I lean my cane against my side as I slit the silver wax seal with a gloved finger, reading quickly. I have a session with Politics' Master Alena this morning ordered by the Headmasters themselves.

I press the letter into Eustace's chest. "I have Runes in ten minutes. Tell Alena I'll see her after that."

I start walking along the balcony and the annoyed page trots after me. "Did you not see the seal on the envelope?" He comes up alongside me and shows me the broken wax. "*Silver.* That's directly from the Headmasters."

I finally slow at the top of the stairs and sigh. "Okay. You can tell Runes' Master Arno I'll have to miss today's lesson, then."

I leave a mortified Eustace atop the stairs. Arno told me the pages are frightened of him and he rarely gets service from them, living on the subterranean floors. At least Eustace will have a story for the others in the pages' barracks tonight.

I know where Alena's office is, having walked past it every morning. The door is half-open when I arrive but the room is empty, the candles unlit and the fire barely smouldering in the hearth. Her desk is messy and cluttered with random bits of paper, pens, pots of ink. A small white jar is half-tucked into a drawer—she left this place in a hurry.

"Sorry, Rose. I had an urgent meeting with Mal—I mean, the Governor." She pushes past me, opening the door wide. I waddle in after her. "The Headmasters have asked me to explain the ticket system to you."

"Oh, good," I intone. "Seeing as mine already has ten years on it."

I sit heavily as she does behind her desk. "I know, I should've explained this earlier. If you'd come to see me like the others... Never mind. The Headmasters agree that you might not have broken the rules so severely if you knew of the consequences." She leans forward with a sympathetic smile, and I brace myself. "They've agreed to reduce your sentence by three months."

I meet her eyes and pinch myself under the table. "Thank you. That's very generous of them."

She smiles wider, pleased with my response. "Now, the ticket system. What do you know about it?"

"I know everyone graduates with one, and the amount of years on it is dependent on"—I almost say 'good behaviour' but refrain—"an assessment of your time at the Academy."

"That's correct. After a student graduates and receives their Silver Wings, they will be stationed in an area of their choice, or the Headmasters will provide a pathway for those with no special interests. The Headmasters will receive fifty percent of your wages in tax for the number of years on your ticket, and you'll be required to live in regulated boarding houses in the area you settle in. Each major town and city has one, and your stay will include all food and laundry, like here."

Something settles deep in my stomach as I absorb the information. "So for the next ten years after I graduate, the Headmasters still have almost complete control of my lifestyle."

"Not *complete* control—"

"They choose where I work. They take half my wages. I don't decide where I live, or even what I eat."

Alena clears her throat, her gaze on the table. "Yes, but—"

I talk over her. "And travel? I'm guessing I can't leave the country."

She chews her lip for a few seconds before answering. "Mages must have less than eight months on their ticket before being granted a travel pass."

I think of running and escaping overseas, and make a mental note to start learning Tsalskinese from Amisha.

When Alena speaks again, her tone is gentle. "Miss Evermore... Rose. Tell me what happened in Riverdoor."

"No." The word leaps to my lips in a single bound. "I'm late for Runes. May I go?"

Her eyebrows fold upwards softly. "Rose, you need to talk about what happened—"

"The Headmasters already decided what happened," I remind her. "We were just discussing the consequences of that."

"You have to realise, you're the only one who knows what happened on the moors. It's your word people have to trust."

"It should be enough," I mutter. "For something like this."

She wants to say more, but I get up and leave. I grip my cane tightly as I limp down the passage towards the dungeons and Arno. I have a sudden need to burrow into the depths of the building and lose myself in the pages of some musty runes manuscript.

But the bell tolls as I reach the top of the stairs that lead into the dungeons, and I hover, undecided. I know I have to face my friends at some point. It might as well be now.

I reach Jett's class a little early, meeting Dena on the way. Her sleeves are pushed up and her arms pink, smelling of fresh soap.

"Hi," I say uneasily as she nears with a strange look. "How was Heal—"

She draws me into a huge hug, and I nearly lose my grip on the cane. Her hold is so tight we're squished together, but something deep inside me threatens to wiggle loose. I squirm from her hold before it can.

"Hello to you too."

She punches me in the shoulder. "Where was my invite to Riverdoor?"

My gaze darkens. "You don't mean that."

She sets her mouth in a mulish line. "I wanted the opportunity to help you. I know you like the mages you hang around with, but you're still humanborn, Rose."

Something about that pisses me off, but I ignore it. "Yeah, well... I don't think they like me much anymore."

The rest of the class arrives, and I sit at a lonely table near the windows. Dena sits with her soulmate with a glance over at me, and I smile tightly.

"This seat free?" Orin dumps his bag on the table before I can reply. "Amisha, pull another table over."

I watch in disbelief as my mage friends sit on either side of me. Amisha's eyes are red and raw, and Orin is paler than usual. We don't speak as the door reopens. A familiar figure in dark leather armour steps through the doorway.

Jett, who's been setting up at the front, frowns before winding his way through the tables as though he expected Captain Marks to pop by.

"Just a routine inspection," Marks says in a low tone. "The Governor is interested in the education of his new mages."

"So he sends you?" The hum of classroom chatter almost drowns out our teacher. "A captain of the guard?"

Marks shrugs. "He knows I'm enjoying my time back here."

Back here? But Marks is non-magi. Why would he have spent any time at the Academy?

Like a divine tap on the shoulder, a page trots through the open door and lays a sealed letter on the desk up front, then leaves. I almost laugh—Captain Marks, a strong, muscled fighter who commands respect, must've started out as an Academy page. I wonder if Eustace aims to wear the black armour of a capital guard one day, but it's the image of Marks in a page's uniform that lightens my shoulders.

He settles in close behind me and my friends, and a wave of spiced scent washes over me. It's not unpleasant, but I feel my spine stiffen as I sense him from the corner of my vision.

So the Governor wants a report on how 'his mages' are doing, as though we're a field of crops coming ripe and ready for harvest. I guess in a way we are; the more mages out and working off their ticket years, the more revenue the Governor and Headmasters receive.

I must look like a big, fat paycheck to my superiors. Ten years of half wages must be many expensive blouses for Netalia.

"Back to your practical application of magic today," Jett calls. "You have exams soon and how you do will reflect on me. I don't need that sort of bad press."

A rumble of laughter follows.

"Speaking of," our teacher continues, "Miss Evermore, can I see you for a moment? Just before we begin."

A mage girl up front laughs, and I scowl at her as I limp

to Jett. She meets my look in a challenge, but I turn away first when I reach our teacher.

"Come for a walk," he says, and I follow him into the corridor. Marks watches us with hawkish eyes but stays put.

The hallway is empty, and he closes the heavy door separating us and the curious class. "I wanted to check on how you were doing."

The unexpected kindness of him keeping his word to Carrier Bayde raises a lump in my throat. I clear it and flex my fingers on my cane. "I'm doing... all right. Considering."

"I know you don't want to talk about it, but it will help."

The tangled knot in my stomach is so unappealing I cannot even imagine beginning to unravel it. I look up into my teacher's eyes, coal-dark with tiny lines between his brows. I can't decide if it's pity that rests deep in his gaze.

He knows I won't answer. "I'm thinking of starting a strategy club. Would you be interested in joining?"

The change in conversation throws me for a moment. "A what club?"

"We gather to play a strategy game called Kingdoms and discuss war history of all the countries. I thought you'd find it interesting."

We stand in silence for a second or two, and I tap my cane on the floor as I think. I'm worried that'll become a tell for when I'm deep in thought.

"Sure. I could use a bit of fun in my life."

"Not too much, though," he warns as he turns to go back

inside. "The Headmasters will shut us down if they think it's fun."

When the bells ring, I pack my belongings with a bit of nervousness. In past lessons, Arno has shown no reservations about grilling me for information. An hour with him will be hard to bear.

He'll get the truth out of me. My shoulders sag as I wonder how my mentor will take the news that I killed.

I'm buried so deep in my thoughts that I don't hear Amisha's or Orin's gentle goodbyes. It's not until I nearly bounce off Phoenix that I realise he was waiting for me outside the room.

"Where are you headed?" he asks as I look over his shoulder. Gods darn it, he has a really nice voice. All mellow and smooth and reassuring.

"I have Runes. Arno is already unhappy with me, so I shouldn't be late."

I try to cane past him, but he speaks again. "Rose. I know you must tire of people asking you this, but would you like to talk about Riverdoor?"

It's spoken so softly that I nearly look at him. A tiny part of me quivers, wanting to tell him everything—what I did, whom I killed. But I back away.

"I'm late," I say finally, and incline my head down the hallway. "Remedial Runes. See you around."

He frowns. "Around what?"

But I'm already caning my way down the corridor as fast as possible. I'm not ready to connect with my soulmate, not yet. There are secrets in my skull that must stay my own, and I still don't know how much he'll know if we bond. Does he get to dig around in my head? Rifle through my memories? Examine thoughts and feelings like they're written down for his enjoyment?

I suppress a shudder as I shoulder open the door of the stairway to the dungeons. Maybe Arno knows more about soulmate interaction, though he's never spoken of his own in the past.

The way to his rooms is ingrained into my head, and I cautiously step over the wet stones and slippery moss, weaving through the vast underground labyrinth. The gas lamps burn steadily, a little greener down here due to how close they are to the natural source, according to Eustace.

Arno's study is well-lit when I arrive. The man sits at his desk, transcribing from the looks of it.

"You're late." He doesn't look up.

"My other class ran overtime." I lean my cane against his desk and lever myself into my customary chair. "Trust me, I would've rather been here."

He snorts, but I can't tell if he's amused or pleased by my words. "I want you to tell me what happened in Riverdoor."

Even if it was expected, I didn't think he'd plunge straight in. "What?"

"I'm one of the few who've read Captain Marks' report. I know what they found at Deadman's Keep."

Searing heat and oily smoke suddenly surround me as though I'm back on the battlefield. Long-dead screams echo in my ears as I relive the final moments of my enemies' lives. "And what was that?" I ask, colder than I intend.

Arno looks up at me before lifting a sheet of cheap parchment onto his desk. "'The corpses of eight deceased men, one of whom was an Academy student. Another student, badly injured but alive, recovered and returned to the Riverdoor estate. The tower that stood on the site, previously known as Deadman's Keep, blown apart by unknown forces. Citymen had to be recruited to extinguish the fires or risk them spreading across the moors.

"'One boy, unburnt despite being bound to a post inside the destroyed tower remains, was unable to offer any explanation of what had transpired because he would not, or could not, speak to us.'"

Arno finishes reading. "Would you like me to continue? Griffin was kind enough to include some of his theories."

"No." I don't need to hear the crackpot thoughts of the first on the scene of my massacre.

"Then talk. Everyone else might've wrapped you up in cotton wool, but you know me better than to think I'll step softly around this subject." Arno points the nib of his pen at me. "You worked some magic that scared you enough that you won't talk about it. What was it?"

I pinch the pen between my fingers, my mouth set in a mulish line. Something tells me not to give in immediately.

"What kind of bonds do soulmates have?" I ask instead.

Arno sighs and leans back in his chair. He rubs his face. "What?"

"Can they read your thoughts? Use your power? What's the deal?"

My Runes' Master twirls his pen. "This is a question for Alena. Didn't she go through this with you?"

"If she did, I wasn't listening."

He grunts. "Somehow I'm not surprised."

I lift my eyebrows expectantly when he looks at me.

"You're not bonded yet, are you?" he asks finally.

"Nope. One of the last."

"So you have the luxury of knowing who your soulmate is without joining with them first."

I wait to see where he's going with this.

"Enjoy your time alone, Evermore. Some people prefer being on their own. I get the sense you're one of them."

"Like you?"

He starts transcribing again, and I recognise the dismissal. I tap my pen, wondering what else I can get out of him.

"What's your soulmate's name? Where do they live?"

"Not here."

"And their name?"

I'm fixed with a resigned glare.

"Jahan," he says finally, looking away. "Tsalskinese mage."

I straighten in my chair. "Oh. Not many of those around. Amisha is Tsalskinese."

He refreshes his pen in a pot of ink. "The little mapmaker? I like her. She has spirit."

A small snip of jealousy tugs my eyebrows inwards. Arno ignores it.

"Pay up, Evermore. Tell me what you did."

Everyone else asked. Arno is *commanding*. The words stick in my throat like honey. I tell it haltingly. "Petre was convinced they were keeping his brother at Deadman's Keep. His father didn't want to take us onto what he thought was haunted ground."

Arno nods, digesting the small snippet I've given. "The ones who live on the moors are often more suspicious. I heard the Lord obeys the old laws, as he should. By giving you bread and ale, he postponed Griffin's retrieval by twenty-four hours."

I hear what he's trying to say, and shake my head. "Captain Marks arrived when we were out on the moors already. Whether Hugh delayed him at the beginning had no effect on the outcome."

Another nod. "Continue with your story."

I describe the slow trek through the moorland scrub, how rain made it hard to see anything in the distance.

"But we found the tower. We found the Keep and the northerners who'd taken Samlin."

My voice dies as I remember the scene. Petre by my side, hovering in the damp brush, his eyes darting across what would soon be his battlefield and grave. The men I was about to kill, milling around the fire I would use.

"Here." My mentor hands me an earthenware mug. The mead inside is warm and surprisingly familiar. I look up at Arno, who leans back in his chair easily. "This came from the Pike girl. I see a lot more than you tell me, Evermore."

Tears prick at my eyes as I think of Laela and that first sip of mead she gave me. I drain the mug and let the liquid strength flow into my belly. I set it back on the desk and tell the story to his inkpot.

"Petre... lost control of himself when he realised they'd lashed his brother to a post like a dog. He rushed the camp and demanded Samlin's release."

Arno sets all four chair legs back on the ground. "Hotheaded nobles. They grew up with the world obeying their commands and are never ready when it doesn't follow through. Where were you?"

"I was frightened," I admit. "I stayed back in the trees until they attacked Petre. Then I..." There are too many little details: the slashing of my sword, the cries of the men who fell to it, the crack of Petre's war magic. "The commander knocked me down with his mace."

"And that's how you got..." He indicates my leg with a jerk of his head.

"Yes. Before the commander could land a killing blow, Petre tackled him to the ground. They killed him." I fumble for the mug even though it's empty and toy with it as I see my friend's lifeless eyes staring accusingly at me. "The commander came back to finish me. I was angry. I... I burned them all."

The mug is taken gently from my grasp. Liquid sloshes as Arno refills it from a skin. "That's stronger than mead, love."

I sip anxiously as he strokes his beard. "Your fire affinity is stronger than most. This usually happens to the offspring of one with unusual magic. I've gone through the records, and no Evermore has attended the Academy within living memory. You don't know who your father is?"

"Not a clue," I wheeze. The whisky burns my throat. "Mum never spoke of him."

"And your mother is humanborn?"

I get a random memory of Mum curled on the couch under a crochet blanket, beer bottle resting on the carpet below her as she watched television.

"There's not a drop of magical blood in her."

"Then your name isn't your own. Someone is lying to you."

I down the rest of the whisky. "My name has always been Evermore."

Arno doesn't answer. He gets up from his chair with a creak, grabbing his wineskin to lean against the mantle with. The fire within flickers curiously, washing my Runes' Master in golden light.

"Have you told anyone else this story?"

I shake my head.

"Good." He lifts the wineskin. "Tell no one. It is unusual enough to invite questions."

"Everyone knows fire—"

"Mages with an affinity for a certain element can only influence what it does. They cannot encourage it to act like an extension of themselves. Jettais can request that metal does as he wants. Master Orin can speak with fog, did you know? Why do you think he chose weather magic? It calls to him.

"Their affinities are weak. They will assist but not serve. But you"—Arno sits again and pushes a lit candle before me—"you control it. You are master of fire at seventeen summers. In addition, if you continue working as hard as you have been, you will be the fourth master of runes to graduate from this Academy."

The candle flame stands tall and steady, bathing me in its pearly light. My voice catches as I say, "I don't want to hurt anyone."

Arno nods. "Then you must learn."

From then on, my runes lessons become a mix of fire and scribing. I progress quickly through each country's native rune set as exams loom, and time spent on fire magic—calling it, creating it, stopping it from burning—doesn't eat into my studies like I feared it would.

"Let me see your practice book," Arno says one evening.

I hand it over. The roughly-bound tome has become my bible of everything rune-related. It contains not only my studies on the official languages, but also drafts of my own language, scribbled theories, and sketches of runes half-lost.

At the top of each page, Arno's *halt* runes are beginning to erode. He starts inking them back to full strength.

"You should know I have to burn this at the end of the semester," he says. "To stop anyone using your work."

I shrug, toying with the corner of a manuscript. "There's nothing in there I'd save."

Arno flicks through the pages. "These theories aren't terrible. The Rune Guild in Castor would be interested if you include these in your application."

I've decided with him that after my years at the Academy, I'll continue my study, applying at the Guild to become a rune novice; from there, I'll work my way up to Master. Arno brought me a practice pack from the Guild on his last trip to the capital, and I perused it with rising excitement. That night, I forgot to visit Tyson again.

Seeing him is becoming harder and harder. Though I've held my depression at bay with hard study and so many practice sessions that my bad leg aches and I don't dream, every time I see my oldest friend he inevitably brings up Riverdoor or The Other. Dodging his questions about returning home is getting tricky; frankly, I don't have a clue how we'll do it.

And though my mental state is worse than ever, I'm not sure I even want to anymore.

How can I return to that world with everything I've seen? With the power I've wielded? If I finally caved and spoke to someone about what I've done, they'd have me committed.

"Ale?" Arno hovers a jug over my favourite cup.

I nod and watch him pour. Though my story is hard to

tell, it has bound us closer than ever. "Right. These stopping runes should hold against even your Sikali. Continue with Halfaan for now."

Ancient Gannameaden runes—he knows I hate them. I take the book with both hands.

"How do we know this'll even burn?" I turn it. "It's heavy. And thick."

My mentor shrugs as he sits. "I've burned books in that forge. It'll go up."

The thought of my beloved practice book crumbling into ash saddens me. I open to the page I've been working on and roll my eyes at my lame attempt at old Gaan.

Arno spots me. "Stop it. Remember what you were like with Melacorean and Tsalskinese runes?"

I learned Thyvventh and Sikali last semester after we returned from Riverdoor—quite a lot faster than I'm managing Gaan. Instead of being alone with my thoughts, I delved into dusty manuscripts, refusing to sleep until I could no longer resist it.

"At least they still exist," I retort. "What's the point of learning a dead language?"

Arno leans forward. "Because *magic* still speaks that language. That's what I'm teaching you, girl."

I sketch the rune for *power*. In Gaan it's a curled scythe with two flecks on the blade, which makes doing it in one go pretty difficult. I twist my practice book to examine the rune from other angles, my mind wandering into other facets of my favourite subject.

"When do I get to learn Larussian?" I've become enamoured with the northern border country of Melacore after reading about its animals. The whole country has a fixation on the environment.

"Next. It's similar to Thyvventh, so you'll pick it up quickly."

I scrawl the rune for *health*. "Then Sudafraen?"

Arno pauses long enough that I look up at him. "Can't learn too much at once," he says haltingly.

I scowl. "I already know four Lotherian rune languages, the Tsalski Empire's charm songs, and the Melacore's enchantment hymns. With the Larussian nature classicals and Gannameaden plague marks, you're seriously saying one more language is too much?"

After that, Arno seals up tighter than a clam. I leave the classroom, past the bookshelves with the backwards books he claimed was a weird habit he acquired to stop thievery.

My own practice book is tucked into my bag. I wonder if the library page can find me anything on the Sudafraen rune language.

CHAPTER TWENTY-THREE

EXAM PREPARATION FEVER sweeps the campus like a winter breeze.

"I don't get it, I don't get it, I don't get it," Dena moans, slumping in her chair. Theresa leans over her and plucks a book from her lap. "They'll want to know when we started performing lanan transfers on patients, but I can't find *any* mention of it in the past hundred years!"

"That's because it's now called a bearing pass." Theresa holds a sheaf of pages away from which Dena had been reading and points out a paragraph. "Maybe try researching on this side of the century."

Dena dives into her notes, scribbling furiously. The rest of my friends, both humanborn and nativeborn mage, follow suit. Ever since our return to Fairhaven, Amisha, Orin, and I have drawn closer to the two humanborn girls. Part of me wonders if we're doing it to fill the gap Petre has left. Currently we're clustered in a circle at the back of the library, studying for our first exam: our majors. I know Arno will test me on Halfaan, so the biggest, most boring book I could get my hands on is open on the table before me.

We manage another five minutes in silence before Orin has a little breakdown when he can't remember how to tell a low-pressure system from a high-pressure one.

"It's clouds," he mutters, feverishly leafing through a large book called *Whether the Weather Allows!* "It's always the damn clouds."

We let him go until a small mist rises from the carpets and dampens the books. Then we boot him furiously until it fades. No one wants damaged books on their ticket.

Our next crisis is Amisha studying cartography, who suddenly forgets every country, including her own.

"You're *Tsalskinese*," I remind her, sliding to the floor. She's surrounded by huge rolls of paper with wonky maps of Gardhillan drawn uncertainly on them. "You moved here, remember?"

I help her with the empire's three main islands but have no idea about the smaller ones dotting the surrounding tropical waters. She pencils those in, then proceeds to the democratic nation of Melacore.

"Damned islands," she growls, sketching in approximations of where the independent islands between Melacore and Larussia lie. "Can't you just write a crafty little rune and finish this for me?"

I pretend to consider it and rub the flimsy paper between my fingers. "Cheap craftsmanship. Almost no effort put into the production. This would burn up as soon as I finished the first rune."

Amisha sprawls protectively over the papers. "Then no thank you."

Everyone laughs except me. Heaviness weighs on my shoulders as my brain registers for the sixteenth time that Petre isn't laughing with us.

Alena has mentioned a few times that she wants to get me into a room. Woman seems to consider herself some kind of psychologist. Phoenix, who's taken to escorting me around the Academy whenever he finds me, just thinks she's nosy.

"Like being the Governor's soulmate gives her the right to pry," he said sourly after she first approached me with the idea.

We'd stood in solidarity for a second before I turned and walked away.

"I want to travel," Theresa moans suddenly. She's almost upside-down in her chair, a book on Gannameade open on her legs. "I want to see all this in real life."

"Gannameade is a bit of a rough place," Orin says, closing *Flinching at Flenches; When to Trust Your Gut!*. "My sister visited a couple years ago. Got beanfoot."

"Beanfoot doesn't exist anymore," Dena says, lying on her stomach and kicking her legs absentmindedly. "We eradicated it in 901."

Orin wrinkles his nose and shakes his head. "I guarantee you, it exists."

"What's beanfoot?" Theresa asks eagerly, scooting closer. Orin half-glances at her and stumbles over the beginning of his sentence.

"Well, the foot goes brown, and the toes—"

"*Don't* describe it," Amisha interrupts, cutting off her soulmate. "Theresa, if you really must see, get Dena to show you an illustration."

Dena shows her a picture from one of her books. I look away from the withered appendage with a grimace.

"Miss Evermore?" A young woman approaches, holding a slip of paper.

I recognise Aeryn, the library page. "Gonna take a break," I say, standing up and stretching. I grab my cane and hobble away, but they're too busy ogling the beanfoot to notice.

Aeryn waits for me to approach. "You were the one to leave the research card, miss? The one on the runes?" she adds quietly.

I frown and guide her into the shelves. "That card was supposed to be anonymous."

She gives me the most respectful but condescending look she can muster. "I'm a librarian, Miss Evermore. You left an inquiry about runes and you're the only runes student."

Impressed but not wanting her to know, I keep my face blank. "What did you find?"

"Well, I searched all our archives, our older catalogues

that we wrote by hand. Took ages, and you should have seen this spider that almost—"

"Aeryn."

Her shoulders slump. She pushes her glasses back up. "Everything to do with Sudafraen runes was destroyed. Our catalogue was burned or stolen. There's nothing printed about them in Lotheria."

I look at the librarian page who can't meet my gaze and realise she's genuinely cut up about not being able to find some random runes.

"Hey. It's fine. I just thought Runes' Master Arno might have been testing me to see if I could discover them on my own. Don't worry about it."

She gnaws her lip. "Are you sure?"

"Yeah. With exams coming up I thought that was part of his test." I clap a hand on her shoulder. "Thank you for trying, Aeryn."

I turn to join my friends but catch movement from the corner of my eye. She made as though to touch my hand.

"What is it?"

"I just wanted to thank you on behalf of my Uncle Maurice. He liked his whisky." She smiles shyly behind her glasses.

"Oh." I cannot, for the life of me, see the family resemblance. Aeryn is blonde and tiny, clad in a dark silken waistcoat and long-sleeved white blouse with lace trimmings. Her tailored pants end in more lace at her shins, revealing shapely calves and tiny ankle boots that have been polished until they gleam in the gaslight.

I think I *might* have seen Maurice in a shirt without holes at some point.

I turn back. "I'm glad he enjoyed it. He took a risk for me. I won't forget that."

She steps forward eagerly, lowering her voice. "Miss Evermore, if you ever need more help—"

The old, healed whip weals on my back suddenly ache something terrible. "Thank you for your assistance with the runes."

I cane back over to my friends, unable to help but feel I've left her disappointed. I don't look over my shoulder when I sit back down. Somewhere in my head, Iain intones from his dark spot on the stairs.

"Any non-magi caught in a tryst with a mage, or any kind of friendship... The punishment is severe. There's a reason we discourage relationships between different kinds of blood."

I imagine pretty Aeryn tied to the whipping post, her uncle watching helplessly.

All the lamps in the library flare red-hot, annealing their bronze holders in rainbow colours.

CHAPTER TWENTY-FOUR

FOR SOME REASON, guilt gnaws at me as the sun falls. I watch its descent towards the horizon from my bedroom window, runes revisions lying unread on my desk before me. The line that separates ground and sky is purple and misty.

Riverdoor would be slightly east of where I'm looking, so I hold my thumb up to block the bright sun as I squint into the distance. Smoke rising from Fairhaven blurs the horizon, and I can't see beyond the trees lining the great-road. When I lower my hand, I know why guilt soaks me. It's happened before, with things like a bowl of hot soup or a moment of laughter with my friends, but not yet with sunsets.

It's because I'm still alive to witness and experience these things and Petre is not.

I dress, grab my cane, and lock my door as the horizon swallows the ball of fire. The stable courtyard is almost empty, with a few groomsmen tending the horses of some nobles staying. The guards, Captain Marks included, have returned to Castor. Watching them ride out the Academy gates with the intense little governor between them was like breathing fresh air. I know I wasn't the only one pleased to see them leave; Jett was in a better mood than I've ever seen him.

"Maybe I just don't like authority," he'd quipped brightly as I beat him in Kingdoms last week.

"You're a *teacher*," I'd reminded him.

The post I was whipped at is gone. I've been hearing whispers around the wait staff and pages that a big sentencing day is coming up—a day when all misdemeanours committed by non-magi and 'lesser citizens' are punished at once.

"One of the downfalls of living in Fairhaven," I heard a page remark with a shrug.

A flicker of movement bounces by my elbow. "Would you like the gate opened, miss?"

I glance down at Thompson. He's taken to appearing whenever I set foot in the yard, which seems to be the only place he's allowed. I wonder if he's after another jar of jam.

"Have you been promoted to doorkeeper, then?"

He waggles the dull key and winks. "Sure."

The cheeky bugger lets me out and bows as I limp into the town square. The gas lamps are lit and the town cleaners have been hard at work—there's not a single beggar or piece of rubbish on the cobbles. Governor Malico apparently hated the homeless and had them removed from his path whenever he came through a district.

I wonder what he thinks of Halvers.

With both legs intact, the journey to Tyson's shop seemed short. Now, I have to rest on a doorstep as I try to stop the leg from shaking. The night air nips at my ears, and I tug my hood up and over my head.

"Oi! You!"

I still, wondering if I can blend into the bland grey and brown behind me. But the Fairhaven guard marches directly toward me, his Silver Wings glinting on his shoulder.

"We moved your rabble out of here, or did you miss the memo?" He towers over me, silhouetted against the lamplight. "Get moving."

I stand, leaning on the cane and hunching my shoulders. Better he think I'm a wayward homeless person than an escaped student with a decade on her ticket. I finally get to my feet, head down, and begin to shuffle away.

Suddenly, magic flares behind me, throwing my shadow into sharp relief against the cobbles. I don't turn, knowing it'll illuminate my face under the hood.

"In case you need a reminder." Laughing, he lobs the handful of magefire at me.

It lands on the cheap cotton of my cloak and catches. I'm torn for a second about revealing myself as a student and blasting him into ash.

But the smell of burning men reeks.

I turn and hobble away as fast as I can.

The door creaks open as wisps of smoke drift up into the night. I try not to jiggle anxiously as a face appears.

"You're burnt," Laela says.

"Yes." I try not to look over my shoulder.

She looks me up and down, taking in my nervous dance, then stands aside. I cane past her and shrug off the cloak when she closes the door.

"Turns out the Fairhaven guards delight in going the extra mile in their job," I say, having a look at the charred fabric. Darn it, I'm no good at mending. "One of them tried to set me on fire."

Which doesn't work particularly well. I pull my shirt aside and peer at the slightly-pinker-than-normal skin, completely unperturbed.

Laela takes the ruined cloak and carries it farther in. I follow her lead and sit by the cooking fire. Though I've only been in this house twice, it carries an unshakeable familiarity, one I sometimes find myself craving while lying awake.

"How's your father?" I ask as she takes out a sewing kit and examines the hole.

"He's good," she says around the pin in her mouth. "Out fishing."

"Not for another student, I hope," I say before I can stop myself. Laela only snorts.

"Whatever you brought us did the trick. It broke his

fever and he started recovering a few days later. Mother says even the poisoned blood cleared."

I nod solemnly, but I'm flabbergasted. That tonic is meant for mild headaches. At best, it numbs a sore tooth, clears an aching skull. Dena learned to brew it during her first week of healing lessons.

There's no way it fixed blood poisoning.

"Do you still have the bottle?" I ask. Laela points towards a shelf amongst the drying roots and herbs, where green glass glints like a prize.

I examine it as she sews a patch over the burnt section of my cloak. It looks like a regular bottle—no markings, no label. I'm about to set it back down when I see the rune near the mouth of the bottle.

It's good, tiny and well-drawn. As it was incorporated into the bottle's original design—placed there when the glass was still molten—the rune would've been extremely influential over the liquid within. Though my Halfaan is still half-baked, even I recognise the strongest symbol for *health* that Gannameade, a country renowned for illness and plague due to open borders, managed to create. There's a reason their runes are called 'plague marks.' Their language was derived from the symbols drawn on the doors of the sick, the magic marks that kept district gates pure against plague. This rune for *health* is the reason Syran, the capital of Gannameade, is still standing.

Arno knew I'd take a healing tonic to the family who tried to help me. He would've had to have this bottle designed and created, Carrier Bayde would've accepted it, filled it with a 'headache' cure—probably a *tiny* bit stronger than normal—and waited for me to request a solution from Dena.

I see more than you know.

Was Dena in on it? No. That girl is so honest anyone can read her like a book. She would've straight-up told me this would cure every ailment Markon had.

"You were going to visit your friend, weren't you?" Laela calls from the fire. I set the bottle down.

"Until the guard caught me. I realised there has been less time between visits than I should allow."

She bites off a length of thread. "He's a lucky man."

I return to the fire and sit. In the flickering light, her face furrowed as she stitches neat rows, I know Iain never got close enough to her to describe her as 'plain.' Her nose is small and slightly turned up, her cheekbones high enough to lend her eyes an almost catlike quality. Her fingers move deftly with a glinting needle weaving in and out of the fabric, almost like magic.

When shadows pass on the street, we still. Loud voices chatter as the guards patrol past, and Laela shares a look with me—I know she's thinking about her father, out fishing in the moonlight with curfew in effect.

"He's not my man—just a friend. Have you found a job?" I ask when they disappear.

"I do some laundry for a noblewoman visiting her soulmate at the Academy, but it doesn't pay much. I've been thinking..." She pauses, pulling a long thread through.

When she glances up I twitch my fingers in a 'go on' gesture. "I've been considering moving to the capital."

Castor is three days south of here. My heart sinks a bit.

"More work?"

"More work, less overbearing Academy. Sorry." Her eyes flick up to mine.

"I'd move if I could," I reassure her. "But I have ten years on my docket already. I won't be going anywhere anytime soon."

Her chocolate-brown eyes widen. "Ten years..." Her small mouth purses. "You were one of the students who left, weren't you?"

Half of me clams up. But the traitorous other half finally wrestles control of my mouth, and I hear myself say, "Yes. I left the Academy to go to Riverdoor with four of my friends."

She bites off more thread with raised eyebrows. "For fun?"

Words stick in my throat, and I clear it with difficulty. I watch as understanding dawns on her face. "They were having an issue with raiders. We went to assist when the Academy told us not to."

Her eyes dart to my cane.

"Yeah, that's when I got... that." Before I can second-guess it, I tug up the hem of my trousers and show her the twisted remains of my right leg. She's like porcelain in the firelight, her expression unchanging at the mangled limb. "Lost... more than that, even."

She lays my cloak on the bench beside her and comes over. Her arms around me threaten to undo me even more, so I return her hug then move away. Anyone else would've been miffed, but she takes her cue to stand and fetches two misshapen clay mugs. She lifts another homemade bottle from a shelf and pours into the two mugs.

"Mother says this is the best fix for anything broken." She toasts me and downs her entire mug.

I follow suit, the spiced rum burning to my stomach. "We'll need more than a single bottle."

She grins, cheeks pink from rum, and I think she's beautiful. We pass the rest of the evening with the bottle between us as guard patrols continue past, and she teaches me some basic stitchwork. I find myself wondering what would happen if I were to stitch a rune into something, if it'd be the same as smithing a rune.

When she catches me deep in thought, she waits for me to speak before asking. She laughs at all the silly stuff I say, and in return I teach her all The Other curse words I remember. There's something endearing about hearing them in her voice.

When Markon returns from fishing, he helps us finish the spiced rum and doesn't even get mad that we drank most of it. When I go to leave as dawn threatens to break, he hugs me tightly. Laela's father smells like sawdust and smoke.

"My girl… If there's anything you need, you come to us, understand?" he asks before letting me out.

"Markon," I say, his hands clasped in mine. "If I need anything, I'm going to stay as far away from your family as possible. You've done enough."

He nods and disappears inside his house. I pull up my hood.

As I sneak back to the Academy in my repaired cloak, guilt dredges deep in my stomach as I remember Tyson, alone, waiting for a visit that never came.

CHAPTER TWENTY-FIVE

I NEVER THOUGHT I'd see Theresa cry, but halfway into exam week, the impossible happens.

"Full marks," Orin reads from Dena's report, returned early from a pleased Carrier. "Distinction of the highest honour, awarded to Miss Dena Brungarra, along with a recommendation that she continues her studies in this subject."

He looks up. "Are those tears?" Everyone looks at Dena, who looks dry-eyed and bewildered.

"Can it," Theresa snaps, and with a jolt I realise tears streak down her cheeks. "I'm just... She worked so hard."

She throws her arms around her soulmate, who looks even more pleased. Amisha clasps her hands under her chin and just looks thrilled.

"You're not softened by this at all?" Orin asks, nudging me.

I lift a shoulder in a half-shrug. "I've told you before, there's just a black mass where my heart is meant to be."

"Also, you have Runes next," Dena reminds me over Theresa's shoulder.

I grow cold to my stomach and tighten the grip on my cane. "Yeah, but I'm totally ready for it. Studied all last night. And nothing bad happened."

Orin lances me with a look. I sigh and take the book on native Gannameaden animals out of my bag.

"I was up super late and accidentally knocked this off my desk. It fell in the fire, but I got it out pretty quick."

Orin takes the book with its charred cover and singed pages from me. "Aren't you supposed to be fireproof?"

I shrug. "I am. My possessions are not."

"You'll have to return it to Aeryn, and she'll probably fine you. All the books in our rooms are on indefinite loan from the library."

As I open my mouth to whinge, Orin turns the book to look at the spine, and a very familiar sight greets me: a sheaf of scorched pages, like the ones in Arno's study.

"Our catalogue was burned or stolen."

Has Arno been hoarding the rune books?

I must be looking more gormless than usual, because Orin hands the book back saying, "I promise it'll be okay, Rose. Aeryn's a reasonable girl."

When the bell tolls, our little group disperses and I begin the familiar trudge downstairs. Would Arno let me look at the books? Surely, a fellow runes enthusiast...

No, I decide as I step over puddles and moss. I remember the way he reacted to the barest mention of Sudafraen runes. No way will he let me study them in detail.

"You're late," my teacher greets as I enter.

"Hardly."

I sit at his desk, trying not to look at the books on the shelves beside me. All this time, they've been right here; Aeryn would be so mad. But how to get my hands on them?

"We're starting with Halfaan." He's standing behind me with a small booklet. "Fill this out within the hour."

I examine it. It's the cheapest paper he could print on without it falling apart, and the top and bottom of the pages have the rune for *halt* linking across them. Makes sense. After an hour, many strong runes will be written in this book.

I start immediately but skip over Halfaan to work on my favourite language, writing a small paragraph on the history of Larussian nature classical. Their runes came from generations of farmers who passed down handwritten music sheets dictating ancient herding calls, until the marks used to transcribe the music began absorbing the power of the people who used them. I want to hear a Larussian herding call in person.

Arno, to his credit, disappears into his backroom to let me work in silence. The first twenty minutes sail by while I immerse myself in my favourite branch of magic. With each sentence of flawless runes, I grow more confident. My speed increases.

I'm so engrossed that when the door bangs open behind me, I whirl with my pen in hand as though to sketch a protection rune in mid-air. Eustace stands in the doorway, chest heaving, an envelope with a silver wax seal in his right hand.

Arno appears from the other room, scowling. "What's the meaning of this interruption? My student is halfway through her exam."

"My apologies, Runes' Master Arno, but I was bid to come immediately." He holds out the envelope.

Arno snatches it, tearing the delicate paper with rough hands. I crane my neck for a look at the letter within, which seems to be just a few lines.

Whatever is written does the trick. Arno turns back to me, eyes glinting behind his mass of sandy hair. "Continue with your exam. I've removed all material you'd be able to cheat with in here anyway."

I gesture towards the half-filled exam booklet. "Like I need to cheat, sir."

I think that almost gets a begrudging smile out of him, but then he disappears out the door with Eustace. I lean back in my chair and exhale.

Right here. This is the opportunity someone divine is trying to hand me.

I wait a full thirty seconds, scribbling about the basics of Sikali. When Arno doesn't come hurtling back, I open my bag and pick up my beloved book on Gannameaden animals, stroking the cover one last time.

I scramble over to the bookshelves as fast as my leg will allow. I pull a random book free, angling it towards a branch of candles to illuminate the title.

A History of Lotheria.

Boring. No Sudafraen runes there.

Land of Power: World-leader or country of heretics?

Religious text, cool. Come to think of it, there are no books about the gods I've heard mentioned in passing. Belatha, who seems to be the patron god or saint or whatever of Lotheria, has a few churches here and there, but no one ever attends. Even the priest at Petre's funeral seemed more of a wandering monk.

I grab the next one. *Small Gods, Big Leaders.*

Again, no runes. I return it hesitantly. I kind of want to read something derogatory about my Headmasters.

She Split the Land: A Memoir of Lotheria's Queens.

I finally pause my ransacking. These aren't materials on the Sudafraen rune language or even generic Lotherian runes. This is stuff on the long-dead kings and queens, like the battlefield of the Siege of Ten and the statue of Fleur in the township, but someone hid it for a reason. An inkling of curiosity surges, and I stuff the memoir into my bag, covering it with other books and crap I should've removed long ago. I shove the burnt book on animals into its place.

I return to my chair, continuing with the exam until Arno returns, at which point I twist in my seat and fire questions at him until he's so annoyed he releases me early. My completed exam rests on his desk, and I leave knowing I passed with flawless marks.

CHAPTER TWENTY-SIX

THOUGH WE'RE NOT yet bonded, Phoenix and I begin seeking each other out.

I watch the northerner on the snowy practice fields, crunching his way through a drill with Yu with a blade in hand. Apparently he's chosen the sword-fighting major, and he's good. I flex my right hand, suddenly missing the hilt of my longsword; I haven't sparred since I lost my leg. I watch my soulmate-to-be lunge at my teacher. They exchange blows in a flurry of cold steel ringing over the field.

A chilly wind makes me pull my cloak tighter. Under the castle's eaves, a few dried leaves swirl around my boots and dirty slush accumulates beside me at the entrance. A cold snap this late in winter bodes ill for the harvest, according to Markon. I visited Laela's family again last night, avoiding the unnamed guard who set me on fire last time and ignoring the voice in my head that said to go to Tyson.

The deep hole in my chest asks again to be filled. I ignore it as Phoenix and Yu take a break. Despite the cold, Phoenix removes the protective armour. Even from here, I see his chest heaving, covered in sweat.

I miss sparring.

Maybe pairing with him won't be so bad. His voice is nice and deep, and he seems like a genuinely nice guy, though a bit of a loner. A northerner, he's ostracized by the other mage students, and the humanborn kind of grouped together at the start of term—except Dylan, who's bonded quite well with Brin, the other international student from Melacore.

When Phoenix turns to place the armour on the ground beside him, I forget my thoughts for a second. The weak sun brings out the scars on his back.

I nearly take a step forward as the pull between us strengthens. Seeing my scars mirrored almost bonds us even at a distance. Phoenix looks up and sees me watching, turning slightly so I can no longer see his back. He nods in my general direction, then turns away. I ignore the twinge of disappointment as the pull lessens.

"There's a reason not many mages make it here from the north," Petre said once. *"They have to survive it first."*

Exam week comes and goes. I perform dismally in every subject except Runes, landing myself in remedial sessions with Jett and Yu. The latter at least seems sympathetic to my poor progress.

"One leg, too bad!" Yu snaps during my first make-up lesson. "You learn to hit harder with fists and stick!"

I struggle on with classes, becoming an expert with my cane and learning to fight with it a little, though I'm assigned a new room on the ground floor to account for my leg. It helps only a bit; the Academy houses so many flights of stairs that I sweat from class to class, and my leg shakes when I retire for the evening.

Finally, the weekend looms, and I begin to hoard a secret bag of candies and food for Tyson.

"Morning," Dena greets me brightly before class. "Sleep well?"

She's far too cheery. "Sure. What's up?"

Dena pulls a face. "You haven't heard? The Headmasters canceled our day off."

My stomach sinks. "What? Why?"

She just shrugs and holds the classroom door open for me to hobble through. "They didn't say. But we're forbidden from going into Fairhaven this week."

If she hadn't said anything, I wouldn't have noticed Jett's bad mood. I've gotten so used to him in recent months that him being in a *good* mood is odd—such as every time we meet to play Kingdoms. The strategy game is weirdly addictive, and I didn't even mind when Jett hijacked a session to recreate a famous Lotherian battle using the figurines.

We get to work on our assignments: ledger-reading and book-keeping. My brain melts out of my skull after the first few pages of numbers. Another professor enters, and the two teachers have a hushed—frustrated—conversation in the corner.

Something has them all on edge.

"Halvers," Maurice grunts at me later that afternoon. I'm perched on the wall of Echo's stall as he files her front right hoof. She lances me with a glare as though she knows I'm the one who reported it. "They moved overnight, popped up out of nowhere right next to Fairhaven."

"Why don't they just move them?" I ask, trying to tempt Echo with a nose scratch, but she flattens her ears and moves her head to avoid me.

"No notion. Prob'ly scared of 'em."

The Headmasters? Scared of Halvers? Not likely. I'd say the implications of the victims of their war crimes moving this close to their home was probably what they really feared.

Kaya has answers for me; I remember the night I spent talking with her.

An old task seizes me. Maybe she knows how I can fulfil my promise.

Sneaking out takes longer than usual.

"Do you really need all this stuff?" Thompson asks.

Kid resembles a walking stack of coats. I acquired all the clothing I could—Halvers don't feel the cold, but their bodies do.

"Yes. Trot faster."

He increases his pace and loses a coat. I scoop it off the ground and add it to the pack on my back. "Thompson, you don't have to come with me."

"I want to."

"It might be dangerous."

He turns to look at me, peering from underneath a hat that's way too big. "Sergeant Hall comes off duty tonight."

We duck under the shadowy eaves of a nearby shop as a pair of guards passes. Hunkered near the door under the piles of clothes, it's almost comfortable. I press a finger to my lips, warning him not to speak. In the weak moonlight, we're practically invisible.

But the streets are empty again, an eerie echo of the last time I snuck out. I can't tell if it's because the Halvers moved so close. Thompson didn't know and insisted on accompanying me.

When we reach the edge of town, I try only half-heartedly to make him go back again. He shouldn't walk back alone, and he's good company. I estimate him at ten or eleven years old, but he won't answer my questions about his age nor how he wound up working in the Academy stable yard.

The only time he falters is when the tent city comes into view. Their spooky silhouettes bring him to a halt.

"It's okay. They know me."

But nerves bite as we draw closer. My cane digs into the dirt, and Thompson kicks rocks out of my way after I nearly fall.

Halvers step into our path, towering against the moonlight. The kid steps behind me with a strangled yelp, like I'd be able to do shit with my cane and half a wardrobe on my back.

I raise my free hand. "I'm here to see Kaya. She knows who I am."

No response. One Halver steps closer, and Thompson seizes my shirt.

How are they so tall? Does having your soul ripped in half give you a growth spurt? The closest one must be well over six feet. He leers closer. Light sparks in his hand. Strangled magefire blooms, sputtering and flickering.

"We're unarmed," I say tightly. My temper is rising. "I'm here to help, not hurt. Take me to Kaya."

He raises his hand like he's going to strike. I dump the pack from my back, smothering Thompson beneath it, and raise my cane in the same movement. I smash it into his wrist and twist, jerking him forwards so I can knee him in the guts. The air shoots out of his lungs, and I smack him in the jaw with the heel of my hand. It knocks the giant back but just seems to piss him off more than anything. I take up a guarded stance, my dead leg aching after being used as a weapon.

I really don't want to burn anyone again.

"I'll help, miss!" It's taken Thompson a few seconds to wriggle free of the pack, but he emerges with a rock in hand. I'll admit to feeling slightly better—I've seen the servant children throw rocks at rodents. Better than cats at keeping the castle free of mice and rats.

But at the sight of him, the Halver stumbles back. The rest of them seem as interested as half-souls can be in another human. Taking a chance, I grab Thompson and shunt him before me.

"That's right, there's a kid here. Don't want to be hurting children, do we?"

It's a wild move, but Thompson plays along and stands at the ready with his rock. It's a stand-off under the pale Lotherian moon until another figure emerges through the towering half-souls.

"Stand down." Kaya's voice has me relaxing on the spot. "I told you she'd come."

I nudge Thompson, who drops his rock. "You knew I'd be here?"

She shrugs. "I hoped."

We pick up the pack I brought. Despite the cold, she's wearing a knitted top with a huge tear in one of the shoulders and only a thin shirt underneath. The others are dressed even worse—one dude doesn't even *have* a shirt.

"I know you don't feel the cold," I begin as we duck into her tent. Another fire is going in the brazier, and Thompson shoots to it. "But I thought you might want these."

I put the pack down, clothes spilling from it. Kaya examines me for a second.

"Is this charity?" she asks finally.

I shrug. "Maybe I don't like coming empty-handed."

We look at each other, and I'm suddenly very aware of the large, child-sized eyes examining us curiously.

Luckily, I've planned ahead. "Thompson, you want tea?"

He nods eagerly, and I use the packet I brought to brew a little tin cup of tea. He drinks the sweetleaves and within minutes snores happily on Kaya's bedroll of wild furs.

"You are doing well with your cane," Kaya comments, sitting opposite me. "Much better than last time."

"I forget I have it sometimes."

She pours a cup of ale, like I hoped she would. "Why are you visiting?"

I take a sip of the heated liquor. "You knew I was coming. Why don't you tell me?"

"Last we met, you were on your way back for punishment. What did they do to you?"

I twist, and pull the corner of my shirt to reveal the top of a whip weal. She's nodding when I turn back, like she expected no less.

"One of their favoured punishments, though they never got me under the lash. They usually reserve it for non-magi."

"They must've made a special case for me." I lift my cup. "They convicted me of manslaughter."

"We heard about the noble's death." Kaya's eyes flick to the sleeping child on her furs. "Why didn't you tell me when last we spoke?"

"It was too fresh," I admit. With Kaya, I can speak freely. I know she has suffered too—knows I just want to talk about loss rather than apply useless remedies to an unfixable situation.

She nods. "Sometimes we need to heal before we can pass the hurt."

Thompson snuffles in his sleep, and she half-rises to go to him. Coupled with the reaction of the Halvers outside, I ask what's going on.

"Half-souls," Kaya says quietly, "are unable to have children."

I'd thought they didn't want to catch Thompson in the crossfire. "So to you, kids are... special."

"Treasured," she corrects. "Those of us who had children before the split lost all contact with them. We are unable to interact with them, play with them, but we still love them."

She's lost in her thoughts. I noticed this happening more and more when I last met her and fear the Halver symptoms are worsening.

"Tell me more of what happened," she says.

"The noble was my best friend. We were trying to rescue his little brother when the Academy refused to help. The mother and I spoke before we left Riverdoor, and she sent me on my way home with blessings and forgiveness."

Kaya is nodding, her eye fixed on me. "So the healing had begun."

"So to return home and be officially sentenced..." I can't finish. Anger chokes my words.

The Halver mistress leans forwards. "Whipping wasn't the worst of the punishments."

I drain the cup. "Not by a long shot."

She refills it. "Do you know why I moved our camp again?"

I thin my lips and shake my head. Nerves tickle my stomach.

"The last time I saw you, I had a dream." Her eye widens slightly. "I haven't dreamt for months, not since Jax died. But I dreamt of you as a queen. I tried to join the Monarchists, but my soulmate talked me out of it. He told me the time of kings and queens was past. But it's not, is it?"

I remember the conversation that feels like a lifetime ago, of Lotheria choosing its own king and queen. That *this* is the conclusion she drew from our last meeting feels bizarre.

"I'm not a queen, Kaya," I say, and her look hardens. "I'm just a humanborn mage. Not even a very good one."

"You are gods-touched," she counters.

The old bite marks in my left arm tingle. "Maybe. But I'm not royalty."

She looks at me and I can't work out if she's disappointed or angry. I half-brace myself to grab my cane and Thompson. But then she leans forward, far too close to the brazier. I mimic what I did with the soulwitch and pull the heat away from her skin so she doesn't char.

"How many men did you kill?"

"Who says I killed anyone?" I reply, eyeing the sleeping stable boy. For a moment, I see Samlin tucked into the crook of my arm and fast asleep.

She smirks. "You think I don't recognise the mark of death on someone when they were the cause? You took lives, Evermore. Don't be coy."

That pisses me right off. "Do I feel it wrong to brag about

the lives I took? Of course I do. I killed, yes. But it isn't something to be celebrated, Kaya."

"Not celebrated, no. But it is something." She taps the tin cup against her lip. "How many summers are you?"

It took me a while to get used to mages asking this. "I will count my eighteenth during the coming year."

"Seventeen summers and already a killer of men. You have skill, Evermore. Skills should be shared, discussed." The glint returns to her eye. "So I ask you again, young mage. How many lives did you take?"

We talk into the night. I tell her of the men I killed, but not how I did it. When dawn begins to rise, she thinks me a competent swordswoman.

"I am impressed by your skill set at such an early age," she says as the tent fabric continues to lighten with the sunrise. Thompson still snores happily in his furs.

"I shouldn't have had to test them yet," I mutter, drumming my fingers on the long-cold tin cup. "The Headmasters should've mobilised their army when Longrock was attacked."

"I agree. Even we heard of the atrocities committed at Longrock. They have proven themselves unworthy leaders." Kaya pokes at the fire as though out of habit; she cannot feel the heat on her skin. "Miss Evermore... Rose. You may be surprised to hear we did not move our camp to Fairhaven for this happy reunion only."

I run my fingernail down the tin cup, my eyes on the rim. "I did wonder."

"My half-souls have been wronged by the Headmasters and ignored for too long. I would see justice for my men."

Silence falls. The other woman stares at me, her fist half-curled and ready to summon, waiting for some reaction that could be my last if it's the wrong one. The fire blazes in my mind's eye as a strong source of power; Kaya does not know my affinity. I could blast her and the tent, cover Thompson, and run.

But I don't.

"What does justice mean for you?" I ask.

Kaya smiles. "Respect. Care. Treatment. We should be honoured war veterans, not unsightly cripples in the eyes of those we fought to protect. I want to give my people the leader who will see them for what they really are."

"I take it you won't petition the Headmasters for this justice."

She leans back. "No. The Academy is well-defended, but we are seasoned warriors, hard fighters who feel neither fear or pain. We will take the building, and I will instate myself as the new leader of Fairhaven. The village will become a home for the Halvers and earn its name for the first time in history."

I lick dry lips. "Why are you telling me this? You're going to attack my school, my friends... I have non-magi friends who will be affected."

"Because I think you can help me," she says. "You are a strong warrior, sound of mind, crippled of body, who has also suffered a loss at the hands of the incompetency of our Headmasters. We share much in common, Rose."

"Except motivation," I say, trying to gauge her reaction.

The Halver assesses me. "So what does someone like you desire? A humanborn mage, already disgraced, already a murderer and a liar."

"You say that like you're any better, Kaya."

She hesitates, but a slow smile draws across her face. "As I said. We share much in common."

This woman plans to turn Lotheria on its head.

"If I help you... if I become your inside woman, I want something in return."

The fire lights her eager face. "Name your price."

I dare not risk telling Kaya who Tyson really is. But after his recent exposure to Griffin, who allegedly bought my excuse of a hired blacksmith, and his introduction in Riverdoor as a mage student... I can't risk him remaining in Lotheria.

Plus, I promised.

I hold her gaze.

"I want to go home."

CHAPTER TWENTY-SEVEN

KAYA'S EYE WIDENS, but she lowers her voice to avoid waking the boy. "You demand the impossible."

"It can't be. They open the portal to lure the humanborn through. There must be a way."

She looks far off, unseeing the inside of the canvas tent.

"We're mages. We can do anything." I let her contemplate again, my heart thundering. For the first time since arriving, I start imagining returning to The Other.

Oh my gods. Hot showers. Internet. Tampons.

A warm glow has spread to her cheeks since I called her a mage. "There was another sent to Thyssen in my unit who did not survive. Jahan had the same mind as you. He loved a humanborn girl who longed for home. Her cause became his."

It shouldn't surprise me that another humanborn wanted to return home, but it does. "Did she ever make it?"

"I lost interest in her plight after I became a half-soul," Kaya replies pensively. "Yes... I think I could find a way to send you home."

She considers me for a long moment. Between us, the fire crackles and pops. Thompson snores suddenly behind me, and her eye lingers on him.

"Swear it that you'll help the half-souls," she says, looking back to me. "In blood."

"And you will swear also?" I say with a hard stare.

She nods, and I extend my hand as she nears. I don't flinch when she pulls a dagger free or when she lays its point on my palm. Petre explained blood oaths to me before he died. She flicks the knife expertly. Warmth rushes to the cut, and I examine it as she repeats the action on her own hand.

My eyes widen. It's not just a cut to draw blood; she's carved a rune *into my skin*. I don't recognise it, but it's done well. Blood rises in the lines but doesn't spill over.

"Rose Evermore," Kaya says, holding her hand out. The bloody knife lies next to us. "Do you swear to assist the half-souls, to raise us from this life as vagabonds and celebrate us as war veterans, to the best of your abilities?"

My stomach turns. I didn't know she could draw runes— this is getting out of control. I fight down my panic, my eyes on the knife beside her. "I swear it," I vow. We clasp hands.

The runes activate with a rusty red glow, lighting the tent. The fire pales in comparison, and scarlet streaks of light flit around our joined hands. Heat sears the rune closed, leaving a thin white scar on my right palm. I break the contact and look at it, my heart slamming in my chest.

"That's a Sudafraen rune," Kaya explains, cleaning the knife with a rag. "One of twenty-six in our *caesis alledari*— our blood alphabet."

The breath leaves my lungs. The Sudafraen rune language. Kaya knows it!

"What's this rune mean?" I hold up my hand.

She lifts her own, and some part of me relaxes when I see only the one slender rune scarred into her palm. "The closest translation to Basic is *promise* or *oath*. You know runes?"

"I dabble." By now I know the Lotherian basics by heart, with Larussian and Tsalskinese as close seconds. Melacorean and Gaan still does my head in, but I've pursued the Sudafraen language since Arno fumbled my question about it. With information about Sudafraen runes so throttled in Lotheria, a thesis on them would guarantee my rune mastership.

"I can teach you if you want," Kaya says. "Our language is a little different from the Lotherian ones."

Doubt gnaws at the edges of my excitement. I learned early on that without understanding a country's culture, their rune language is harder to study. I know nothing about Sudafrae.

"I would love to learn. But I'm very ignorant of your country, and information is hard to get in the Academy."

Her eyebrow lifts. "Is it now? Iain must've removed everything. Even when I was at the Academy, he was touchy about people discussing our homeland. I never learned why."

As Thompson slumbers, Kaya teaches me about Sudafrae over cups of ale. About the capital city, Ancana, the smaller cities on the coasts, and the inland villages amongst the jungles. She walks me through vibrant streets lined in gold and red (the national colours), tells me of summers spent in humid heat with insects buzzing, the heady smell of the white *kambrai* flowers that grow over everything as a vine. She teaches me a little of the language; it's heavy and my tongue stumbles.

"Blood is the most important aspect." The fire has burned down to glowing coals. "We use it to swear oaths, as an ingredient in our witchcraft. If someone has your blood, they have control over you. With the *caesis alledari*, anything is possible. We exchange vials of our blood as wedding gifts, as a sign of complete and utter trust. Duels have been fought for the blood of the loser, and allegiances spanning generations have been commanded by the losses of ancestors."

"Your runes were born from this?" I wish I had my notebook. I can see my acceptance letter from the Rune Guild in my mind. "Other cultures seem to have developed their runes from such things."

Kaya eyes me. "You are eager to learn, for someone who wants so desperately to leave this world."

My enthusiasm ebbs. "Until you know of a way to return me, I might as well spend my time being useful."

Thompson snuffles as the tent lightens further. I prod him awake with my cane and say goodbye to the Halver leader I've sworn allegiance to, then we slink back to town as the first non-magi merchants wake.

I tuck the metal platter between my body and arm, caning my way across the busy dining hall. My heart thrums, but I shove through people and blurt the question before I can second-guess myself.

"Can I sit here?"

Phoenix looks up, but I can't tell if he's surprised by my request. At his tiny nod, I seat myself on the other side of the table. He ignores me for a second, which is fine; I'm trying to work out if this was a good idea.

"You snuck out last night." He takes a sip of water. He's pretending the bread doesn't need softening before eating, but then he tucks a crust into his mouth to chew with the water.

Smart boy. I cracked a tooth last week on a loaf of what the cooks had the audacity to call sourdough.

"What if I did?" I get to pulling the skin from the three large beans on my plate. I don't know what they are, and I won't ask. All I know is they taste kind of like boiled cabbage. "You want to come next time?"

"No," he says, and I'm a little crushed. "I don't need years on my ticket before I even graduate."

A cold trickle of anger seeps into my belly. "You should try it. Very motivating."

I push a bean around my plate but suddenly I'm not

hungry anymore. I'm contemplating going to sit with my friends when I realise Phoenix watches me with a furrowed brow.

"I offended you," he says, but it's half a question, so I nod. "How?"

"I don't like people mentioning the years. It reminds me how I got them."

"Ah." He disappears behind a facade of calm, and I wonder how I'm ever going to read this dude if he can look so like a statue. "The Riverdoor mage."

"Mhm."

"My apologies—no offence was intended. I merely want to graduate as a free mage."

"Everyone gets some years on their ticket, buddy." I point at him, a bean in my fingers. They're easier to eat by hand; nothing will stop them from mysteriously sliding from the tines of a fork. "No one graduates from here free."

He looks puzzled. A tiny line appears at the corner of his mouth.

"There were some mages who started working for themselves or traveled overseas immediately upon graduating. I read about them in Norrimoor."

I stop gnawing on the bean's tough outer layer. This is the first time I've heard about Orthandrell's self-proclaimed capital from someone who actually *lives* there. "You did?"

"I found a book or two in our library concerning the graduates of the revered Stanthor Academy. It's what made me decide to leave."

"A book?"

He drops his gaze to the table. "Freedom."

I say nothing, just sitting opposite my to-be soulmate with greasy bean fingers. I wonder if I should dig deeper, but then Phoenix clears his throat and stands with his half-eaten breakfast tray.

"Have a good morning, Rose Evermore." He heads towards the cleaning station.

I watch him go with mixed feelings. I suspect he's just told me more about why he came to the Academy than anyone else here—he has no close friends I've seen. As I watch him clean his tray neatly, pieces fall into place. He's not here to make friends; he's here to graduate as a full-fledged mage without a ticket. He's the best student in most of our classes, attentive and intelligent, intuitive and polite.

If I'd thought about it at all, I would've guessed it was the prejudice against him that made him want to show people he was different. But now I wonder if he's not just a man with an idea of freedom who now has a way to get it.

When I leave, guilt nibbles at me for the first time. If he's watching me, even with my hood, Phoenix will recognise my cane and gait. He'll know I snuck out again, though it's becoming harder to do so.

New guards posted at the ends of corridors and additions to the fence at the back of the stable mean I must find another route. With Amisha's help, we've mapped the secret tunnels and passages by spending our free time looking behind tapestries, investigating statues, and researching the oldest blueprints of the Academy we can find. Her cartography magic has come in handy for finding the hidden nooks built by the Academy's first owner, and I use them freely without threat of discovery, emerging unnoticed from a small, unused hatch behind an abandoned shop late in the afternoon.

My stomach squeezes, but I have to face Tyson. At least I can bring good news. I have become so adept with my cane that I almost don't feel it in my hand as I plant it between the uneven stones, unintentionally vaulting over something questionable in a gutter.

The trade quarter opens up around me, heavy with thick smoke and the smell of carpenter's glue. Chips of stone and wayward pieces of coal crunch under my boots as I approach his workshop.

The master is working the main forge, and I stand and watch Craige hammer a glowing chunk of metal, sparks flying. Some land on his bare arms, but he doesn't pause, flipping the chunk to continue flattening it. Some glowing embers drift to me, and he looks up.

"Come over, little fire whisper, before my forge fire runs to you like a loyal dog."

I oblige, stepping under the open door. Inside smells like iron and rust. Tyson is nowhere in sight.

"My apprentice is fetching lunch. Stay close to the flames for me." He begins hammering again. "Had to use the shitty coal Garren has been peddling."

I feel the fire's eagerness for me and hesitate.

Craige frowns, annoyed. "Go on. What's the matter?"

I tug my glove off. Fire whispering works better with bare skin.

"It's just… the last time I did this without my mentor…"

The blacksmith shoves the metal back into the coals and finally looks at me, squinting against the iron-grey light from the gloomy day. His dark eyes examine me closely, and I look at my boots.

"Ah, you finally hurt someone with it." Unperturbed, the smith retrieves his metal and continues working. I blink with every fall of the hammer. "Those idiots at the Academy didn't realise how strong your affinity is."

"You seem to know a lot about magic, for a non-magi."

I extend my hand and feed a slender tendril into the fire. The coals glow golden as the smith returns his metal to their heat.

"Only a fool would be blind to your strength in fire," he says. "It doesn't take a genius."

"What doesn't take a genius?" Tyson appears in the doorway with two small wooden boxes balanced on one hand.

"Fetching lunch faster than a tortoise," Craige says smartly. He jerks his head to a bench. "Leave mine near the little smelter so it stays warm."

Tyson delivers a pie-box to the clay smelter and gives me a funny look before sliding the lid from his own. Inside is a small pastry, misshapen but golden on top.

"I didn't know you were coming, or I would've gotten one for you too." He bites into it. Flakes of pastry drift down. "What's up?"

Hearing a phrase from The Other is such a relief that I smile. "Thought I'd come and see you. Do I need a specific reason?"

"Mages don't sneak out of the Academy for social visits," Craige says from the forge. "Keep that heat steady, girl."

I lift my hand again. "This mage does."

Only the clangs of Craige's hammer break the silence. Tyson finishes his pie wordlessly. A tiny seed of dread settles in my stomach. He's mad at me.

And rightly so. How long has it been since I visited? The last time would've been a week after we returned from Riverdoor. He requested the full story about what had happened at Deadman's Keep. Without telling him, I left soon after and haven't returned.

"Well, I can sense you two need to talk about something," Craige says finally, mixing what looks like clay and water. "Go up to your room, kid. Be back for the quenching."

"Yes, sir." Tyson replaces the lid on his empty pie-box. Together, we climb the rickety stairs that lead to his room. He opens the door and gestures to his bed. "I'm glad you came today. Missed you."

"I missed you too." I sit on the straw mattress and realise how sore my leg is. I stretch it with a groan. "But I know you're mad at me."

He grimaces. "I'm sorry it's so obvious."

"I'm sorry it took me so long to get here." I look to the set fireplace and send a wash of sparks that settle on the tinder and ignite. A new fire gently swarms to life. Heat washes over us. "I've had some stuff to work through."

"I know you have. I just wish you'd let me work through it with you," he says. "I know he was your friend, but I liked Petre too. And seeing them carry you off the moors, covered in blood and lying on the stretcher... gods, Rose, I thought you were dead."

Thankfully, I'd been unconscious until after my surgery.

"You won't even tell me what happened," he finishes bitterly, staring into the fire I conjured.

I lean forward on the mattress. "How about I tell you something better? We have someone helping us get home."

His expression changes to a mix of hope, worry, and finally excitement. "Who?"

I falter. It sounds so much better on the surface. "Trust me, the less you know, the better. But it's something. It's more than we've ever had, Tyson."

His suspicion doesn't fade. "As long as you haven't done something foolish, Rose."

The blood rune on my palm tingles. "Getting you home safe is all that matters to me. Especially after Riverdoor."

He winces. "I shouldn't have come."

"Probably not. But there's not much we can do to change that now. While I organise this, I want you to keep your head down. Stay close to Craige and do what he tells you, okay?" I press my lips together but say, "And stay away from Amisha."

Hurt flickers in his eyes, but he nods. "Do you have an estimated time?"

I wonder how long it'll take Kaya to get impatient and enact her coup. I doubt she'll let me return to The Other before she's taken power.

"Soon," I say vaguely. "And don't... go too close to the edge of town."

"You mean the Halvers?"

"Yes."

He frowns. "The Headmasters will clear them out soon anyway. Craige said they've never moved so close to the Academy. They're putting a lot of people on edge."

He tells me how the baker he bought the pies from has stopped sending daily deliveries to the farming district nearest the Halvers' camp. The inn I lunched in with my friends on my first day has boarded its windows and doors.

"Merchants won't come from the north anymore. Only the trade route between Castor and Fairhaven remains open, Craige says. It means there won't be as much to go around."

Hence why Craige was forced to buy the substandard coal.

"The Headmasters will try and move them," I echo slowly.

This will force Kaya's hand. A contingent of soldiers, probably the village guards, will be sent to clear the entire camp like in times past. But this time they won't leave. This time, they're united behind a leader who wants revenge.

I rub my brow with my thumb, wondering what I've sworn myself to.

"What the hell is that?" Tyson asks. A large hand wraps around my forearm, yanking mine from my head. He turns it over, and I make a fist.

He looks at me. I uncurl my fingers slowly until the oath rune is stark against my skin.

"Things are done differently here," I say. "Sometimes a promise will only be accepted if it's sworn in blood."

"Gods," he mutters, letting me take my hand back. "So our way home isn't exactly legitimate."

"No. We'll never return if I leave it up to the Headmasters." I think of the years on my ticket and how I got them. "They'll keep me close until I die."

CHAPTER TWENTY-EIGHT

AS WINTER YAWNS to a close, I realise how frustrated my lack of progress makes me. Neither Kaya nor I have discovered a way to reopen the portal Tyson and I fell through. I take to peeling open ancient books in the evenings, choking on the thick dust keeping them intact, and reading tiny, grimy writing until birds signal a new morning. My fingers blacken with old ink.

I slam the lid of another useless book closed, coughing on the resulting dust cloud. I lean back in my desk chair, getting my sore leg stuck on the bag I tossed under it.

"Rack off," I mutter, and give it a good boot with my healthy foot. Something jabs me between the toes. "Ow!"

Determined to find what fought back, I wrench out the bag by the strap. When my fingers scrabble against the hard cover of *another* gods-cursed book, I haul it from the depths and prepare to launch it across the room.

She Split the Land: A Memoir of Lotheria's Queens.

I hold it for a second, remembering my heist in Arno's office. I pick at the edge of the pages, loosening crumbs of burnt paper that bounce into my lap. Someone tried their darnedest to destroy this book and remove it from the library catalogue. For some reason, Arno saved it, and for some reason, I stole it.

The first chapter of *She Split the Land* is more interesting than the last seven books I've forced myself to read combined. The bloodline of Lotherian queens stretches back further than any other country's, and a chapter prelude casually mentions that Lotheria is widely regarded by academics as the First Country—the gods' first experiment with creating life on a continent. The middle of the book is a tangle of bloodmaps, illustrating the families that sprang from royalty to be forgotten in the annals as the queen died and was replaced by an unrelated woman. I nearly manage the whole book in one night, but a searing headache forces me to abandon it near dawn. I crawl into bed, family trees burned into my retinas.

Classes continue into the newborn spring, but frost still ices the morning air. I'm shaking slush off a boot when small feet rocket up behind me.

"Miss Evermore!"

I groan, pushing a fresh headache back into my eye sockets with the heel of my palm. "Thompson, I told you the other day, I don't have any more jam yet. I'll get—"

Strong hands seize the back of my Academy cloak. "*Rose.*"

He could've slapped me around the head, but the use of my first name makes me look at him seriously. His eyes are wild, his chest heaving. If he'd come from the stable yard, he wouldn't be nearly so out of breath.

"What's going on?"

"Today is Hearing Day," he says, my cloak still fisted in his hands.

I think of the whipping post that disappeared from the stable yard after my punishment and begin lacing my boots.

"Who've they got?" I ask quickly.

"Maurice had a bottle of whisky in his cot and there's a baker who didn't open his doors early enough for the Headmasters' breakfast. A waitress stole some silverware from a restaurant, and a girl had a bottle from the Academy in her house."

The laces in my fingers go limp. My vision mists as guilt swarms me. The whisky they found on Maurice was his payment for helping us leave for Riverdoor, and if it's Laela... I brought her that bottle.

"The girl," I force out. "Do you know her?"

"No."

Fire races through my limbs, lending strength. I grab my cane and set off. "What did she look like?"

Thompson scrambles behind me. "Um, shorter than you. Reddish hair, like a chestnut's mane. Brown eyes."

I squeeze my eyes closed. The Headmasters have Laela.

I curse the man who took my leg as we hobble across the yard. It's Hearing Day, so the place is empty; people are either being punished or watching co-workers, family members, friends endure the whip or knife. I force breaths as we approach. Maurice stands to the side, his shirt bloody with fresh whip marks. My stomach sinks.

He lifts a bottle of golden liquid to his lips in full view of the guards. When they do nothing, some of the urgency trickles away.

Thompson relaxes also. "He's already been judged. The bottle is his to keep now."

"Why," I start, nearing the crowd, "was he whipped for having a bottle of liquor in his own cot?"

"They thought he stole it."

According to Theresa, who's branching into history as well as politics, the Headmasters dissolved the court system shortly after taking power. I'm guessing a non-magi farrier would have no way to fight false charges.

We start pushing our way through the villagers until we can see the platform raised above the crowd. The whipping post is on one end, Sergeant Hall on the other. Thompson shrinks behind me.

"For the crime of theft, Maurice Lorrington received seven lashes. Make this offence your last, Mr Lorrington," the sergeant calls. Across the square, Maurice toasts the guard with his 'stolen' liquor. My respect for him rises even as guilt boils.

Mage guards in black armour escort the next villager up. They part to reveal Laela, her hands bound before her. Her skirts billow in the early morning breeze. She lifts her chin.

"Laela Pike, you were found with Academy property in your home. This is forbidden under the Charter of 917 Section R, Variable 17 'Relations Between Mage and Non-Magi.' Do you understand this?"

I don't hear her response.

"Thompson, what can I do?"

"Um... I don't..."

"You will receive fifteen lashes," the mage guard calls.

The crowd stirs. I go cold. Fifteen is three times the amount I received for *running away* from the Academy.

"Theft seems to be our recurring theme today." Hall addresses the gathered like he's a friggin' comedian. No one smiles. "Undress her."

I grip my cane. "Thompson!"

"You could shoot fire at them?" he suggests weakly, and I remember he's just a kid.

The first guard reaches for the button at the back of her dress. Seeing his rough fingers on the nape of her neck, something in me snaps.

I hobble forwards through the front row. "Wait!"

The only sound in the square is my cane against the cobbles. My cheeks burn as eyes land on my ruined leg, my cloak swept away in the breeze.

"Yes, Miss Evermore?" Hall snaps. My shoulder tingles.

"I gave her the damn bottle." With my left hand, I unclip the brooch from my left shoulder and let the slate-grey cloak, worth more than most families here earn in half a year, slither to the ground. "I'll take her punishment."

327

Something greedy lights his eyes, and disgust fills me. This isn't a chore for him. It's a perk of the job.

I climb the stairs and toss my cane to the nearest guard. He catches it, eyes wide. I peel my tunic off and chuck it onto the platform, then unbutton the white shirt underneath until I stand in just my singlet. My scars are bare to the crowd.

"Rose—" Laela starts.

I wave her away. The echoes of pain come rippling back; fifteen lashes are a lot more than five. I clench my fists, wobbling on the spot. The guard doesn't offer my cane back.

"You understand that taking her place of punishment, you waive your right to Academy treatment afterwards?"

I didn't know that. I wonder if Maurice will share his whisky.

"Sure. I also understand you're a prick."

The guard holding my cane stifles a smirk, and I regret my cheap shot. But in my defence, I'm pretty pissed and am about to be whipped for giving my friend medicine.

They tie me to the whipping post this time. When I'm kneeling before it, I realise the dark patches staining the wood are fresh blood. Probably Maurice's or the baker's.

As Hall uncoils his whip, I see Laela with unbound wrists embrace her mother.

Something squeezes my heart as the first hit opens an old scar.

My fingers tighten on the rough rope. Tears blur my vision. I wish I'd had the presence of mind to send

Thompson away. Instead, he's picked up my clothes from the cobblestones and waits in the crowd.

I groan at the second hit and bite my lip. At the third hit, a tear escapes.

At the sixth, my hands tug against their binding. I want to take my words back.

At the tenth, I'm ready to give the whole thing up. This isn't fun or daring or majestic. This is misguided and painful. My blood stains the post with each lash. I watch specks of it land on the backs of my hands, and the oath rune digs against the rough wood. The promises I've made pale against the coarse reality I face now.

I remember how naive and hopeful I'd been when carrying the bottle through the streets late at night. How I thought I'd outsmarted those watching at the Academy, when Arno and Bayde had been waiting for me to do exactly what I did.

Allegiance to a woman with only half a soul? A coup? Who the hell do I think I am?

The last hit lands across three new ones, and my vision darkens. I come to when I fall forwards, free of my bindings.

I hear Hall through the fog. "Next."

I lean on my elbows, my breath heavy and grating.

Get up, Rose.

The voice sounds a lot like Petre's.

Get up, he urges.

I slide one foot under myself, then the other. I use the

post to stand, and a wave of fresh blood streaks down my ruined shirt. Strips of cloth stick in the new wounds while others strain in the breeze like tiny flags of surrender. I blink in the bright sunlight and extend my hand. My cane is returned.

I limp down the stairs, my head heavy, vision dark. My ragged breathing thuds in my ears until my boots hit the cobbles. I head for Thompson with shuffling, agonised steps until I realise the kid won't be able to do shit. Indecision slows me again, and I close my eyes against tears I don't know what to do with.

I don't have a plan.

Shadows flicker as people close in around me. A strong hand seizes me in the armpit. Someone takes my cane. My arm loops over a strong shoulder.

"Fifteen lashes, girl. You've set a record."

I recognise Maurice's gravelly voice and try to mumble a response. Instead, someone ducks under my left arm.

"No one's taken that many and walked themselves back down the stairs," Markon says.

I'm pretty sure they're bullshitting me, but it's helping. I try to walk, but the men scoot me forwards, so it's easier to let my toes drag. Behind us, voices raise. Those carrying me shuffle faster.

I catch glimpses of where they're taking me when I manage to crack my eyelids. By now, the way to Laela's house is familiar. The smell of drying herbs greets me like an old friend, and I relax slightly in the comfortable house.

The men lay me facedown on the same bench Markon laid prone on a few months ago. My blood, thickening as it slows, drips anew onto the wood. I press my cheek into the bench and try not to cry.

A cool rag sweeps along my sides, cleaning the blood that leaks freely. I hear Maurice refuse assistance and accept a rag to clean himself. My shirt drapes over the bench like a bloody doily. Any concern about bare skin before the men is overpowered by the agonising mess that is my back.

Laela's mother murmurs something to her daughter, then her footsteps glide away. As the three voices gather in the corner, Laela's fingers slide up my back, the rag trailing. She plants her lips softly on my cheekbone, catching a tear, then rests her head against mine.

"Thank you," she whispers. A soft fog rolls over the pain. More tears swell.

She cleans my back, then opens a jar of something that nearly makes me faint. But the sensation of her smoothing it along the smaller cuts melts the pain, and I relax back into her care. Some of the agony leaks out, and I'm at ease until there's a knock.

Markon opens the door. A burst of pale sunlight floods the room. A tall man, his face silhouetted, pushes past Markon. "They're looking for her."

My heart jumps. What the hell is Phoenix doing here?

Laela gets to her feet, jar of smelly ointment in hand. She positions herself between me and Phoenix. "Who are you?" she demands.

Phoenix's response, cold and hard, takes me by surprise. "She's my soulmate."

Laela doesn't budge. "She's not bonded."

The air between the two is charged; neither is going to back down.

"Who's looking for me?" I manage to groan.

They both turn, Laela kneeling beside me again as though she never rose. Phoenix, with a wary glance at the watching adults, steps closer.

"The Headmasters. They've arrested Hall for whipping a student beyond the Academy walls, and they're looking for both you and Miss Pike."

"Relations between Mage and Non-Magi," I recite weakly.

"Charter of 917," Laela finishes. Her fingers rest upon my back.

I want to take her hand in mine so badly my stomach aches, but the ointment has some numbing property and I'm working on keeping all the drool inside my mouth instead.

"They'll want to punish her," Maurice says from his corner. "She'll become a martyr. First mage to take lashes for a non-magi."

"Rose, do you know someplace you can hide? Somewhere they won't find you?" Laela's mother asks. There's a hint of real worry in her voice that weirdly reassures me. I thought she'd merely tolerated my presence in her home.

Kaya flashes into mind, followed quickly by Craige and Tyson. Indecision squeezes me, but I know the Headmasters will never look at the Halver camp, and I can blend in with my bung leg and cane.

I nod. "I have somewhere to hide."

"Laela will have to go, too," Phoenix says. "They're looking for her as well."

They'll make an example of Laela if they get their hands on her. There's a good chance I'll never see the light of day again, but my talents as a mage are too valuable to them for me to disappear permanently. But the life of a non-magi is worth nothing to them.

Laela curls her fingers around mine. "Is it safe for me to go with you?"

I squeeze her hand. "I won't let them hurt you."

Phoenix kneels closer, and I fix my gaze on the splintered floorboards. I know he'll touch my skin, and resisting the bond will be harder than ever. Careful fire lights the opposite wall as he begins a basic healing spell to seal the larger wounds. I remember he chose History for his major, minoring in Healing. The choices struck me as odd for a northerner; now I'm glad.

His fingertips brush me lightly, and my soul tugs towards his like a magnet before I withdraw. Laela senses it and leaves. A part of me goes with her.

"Is this," I begin softly, "the kind of freedom you wanted?"

Phoenix works for a few lengthy seconds before saying, "No."

I slip into comfortable sleep as he works magic across my

back, the pale orange light comforting and warm. When I come to, his brow is sheened with sweat, but my back is bound in new scar tissue.

"Will you be safe in the Halver camp?" he asks when I wake, and I wonder how he guessed that's where we'll go.

"Their leader and I have an understanding," I say, my voice low. "She won't let any harm come to us."

His fingers tremble almost imperceptibly. "What do you mean?"

Do I tell him about the coup? Would he support it? Of all the mage students in the Academy, he's my best chance at a supporter. But the oath is too fresh, the plan too wobbly. I can't request his backing when there's nothing to back yet.

"We'll be safe in the Halver camp," I mumble.

I really hope Tyson wasn't at Hearing Day. Firstly, he's seen me pull the corpse pose more than enough for one lifetime. Secondly, he'll rip the Headmasters from their stone nest on his own. I don't need my friend burning for vengeance; I need him hidden and safe while I recollect myself.

One of the curtains over the front-facing windows puffs out, and Thompson, sent as a scout, falls lightly to the floor.

"They're coming," he says, out of breath. "They just passed Miller's house."

Phoenix helps me off the bench, and Laela wraps a pillowcase around my torso. There's no point wasting a shirt on the bloody, gooey-with-ointment mess that is me at the moment. After all, we're Halvers now, and Halvers have nothing. She's wearing a plain cotton dress with a long, pale blue coat fastened at her waist. She quickly plaits her hair around her head in a crown, then jams a knitted hat over it.

Her mother ties another coat over my arms. My trousers and boots are still good and too valuable to leave behind. Nothing distinguishes them as Academy property—I picked off the logo from the waistband months ago.

I tuck my long brown hair into a plain knitted hat. Laela cups my elbow and steers me toward the back door.

"We'll make contact when we can," Markon says, sounding uncertain.

"Send him." I jerk my head at Thompson, who brightens. "They love kids where we're going, and he's small enough to leave the Academy unnoticed."

"Yes, can I please?" Thompson implores Maurice, who shrugs and drinks from his bottle.

"Do what you want, kid."

"You never saw us," I remind the room. Phoenix watches us go, stony-faced, and something squeezes my chest. "Find the townsfolk who saw us leave together and convince them otherwise."

"That won't be any trouble," Maurice growls. "Like I said, you're a martyr now. They'll protect you."

I so badly want to believe him.

Laela leads me through the back of their house, down some rickety steps, and into a muddy yard shared by three other dwellings. The sun overhead is bright and cold as we race through the alleyways, our heads down.

"Laela," I say between breaths. "Grab those cloaks."

Two patched brown cloaks flutter from a line, alluringly close to the fence. Laela looks horrified.

"I can't steal!"

I raise my eyebrow as the Academy bell starts ringing an unfamiliar pattern. Even at the edge of Fairhaven, the sound touches all. We're still very much in the Headmasters' reach.

"Right." She hops the fence neatly despite her long skirts.

We don the cloaks, letting the folds drape to the ground. With our hoods up, we're two Lotherian peasants.

Past a tavern empty at high trading hour, through a field of skinny stalks that should be almost ready for harvest, the Halvers' tents come into view.

Laela's hand sneaks into mine. I wish I could tell her it'll be okay.

CHAPTER TWENTY-NINE

THE FIRST THING I notice: their camp is much more organised than at Mornington. Rows of canvas peaks stretch back into the field until the wall of trees stops them, and there are a few more than usual. Fresh Halvers?

I get through Kaya's now customary front guard using my oath rune. Apparently pictures carved in skin are more memorable than faces. Laela clings to my left hand as I lead her through the camp past the smouldering fires cooking what meagre game the half-souls brought down. They still eat out of habit, but Kaya says the urge to catch, cook, and eat fades after a few years. Even now, I have to prompt her into eating when she gets food for my visits.

Like usual, the half-soul leader awaits me in the middle of the camp. Halvers ring the clearing. I can almost feel Laela's pulse through our hands.

"Who've you brought?" Kaya demands.

"Her name is Laela Pike. Non-magi." I pull back my hood so Kaya can read my expression. "You'll want to hear what's happened."

Kaya's expression is grim, and I know she's about to sling a speech about using her as a drop-in zone, so I hold up my oath rune. Her eye flicks to it before she jerks her head into her tent. I hold the flap open for Laela, and we enter with joined hands. I lead her to the fire and take my cloak off, folding it so she has something to sit on. She nods at me, her eyes wide with fear.

Kaya is watching us on the other side of the tent. "She your consort?"

I stop tucking the corners of the cloak. "My what?"

"She thinks I'm your lover," Laela mutters to me, and I go pink.

"No, she's... she's not, just my friend. She's just a friend."

Kaya shrugs. "It is not a strange practice in Sudafrae. Queen Laraba had a harem of women for her enjoyment."

I recognise the name of the Sudafraen queen from our talk. The queen never had children and passed her crown to her favourite lover. That woman reigned successfully for fifty years, eventually passing her crown to her reluctant son.

"Rose," Kaya says, a bit sharper. "Why are you *here*?"

"Today was Hearing Day. Laela was caught with a bottle from the Academy."

Kaya's expression softens a little. "How many lashes?"

"Fifteen," Laela replies. "But Rose took them for me."

Kaya looks at me in disbelief, then anger heats her face.

"You fool. You've been kicked out of the Academy for a non-magi?"

My own temper rises. "Not officially. They tried to arrest me."

The Halver runs a hand through her short hair. She's still wearing her torn knit shirt; the clothes I brought have disappeared into the camp, hopefully to the fresh half-souls who've arrived.

"So my insider has become my outsider," Kaya remarks with folded arms. Her eye gives away nothing as she paces. "Meet me later. We have plans to discuss."

She disappears as the sun sinks towards the horizon. Requiring maintenance again, I strip in Kaya's tent. Laela tends to the fresh whip marks.

"She seems nice," Laela ventures when we're left alone. Apparently we're getting our own tent.

"I don't know if 'nice' is the word for Kaya. She's... hungry," I say, trying to ignore the pattern Laela's fingers trace on my skin.

Laela works in silence. Outside the thin canvas, more fires are lit. I think they're just for show rather than warmth or food. Proudly displaying their numbers to the Headmasters? From here, the Academy is a misty blight tucked into a cluster of smaller buildings. But I know where Netalia's office is—they can see the fires of the soldiers they abandoned. It must be spooky.

I can't help grinning.

"I feel like there's a lot of magical culture I don't

understand," Laela says quietly. "I don't really know the difference between Kaya and you. You're not bonded."

"Kaya is a half-soul," I explain, trying not to groan when she massages bruised muscles. "Her soulmate was killed *after* they bonded."

"But you don't have a soulmate yet. At least, I thought you didn't." Her tone grows bitter.

"Phoenix and I aren't bonded, but we can feel the match. We know our souls are trying to reunite, but..." I don't know how to finish this bit.

"You're not ready to let someone else in."

Something hits a little too close to home for us both. I let her work in silence, gnawing my lip.

"What does she want to talk about tonight?" Laela asks.

Do I tell her Kaya wishes to remove the Headmasters from power and that I agreed to help her in exchange for a ticket home?

Lies settle on my tongue. "Kaya wants to petition the Headmasters for better care. She wants the Halvers recognised as war veterans and awarded the same treatment."

Laela's fingers waver. "This entire camp have been outcasts for decades. They won't take her demands lightly."

She's right. The mages and non-magi will not accept Kaya as a Halver.

My breath leaves me in a rush as I remember a conversation and tiny words written on a page: *She Split the Land.*

They might accept her as the new queen.

"Utter madness," Kaya snaps, and I wish I had my book to back my theory.

"No, listen. The land of Lotheria, the god, the spirit, whatever," I wave my hand dismissively, "chooses the queen. It's not a bloodline monarchy. What proof do we need to say you're the next queen?"

She falls quiet but continues pacing. The fire gutters angrily between us, and I extend a hand to calm it.

"There have been no queens since Fleur," I press. "Not one. The line broke when the Headmasters seized power."

It's so important that Kaya grasps this. The people won't accept her as a conqueror; they'll fight her every second of her rule. I've picked the underdog, and she's mean. She's hungry for revenge against the wrong people. But if they view her as their gods-gifted queen, they *might* accept her.

"And how would I keep my promise to you?" she finally asks, holding her hand out for inspection. Her oath rune has reddened around the edges, and I examine my own; it's pearly-white and healthy. I have been making steps to keep my promise, but Kaya has no clue how to get me and Tyson home.

My heart sinks. "The Headmasters have something. They must, to still be receiving humanborn students. Take it, open the portal, send us through."

Her brow furrows as she ponders. She looks up through her ragged fringe of dark hair. "Whatever is hidden in the Academy, we will take it."

A sea of tents sprawls before our rocky outcrop, lit with hundreds of fires. More half-souls join by the hour, seeping from between the cracks of society like earthworms after a spring rain. Kaya has prepared for their number. Her most trusted lieutenants house new arrivals as we speak.

Fairhaven glows to the south of the camp, strong stone houses and shops blocking the spring night chill. The Academy looms over it all, though most of the leadlight windows are dark. A stone wall's remains ring the training field; no one commissioned its repair after Fleur died.

The town is ripe for the sacking.

I feel a war brewing, and I know which side I've chosen. But looking at the slumbering school, knowing my classmates—whom I learned beside, sparred with, supped with—are tucked inside, a cold fear leaks through my bones and sets my heart pumping.

I'm doing this to keep Tyson safe, but how many innocent lives will be lost doing so?

Thompson returned to us in the evening with news of more troops arriving from Castor. The yard-boys are tasked with preparing the war stable, which can house a large cavalry. I wondered if Netalia has ever played a game of Kingdoms. Jett would be appalled at the idea of using horses within close quarters. Infantry—the Halvers in this case—will mow them down.

"So we present me as the new queen," Kaya says. "We fake my credentials, and the Headmasters will bow to me?"

"I doubt it. They'll fight you. But if we convince the

people, there aren't enough mages to hold them down. And if the mage guards believe the ruse..." I shrug. "Then it's them and what army?"

She's nodding eagerly, perhaps imagining herself on a throne ringed with advisors. Something about the image scares the shit out of me. I don't pursue the thought.

"I just wanted to take Fairhaven, but this makes much more sense," she mutters, rubbing her chin. "I could care for half-souls everywhere, and no new ones would be created under my reign."

She turns to me and sits on the boulder she stood on.

"What information do you have so far?"

I try to think of the night I nearly read an entire book in one sitting. "You would've chosen your king. The man you loved, crowned at your request."

"I am not familiar with love."

I press on. "Pretend to be. How did you feel about your soulmate?"

She looks away. "It is for Jax's sake that I'm doing this."

An image of Petre laughing at one of my jokes, trying to waddle behind me, flits unbidden through my mind. My throat tightens.

"You will have immense power," I continue. "Enough to split the skies and the land with your magic, and the token of Lotheria shall choose you as its companion."

She frowns.

"A bird," I clarify. "Hence why mages work for their Silver 'Wings' and why there's a big stone budgie carved above the doors of the Academy. The thing I can't work out is how to make you so powerful you can 'rattle the stones of a god's grave and make the skies roar.' I know you're talented, but..."

She laughs easily, and I'm surprised how much it softens her, how young she looks. Something relaxes in me. Perhaps she'll lead well.

"If only we could combine the power of all mages," she says. "There is a rune in the *caesis alledari* that would serve this purpose, with small modification."

A phantom ache develops in the crook of my elbow, and a yawning suspicion grows in my stomach. The missing books... "Kaya, how much does Iain know of his homeland's rune language?"

The topic change throws her for a second, but she recovers quickly. Tonight, the chill doesn't have her mind. "He would know a basic amount. All Sudafraen children are taught the importance of blood from an early age, lest they are fooled into giving it freely."

"When you arrived at the Academy, did they do tests on you? Did they take your blood?"

Realization dawns on her. She clenches her fist atop her knee and her breath leaves in a puff. "He saw an opportunity to exploit foreigner ignorance. Every mage tutored under him and his soulmate is at their mercy."

I dig in my inner cloak pocket and withdraw the small notebook I had on Hearing Day. "Kaya, you need to tell me everything about what a mage can do with someone else's blood if they know the *caesis alledari*."

She starts talking as I jot rough notes, cheap ink bleeding into the pages. Though my eyes widen several times, I don't pause my writing. My hand cramps around the pen as she reveals what Iain could do with blood: influence the mages to go against their bidding, make them think or see things that aren't real.

He could kill them from a great distance.

I rest the pen in the middle of the tiny notebook and rub my eyes. The sky is fading from darkest night into navy morning. Laela will wonder where I am.

But now I can't stop wondering if everything I know is true.

"He could make me see things that weren't there," I mumble. "He could make the graduates do anything he wanted."

All this time, I thought Netalia the mastermind of the pair. But Iain, the quiet danger, stewed in the background. Hells, I even had the audacity to think him the reasonable one.

Fear what does not need to roar. I think Arno said that to me once about runes. That man loves runes.

Kaya's skin is paler than usual. "He controls through blood, through the power it lends him. Rose... With that magic." She meets my gaze. "He could be opening the portal with it."

CHAPTER THIRTY

THE COALS FLARE when I enter the tent, and it's enough to wake Laela in the furs.

"Where've you been?" She blinks sleepily. Her auburn hair curls around her neck, and her cheeks are pink. "What hour is it?"

I wince. "About three past moonfall."

Every inch of me hurts. Kaya insisted on meeting on the rocks that foot the forest so we weren't overheard, but without Thompson to clear my path, my bad leg had a tough time scaling the path. It throbs when I limp to my own bedroll. As I sit, some of the dried ointment on my back catches on a ragged bit of shirt and tears my skin. Fresh blood trickles from a re-opened whip weal.

I lay my cane down and rub damp eyes. It's almost too much.

Careful hands grip my shoulders as I relax onto the furs.

I hear her unstopper the jar containing the minty ointment, then she tugs aside my shirt.

"Do we really have to stay here?" she asks quietly, working the soothing treatment.

The Halvers don't sleep. Even now their footsteps fall heavily and far too near our tent. Their ragged breathing and utter silence are discomforting beyond words.

"Yes," I murmur. "But it won't be long."

"Surely if we reasoned with the guards—"

I look at her over my bare shoulder. "Do you really think we would've been seen again if the Headmasters got hold of us today?"

She bites her lip. I stare a little too long.

"No. I don't think we would've been heard from ever again." She squeezes her eyes closed. I rest a hand on her folded leg.

"We got out. We'll be okay. Soon you'll be safer than ever."

She nods. "I trust you."

Something warm and golden fills my chest like the friggin' sun. The smell of mint makes me float, and I push to my knees so I'm kneeling. Annoyed by the crusty tatters of my old shirt, I struggle to pull it from around my neck.

"Let me find something to cut it free," Laela says, unsheathing my Academy knife. She slides the blade under the ruined shirt. "Hold still."

I swallow. "I trust you."

She saws gently, the fibres breaking in the blade's path. Eventually, the stained undershirt comes undone. She holds it in a wad of bloody material.

The breeze washes over my bare skin, but the ointment numbs me. I watch her carefully as she considers the shirt.

"You did this for me," she whispers, closing her eyes. Her fingers dig into the fabric. "You bled for me."

"It's just blood," I say awkwardly, then flush pink. "I'd do worse for you."

She looks at me, knife in one hand, shirt in the other. Then she places both down, cups my face, and presses her lips to mine.

I freeze, then pull her into me, kissing her. I don't feel the whip weals when she pushes me to the canvas floor, but I feel her fingers trace down my chest, and I forget everything but her.

A few hours later, when the sun burns through an early morning fog that reminds me of Orin, Kaya enters our tent.

"I brought food." She slings a limp bundle of limbs and fur to us. Laela catches the rabbit and extends her hand for a skinning knife. "Rose, I'd like us to return to the Academy at moon high."

I feel Laela's stare across the tent. Though I appreciate Kaya framing it like a request, I haven't quite gotten around to telling Laela what we discussed on the rocks.

"You're going back into the Academy?" Laela echoes.

"We have to," I say. "There's something in the Academy we'll need."

I watch her process it, then she bites her lip and nods. As she returns to skinning our breakfast, something digs painfully into my chest.

I hate lying to her. She'll hate me when she discovers the truth.

I turn to Kaya. "Which area of the Academy?"

She takes a seat on the bare canvas floor. "I suspect the dungeons beneath the castle. You've seen them?"

I nod. "My runes class is down there."

"Good. I visited once or twice. I need someone more familiar with the area."

I want to ask why we're going to the dungeons, but Laela's ears are too close. As the rabbit roasts over our small fire, my stomach growls at the smell of greasy meat. Kaya doesn't seem to notice. We discuss the logistics of the Halver camp until she leaves around midday, promising to fetch me for our midnight operation.

Our first day in exile drags by. Though I roam the Halver camp freely, knowing I could fight, blast, or burn my way out of danger, Laela stays tucked in our tent without the same advantage. She gives me a list of things she wants and I go from area to area of the camp, trading ragged bits of cloth for a roll of coloured wool, then a few bones from our breakfast for some pins, before finding some flowers underfoot in a part of the meadow not crushed by tents. While Laela prepares the wool and clicks the pins together,

I make a daisy chain and place it on her hair like a crown. When I tell her she's beautiful, she giggles.

When the moon is a pale blip about an hour from its peak, I wrap her in furs as the night chills our tent. I await Kaya nervously, wondering if Thompson can reach us tonight.

As though summoned, the kid pushes through the tent flap without knocking, followed closely by Kaya. I glance at Laela, who returns the look with pink cheeks, and I know we're thinking the same thing.

"They're still searching," Thompson says, taking a cup of water from Kaya. She's in full doting mode already. "Going through people's houses, questioning your friends. The man who came and warned us has been with Sergeant Hall, but they're the only two who've been taken in."

Maurice and the others are safe. Laela relaxes upon hearing of her family's safety.

"They'll do another Hearing Day soon, though," Thompson says after a slurp. "They've found a lot of stuff in people's houses."

No, they won't. They'll be powerless before they get the chance. Laela hands me a cup of tea, her fingers lingering on mine.

"We'll need this," Kaya says, tearing her gaze from him. She lifts a silver device. "I had a half-soul with a smithing background make it for us."

It looks like a small hand-held drill with a needle point and plunger. I have no idea what it's for. She notes my expression.

"Your job is to get us through the dungeons. I'll handle the rest. The less you know, the better, in case we're captured and questioned." She pats the knife at her hip so she doesn't have to say 'tortured' around Thompson. "I need your word that you're ready to go through with this."

I nod sharply before she's finished speaking. "I'll be seeing it through, Kaya. I promised, remember?"

I hold up my palm. Laela examines the rune scarred into my skin, but I don't cringe from her watchful gaze. I'll tell her when we return.

There will probably be worse to explain.

The moon peaks as Thompson falls asleep on Kaya's bed without sweetleaf tea. Laela tucks him into the furs while Kaya and I dress in the cheap cloaks we wore here. Our only weapon is the knife that carved a rune into my hand.

At the door, Laela asks, "When will you be back?" She'll stay here tonight to keep an eye on Thompson and has no idea that I've drawn protection runes all around the tent. No half-soul besides Kaya can cross the threshold. "When should I get worried?"

Farther up the row of tents, Kaya jerks her head at me, standing with two of her lieutenants—the big, leery fellows who give me trouble every time I so much as think about coming to the Halver camp.

"Rose, we have to leave."

"Be right there," I say, nerves nibbling my stomach. I turn back to Laela, whose face is washed with pale moonlight. "There's no need to worry. We'll be back before dawn."

If not, the Halvers are instructed to take Thompson and Laela to a safe-house. Laela is still looking at me with huge eyes. In a single day, she's been torn from everything she knows.

Without thinking, I take her hand. "I promise I'll come back."

She traces the rune scarred into my palm. "You promise a lot of things, Rose Evermore."

I smile and lift her fingers to my lips. "I deliver on a lot of things, too."

"Rose, we're leaving." Kaya's voice is clipped, impatient.

I let Laela's hand fall, stepping back. She nods and disappears into the tent to spend five nerve-racking hours wondering which direction her life will take next.

I wish I could tell her.

Showing Kaya one of my secret passages feels wrong, but I do it anyway. As I pull open the trapdoor set into the floor of the abandoned shop, I hope Amisha knows I didn't have a choice but to betray our project.

The half-soul says nothing as we walk the narrow passage, dodging the underbellies of clay pipes and gnarled roots. I lead the way up, reaching for the smooth surface of the bookcase that hides this tunnel. It swings open just enough for us to squeeze into the small room.

"What is this place?" Kaya asks.

I shrug, looking around. "Some workshop, I think. No one uses it."

We leave the empty room, slinking into the hall. My heart beats loudly in my ears; we could be discovered any second.

"Feels strange," Kaya says.

"What does?"

We move into the hallway mottled with strands of moonlight and dimmed gas lamps.

"Being back here," she murmurs. "I was so proud when I left, ready to prove I'd earned my Silver Wings. But my soulmate was about to be killed pursuing what they were forged from."

Her face twists with a mix of anger and sadness. I reach out and grip her wrist, feeling time tick away as I waste it comforting her.

"After tonight, they'll never be able to do that to anyone else, understand?" I learned early to get stern with Kaya. "We just have to keep pushing forward."

The way to the dungeons is one I tread eagerly, part of me ready to be the good student I'd pretended to be of late. A few corridors away, my room waits for that student to return, her bed messy and assignment half-finished on her desk. A small ache stabs through my defences.

"Keep going," I mutter. Laela banishes any other thought of defecting.

When we descend the stairs to the dungeons, I half-expect to see Arno waiting at the bottom. If he could read me so well, doesn't this mean he knows what I'll do next?

But no Runes' Master guards his labyrinth of stone paths

and rocky outcrops. "Iain has to keep his blood storage somewhere it won't rot," Kaya explains. "He must have it deep in the ground, where the temperature keeps everything iced. Nowhere else is as cold in southern Lotheria as the Academy dungeons are."

I tread the paths with numb feet, fearing my cane taps louder than usual, that my teacher will recognise the familiar sound. But he doesn't come running. No guards shout down the halls after us.

We wind deeper. The gas in the lamps grows darker, a poisonous shade of green, as we draw closer to the source that feeds them. The longest corridor ends in an iron door inlaid with runes. I don't recognise them; they're not of Arno's hand.

"They're written in the blood alphabet," Kaya murmurs, resting her small canvas bag on the floor. "I don't recognise all of them."

I look at the shapes. "This might take me a moment."

I lay my hands on the door, careful to avoid the protruding metal pictures. My rune magic swirls raw through the iron, seeking, probing... A few interest me but I dismiss them, rifling through the thousands of small shapes until one pulses in my mind's eye. It has been used recently and is eager to be of service again.

"This one." I press the rune. Fingers of rust spread out to choke the others until they melt away. We step back as the door disintegrates around our feet. Wispy tendrils seep from the dark room it hid.

"I've never seen that rune," she breathes. "I have a rough knowledge of the entire *alledari*, but I've never seen that."

I think of Arno creating his own runes for specific tasks. "Someone made it just for this door." A glint catches my eye, and I stoop to pick up the glowing metal from the pile of rust flakes. "It should rebuild when we leave." I feel the power pulsing in the iron, eager to re-establish itself.

Kaya is on a different train of thought. "And if it rebuilds while we're in there?"

I curl my fingers around the guard rune. "Maybe I hold on to this until we leave."

We step into the room. Somehow, it's colder than the passages we traversed to get here. The outside lamps' dim light barely reaches past the threshold, and I'm blind until Kaya lights a lantern.

Rows and rows of small ice blocks with metal tags surround us. They hang on long poles with spaces between them so someone can peruse the collection like a bookshelf. The room stretches back. More ice reflects the lamp back at us.

"Oh my gods," I breathe. My breath billows into the darkness.

Kaya steps forward, lifting the tag on the nearest block of ice. The lamp's golden light falls over it, and the dark heart in the middle of the block becomes clear.

"Whose is it?" I ask.

"Cantrine Selzer," she reads out. "938."

The last lot of mages before the current ones. "What else does the tag say?"

She flips it over. "'Five years on ticket. C-grade."

Like a cut of meat. When I pick up another tag, it's also a C-grade blood sample.

We exchange looks, and I know she's wondering where her blood is stored and what grade she got.

The darkness envelops us as we head deeper into the blood vault. I roll the guard rune over in my hand. It's been smithed well. It's probably been down here for years, breaking down and rebuilding the door when the Headmasters visit. I swallow hard at the thought of them having control of my blood whenever they want it.

"We're doing the right thing by destroying this," I mutter.

Kaya turns back to me. "We're not destroying this vault, Rose."

"Kaya… we can't leave it intact."

She puts the lantern down. "Don't you see? This is the answer to our problem! We mix the blood of mages and cut it into runes."

She's proposing we make her into a false queen with the stolen blood of her classmates. "That's what the drill is for," I say slowly. "You had this planned."

As though reminded, she slings the canvas bag to the floor and begins digging. "You said it, Evermore. I'm a liar and a murderer."

She takes the drill out and lifts the nearest ice tag. "Now, are you going to turn me into the queen like you promised? Or would you like to feel the pain of breaking a *caesi mora*?"

The blood promise tingles on my hand at its name. I

hesitate, then kneel and withdraw the small copper bowl she packed. Kaya presses the point of the drill against the tag she's chosen and winds the handle.

Pain lances through my head. I groan and put a hand to my ear. Kaya drops her drill amongst slender ice shavings melting on the stone floor.

"I feel it too," she says, her eye screwed up against the pressure. She blinks it away and looks around. "Something's down here."

The lamp gutters from an unfelt breeze. Kaya reaches for the dial to feed it more oil, but before she can, the wick goes out in a wholly unnatural way.

I feel for a knife that isn't there.

A dim, pearly glow emanates from the back of the room, nestled amongst the A-grade blood samples. The ice blocks hang, glittering, from their metal prisons. Behind them, a mass of white.

Mesmerised, we draw closer to the largest ice block we've seen yet, led by the light it gives off. It rests gently upon a block of mahogany, into which more runes are carved. The pain in my head beats once, twice, then vanishes. My skin prickles.

"Rose," Kaya warns.

My fingers curl in. I'd reached out to touch it.

"What is it?" I whisper.

The lamp lights itself again, and some of the power from the ice lessens. A name, written like an afterthought, is carved next to the runes.

My stomach boils. "I think it's blood," I choke out. "White blood?"

Kaya stares at the ice. "They blooded her. I can't believe it."

"Who?" I ask, looking at the half-soul. "You knew her?"

She nods. "Lydia Greatcast was my classmate. Quiet. Kind. She disappeared a year before we all graduated."

"Because she was the next chosen queen," I whisper. "This is why. This is why there've been no queens since the Headmasters took power. They killed the only one and took her blood."

I remember a passage from *She Split the Land: 'A queen passed must be returned to the bare earth with only the dirt and flowers as her coffin.'*

They took her magic so it couldn't be reborn in a new queen. I ache for the book in my room.

"They didn't just kill her. They blooded her beforehand," Kaya says in a low tone. "Only Iain would know how to do this."

She undoes her bag again, her hands feverish. The silver tool glints in the light of the queen's blood. "We don't have to fake it at all."

She rests the point against the ice. I throw out my hand to stop her.

"This changes things," she says heatedly, tapping the point against the ice. It leaves no mark. "We have the queen's blood. We want to fake being the queen. Our mission just became a whole lot easier."

"Let's just wait a minute." I rest my fingers lightly on her wrist.

The half-soul turns to me. In the blood's eerie light, I see the growing madness deep in her eyes. Then she blinks, and it's gone, but we both know her time is running out. Her soul is disintegrating.

"What would you propose?"

I look around at the blood samples of the Academy's best students in recent years. "We go with your original plan, and if needed, then we tap into this."

I rest my knuckle against the ice. The liquid within pulses like a heartbeat. Kaya nods even as part of me revolts at the idea of allowing this.

"You're right. Get the dish."

As Kaya stands with the little drill in her grip, I dig for the brass dish again. The Halver has selected another blood sample and begins turning the hand drill. She feeds a tiny bit of rust-coloured fire down the shaft. Red liquid drips into the glass syringe in the middle of the device.

"It works," she breathes.

I hold the drill while Kaya melts the ice with her fire, sealing any breach that might reveal what we've done.

We move on to others. When the syringe is full of blood, we empty it into the brass dish and repeat. My initial disgust wanes after the first two syringes.

My internal clock ticks a warning as Kaya continues to the next row. "We should do this now." She empties the last syringe, but the bowl still seems a bit empty. The dark mage blood reflects our expressions, and together we look towards the queen's blood. Kaya's hand flexes towards the dagger at her belt, and she looks at me hungrily. The chill is back, riding in the forefront of her mind.

"Fine," I relent, trying to calm her. "Half a syringe."

She grins. Pain beats a wary tattoo in my head as we near Lydia's blood. Kaya sets the point of the drill against the ice.

I expect some kind of explosion, some booby trap, but there's nothing. Ice shavings fall victim to the drill, the point burrowing into the icy prison. I read the runes carved around it; none are for protection. They tell the story of a queen who rose like the land intended. It reads like a glorified royal history, and then I realise why the runes look different from the one in my pocket.

Arno wrote them.

Something softens the hard recklessness in my chest. I look up to stop Kaya, but then the first glowing drops begin seeping along the glass.

We are transfixed by its beauty. It shimmers like a liquid star, roiling even in captivity. The syringe fills quickly, as though Lydia is eager to be free of the ice, and when we empty it into the dish it swims through the other blood like oil through water.

"What runes shall we use?" Kaya asks.

I hate the idea of using my favourite branch of magic for something so twisted. "Give me a moment."

Arno had been working on his own alphabet with no idea

that I was doing the same. Drawing from my knowledge of most rune languages in the world, I've written a base material I draw from now.

Eight modified runes will embody what Lotherians see as queenly qualities according to *She Split the Land*. A Sudafraen blood rune for *power*, the Larussian symbol for *lightning*, six Melacorean runes for *metal* and *minerals*. I take a deep breath as I envision merging them with the *caesis alledari* and carving them into Kaya's arms.

"How did you spot that rune on the door?" the half-soul asks quietly.

It was not a question I expected, crouched on the stone floor of a frozen blood bank. "My major is Runes. My teacher taught me how to identify runes written in another hand. This one stood out." I feel the cheap power curled through the metal, even in my pocket.

Kaya looks up, respect in her eyes. "You could become a master, you know. If you weren't so bent on leaving."

I've never wanted anything so badly. Now my runes are just the means to an end. "Are we going to do this?"

She nods, the innocent conversation over. She lowers her knife into the bowl of blood. I roll my sleeves and grab it as she removes her coat.

I rest the point against her skin, then cut quickly. The queen's blood sparks and flashes, and Kaya gasps in pain. Surprised, I yank the knife away as her skin starts burning from the contact. Wisps of smoke carry the smell of scorched flesh.

"Oh my gosh," I breathe. I knew it; this was insane. Halvers can't feel pain, and yet... "Kaya—"

"Draw the damn rune, Evermore," she says through clenched teeth.

I swallow, beginning to trace the pattern again.

Kaya's hiss stops me, and this time her other hand hovers over the bleeding wound. "*Caesi vendoqa!*"

I don't need to know her language to recognise the curse words. "I have to stop, Kaya. I can't do this to you."

The blood smokes on her injured arm and her skin crisps. She trembles. "We can't let the plan fail. My half-souls..."

She looks through me without seeing me, pale blue icing the edges of her dark iris, and I know the chill has taken her almost completely.

"You will take my place, no matter the pain," she orders. "You will be my puppet queen. You will stay."

I nearly lose my grip on the bloody weapon. As a woman who can't feel pain, she'd been in agony. I'll probably die. "I can't—"

Kaya moves quicker than I can, grabbing the knife. The blade is on my throat before I can blink.

She examines me closer. "No, this won't motivate you. But the girl..." She smiles dangerously. "I'll kill her if you don't."

I go cold, even surrounded by ice and mist. "You wouldn't."

"Does it seem like I'm jesting?" she asks, pressing the dagger in. "Laela Pike will be dead before sun-up if you don't do as I say."

My heart squeezes. I see Laela smiling with a daisy-chain crown. "Kaya, please."

She removes the knife and offers it to me handle-first. With shaking hands, I dip it in the bowl of stolen blood. I think of attacking the half-soul leader, but she sneers as though sensing it.

"You think I ordered a safehouse for your girl when we left? If I don't return, your consort will be killed the moment you set foot in camp."

The runes around the tent will keep her safe, but she won't stay inside forever.

I squeeze the handle of the knife, wishing I could hurl it into her chest.

Then I make the first cut in my own skin.

CHAPTER THIRTY-ONE

PAIN SCREAMS ALONG the lines of the rune as mage blood rushes down the blade to fill the new gaps. I carve the final line. When liquid trembles just below the surface of my torn skin, I flick the knife like I would my pen. This time, fire sears it closed. The scar is almost hidden on my pale skin. The pain subsides.

"It used my magic," I say in wonder.

Kaya examines my unburnt skin. "Why does it not injure you?"

I shake my head. "I don't know."

I cut the next rune, then the next. Diamond threads of queen's blood slink into each one, sealing inside the scars. Agony grows in my gut and sweat beads on my forehead. I don't falter, even when my nose starts bleeding. When my vision wobbles, I remember Laela.

The final rune hisses closed with a blast of fire. I fall

backwards, and Kaya catches me. New blood washes through me. Like liquid strength, it roars across my chest.

"Evermore, talk to me."

Light blazes in my vision. I brace myself on my cane and stand shakily.

"Rose." She takes a step back. "Your eyes..."

The ice block reflects two pin-pricks of silver light. I blink, and they go out.

The half-soul grins. "It worked."

A heart-stopping crack splits the air and we look at each other as it sounds again.

I spin toward Lydia's blood. Fissures spider-web across the surface of the ice.

"Kaya," I say. "Run—"

The ice explodes outwards as the blood shatters into a million, razor-sharp stars. Sparks of magic swarm me and force me to the floor as Kaya surrounds herself in rust-coloured light. Several stars attack her but melt under the onslaught of her power.

Then they dig into my skin, burrow under my eyelids. Lydia's power melds with mine, overwhelming it. I try to scream but I'm drowning under a pillar of fire. Flashes of white blind me.

My magic flares, trying to protect me. The fire affinity I've kept hidden from Kaya boils the lantern into an inferno, lighting the vault. The floor dampens under my boots as ice melts. I wrestle with not only Lydia's blood but also my own power spiraling out of control. The runes on my arm pulse.

Suddenly, the magic disappears under my skin. I rise. The lantern calms as the runes fade back to scars.

Sweat runs down my neck, stinging the slight graze where Kaya threatened me. She unravels her knot of magic, seeming surprised to find me standing.

"What was that?" she asks, not bothering to check if I'm okay.

Something pulls me, the same something that burned the northern commander alive, and I want to blast her into the next chamber. I suppress it.

"I guess Lydia's blood can't be halved."

My leg aches, pulsing hot beneath the old injury. I grip my cane harder. My breath comes in ragged gasps.

"We need to leave," I say through gritted teeth.

She strides for the door. "Yes. Come."

Tears form in the corners of my eyes, the handle of the cane digging hard into the rune scar.

I hate that damn scar.

As I pass under the iron doorway, I don't bother returning the rune, and the door remains in a heap of ashes. Some part of me *wants* Iain to know we were here, that we infiltrated his precious storeroom.

I lean against the walls periodically as I follow Kaya, who hisses at me to hurry up.

That surge of fire runs through me again. The few torches flare, and she finally pauses.

"Keep your magic under control," she snaps. "We don't need the entire guard coming down because you're lighting the place up."

The flames tug towards her, and I pull them back regretfully. She eyes them with fear. A sliver of satisfaction draws deep into my body.

She didn't know I had fire magic, hadn't factored it into her plans. Maybe I'm not quite lost yet.

We reach the top of the stairs to the main floor. Through the open doorway, I see the dark, vaulting roof, the low light from the gas lamps. We're almost out. Kaya halts.

"What is it?" I murmur. I want to shove her out of the way and make a run for it, but I hold still.

She mutters, "It's too quiet."

It strikes me then—the silence. Pages or guards always roam the Academy halls, no matter the hour. I'd often adjusted my schedule of sneaking out to avoid the patrols and nosy pages.

I lick my dry lips. "Keep going. We just have to get back to the workshop."

She creeps along like a prey animal, her ragged coat billowing.

"Kaya, I need to rest."

She turns, brows drawn inward. "We're in the middle of the Academy, Rose, you cannot rest here."

Sweat rolls down my face. "I have to, I can't—"

My vision dims as the hallway wavers before my eyes.

Strong, unkind arms catch me, bruise me, as Kaya leans me against the wall. Her face swims too close to mine.

"Be stronger, fire whisper. Your lover is counting on you to return."

Anger struggles beneath the haze of exhaustion. My arms tingle as she returns my walking stick.

"If you are to be queen of Lotheria, you cannot show weakness." She rakes me over with a glance. "It will be hard enough to sell you as it is."

Curse words both Lotherian and Other cluster on my tongue, but she's already walking down the hall. I stagger after her.

The Academy remains a ghost town. Not a single soul roams the halls, and the only lamps lit are those that never die. We pass the courtyard where Thompson would be working if he wasn't currently at the Halver camp. I search for Maurice, wondering if he returned after his whipping.

But the stable is empty, the courtyard abandoned. A low neigh comes from the wooden building, answered only by other horses.

"Something's up, Kaya."

"Nothing that concerns us," she hisses. "Keep moving."

But she's freaked out too. We move from shadow to shadow and hear nothing until we near the front of the castle.

A voice rings out, muffled by the thick stone, just as we reach the door to the abandoned room we came through.

We both freeze. The voice continues, loud and commanding. Even as this distance I recognise Iain's tone.

Shouting answers him. Through the long, high slits in the front wall that serve as windows, firelight flickers angrily.

I take a step forward.

"Where are you going?" Kaya asks.

I don't answer. Around the corner, the enormous double doors that serve as the Academy's main entrance are wide open. Iain's voice booms in the centre of the town square.

"Under the guidance of a loyal servant to the Academy, we investigated. At the premises named, we found the suspect and brought him back to the castle to stand trial."

My blood turns to ice. I move closer to the door.

"What are you doing?" Kaya snaps from the corner. "*Rose.*"

My cane digs into the plush carpet as I hobble faster. My breathing is ragged, an unworded prayer to an unseen god.

No. Please no. Not when we were so close.

I round the double doors and peer into the town square, taking in the gathered non-magi crowd, the battalion of armoured guards with lit torches. The wooden platform from the hearings remains intact. Upon it are three figures. Iain looks out over the crowd as though searching for someone. Beside him, Sergeant Hall holds a hooded person by the arms.

"We gather today," Iain says, "to bear witness to the punishment of this man."

With a sick flourish, Hall removes the hood, and Tyson blinks in the sudden firelight.

CHAPTER THIRTY-TWO

MY STOMACH FALLS through the floor. Ignoring Kaya's yells, I scramble down the steps, Iain drowning out the clacking of my cane.

"This man is a liar," he continues. "An imposter. He is the first humanborn non-magi to cross the river."

A ripple of disbelief rolls through the crowd closest to me. I jostle through some of the villagers.

"That's Craige's apprentice," a man says. "Oi, what's he done?"

Iain appears not to hear. "Though we tolerate and acknowledge our humanborn students, this man does not belong. He has lied to you, he—"

"Tyson Welles ain't a criminal," a woman in a flour-stained apron barks. "He comes to buy pies every day. He's the most polite lad."

Iain looks stunned but shakes it quickly. "The *implications* of his presence here demand that—"

This time, non-magi voices drown each other out. I shoulder another man aside, fighting to reach the front. My leg catches on an uneven stone. Exhaustion from earlier seeps up, but I shove it down.

"He's not of this world—"

"And he's to be executed for that?" the man from before asks. "Just 'cause he's from The Other?"

"Enough!" Iain roars over the gathered. The guards not holding torches reach for their swords, and the people nearest them shrink back. "As Headmaster of the Academy and member of your Council of Three, I hereby sentence this man to death."

Tyson blanches.

"Get out of the way!" I yell, but my words are lost in the crowd. Fire flares in my heart, and I wrestle for control.

Not yet. I can't hurt anyone innocent.

Iain turns to my oldest friend, his hand on the pommel of his sword. "Tyson Welles—"

"Enough!"

I pause, stunned. Phoenix strides from the crowd in his grey Academy cloak. With dark hair tied back and anger in his eyes, he looks like a northern prince.

"I left Orthandrell because your Academy promised freedom. It promised redemption. A new life away from what I've grown up with." He points at Iain with more authority than any sword he ever wielded. "You want to sentence this man because he's a liar? Then you should place your own neck on the chopping block beside his!" A roar rises at his words.

The guards unsheathe their weapons. The crowd doesn't retreat, hurling curses at the people standing emotionless. I'm swept up in a tidal wave of hate.

Magefire scatters through the crowd. I hesitate, then fling off the heavy coat shielding me from the night's chill. Using my cane, I shove people out of the way.

The runes on my arms tingle again.

A ball of magefire burns past me, and I reach out to grab it. Holding someone else's magic feels as familiar as holding their hand, and when I dispel it, a guard pales suddenly. The one beside her sweeps a burning torch at the onslaught of furious villagers. I reach out, searching for the fires, remembering Arno's lessons on control.

The tall flames glimmer and call to me. I can't help grinning as I seize the guards' fire.

On the platform, Phoenix meets Hall and Iain in a clash of steel and sparks. The longsword he won from Yu is finally being used in a real fight, and from here, I see his grimace. He didn't want this.

He was driven to it.

Tyson headbutts Hall in the back of the head, and the sergeant stumbles, caught off guard. My friend tries to leg it off the platform, hands bound behind his back.

Someone knocks me off balance. I hit the cobbles hard and lose sight of the men on the platform—my soulmate and my oldest friend. Worry seizes me, and frustration boils over.

The fire I took from the torch explodes in my grasp. The flaring torches light the square as screams echo off the buildings. I climb to my feet, lean on my cane, take a deep breath.

Then I push harder.

The darkness that gripped me at Deadman's Keep swarms back, filling my limbs, my heart. Bolts of fire streak across the square, accompanying me as I finally wrench free of the mass of people.

"Tyson!" I scream.

He turns just in time to see Hall swing his sword downwards. Tyson ducks out of the way, but the blade catches his arm and he yelps. Blood streaks his white shirt, stained with a hard day's labour.

I go numb.

Clouds gather over the square, dark purple and threatening. Thunder rumbles as the ground beneath my boots shivers.

The runes in my skin are activating.

The balls of fire floating beside me smash into the platform, clinging and burning as cheap wood blackens beneath them. I will them to climb, singe, incinerate anything in their path.

A rough hand grips my shoulder. I spin, glaring up into Arno's tawny gaze.

"Calm, little fire whisper," he says evenly. "Calm now."

"They'll kill him," I spit. My vision is tinted again, flames curling around my irises. Arno doesn't flinch.

"Your soulmate's doing a decent job preventing that. The only one who'll kill him is you if you keep burning that platform."

I turn away. *Fire* will be the thing that saves Tyson, and I mean to use it.

The hand tightens. "*Control*, Rose. Remember Deadman's Keep. Remember what you did."

A man burning, screaming under my touch. Petre's lifeless eyes, his body limp in the mud.

Tears cluster in my eyes.

"I couldn't save Petre," I say. "But I can save Tyson."

The fire rages. With a screech of burnt timber, a support gives way and everyone stumbles towards the inferno. Cinders fly into the dark night as the riot rages behind me.

Another voice, familiar. "Have you got her? She needs to stop this fire."

When Arno nods, his hand shakes me somewhat. "She's deep, but I'll get her out. You get your boy."

A dark-haired man with a leather apron sprints off across the cobbles. He leaps into my flames and disappears behind the searing heat.

"You were my finest runes student, Evermore, did you know that?" Arno's tone is casual, like we're discussing this over ale. "I've turned away everyone before you. But you... you had the gift."

"I *have* a gift." The fire climbs higher.

"You have to stop the flames now. You'll hurt people."

For the first time, a hint of desperation creeps into my teacher's voice.

Maybe he's right.

I shake it off. Burn Iain, burn Sergeant Hall, and Tyson will be safe.

Arno switches tracks. "Rose—"

A new scream cuts him off. My vision clears as a woman comes flying from an alley, running towards the Academy. As the entire square seems to pause, another woman joins her, skirts flying, eyes wide.

A Halver lumbers between the buildings after them.

"Oh shit," Arno says instead. "Rose, we need to go. We need to get your friend and go *now*."

I squeeze my eyes closed. When I open them, I take in the carnage.

Two figures still fight with clashing swords atop a burning wooden platform. Flames tower above and around them. Behind us are sounds of dying villagers and wounded guards.

I begin to shake. "Where's Tyson?"

"Craige got him from the fire." Arno plants a hand on my back and steers me to the dark alleyways. More Halvers appear, sparks of ill magic flashing as they, too, set upon the guards. "He's safe."

We're barely in the shadows when my teacher grabs my arms. I try to yank away, but he runs rough fingers over the scars that now flicker with a soft, pearly white light.

He lets go. "You're too much like me, Evermore. That frightens me."

Arno strides off, farther into town. I cane after him. "What do you mean?"

"You think you're the first to try to harness the power of runes into their own magic, to use them on their body?" He turns, pulling a hank of hair away. Beneath it, a puckered scar, badly-healed: the blood rune for 'stop.'

"What were you—"

He rolls his eyes. "Gods, Evermore, I thought you were bright. I'm a Halver. Haven't you noticed how they all hate me?"

My jaw slackens. "Arno, I had no—"

"Keep walking," he says gruffly. "It's a long story and this is not the time for it."

I take another step forward, then the oath rune blazes into life. I cry out as it sears my skin, turning ruby-red.

"Don't run from me, Evermore."

Kaya's voice slithers into my ears. I curl my fingers into a fist.

"What is it?"

I suck in a breath. "Kaya. She's talking to me."

Arno fills my vision as I fight the pain. "Ignore her, Rose. You've made a deal with her?"

I nod, my eyes full of tears. Pain streaks up my arm. He grips my shoulder.

"Don't listen to her. I know Kaya Aule, she was a nasty piece of work even when she was whole. We were students together. I know her ways. You've gotta come with me now, okay?"

"Okay," I whisper. "Where's Tyson?"

"He's safe, but we need you there too. So keep walking, all right? And ignore her."

We emerge from the alley, cross a wide street, then duck into another. I recognise the way to the distillery—my first adventure into Fairhaven, the day I kicked a man in the nuts.

The memory bolsters me. I've always looked after myself. I hobble a little faster.

"Where's your girl, Rose?"

My steps falter, but I press on. Tears run down my cheeks as the oath rune rages and burns on my palm.

"I have Laela Pike. If you want her, come and get her."

Kaya's presence finally fades. I come to in the middle of an alley. Arno looks at me forlornly. "You're going back, aren't you?"

"I have to," I choke out. "She has Laela."

He just looks at me, and I know I'll have to go alone. But then he heaves a sigh.

"Fine. We save your girl, then we save you." He shakes his head. "I love being a teacher."

We trace our steps back the way we came. More than once, we duck out of the way as people run past, but whether they're half-souls or non-magi or guards, we don't know.

"Where is she?" Arno asks. "Do you know?"

I start shaking my head, but the oath rune pulses. It turns my blood cold.

Kaya wants to be found.

A statue flickers in my mind's eye, a familiar plaque and garden bed. "She's at Fleur's statue."

Arno nods. "I know where it is. Come on."

"We don't have any weapons," I protest.

My Runes' Master looks at me over his shoulder. "We won't need them."

We cross the town. My heart sinks—Fairhaven is in ruins. My fire has spread from the main square, seizing houses and buildings. Burning thatch lights the sky and rains curling embers on the townsfolk. Anguish squeezes me.

I lost control again.

Shame weighs my steps, but it evaporates quickly in the face of the devastation wrought by the half-souls.

Bodies lie strewn around the square, some in commoner clothes, others clad in black armour. Weapons lie bloody and broken at their sides as a second fire guts the buildings that ring the area.

At the centre of it all: Kaya.

The woman stands against the feet of the last queen, her long cloak torn and burnt. She swings an ugly shortsword, commanding her newest battalion of half-soul troops into action. Her short, dark hair whips around in the smoky night air, and as she turns to face me, her eye narrows.

"Evermore. Are you done running?"

I limp forward, Arno at my side.

"Where's Laela?" I ask. I look for her around the square but see only death and destruction.

Kaya tightens her grip on the sword. "When you ran into the crowd, I went back to the camp—"

I continue my approach. "Where is she?"

"I knew you'd abandoned me. You never had any intention of upholding our bargain." Her deranged sneer suddenly melts. Her eye softens. "I thought we understood each other, Rose."

My steps slow as I remember our first conversation. How she'd talked me through the grief, the guilt of killing. I take a deep breath, shoving those feelings away. *Kaya* is responsible for all this. She's not my ally and never was.

"Where is she?" I repeat. "As for our oath, you've been breaking your end since we made it. You had no intention of getting me home."

"No, I didn't. You forgot one little detail, humanborn." This close, I can see the icy blue lining her iris. She holds up her hand with a smile. "I don't feel pain."

The scar is deep red and pockmarked with burns, her arm withering away.

Fear streaks through me. "Where is Laela?"

She grins. "I gave her to my Halvers. Tonight is a great victory against those in the stone castle, and she is the reward."

Silence falls as I grapple with her words. I can feel the fire burning within me, begging for release again. I grip my cane with white knuckles, fighting to restrain myself.

"You—" I manage, then she's swinging towards me.

My cane comes up, blocking her first strike. The blade

bites deep, and I twist with both hands, trying to wrench the sword free. She pulls it away, taking a chunk of wood with it. I take a step back, trying to brace my leg on the cobbles.

"Arno!" I yell.

No answer.

Kaya sneers. "Pathetic. I heard rumours of your prowess with a sword, and now look at you. Unable to stand, unable to fight. Without your fire, you're useless."

She's baiting me, and it's working. I keep my distance, resisting the fire that wants to incinerate her like it did the northern commander.

Kaya takes another step toward me, and I know I can't wait for Arno to intervene.

I explode forward, using my good leg to take a deep step in. With the cane between my body and her blade, I drive the handle into her stomach, then smash into her again. She stumbles, caught offguard, but I don't hesitate. I bring down the cane like a sword. It slams into the side of her head.

"Am I weak now?" I snarl as she struggles to keep her footing. I swing again and smack the cane into her jaw, snapping her head to the side.

She tries to bring her sword up under my onslaught. My seething rage helps me drive my cane into her face. Before she can recover, I swing at her legs with a two-handed grip like I'm playing softball in high school again.

Her knee cracks inwards and she collapses, sword clattering to her side.

I loom over her. "Call them off."

She scoots backwards, dragging her broken leg across the ground. Hatred mars her face. "We're taking this town, Evermore. We won't surrender."

I hit her again, slamming the point of my cane into her stomach. She blanches even though she doesn't feel the pain, and her breath wheezes between cracked ribs.

"Hit me all you want. Look around. We've won."

I glance around the square. The raging inferno is too big for me to control, even if I could spare the attention. Arno is across on the other side, assisting the fallen. Fresh bodies litter the streets as Halvers carve into them with homemade weapons. Sickening thuds silence weak cries.

And Laela…

My shoulders slump. I can beat up Kaya, even kill her, and the Halvers won't be brought under control.

Desperation fills me. The runes on my arms tingle to life.

Rain begins falling, uncertain at first, then heavier as I lift my face. Power curls around a rune near my wrist, singing it to life. Rumbles of thunder growl across the sky. Lightning flashes, illuminating the ruins of Fairhaven with unearthly light.

Then a bolt strikes the ground.

"Yes, you might have won." I take a deep breath and close my eyes. "But you won't live to see your victory."

Finally, I let myself lose control against the one who deserves it.

The fire that rages in the closest buildings twists, tucking into a pillar that surges towards me. I pick up Kaya's sword in my left hand and advance. She scrambles back from me.

"Fine! You can have the girl. She's in the camp, she should be untouched... I told them to await my return, take the town first." She licks her lips and glances at something behind me. "She's unhurt, Rose. Laela is waiting for you."

I lift the sword, preparing to plunge it into her stomach, when something smashes into me from behind.

I fly forward, hitting the sharp cobblestones hard. My breath explodes from me and I wheeze, trying to see what hit me.

The Halver lieutenant leers at me, holding a makeshift weapon. He raises it, but I call the pillar of fire. It plows into him, enveloping him. He struggles against the flames, burning silently. Using Kaya's sword, I rise to my feet, gritting my teeth against the pain in my back. I cough and spit red to the stones.

"Always hated that guy," I groan as he finally folds to the ground. Old guilt wrestles within me, but I lean into the recklessness of self-protection. "Call them off."

Instead, she smiles. "You can't burn them all, Rose."

I follow her gaze. Dozens of Halvers crowd the square, unfazed by the lightning that strikes close and the column of fire soaring above them. As one, they lift their weapons and close in.

With an ear-splitting crack, the ground splits beneath our feet. A yawning chasm opens in the square, swallowing half a dozen men. They pitch into the darkness, tumbling off the sides as I back away, a deep, primal fear now taking hold. Kaya, too, edges away as it widens.

"Leave my student, Kaya," Arno calls, appearing on the crack's other side. "You've wreaked enough havoc for your personal vendetta. Let her go."

Kaya laughs. "You were always a funny one, Veloquis. I liked you."

He shrugs. "I was never that keen on you."

Her expression snaps back. "Well, that hurts."

Arno holds up a small, black stone. Golden threads glitter with reflected flames, showing off the intricate rune carved in the centre. "Let her go, or I'll throw us all to the depths of the earth."

Kaya breathes deep through her nose. "You and your pictures... You should've joined us when you could. *Halver.*"

He ignores the slight. "Come on, Rose."

I limp towards the bit of the square untouched by Arno's earthquake. My leg burns as I lean against my cane, but I suppress the pain. Arno reaches for me, his eyes on Kaya, the small marble slab in his other hand. I take his arm and he pulls me close.

"I suggest you leave, Aule," he calls as he pulls me back towards an alleyway. "There's nothing for you here. Not redemption, not Jax."

She pulls herself up onto the edge of a garden bed, her gaze dark. "She belongs to me, Veloquis. I created her. I'll find her."

Arno's arm around me tightens, but his voice is clear. "I think you should worry that she'll find you."

Shadows close over us as we reach the alley. Arno immediately stoops and throws me over his shoulder.

"Ow!"

"Quiet. She'll have them following us."

I clutch him as best I can while he sets a fast pace down the alley. Powerful muscles bunch beneath his shirt, and the ground slides past at an alarming rate.

"Can you find Laela?" I ask quietly. My back hurts, and my mouth tastes like copper; I know the injury from the lieutenant goes deep. "She's in the Halver camp, Arno."

"I'll find her," he promises, his voice strained.

We leave the outskirts. As he carries me away, I watch the town, the columns of smoke and the purple lightning. A bolt strikes the Academy bell tower, and the resulting crack of thunder is deafening.

"Can you make it stop?" Arno asks as he begins threading amongst the trees.

"I have no idea how it started."

"Veloquis? That you?"

The voice comes from the darkness, and I feel Arno tense then relax as he recognises Craige.

The blacksmith is incensed. "Gods curse it, man, what took you so long?"

Arno lowers me to the ground as lightning flickers. In the brief flash of light, I take in the scene: Craige, pale with worry and soaked to the bone, and Tyson tied to a tree, gagged and looking furious.

Craige follows my horrified look. "It's the only way he'd stay, don't blame me."

I hobble to my friend and half-collapse against the tree. I pull the gag from his mouth.

"Craige, is that the rag from the shop?" is the first thing the damn fool asks.

Craige decides not to answer, and Tyson smacks his lips, trying to clear the taste.

"I'm sorry I wasn't the one to save you," I mutter, feeling behind the trunk for the ropes that bind him. "I made things worse."

He sighs. "I'm not going to argue that, Rose. You know I don't lie to you."

I free him as Arno approaches.

"You have to go back," he growls. "You heard her, Rose. She'll find you."

The runes in my skin ripple with fire. "Maybe I want her to find me."

Arno shakes his head. "You nearly lost this round. You'll surely lose the second."

Beside us, the Lotherian river rages, swollen with rain. Tyson puts his arm around me and helps me to the bank. "I don't know about you, but I'm ready to go home."

I look at him then, in the next lightning flash. Lines crease his boyish face, aging him beyond seventeen years. His eyes have seen too much. I lean into him. He smells like iron and sweat, rainwater and blood. I nod.

I turn back to Arno. "Please, please find Laela. She's non-magi, auburn hair, brown eyes…"

Arno holds up his hand. "I know what the girl looks like. She'll be fine, Rose."

"And Amisha," Tyson cuts in. "The Tsalskinese cartography student."

"Orin," I add. "And Phoenix…"

"We'll take care of them all," Craige thunders. "Now get your arses into the river."

Tears blur my vision as I stumble forward and throw myself into Arno's arms. He holds me tightly, and I whisper in his ear, "I don't want to go. This is my home."

He lets me hang on to him for a second more, then pushes me away. "No. The Other is your home."

My throat closes. Tears streak down my face. "I belong here."

"You'll die here."

Shouting echoes through the trees, the deep bass of broken syllables; Halvers. Fear sinks in.

"I don't know how to open the portal," I whisper.

Arno draws a small dagger and gestures for my arm. I don't flinch when he slices the back of my hand, though we all stare at the silver blood gleaming through the broken skin. He nods slowly.

"You took Lydia's blood. Only a queen can open the portal between worlds." He's paled. Craige looks similarly disturbed. "Now go."

Shaking, I hold my hand over the water. A few droplets

of gleaming white fall into the thrashing waters, mixing and swirling. A portion of the river settles, luminescent.

Tyson grips my hand, looks over his shoulder at his boss.

I think of Laela, of Orin and Amisha. Learning runes, studying in the library, eating pies. Complaining about the Academy food with Petre.

I remember the broken promises, the lies, the hurt...

But I don't want to leave.

Tyson's watching me with dark, unsure eyes. I nod.

I made a promise, after all. I intend to keep this one.

I squeeze his hand, and together we step into the river, giving ourselves to the rushing waters. We're submerged immediately, and his hand grips mine. My eyes stay open against the murky water, watching the lacy threads of silver magic swirl around us, caressing us on this journey home.

Pale light appears, guiding us to the surface. I kick with my one strong leg, but it's Tyson's powerful stroke that breaks the water above us. We gasp for air as a plane echoes through the sky. Traffic roars across the nearby bridge. The sounds of The Other envelop us as we meet each other's eyes.

We're back.

ACKNOWLEDGEMENTS

When I started writing *Her Crown of Fire*, it looked nothing like the book you've just read. It was angsty, riddled with plot holes, and quite frankly I loved it to pieces. I loved it enough to hand it over to the incredible Haley Sulich, who looked through all the mess to the core of a story in which she saw potential. With her guidance and never-ending patience, I learnt to push boundaries and go further than I ever dared to venture in my writing. This book is as much hers as it is mine. Cheers to one fantastic editor and someone I'm lucky enough to call a friend.

Stephi Cham, one of the best poets and copyeditors I know, cleaned up all my 'thats' and 'buts.' She's not only a brilliant editor but also an excellent friend with a sympathetic Twitter ear.

To my partner, William, for making me tea and busting my butt about not writing on my days off. As my original beta reader, he shrieked when he reached the end of my unfinished draft and made me promise to finish it. He's the reason this book is in your hands. Thanks for looking after the chickens while I shut myself away and tippy-tapped anxiously.

To my writing gals, Dayna Watson (also responsible for that incredible cover!) and Danica Peck, for putting up with my breakdowns and rants. Love our cafe writing mornings, ladies.

To the entire writing community on Twitter for banding together and being a ball of incredible motivation. Sofia Aguerre, Nicole Scarano, Paul Grealish, Dave Deickman, Jim Kiernan, Brenton Oxenberry, Heather James, Emm Cole, Francesca Tacchi, and oh my gosh, so many others, I'm sorry if I missed you, yell at me on Twitter! You're all wonderful people and amazing authors.

To Bec Moore and Arden Brims, for being awesome beta readers and finishing the whole book in TWO DAYS, leading to the creation of a book club with some of my favourite people. Danica Carrick, for being a gorgeous person and always having a kind, positive word when I felt down. Brock Lanham, for his stoic support and cool maps; you're gonna write that book one day, buddy. Everyone I ever played DnD with this year. My creative brain was always watching.

To my family, who kept asking when it would come out. My work mates, who asked regularly how my writing was going. All my Camp NaNo mates from the last two years, for sprinting with me!

This book is no longer solely my creation. Everyone who had a hand in it has left their mark. I'm so grateful to have had the opportunity to work with them all and to have written this for you.

Thank you.

(Look, Haley, we did it!)

Renee April is the author of the young adult fantasy novel *Her Crown of Fire*. Not only an avid reader and writer, Renee also streams games badly on Twitch and acts as dungeon master for her D&D group. As a result, she spends far too much time in fantasy realms. She can be found on various writing sites including <u>Wattpad</u> and <u>Goodreads</u> but usually lurks on Twitter, handing out bad advice and genuine sympathies.

CPSIA information can be obtained
at www.ICGtesting.com
Printed in the USA
LVHW040708031119
636167LV00004B/22/P

9 781948 115056